PRAISE FOR

"Nobody writes like Tijan. With addicting story lines and unparalleled prose, she's always an autoclick author for me."

— Rachel Van Dyken, #1 *New York Times* bestselling author

"Tijan knows how to create addictive, fun, and exciting stories that you simply cannot put down!"

— Elle Kennedy, *New York Times* bestselling author

"I can always count on Tijan to write an action-packed, intense, emotional story that will have me invested until the very last page."

— Helena Hunting, *New York Times* bestselling author

"Tijan delivers on the fun, edge, and angst. Her books never fail to please!"

— Kylie Scott, *New York Times* bestselling author

"Tijan delivers a power punch with *Anti-Stepbrother*—angst, tension, and an emotional conclusion that'll have you glued to every page. The characters jump straight from the story and claim your heart. You won't be ready to let go."

— JB Salsbury, *New York Times* and *USA Today* bestselling author

"One of my Tijan faves, with a hero to die for and a heroine you'll want as your best friend."

— Katy Evans, *New York Times* bestselling author, on *Anti-Stepbrother*

"5+ riveting stars! The chemistry between Dusty and Stone was off-the-charts electrifying. I was completely absorbed from the first page to the last. Tijan didn't just get a touchdown with this story—she won the Super Bowl!"

—Beth Flynn, *USA Today* bestselling author, on *Enemies*

"Obsessed from page 1! *The Insiders* is yet another addicting read from Tijan."

—Jennifer L. Armentrout, #1 *New York Times* bestselling author, on *The Insiders*

"A whirlwind of high-stakes suspense."

—*Publishers Weekly* on *The Insiders*

"Hello, book hangover! With captivating, unique characters, this story is so much more than an epic sports romance. Redemption. Friendship. Unconditional love. And that ending! Hands down, my favorite Tijan book!"

—Devney Perry, *USA Today* bestselling author, on *The Not-Outcast*

"Blaise is the perfect rich prick to fall in love with! One of my fave reads in 2020!"

—Ilsa Madden-Mills, *Wall Street Journal* bestselling author, on *Rich Prick*

A

Dirty

BUSINESS

ALSO BY TIJAN

Mafia Stand-Alones

Canary
Cole
Bennett Mafia
Jonah Bennett

Fallen Crest / Crew Universe

Fallen Crest / Roussou Universe
Fallen Crest Series
Crew Series
The Boy I Grew Up With (stand-alone)
Rich Prick
Fallen Crest Campout
Nate
A Kade Christmas (novella)

Other Series

Broken and Screwed Series (YA/NA)
Jaded Series (YA/NA suspense)
Davy Harwood Series (paranormal)
Carter Reed Series (mafia)
The Insiders (trilogy)

Sports Romance Stand-Alones

Enemies
Teardrop Shot

Hate to Love You
The Not-Outcast

Young Adult Stand-Alones

Ryan's Bed
A Whole New Crowd
Brady Remington Landed Me in Jail

College Stand-Alones

Anti-Stepbrother
Kian

Contemporary Romances

Bad Boy Brody
Home Tears
Fighter

Rockstar Romance Stand-Alone

Sustain

Paranormal Stand-Alone

Evil
Micaela's Big Bad

More books to come!

A *Dirty* BUSINESS

TIJAN

 Montlake

Published by Montlake, Seattle

www.apub.com

Amazon, the Amazon logo, and Montlake are trademarks of Amazon.com, Inc., or its affiliates.

ISBN-13: 9781542038416 (paperback)
ISBN-13: 9781542038409 (digital)

Cover design by Caroline Teagle Johnson
Cover images: © Georgijevic, © izusek, © Ivan Ozerov / Getty Images

Printed in the United States of America

To any and all readers! I hope you enjoy.

CHAPTER ONE

JESS

Beer and hockey.

That's where it's at.

I didn't know what "it" was and where "it" was, but I was currently sitting at the hockey arena, a beer in hand, watching some holy hottie hockey gods on the ice, so yeah, I was thinking I was where "it" was supposed to be. Life was good. Beer and hockey.

"I gotta take a piss."

I stifled a grin because only my roommate, who looked like a real-life Barbie, talked in a way that in no way was Barbie-like at all. Made me love her even more for it.

I gave a nod. The second period was ending, and I glanced at my beer. It was a third empty.

I made a decision, right then and there. Because I was decisive—it's a word that I had to recently explain to a parolee of mine, and I had to explain in detail to the nth degree. She didn't know what setting goals was or what being decisive meant. I'd enjoyed the conversation. Her eyes were glazed, and her drug test was negative, so I knew it was the topic boring her. Too bad. We both had to endure that conversation, though it wasn't her that had me needing my current beer. It was the three parolees after her that I checked on. All of them together made me need the last beer, and my *next* beer was being dedicated to the two home visits I'd be doing tomorrow.

Not looking forward to those, but it was part of the job. So as Kelly was making her way to the stairs, I went right behind her.

Kelly drew the eye. Platinum-blonde hair. A slender and almost model-like body. Blue eyes. Barbie, like I said. She got looks from males and females, and I understood, especially after her recent boob job. She'd been my roommate since college and after. The only time we'd taken apart from each other was when she'd moved in with a boy-friend-turned-fiancé, who was now an ex-husband. He'd cheated on her, so she got a decent-size settlement from him, and I got my best friend back. Score for me, sucked for him. But the thing I loved about Kelly was that she was flexible. I came home and told her I needed a drink, and she said she won two tickets to the New York Stallions hockey game. It was meant to be, the way I was figuring.

She glanced back, saw me following her.

I tipped my cup up and drained it to her unspoken question.

She turned, going the rest of the way with a laugh. Almost like we'd done this before (because we had), she went for the bathroom, and I went to the beer concession stand.

"Oh, ho, ho, ho. Hey there."

The jovial greeting sounded out from one of the workers, a big burly guy. I had to take a second to appreciate what I was seeing. I knew this guy. He'd been a parolee in the past, not mine, but I'd been in the hallway a few times he had a disagreement with his current parole officer at that time. He liked to go by the name Jimi Hendrix, but we all called him Jimmy. And with Jimmy, unfortunately, there'd been a lot of disagreements.

So, he was on parole a lot.

"Jimmy." I was scanning him up and down. He'd lost thirty pounds, which I caught because I needed to know that for my job, but on him, it was barely noticeable. The guy was six five and 310. Or now, 280? I was also noting the beer he was serving. "How are you doing?"

He caught my tone, and his grin upped a degree. "I'm off parole. You don't need to be worried about reporting me. Finished it, got a good place to live, and got this job. I'm working at a grocery store, bagging groceries, too, Miss Jess."

That was another thing about Jimmy. I was normally Officer Montell, but Jimmy somehow got away with calling me Miss Jess. A couple of his coworkers were checking me out like I was his ex-lady, and I saw the speculation in their eyes. I had no interest in dating either of them.

"You wanna beer, Miss Jess?"

"Uh . . . sure." Felt odd taking a beer from a past parolee, but okay then. As he was pouring, still seeing some of the interest from his coworkers, I reached into my purse for my phone and my badge. The badge got hung around my neck. I didn't need to brandish it here, but they saw it, and it did the job. The interest fell flat, and I got a couple sneers instead.

I pulled up Travis, a coworker, and sent him a text.

Jess: Jimi Hendrix is off parole?

He buzzed back almost right away.

Asshole Coworker 1: Yeah. Why?

Jess: Just wondering, saw him. He looks good.

Asshole Coworker 1: He in trouble?

Jess: Nope. Bye.

My phone buzzed again, but I didn't like Travis. The feeling was mutual, more than mutual actually. Derek Travis. He'd been up my ass for as long as I'd been working as a parole officer. Didn't know why or what his problem was since they needed female parole officers. I did my job, did it well, and only butted heads with him a couple of times. But I'd asked about Jimmy because I needed to make sure, and he'd answered. The topic was done as far as I was concerned. I wasn't going to give him any reason to bug Jimmy, but sometimes they lied, hence the text.

"Here you go, Miss Jess."

Even with Jimmy's outbursts or disagreements, I always liked him. He couldn't handle his temper at times, but he was usually funny about it, swinging on himself more than swinging on others. Ninety-five percent of the time, he didn't want to hurt anyone else.

"What do I owe you, Jimmy?"

His smile was almost blinding, his two massive hands resting on the sides of the register and his big frame hunched forward and down. That'd been one of his old habits, I was remembering too. He tried to make himself smaller than he was, usually to make others feel more comfortable around him.

"Nothing, Miss Jess. It's on me."

I glanced to his coworkers, seeing one watching us with a bit too much interest for my liking. I leaned closer to Jimmy and lowered my voice. "Are you sure that you got the cash on you?"

He started to bolster up, his mouth opening, a pink color coming to his neck, more than what it was, but I kept on. "Because I know you travel with as little cash as necessary. Your heart's in the right place, but if you find yourself short on the exact cash, I wouldn't want someone to notice and let your boss know, if you get my drift." My eyes darted to that coworker trying to listen in. He'd washed the same two-by-two inches of counter eighteen times now.

Getting my drift, Jimmy's shoulders sank even lower. "Sorry, Miss Jess. You're right." He told me the amount I owed, and I handed over the cash. When he started to give me the change, I waved my hand, indicating he should keep it. He was putting it in their tip jar when I headed off.

Going to the stairs, I scanned for our seats. Kelly wasn't there.

Knowing I'd need a bathroom break myself before too long, I sipped my beer and headed in the direction Kelly had gone.

The line was too long at the first one, but being the slightly buzzed savvy parole officer I was, I knew there'd be more bathrooms farther away from the main area. I kept going, and I had half my beer sipped before I found a door. It said "bathrooms" and had an arrow, so I was following the arrow.

I surged through, and oh crap.

I was in the exit stairwell. I'd made a mistake.

I turned, reaching for the door, when I heard just above me, "—hear about it. I do not care."

I moved back, angled my head. He wasn't all the way up to the next floor, but he was halfway up to the top. His back was turned slightly toward the stairway, and he was talking on the phone. "Yes. Yes."

I should go. That was a private call, not my business.

I pushed the door handle to go out, but nothing. The door was locked.

I was locked inside.

Well, shitters.

I had a beer. I'd soon have a bladder that would need to be emptied, and that guy was still on his phone.

"—wait. Someone is here."

Oh, double shitters.

I turned when he started down the stairs.

I called up, "I'm sorry! I didn't know these doors . . ." I trailed off as he turned the corner, now facing me and coming down the stairs directly to me. And I trailed off because good gracious, this man was one of the most beautiful men I'd ever seen.

He had pretty features. His eyes were a gray-hazel color, and yes, even from this distance, I was struck at how clear they were. His cheekbones were set wide on the sides of his face, but he had such a square jawline that it worked for him. He was rugged but handsome and hot all at the same time. I was putting his height at six four. Weight at 210. He was dressed in some seriously nice threads, all business suit. His shoes were the expensive kind, like what I would joke that a Wall Street dude would wear to a hockey game. At seeing me, he paused, but then a wicked grin slowly spread over his face, and that knocked me back a bit too.

It was almost a nice punch to my sternum, one to shock me more than incapacitate me.

He spoke into the phone: "Excuse me a bit." I could hear the other person talking, but he ended the call and put his phone into his pocket. "Hello."

He was looking me up and down, looking like a bored cat who had come across a mouse and had a new toy to play with.

"I didn't mean to interrupt your phone—"

"On the contrary, thank you very much." He came down a few more steps. "I needed an excuse to get off the call."

I shifted backward, giving him space—or myself space—as he continued until he was on the step right above, looking down. "I was looking for the bathroom."

"These are the stairs." His voice was a low baritone croon, and he was still doing the eye thing where he wasn't just assessing me, but he was reading my soul, and he was enjoying whatever he was reading. If I were a character in a book, I might've likened him to a vampire. I almost started laughing because how ridiculous was I? Getting nervous with this guy, who it was very apparent was in a whole different tax bracket than me. But normal me wouldn't have cared. Normal me wouldn't have stuck around this long either.

I nodded as he stepped down, facing me directly. "I realized. There's a sign that said 'bathrooms' and pointed in here. I came in, not remembering the doors lock behind you."

"Right." He still had that smile, his eyes sparking up. "Because if you read the sign on the door, it would've said 'emergency exit only.' And that it locks."

I refused to flush for this guy. Nope. But the back of my neck did get heated. A little bit.

"Yeah. My mistake." My tone was cool, and I was giving him the look to back off.

That seemed to amuse him even more. "What's your name?"

I bristled. "None of your business, how about that?"

His eyes went to smoldering. This guy wasn't normal. "Sass." His tone went soft. "I like it."

That made me bristle even more. "Excuse me?" I shifted back, getting in a stance as I automatically started thinking how to handle him if he made a move.

As if reading my mind, or feeling the air shift, he drew back. The smoldering effect lessened, but just a little. It was still there. I was still amusing him, and I didn't know how I felt about that either. "You have no idea who I am."

I frowned. "That gets you off or something?"

His grin turned inward, showing off a dimple.

God. The dimple. What female didn't have a thing for a cheek dimple? That wasn't fair. Some of my bristling eased up.

He chuckled, still in that baritone, and it was *sensual too*. "Apparently it does with you. Trust me. I'm just as shocked as you seem to be." His eyes sharpened. "Are you here with someone?"

I straightened out of the fighting stance I'd assumed and relaxed, only slightly. "My roommate."

Another spark of interest in those eyes of his. "Is your roommate a significant other? Or *just* a roommate?"

Damn. He was direct, and fast about it.

If I'd been at the bar and in the mood for a one-nighter, this conversation would have a whole different ending. I liked guys who were direct. *A lot.*

"She's my best friend." I saw the next question forming, so I added, "And she's straight."

His head lowered, those eyes of his softening. "And you? Who are you into?"

My throat swelled up. I didn't know why, but I felt entranced by him.

He took a step closer, slowly.

I couldn't tear my gaze away, and I couldn't take a step back. I didn't want to.

A part of me was railing at myself, in the back of my head, but my heart was pounding, and my throat was still swollen. My body was heating, and an ache was forming between my legs.

This man, what was he doing to me?

This reaction didn't happen to me, ever.

"Who are you into, Miss . . . ?" His head cocked to the side, like he could lure me into answering him.

I wanted to do just that too.

My lips parted from surprise, but then his eyes shifted to my shirt, and everything changed. Abruptly.

He'd been seductive and coaxing. And then nothing. Frigid cold.

I even shivered, feeling his withdrawal though he hadn't moved a muscle.

I followed his eyes down to my sternum. My badge was sticking out from my jacket, but when I looked back up, I sucked in my breath. His eyes were on me, and they were *not* friendly. They were hostile. All that flirting was gone in an instant.

"You a cop?" His tone was flat, cutting.

"I'm a parole officer."

His phone started ringing again, and he fished it out of his pocket. Without saying a word to me, he hit accept and turned to go back up the stairs. "Hey. Hold one moment. I'm heading for the door. Open it for me."

I couldn't suppress a shiver as he disappeared around the turn, going up the last set of stairs.

Thump!

The door opened. Sounds from the hockey game filtered into the stairwell, and then they were muted again.

I waited, but nothing.

He'd gone.

What the hell had just happened?

Also, I was still locked in.

CHAPTER TWO

JESS

"Girl." Kelly was laughing when she opened the door for me. We'd had a good chat while I navigated her to where I was. It had been an elaborate game of Marco Polo, with Kelly laughing as she'd called out the Marco part and me half growling when I'd answered the Polo part. We were in our older twenties, and even though my bladder wasn't amused, it was a fun game. I guess some part of us would never grow old.

I stepped through, the sounds of the game coming full force.

"How did you end up in there again?"

I'd already explained, so I ignored her, tossing my now-empty beer cup in the recycling bin. "Where's the bathroom?"

She kept laughing as she showed me, and since we were smack in the middle of the third period, the place was empty.

And filthy. Paper towels were everywhere, some hanging half out of the garbage and a huge pile around the bottom. There was water pooling under one of the sinks.

Kelly went toward the sink area while I grabbed the first clean stall I could find.

It was the sixth one.

"You said there was a guy in there with you?"

I grinned. "In here?"

"You know what I'm talking about. Who was it?"

I didn't know what to say. This was Kelly. Recently divorced and heartbroken, but she was a romantic at heart. I mention anything about him, his reaction to me, and she'd be building him up to being some wealthy Romeo.

"No one. He thought I was a cop."

"Why'd he think that?"

"He saw my badge."

"Why's your badge out?"

I finished peeing, flushed, and came out. She was waiting at the end, leaning against the wall with her arms crossed over her chest. I felt sheepish about this, but I didn't know why. "I saw an old parolee and wanted to scare some of his coworkers away."

She burst out laughing.

I went to the sink, washed my hands, and did a cursory hair fix.

I was a mess on a normal day, but there was an extra sparkle to me. My skin glowed a little more. I had a little bit more pink to my cheeks, and my eyes were crystal clear, which said something because they were normally dark almond.

"I don't believe you."

"What?" I shot Kelly a look, taking my badge off and putting it back in my purse.

Then I studied myself.

I was normal weight, normal height. Five six. I kept myself in shape and conditioned, because it would be stupid not to be for my job. Especially being a female. Since I'd decided to go this career route, I'd been married to my job. Had to be, but I also had to roll with the punches, or the caseload.

A decent rack.

Some ass behind me.

I liked my body. I liked that it wouldn't break if I got into a situation, but I knew I was easy on the eyes too. A heart-shaped face that was a little long but fresh. Guys tended to like how I looked. An ex once told me it was my eyes, how dark they got, and he groaned every time I walked into a room. Said my legs were the type that guys longed to have them squeeze around their waist.

I became aware of Kelly studying me as I had been studying myself. "What?"

She shrugged, a secretive grin tugging at her mouth. She shifted, resting one shoulder against the wall. Her eyebrows went up. "Nothing. You wanna finish the game or get out of here?"

"What's the score?"

"Kansas City scored two while you were in there. It's going to be a blowout."

Shit. "Yeah. Let's take off."

"You want to head home?"

It was Thursday night. I had a full day tomorrow. Normally, yes. I'd be in bed by ten, but something different was in me tonight. It was that guy, I knew it, but I was going to ignore it.

"Nah. Let's go to Octavia."

"Nice! Why not Katya?"

I shook my head. Being a PO didn't pay all my bills, so I bartended at Katya every Friday and Saturday night in Manhattan. I didn't want to go where I worked; I wanted a full night off, and Octavia was just that. It wasn't a new club, but it was dark and sinful and anonymous.

I was thirsting for some of that sin tonight.

Or maybe it was the guy I just met.

CHAPTER THREE

TRACE

We were heading out to our Escalade when Caleb asked us to hold up. "I need to double-check something real quick. My apologies, Mr. West."

Ashton came to stand next to me. We were best friends—had been all our life and would be when we both left this world. Every step of the way. It was how we were.

Because of our history, we weren't friends that needed to speak. I wasn't waiting with a nervous employee or business worker, and probably because of that silence, we heard the shriek of laughter that sounded from farther down, outside the main arena's entrance.

It was her.

I would've recognized her voice anywhere, and I was ignoring how that was alarming to me when I looked over.

My body locked up, and I lifted my head higher.

"You a cop?"

"A parole officer."

She'd been intriguing at first glance. A longer look and I wanted to fuck her, but it was *more*. I wanted her for a full weekend. I wanted to twist her in so many different positions, introduce my dick to so many enjoyments of her body, but that badge. Everything went cold in me when I saw that.

She said a PO, but she was a cop. A fucking cop.

But seeing her again, and not even that, hearing her again. Her laugh got my attention.

I *wanted* her.

I couldn't have her, but I wanted her anyway.

This was going to be a problem.

"The blonde or the dark-haired one?"

Of course Ashton would take notice.

"The dark-haired one."

I kept watching her, but I knew Ashton was giving her a more studious look.

"You know her?"

"No." I looked at him as Caleb came around and opened the back door. "Find out who she is."

Then I got in, and Ashton was pulling his phone out even as he got in behind me.

He had the quicker connections. He'd have her name within an hour.

CHAPTER FOUR

JESS

Dancing and drinking at Octavia had been a good decision, but the morning after, my head was pounding a whole different decision. Coffee, coffee, coffee. I needed all the espresso shots I could get in, and still, six shots later, it wasn't enough.

Parking my state-issued sedan, I was walking in when I heard from the side, "Incoming, Montell."

I ignored him. If I couldn't see him, he couldn't see me. I was using my four-year-old reasoning.

Unfortunately, he started walking next to me. "Stopped at Cleo's, huh?"

I groaned. "Go away, Travis."

"Why didn't you get me anything to drink? I could use coffee. Was up late covering your ass, after all."

Those were fighting words. I ground to a halt and faced him. "What are you talking about?"

The same Derek Travis I texted last night. A PO for the last three years, and I was so beyond his gripes. He was decent with others, so I had to give him that credit, but he went out of his way to make my job difficult.

His smirk was next level. He was wearing shades and his usual work attire: khaki cargo pants and a black long-sleeved shirt under the vest we all wore. "One of your parolees violated last night. He got picked up, tested positive for cocaine and meth. You messed up, Montell."

See. Busting my balls. I had nothing to do with what my parolee did. "How'd you find this out?"

"I was here when he was brought in. Team Leader wanted an update for the board. He's doing a call with them, right about now." He said that so casual and slow as he was pretending to look at his wrist, the one without a watch.

I cursed because this guy. It was none of his business, and our team leader knew that.

Leo should've waited for me to let him know what was going on.

I tossed my things in my office and walked right into our team leader's. "Hey." A quick head nod to him and I sat down, grabbing the file he had open on his desk.

Leo, short for Leland Aguila, was my boss, but also like a father-slash-mentor to me. He was the reason, or one of the reasons, I came into this line of work. There was a time I needed guidance and I needed the world to make sense again. Leo gave that to me. Because of that, I didn't like seeing the thin line of disapproval on his flat mouth. Or how the wrinkles on his forehead were pushed together.

He was a big man, over six feet. Two eighty. Bald, because he said this work didn't allow him to grow any hair, but he kept himself mostly in shape. A solid lineman.

He was putting his phone away. "What are you doing?"

"You're calling about my guy, right?"

Leo paused, his big head tilting to the side. His eyes gentled. "No. That's for you to do. You got time. Why are you asking?"

Oh.

I gave a tight shrug. "Travis."

16

Understanding dawned. "Ignore him. You know how he is. He wants to get a reaction from you."

Yeah. I didn't appreciate it.

Leo gave me a grin and motioned for the door. "Get out of my office, Montell. Go find Officer Hartman and do whatever you both need to do today."

I gave him a mock salute, which he snorted at, and did just that.

Hearing Val's tone, hearing the irritation from her, I knew exactly where she was and headed over to her office. She was on the phone but just setting it down. Seeing me, she wheeled back her chair. "Ready?"

Home visits. Not fun.

I clipped my head in a nod. "Ready."

CHAPTER FIVE

TRACE

"She works at Katya?" The laughter in Ashton's voice was barely contained.

He was reading a copy of the report our guy had put together in the last two days of following her. I'd gotten it earlier in the day, but that didn't mean hearing it again was any less of a rub than when I'd first found out that she worked for me.

I made good money. Had a good life. And I slept with women when I wanted them, but it hadn't always been like that. I'd had a steady girlfriend in high school and another one in college. I'd been faithful. Felt appropriate. If they were giving me their heart and body, I'd do the same. But I got older, and my dad's "helping" in the family business was him "fucking it up," and my uncle started calling me to take over and fix the mess my father always made.

I was tired of it. My uncle was tired of it.

But that part of my life began rearing up more and more, and I knew it wasn't right to have another girlfriend, not in this life. It was too much with the two worlds already. So, casual sex or women who knew the score. They got dinner, drinks, a night where they felt important being on my arm, and I got sex with no strings. They were women who didn't want a relationship, either, so it was a win-win for both of us.

But now, I wanted her, and for the first time in a long time, I was considering throwing out my rules.

For her.

But only one weekend. That was it. That was all I could take. Fuck her out of my system and move on, go back to my normal routine. All would be well then.

"You're so screwed." Ashton was back to laughing.

I gave him a dark look. "I have a gun in my drawer, you know."

That made him laugh harder, and he leaned forward, shaking his head. "You want her to know you own Katya?"

"*We* own Katya." It was our club, his and mine. Ashton had his family, too, similar to mine, but Katya was one of our endeavors that had no connection to either of our families. We wouldn't allow it. If anyone tried to push in, it would be an internal war.

"Yeah, yeah. You know what I mean."

Did I want her to know? No. "Call Anthony. Tell him the arrangements. I don't want her to know, not yet."

Ashton was pulling out his phone as my own began buzzing. It was our PI.

I answered. "You have something more on her?"

"She bowls."

I frowned. "Bowls?"

"You wanted the file quick, so I didn't get it in there, but every Sunday, her and her roommate go to Easter Lanes. It's almost a religious event."

That . . . was helpful. "When do they go?"

"They're there by six, play till eight, and hang out till nine thirty."

Easter Lanes. "Who owns the place?"

"Molly Easter. Bought it from her father, turned it around, and it's doing well."

"Who's her father?"

"Shorty Easter, real name is Marcus. Gambler. He owes big to Ashton's family."

I glanced to Ashton as our PI was telling me this, and feeling my gaze, Ashton looked back to me. His eyebrow rose. "What?"

"Anything else?"

"Back to your parole officer. She's tight with her brother, incarcerated for killing their father."

My blood went cold hearing that. That hadn't been in the report. "You just found that out too?"

He hesitated on his end. "I need to follow up on one more thing before I can answer that. Trust me, you'll want me to wait."

"Fine. Get it to me as soon as possible."

"Will do."

"What's going on?" Ashton asked after I hung up.

I filled him in about Easter, and he snorted. "Yeah, I remember that guy. Family keeps him around because he's funny, tells good stories, but he owes out of his ass."

"You know the daughter?"

His eyes narrowed. "You're going to make your approach at a bowling alley?"

I sighed. "Might have to, and you're not coming."

"I met the daughter once, when we were kids. She won't remember me."

"I don't want to risk it, not yet."

"A lot of work you're putting in to get some ass when all you normally need to do is wave a hand, and they *come*."

I shot him a look, because I was completely aware of that fact.

This was aggravating.

CHAPTER SIX

JESS

He was here.

Sunday nights at Easter Lanes was our jam: me and Kelly. I was a pain up people's asses all week long. Friday and Saturday were given to pouring drinks and hoping none of my parolees violated at my second job, but Sundays were ours. Night off. We loved Molly Easter. She'd become a friend from doing a pottery class with Kelly, and when she'd told us she was taking over her dad's old place but going to make it better, we were here. Every Sunday. We showed up. We supported how we could, but in the meantime it became a sanctuary to our group.

When I bowled, I was a whole different person.

No worries. No rules. I could come in wearing a mustache on my face, dressed as a trucker if I wanted. No one cared. They loved our bowling outfits, and everyone should bowl in an outfit. Serious business with a side of fun. Also, Sunday nights were not date nights. Those people never understood the mission of dressing for bowling.

I ground to a halt coming into the door, seeing him there. He was in a back booth, alongside the wall with another guy across from him. There were only a few booths on that wall, set across from the bar. I stopped and stared. I couldn't help myself, and Kelly walked into me.

"Hey, what are you—*ooh*." She breathed in. "Who is *that*?!"

"*You a cop?*"

The condemnation from him as he asked that question, how cold he'd been.

I shivered now, remembering, but more remembering from the warmth I'd felt a second earlier.

As if feeling my gaze, his eyes turned my way.

I waited, expecting shock. There was none, and *that* spread shock through me.

I frowned, but then I was just sucked in by his gaze because he was all-consuming. I felt burned from the inside out. God, he was gorgeous. He'd been in a business suit at the hockey game, but this time he was in a white shirt, a leather jacket, and I knew without seeing that his jeans were some serious quality. He leaned forward, those clear eyes never wavering from me, and then he drew back. His drink in hand and still holding my gaze, he raised the glass to his mouth. His throat moved as he took a long drink, and god, I hated how pretty he was.

My heart was pushing out into my chest, trying to get free.

This guy. I didn't know him, and I made up my mind. I did not want to know him, ever.

"Jess—" Kelly's voice tore me out of whatever spell I'd been in, and I wrenched myself around, forcibly walking in the opposite direction. It took a second before I comprehended I was going straight to the arcade game area, but dammit, I gritted my teeth and kept on. I needed to be away from him, so I was committing, going to the bathroom in the back. I needed a breather, because even walking away from him, I could feel his gaze on me.

I pushed through to the bathroom. Two teenage girls were in there, and both jumped at the ferocity of me.

"Get out," I said.

One squealed. The other started to glare. "Who do you think—" She cut herself off, grimacing as her friend grabbed her arm and yanked her behind her. She rushed out as Kelly was stepping inside. She held the door for them, watching them run out before letting the door close and coming in farther behind me.

I was at the sink, glaring at the mirror, watching her warily because there was no way that response from me was going to go unspoken about.

She was cautious, moving to the sink beside me. "Uh . . . you going to fill me in? Who was that guy?"

"The asshole from the hockey game."

Her eyebrows pinched down. She took a moment, and then understanding dawned. "Him?! That's the dude who's pissed you're a cop?"

I was gritting my teeth again because it didn't matter. "Why the fuck is he here?"

"Let's go ask him." Her voice was upbeat, and she was all smiles now.

"Why are you smiling?"

Her grin turned more Cheshire, and she leaned back, getting settled as she folded her arms over her chest. "Because that guy, my friend, wants to bang the fuck out of you, and you're going to let him."

"What? No!" *Yes!*

She snorted. "I took him in for only a few seconds, and I could tell right away that that is not a dude who comes to Easter Lanes for bowling. He's here for you. He totally knew you were coming, and that means he asked around about you."

I was shaking my head. "No way. That's—"

"Totally what's going on. He wants you."

"I'm a cop. That's an issue for him. I don't want to fuck someone who has a problem with that."

Kelly snorted again and turned on the water. After wetting her fingers a bit, she turned it off, took my shoulders, faced me toward her, and then began running her fingers through my hair.

I knocked her hand away. "What are you doing?"

She ignored me and went right back to shifting through my hair. "Giving you a little bit of a 'wet' look. Guys love that shit."

"Agh." I twisted away from her.

He came here. *Here.* I was always happy here. It was my happy place, and he had invaded it. I was in the bathroom, stewing and avoiding him, and that wasn't me.

Kelly took my groan the other way. "Totally. You go out there and show him who's boss. Just make sure that extends to the bedroom, and"—she lowered her voice because I was opening the door, and whispered loudly—"tell me all about it in the morning."

I shook my head because none of that was going to happen. Raising my hand up, I gave her the middle finger over my shoulder. Kelly just laughed. When we went back out, bypassing the arcade section, I saw the two girls that I'd barked at hadn't left. They stood off to the side, whispering with each other, and had joined a whole other group of teenagers. Boys and girls. A few of them looked like future delinquents, but maybe that was just my profession coming out of me.

I refused to look at his booth, even though I felt his attention as soon as I cleared the teenager section. Yep. Totally refusing. The back of my neck was getting hot, but still refusing.

I marched up to Molly, who was behind the counter tonight. Five five. I would've classed her weight at 116. To me, she was tiny. A few freckles on her face. Strawberry-blonde hair. Wide blue eyes. Molly was so pretty, but it was almost wasted since she took care of this bowling alley with most of her time. I knew there was bad blood between her and her dad, but we weren't the type of friends who shared that kind of personal stuff. It was mostly bowling, lighthearted laughs, though Molly was a kind soul. There were stories about how she could overreact. Her staff called it "the switch." But I'd not seen that side of her. Sometimes she manned the bar; tonight it was the bowling section. She took one look at me, and her eyebrows shot up to her forehead. Her gaze trailed behind, and she asked Kelly, "Do I want to know?"

"No," I answered.

Kelly came up to the counter beside me and breathed, excitedly, "*Yes.*"

"Now I really want to know."

"It's so exciting." From Kelly.

I was going to ignore both of them, except I pointed at my usual shoes. "Please tell me you haven't rented those out to anyone this week?"

Molly didn't move at first. She stood back, her hands still holding on to the counter, and her gaze went from me to Kelly, who I could tell from the corner of my eye was nodding her head, and Molly sighed, reaching back for the shoes I always wore, the ones I bought specifically for me. She placed them on the counter. "You know I wouldn't. These are yours. I just hold space for them."

"I want mine too!"

Kelly's exuberance was getting on my nerves. I knew this was how she'd react, the ever romantic she was. She also just really liked sex, and good sex. I heard porn sounds coming from her room on a regular basis, and I was pretty sure she just had it as background noise sometimes.

Molly was chuckling and shaking her head to herself as she set us both up. We'd play four games. It was our usual number, but I was tempted to say we'd only do two tonight, but then Kelly nudged my elbow. "Our bowling friends are here."

It was time to bowl.

CHAPTER SEVEN

TRACE

We watched while she played three games.

"Not that I don't mind a field trip every now and then, how many games are you going to wait—" I could hear Eric's laughter in his voice.

"Shut up."

He laughed, a bit darker than before, and began to slide out of the booth. "Fine, but whatever you're hoping for here, I'll need a ride home. I'm too far gone to drive myself."

I gave him a look. "You have millions. You can afford a car service."

He snorted, taking out some cash and throwing a wad of it on the table. "Yeah, but you have entire drivers at your disposal, and I'm here for you tonight. Trust and believe I'm going to be grilling Ashton on why I'm here and not him." He began to turn away when he nodded to the cash. "I gotta piss. Next round is on me."

I pulled my phone out and sent off a text.

Trace: Eric's curious what's going on. Don't say a word to him.

We'd all been fraternity brothers in college, and while I shared that history with Eric, he wasn't in the same world Ashton and I both were.

Eric only knew about Wall Street. He knew that life, not the one Ashton and I kept hidden, and me asking him to meet me at a bowling alley was not in the realm of nightclubs and cocktail lounges that we usually frequented.

Ashton: Fucking duh, man.

I laughed, a dry one, but that cut out as soon as *she* slid into Eric's abandoned side.

I grinned, slow and steady. "Finally."

My god, she was beautiful. Her hair had been hanging free and loose when she'd first walked in, but it was now put up in a braid, perhaps to match one of her bowling companions. Either way, her skin was glowing, her lips a little fuller than what I'd remembered, but she was seething.

Her hands clasped together, and she rested her elbows on the table, leaning toward me. "What do you want?" Her words were clipped.

I picked up my drink, swished the liquid around as I slowly leaned in to match her posture. I breathed out the word right before I took a sip. "You."

I did not miss how her chest rose. She sucked in some oxygen, but her eyes flickered. There was a wildness there, a brief second before she slammed a wall down and shot back in the seat. "Thought you couldn't stand me. I'm a cop."

"You're a parole officer. There's a difference." My tone was bored, but I was anything *but* that. I was invigorated. "I'm also aware you've been doing your job for years, and you're quite good at it."

She was glaring at me, and for a moment, she couldn't speak. Or she didn't want to. "How do you know that?"

I lowered my head, my eyes never moving from hers. "I hired a PI. For being a PO, you're not perceptive about a guy following you."

Her nostrils flared. "I met you three nights ago."

"Exactly."

"You got all of that in three days?"

"Two, actually, but he's updating the file each day. I'm enjoying every tidbit he's finding out about you."

"Stop it." She jerked forward, but I loved it. It only brought her closer, and my gaze went to her mouth.

Those lips. Those very full lips that I hadn't tasted. Not yet.

My dick was trying to tunnel its way out of my pants.

"No." I whispered those words, loving how they produced that wildness back in her gaze, just for a moment.

I wanted more of that.

I wanted to be the one to let that person loose, whoever she was inside.

"I have a case for harassment here."

I chuckled, leaning back, but I held my glass in the air between us. "Try it. It's my foreplay."

That wild look came back, and it was staying longer each time it did.

I started to wonder what she would do if I got her to stay longer. What did I need to do to make that happen?

"I don't even know your name."

I glanced to where she'd come from, seeing her remaining friends all looking our way. They were trying to sneak their looks, but they were horrible at it. The one friend, the one I knew was her roommate, wasn't hiding at all. She was grinning widely at us and almost clapping her hands. Her delight was obvious.

"Your friend has horrible taste in men."

She sucked in her breath, and I saw her fingers tighten on the edge of the table. She'd been holding on. I'd missed that part, but now even that captivated me.

"That's what I thought." Her eyes locked with mine, growing heated, some anger shining through. "You're a bad guy."

28

I paused before I responded because there was more here.

She wanted me back. I knew the signs, but she was fighting herself, and it seemed I had just confirmed her suspicion.

I gave her a slow smile, knowing it was a predatory one. "You already knew that much, but you also know that it won't stop what will happen between you and me."

She leaned back.

Eric was returning, pausing when he saw she was across from me. He gave me a slight nod, flashing two fingers, and moved to the bar, where he slid onto one of the stools. The owner, who had been sneaking looks at us, moved to serve Eric.

I scanned the room. For a moment, no one was watching us.

I moved, grabbing her hand, and before she could yelp, I whisked her through the exit door.

"What are you—"

My mouth found hers, and she froze.

Finally. I know how she tastes.

I waited, my lips coaxing over hers, waiting for her reaction.

Then she gave in.

I angled my head, taking advantage because I knew this wasn't going to last, but my god, I was going to savor every taste I got of her.

CHAPTER EIGHT

JESS

He had me against the wall, and my arms were around him.

It happened so fast. With his touch on my arm, he had me out of the booth and through the door, and then bam, his lips were on mine, and I hadn't been expecting it. Not that touch. Not any of it. As soon as his fingers were on me, there was an explosion of sensation.

A feeling of familiarity, and of home, and excitement, all at once.

But then his lips were touching mine, and that was a whole other ball game.

My body was burning up. The looks. The feeling of him watching me all night long. How he had enjoyed me at the game, all of it was rolled up in one burst of electricity.

I could've climbed him like he was my own pole, but all I did, for one brief moment, was give in.

I surrendered, because he hadn't been the only one thinking of this since that Thursday night. My body had been aching, but then sanity came back to me, and I shoved him off.

I was panting, my pulse pounding. My whole body was flushed, and I was sweating.

His gaze was unsteady, and I felt a moment of triumph, because I did that to him. Not that he'd been quiet about wanting me, but he'd felt in control. This whole time, he'd been toying with me, but now he was off kilter, and I was the reason.

This wasn't just a one-way street. I had power over him too.

His eyes glazed over, and he began to move in again.

I shot a hand against his chest. He held back, but his hands moved to my legs, where they gripped me in place. He had one holding me up against the wall, cupping half of my ass. His fingers pressed in, and he moved his pelvis into me.

I started to make a noise, to stop him, but then he was there and he was touching me, and dear god, he felt so good.

He ground against me, and I almost forgot where we were. The haze of wanting his lips on mine again was so strong, but a burst of laughter sounded on the other side of the door. It was like a bucket of water drenching us. We were brought back to reality once more.

Reality sucked.

His eyes closed, and he pried his hands off of me, forcibly taking a step back. He raked a hand through his hair, his eyes flashing an apology, one that seemed genuine. "I hadn't intended that when I brought you out here."

Breathing was hard around him. "What did you intend?"

"Honestly? I have no idea, so maybe I did intend for that to happen." His gaze lingered on my mouth, and his eyes darkened.

He was about to go back in when I sidestepped him. I reached behind, finding the door handle. My chest was still rising and falling at a rapid pace, my heartbeat a loud drum in my ears. "I think"—I winced at hearing how raspy my voice was because he did that. He had that power over me—"it's very obvious, whoever you are, that you are not good for me, or me for you, so let's leave this behind us." I was half whispering those words, and my heart was squeezing again because my body was screaming for the opposite of what I was saying. But I knew, I

31

just knew, this wouldn't end well. One night wouldn't do it for me. He was already under my skin, and that was from one kiss. I shuddered at what would happen if we did have sex. This guy was disastrous for me.

His eyes were pained, but he was listening to me.

I paused, because this had to be final, and I hardened my voice. I hardened everything inside of me. "You should stay away."

I didn't give him a second to argue or, worse, touch me.

I opened the door and slipped through and pulled it shut right behind me.

I paused, one beat, but then as I felt him start to open the door, I did what I never thought I'd do.

I fled.

CHAPTER NINE

JESS

I woke early the next morning, and I was telling myself it was because I needed to check on my mom and not because I wanted to avoid Kelly. Like I'd avoided her last night. I'd taken off, sending her a text that she'd need to get a ride from one of our bowling friends.

I'd been in bed by the time she'd rolled in, which was late because I knew they liked to have a couple extra beers after, sometimes going out dancing too.

It wasn't that I didn't want to fill Kelly in on this guy, whose name I still didn't know, but it was that if I forgot about him, didn't talk about him, I wouldn't remember how he made me feel. Or how my body reacted to him, because it was too much and it was out of control, and in all of my life, I'd never felt that.

I was twenty-nine. I didn't know if I should be sad about that or pissed off that it took this long.

Either way, it didn't matter. Whoever he was, he was bad news.

I needed to forget him, forget the whole thing. The two meetings. The constant thinking about him. Now the continuous remembering how he felt, his kisses, his touches, how he felt pressed up and into me—on a constant loop. I needed to forget that too.

I groaned, shaking my head, because the only thing that would dash all my dreams and hopes—a visit to my mother. That's not why I was going to see her. It was just time to check on her. I didn't like to go longer than a couple weeks if I didn't hear from her, and the two weeks was up. I was planning on dropping by an hour before work. That gave me time to grab coffee and also time to handle whatever needed to be handled at the house, because with my mom, there was usually something that needed to be handled.

I stopped before heading to Mom's and got coffee from Marco's Corner Stand, which was the most divine Cuban coffee I'd ever had in my life. Knowing Chelsea would grumble if I didn't bring her some, I grabbed one for her as well.

We were in the same brownstone we'd been all our life. It was inherited from our grandfather's grandfather. Since my dad died, since my brother, Isaac, went to prison, the place wasn't being kept up. My mom lived here, but she didn't handle any of the maintenance. I grimaced, coming to the front steps and seeing two of them cracked down the middle. The frames needed a new paint job, but that was cosmetic. I knocked, rang the doorbell, because Chelsea Montell didn't like me walking in and scaring her. I was more under the impression she wanted a few minutes to stash her stuff, whatever it was that she knew I wouldn't want her having. So I did it, because I'm a good daughter, despite her complaints.

I waited a little before I used my key to go inside. *"Ma!"*

"Oh gawd, shut up." A stair creaked upstairs. She was coming from the bathroom. "What are you doing here at this hour?"

I did a full scan as she came around the stairs corner, tugging her robe closed in front of her. Chelsea Montell was a spitfire sixty-four-year-old. Dark hair that had only a few grays in it and a naturally beautiful face that had aged well so she looked in her older forties instead. She was rail thin. What calories didn't fill her body, her spirit did instead. A crass mouth at times, a penchant for cursing like a trucker, she really enjoyed her booze. I got a strong whiff and guessed that she'd stuffed a bottle of vodka away before coming down here.

"Hey, Mom."

"Mom." She made a face, the makeup from last night still caked all over her, but she wasn't looking me in the eye. Her free hand was holding tight to the railing. "I was just 'Ma' a second ago. Now I'm 'Mom.' What happened to the 'Ma' greeting?" She came to the bottom step and paused a second to get her bearings. Her body was unsteady before she turned, still not looking at me, and headed for the kitchen.

I went around through the living room and the dining room and used the second entrance to the kitchen. She was just making her way past the fridge. I put her coffee on the middle island. "I got you Marco's."

She raised her head a little, making a show of taking a whiff. A genuine smile pulled at her mouth, but she didn't look at me. Still focusing on the steps in front of her. "Smells delicious, honey. Thank you."

Honey. I was a "honey" now that I got Marco's for her.

I coughed, clearing my throat. "Is the bathroom still not working down here?" I didn't wait, heading for the stairs. "I'll be right back."

"Wait. No!"

I ignored her, hurrying up the stairs. "Hold on, Mom! I've got the flow. You have any old tampons up here?"

She yelled something back, but I went into her bathroom and shut the door.

Then I went to town, but she always hid the booze in the same places. It just changed rooms. This time, I opened the bathroom closet door and took a breath before reaching back behind the pile of towels reserved for guests. My hand found something round and solid, and I pulled it out.

Vodka. I'd been right.

It was a new bottle too.

I reached back, seeing if there was more. There wasn't, not in this room, and she wouldn't let me check the other rooms. She'd be hammering up at me, so I unscrewed it, poured 80 percent of it down the toilet, flushed, and refilled it with water from the tap. I wiped it off, screwed the cap on, and put it back.

I hated this, whatever this was. A game? What we both knew, what we'd had so many fights over, all the insults, the ultimatums, the tears. All of it reduced to this game now where we both knew, but we both didn't speak up. Losing Dad, and then Isaac, had taken its toll on both of us.

I said a prayer under my breath that she wouldn't realize the vodka was watered down for a while. Was I even right to do what I just did? I had no idea, but it was what it was.

I hurried back down the stairs and smiled. "False emergency. I found one in my purse."

She was at the end of the stairs, suspicion on her face. One of her hands was propped on her waist, and she'd forgotten her robe wasn't tied closed. There was a small opening now, and I saw she was dressed in black leggings and a sweater that she usually reserved for bingo down the block. She hadn't changed clothes.

She'd slept in those clothes. Or passed out in those clothes.

I blinked, pretending I didn't see them, and sailed past her to the kitchen. After grabbing my coffee, I went back out and stepped to her. "I gotta go, Mom. Love you. Let me know when you want me to bring dinner, yeah?"

She didn't say a word but moved in when I kissed her on the cheek.

I moved back, going for the door. "Love you again."

The door closed behind me, and I took a breath, one, before resolving that I needed to get those steps fixed.

CHAPTER TEN

TRACE

Uncle Steph was the head of our family's business, and when Uncle Steph called to have you come by, you did what he said. I'd put the call through to my assistant to have all my meetings rescheduled for the day, and instead of heading toward my office on Wall Street, I was being driven back to Red Hook.

We were halfway there when my phone began buzzing.

Ashton calling.

I hit accept. "Hey."

"You're heading to your uncle?"

I had texted him earlier. "Yeah."

"You want me to come?"

"No. Uncle Steph only calls for a few reasons, and I'm guessing this has something to do with my father."

"Let me know when you're done."

"I will."

Ashton's family and my family worked together at times and at other times were very separate. I had a feeling this meeting was a very separate thing, but I'd have to see. We were pulling up to my uncle's house when I got a text.

Blocked Number: Here's more information on her. Check out the mom situation.

I sighed but put my phone away. I'd have to look into that after the meeting. We pulled into the driveway and went to the back, and there were some of our family's men waiting for me.

They were dressed in sweatsuits, white shirts under, and gold chains peeking out from under their jackets. All my uncle's men were heavier, from either fat or muscle. All big. All imposing. Some was just for the intimidation factor, but I knew most of my uncle's men were violent and had to be for him. That was the business they were in.

My car door was opened for me.

Bobby gave a nod. "Tristian."

Bobby. Barrel. Buddha. They were the three main security guys around my uncle.

I didn't care for any of them, but my uncle had his ways. I considered them to be in the "old" way, but it was what it was. I gave each a nod, noting none of them used my nickname, which was how it was supposed to be. Trace was used for those I liked.

I headed for the house as a door was opened by one of my uncle's men.

I stepped in, seeing my uncle at the stovetop. A warm smile spread over his face. "Nephew Trace. Come here." He put down his teapot and moved my way, his arms up and held out.

I stepped in, giving my uncle a hug. He held me tight a second before pounding my back one last time, then stepped away, but his hands remained on my shoulders. He was looking me over, a proud smile on his face. But he was always proud of me. He never kept that a secret. He shook me slightly. "My boy. My nephew. A big Wall Street guy. You're doing well. Making our family proud. That's what you're doing."

My throat swelled for a beat.

Dominic West was my father, but in so many ways, my real father was the man in front of me. They were brothers; my father was the eldest, but he was a screwup, and I meant that in a respectful manner, but it was what it was. He *was* a screwup. My uncle had stepped up to the plate and taken over the family business, and he'd been running it ever since he was twenty-two. It'd taken its toll with three divorces and one son who was dead from a drug overdose and another son who refused to acknowledge his father. My cousin wasn't exiled by my uncle, but there was an unspoken understanding that no one brought up his name unless Uncle Steph did.

"How's your sister?" He patted my shoulders one last time before moving back to the teapot and turning on the burner. He motioned to the table. "You want some tea? It's a new thing my doctor turned me on to, and I have to say, I'm a fan. Once I had the Bengal spice tea, I was a goner. Also doesn't hurt that my doc is a beautiful woman. I'll do anything she says."

I snorted because it was guaranteed she was sleeping with my uncle, but I moved to the table and slid into one of the chairs. The water must've been boiling when I first came in because he got two cups ready, dropping the teabags in, and brought them over to me. He grabbed a plate of bread and oil for dipping and also a small bowl of prunes.

I gave him a look, but he just laughed. "It's why I called you, or part of the reason. My health."

"Ah. I see."

Uncle Steph was a big man, but not how his men were. He was tall, six three, and kept himself in shape. If something was going on with his health, it wasn't good.

He motioned to the prunes. "Have some. They're good. I actually enjoy healthy crap now. I can't believe it. Eating so many fruits that that's all I'm shitting out of me nowadays." His eyes grew serious, and I felt the mood shift.

I leaned back. "What's going on, Uncle Steph?"

He leaned back, mirroring my posture, but he put an arm up on the back of the chair next to him and glanced away. "I need your help, and you know I don't like to call on you if I don't have to, but in this case . . ." He looked my way, and he swallowed before going on. "I need you to do some things for me, and you're not going to like them. Any of them."

I knew. I hadn't wanted to know, but I knew being called here today, it was serious.

"What is it?"

His eyes flickered before growing firm again. "If Nico wasn't all the way in Hawaii and wanting nothing to do with this family, I'd call on him, but . . ."

I leaned forward, my hands folding together. I rested my elbows on the table. "Nico wants nothing to do with us. You've lost a son, and I've lost a cousin. That's his decision. I'm here, Uncle Steph. Tell me what you need."

He'd been watching me intently as I spoke, and when I was done, he drew in a deep breath. "Thank you. I—I was worried, but thank you. I've always considered you like a son, especially when Dom passed."

I nodded.

Dom was the opposite in so many ways of Nico. Nico was law abiding, rigid; everything was black and white, and we were firmly on the wrong side to him. Dom was the opposite, and sometimes I wondered if some of my father's ways had slipped through his name, since my cousin was named after my father. Both Dominic. Nico wasn't short for any other name. He was only Nico, and Dom was only Dom. But Dom had liked being a criminal from early on. That led to drugs, alcohol, and his stints in rehab never took. The last rehab had been his eighth time. He'd gotten high the very night they'd released him, and it had been too much for his body.

It'd been three years since Uncle Steph had found his body. He didn't talk about it, but I knew it affected him. Had and still did.

"I'm guessing that part of the reason I'm here is because of my father?"

He nodded, his face shuddering closed. "I got a call from Benny Walden."

I tensed because this was going from bad to really bad. That was Ashton's grandfather.

"Your father was at one of their hotels last night, up north, and he made a mess."

I was not liking the grave look he was giving.

"What kind of a mess?"

"One that I need you to go and clean up. You'll see when you get there."

Fuck, fuck, fuck.

He kept on, picking up a prune. "It will help if you have Ashton go with you. Your father's been taking advantage of our family relationship with the Waldens and especially of your relationship with Ashton. Benny adores you, and he's agreed that nothing will happen to your father if you yourself go up to handle it."

That got a sharp look from me. "My father's still there?"

He gave a nod. "I'm going to send Bobby—"

"No. I have a driver, and I'll have Ashton. No offense against your men, but I want my own around me."

He barely blinked at that, looking more aged for some reason. "Understood, and I do get that, but I'm not sending them up for you. I'm sending them to retrieve your father for me. You go up. Handle the situation. Smooth things over, how you see fit. You have freedom to deal with your father how you'd like, whatever way you'd like, but then I want him sent here with my boys."

My father had *really* messed up.

"They can follow in their own car."

41

"That's fine. But there is another matter . . ." He hesitated. "You deal with this situation first, and the rest can be talked about after. How about that?"

I frowned. That's not what he had been planning. I could tell. "You sure?"

He nodded, looking relieved but also worried at the same time. "Yeah. I'm sure." He motioned to the mug in front of me. "You haven't tried your tea. Try your tea, boy."

I tried my tea.

I didn't care for it, but I drank it. I ate some bread, some prunes, and when Uncle Steph asked if I wanted a second cup, I agreed because he wanted me to stay a little longer.

So I stayed.

CHAPTER ELEVEN

TRACE

Ashton's cousin met us at the back of their hotel. He opened the door, stepped out, and greeted Ashton first. Hugs. A couple pats on the back. Ashton's family was the opposite of mine. They had larger numbers, and there was a general love and trust for each other. There was respect and fondness between Stephano and me, but there was still distrust. I did what my uncle said because he was the closest thing I had to a father, but I wasn't in denial of what he did.

Mafia was Mafia. The only gray area allowed was toward blood. Family members got a lot of leeway unless they went after their own family members. Our bloodline was needed to keep going, keep the family business, but even with that, I was starting to feel some chokehold pressure around my neck. It was down to me to keep the family business going. Stephano knew this. I knew this.

Everyone else, they messed up once, and the consequences were dire.

I suppose there were times I didn't have the stomach for what we've done, but I didn't allow myself to have many of those moments. It was what it was, but having said all that, I was envious of the fondness each had when Ashton stepped back and Marco Walden turned toward me. He was a few years older than us, more ingrained in their family, but as far as I knew, he was the one who oversaw all their hotels.

The fact that Benny, their grandfather and the head of their family, was the one who'd reached out to Stephano told me they were done with my father. Blood would need to be spilled to make sure my father knew they would not be giving him any more allowances. This was a very major fuckup on my father's end, but it was one that'd been coming for so long I wasn't surprised to be in this position. Ashton would've been called in for this anyway. They were showing respect by giving the message to Stephano, who'd handed it down to me. When I'd called Ashton, he'd just gotten his own call from his family.

Everyone was aware of what would need to be done.

"Tristian." Marco held a hand out, and I met it with mine as we half hugged, clapped each other on the back at the same time. "It's good to see you. You and my coz need to come up and spend more time with us."

I nodded, stepping back. "You name the time, and we'll be there."

He tipped his head up, laughing. "Yeah, right. You and Ashton here are building your own empire. We hear the rumors. We know both of you are doing just fine. Huh?" He clasped Ashton's shoulder, giving it a good-natured squeeze. "Am I right? You and Tristian here, both the golden princes of our families. We're proud of you. You hear that? Proud." His tone grew thick with that last word, and he blinked a few times. "Real proud, Ashton. Grandpop says it, but you need to hear it more than you do."

Ashton was blinking a few times too. "Thanks, Marco."

"Yeah."

I waited a beat, giving them a second before I cleared my throat. Ashton saw his family on the regular, but it wasn't as regular as they'd like. That was because of me. He was firmly in our in-between world, focusing on our businesses. Or that's what they felt was the reason. That he chose our friendship over them: there was a grain of contention underneath everything because of that fact. That contention was not known to my uncle or my father. It was known only to me, Ashton, and Ashton's family.

That was another thing that added irritation about my father. Besides being a general asshole in life as a husband, a father, a brother, this was the latest straw that was breaking my back. And I was pissed at myself at the same time because we'd enabled him. Myself. Stephano. Even Ashton's family, to an extent. We all let him do his shit, let him get away with it, and now, when he'd probably gone too far, we were coming in only to make things correct.

I was suddenly so tired of my dad's bullshit that I wanted to get this done. We'd do what we needed to do, and I wanted to get to business. Get it over with, handle everything, and let Bobby have my father when we were done.

"My father?" It was time to ask.

"Right." Marco's tone and eyes both chilled. He straightened up, nodding behind him, and one of his men stepped around us to hold the door. Another two of his men began leading the way. Marco behind them. Ashton. Me. The door guy fell in line behind me.

We walked through their loading area, their kitchen, and a banquet hall, and then he led us to a back elevator. I recognized it from their other hotels. The elevator and this lobby were used for the high rollers or the celebrities. Maximum privacy and confidentiality. I glanced up, seeing a rounded mirror set in the corner, but I knew this family. There was no way those cameras were on. They were permanently "broken." Their excuse for any authorities who might try to get a warrant for their security footage.

Once in the elevator, Marco still didn't say a word. Two of his men stayed back, guarding the elevator. The third one, the door guy, came with us.

Marco hit the button for the top floor. He shot me a look. "He didn't have that room initially. When the incident happened, we moved everyone up there. Easier to keep a handle on the collateral."

Fuck.

It wasn't just my dad involved.

I refrained from letting out a curse, but *goddamn, Dominic.*

The hotel was attached to their casino. My guess was that I was walking into a possible overdose? A hooker? Or a high-end escort? That's what I was hoping for, because if it wasn't a working girl, we'd be wading into an area that, if I let myself, would turn my stomach more than it was already going.

I couldn't let myself go there.

I was aware of Ashton glancing my way and Marco watching his cousin. Both were tensing up, both knowing there was a small chance I'd lose my shit inside.

I locked down. I had to.

We arrived.

The doors slid open, giving us immediate entrance to the entire top floor, which I was guessing was the presidential suite.

I saw the reason for the relocation. Three bedroom doors were open. Each had a guard standing in front of it, and at the ping of our entrance, I heard my father before I saw him.

"Finally! Goddamn, motherfucking. This is—" He cut off, coming from the bedroom closest to our right side. He saw me, and his words dried up.

He swallowed, and I'd only seen my father pale one time before. That was the night my mother died.

He paled this time.

Goddamn! I knew what that meant.

"Son." His tone was all different this time. Way more congeniality, but I heard the caution in there.

I began shaking my head as I went to the far-left bedroom, rage filling me up. I was losing my battle over my self-restraint.

"Trace—"

"Do not call me that!" I pointed at him as I kept going.

Churning. More churning.

My stomach was twisting.

The guard moved aside, but I only looked. I didn't go in the room.

A girl was laid out on the bed, her arms spread out, one of them falling off the bed. Her legs were sprawled out too. She was in a bra and a skirt. The skirt was pushed up around her waist. Her eyes were closed. I tracked her chest, seeing if she was breathing. I couldn't see any needles, and there was no white around her nostrils.

Fucking hell.

"Is she alive?"

The guard looked at me, no expression. "Yes. Checked her pulse fifteen minutes ago. It's there."

I went back to watching her chest, counting her breaths. They were slow, and I was having a hard time seeing much movement.

"You guys have been waiting for me to come before handling this?" My tone picked up. My shit was easing out. My control was breaking.

I went to the other bedroom.

Marco was the one who answered. "We made the call to Stephano. This won't be happening here *ever* again." His voice changed, growing the tiniest bit distant, and if I were to guess, he was looking at my father as he said that.

And my father, fuck my father. He was quiet *now*.

Waiting. Biding his time.

I really loathed Dominic West.

He hadn't been a father to me. It'd been Uncle Stephano at my ball games. Uncle Stephano who helped me learn how to drive, who took me to the batting cages, who was there when I graduated high school, Columbia, Yale. My dad? Not fucking there. He'd been getting high. Cheating on his wife. A liar. An abus—I had to stop thinking about him, letting all the past rise up. I went to the second room.

It wasn't much better, except the girl there was fully awake and barely clothed. She was huddling in the corner, her arms wrapped around her knees, and she looked at me, makeup streaming down her face. She was in a bra and this time only underwear. The bed had been stripped. I was guessing they'd pulled everything to keep any more evidence from being left behind. Helped with the cleanup, and because we were Mafia, that'd been their fucking first thought.

Ashton hadn't moved from just beyond the elevator. His gaze was solely focused on me.

I was aware of how much *he* was aware that I was fast losing any and all restraint I had in me.

I turned, facing Marco and my father in the same direction. "Who are these girls?"

Please be working girls. Not that their fate was any less tragic—it might've been more, but because they'd been caught up in this life before now, before my father. He hadn't been the first to victimize them, just the latest in a long line of others. That, by itself, eased a little bit of the tension in me. Just a tiny bit, but not enough.

And seriously, how sad and pathetic of a thought was that?

"Your father brought them with him. He's been gambling all week at the casino, getting high and loud in the hotel the rest of the time. We've had too many complaints. The last few were calls straight to the police. We cannot give them any more reason than what's already necessary to come here—"

He would've kept going, but I held up a hand. I got the picture.

Ashton's family bribed a lot of the police, here and in the city, but they didn't like using favors if they didn't need to. Especially favors for a jackass like Dominic West.

I locked on my father. "Who are these girls?"

He was big like Stephano, but while Steph kept himself in shape and any excess weight was turned into muscle, I doubted my father could remember the last time he saw the inside of a weight room. He had a paunch on him, and his hair was graying. Right now, it was greasy and messy. He hadn't shaved in a few days. The bags under his eyes had bags, and *they* had bags.

I could see the white under his nostrils. He'd recently done a drag.

He also hadn't answered my question.

"Who are they?" I barked.

"I know you, son—"

I was railing inside. "I'm not your son. Your sperm helped create me, but you and I have never been father and son, so do not start trying to pull that card right now."

His eyes widened, and his face jerked back a little.

In public, I held more decorum. I let him parade around the father/son charade, but Stephano, my sister, Ashton—they knew the truth. They got the real show. They knew how very, *very* estranged my father and I were, but I still walked the line in their presence. I played my part in the pretend game, because that's what we did in the West family.

It was a rule.

Nothing got addressed. Everything got ignored.

But this, how my father took advantage of my relationship, how many times he must've gotten high, had sex parties, made a scene— this was only being handled now because another family was fed up. Dominic had committed the cardinal sin in our family. Nothing messes up business, and he'd done that. We needed the Walden family, like they needed us. If there wasn't harmony between the two, both sides would take a hit. Our alliance was protected at all costs, and now because of that rule, we could finally do something about my father.

My father very much knew that he had truly and royally fucked up. His time for having fun at the expense of my friendship with Ashton was long over. He was getting all of that right now, and I waited, biding my time to see what card he would pull next. He'd either shit his pants, or he'd get self-righteous.

I was hoping for the latter because it wouldn't feel right hitting a crying man.

He swallowed, taking a step backward, his hands raised. "Tra—"

I let out a low growl.

He amended, "Tristian—"

"Who are those girls?!"

He let out a sigh. "I got 'em from Nemah."

Nemah.

I didn't know if that should make me feel better or not, but at least I had options now.

Nemah was locally known for being in the sex business, so that meant these girls knew the score.

"That one needs medical attention now," I said to Marco.

He nodded to the guard at her door, who went in. The guard came out a second later with her body in his arms, and Ashton hit the elevator door. They opened right as he got there.

"Take Josiah. Take her to the hospital, back entrance. Call our doctor," Marco instructed. The man gave Marco a nod right as the doors closed on him.

I turned to the guard on the other girl. "Give her something to cover herself."

He went to the closet and pulled out a blanket, then took it inside the room.

Marco approached as his men did that and asked under his breath, "What do you want done with her?"

I ignored his question for a moment, focusing on my father again.

Dominic West, even though he was a fuckup, was still a West.

Despite the general rule of not killing each other, I wondered, deep down, if I could give the order. If I told Marco to execute my father, would he? Maybe. Ashton, yes. Ashton's family? I wasn't sure. It would put them at odds against my family, but Stephano, would he let me do what we both knew needed to be done at some point?

I didn't know. There was no love between them, and I had no idea if there ever had been.

I was tempted, so really truly fucking tempted.

My mother was dead because of him. He used to beat the shit out of me on the regular until Stephano caught the bruises on my arms. The beatings stopped after that, but I knew he only intensified on my mother.

Family rules. I couldn't say anything. She didn't either. Whenever he did whatever he did, he did it in private, and she never talked.

I wished she had.

The *only* grace from her death was that he'd stopped, and I could tell that he'd never touched my sister. If he had, she wouldn't have grown up a pampered, privileged brat. Love my sister, but she was, and it made me breathe easier.

But, seeing my father watching me, reading me, maybe he was seeing my temptation to try an order that I knew would turn my soul, but my god—I was still tempted.

For once, he kept his mouth shut.

"Bobby is downstairs. He's waiting for—"

"Goddamn, you motherfucking piece of—" My father flew past his guard, who had eased up on his alertness. Dominic got past him, and he was coming right at me.

Marco started to step between us at the same time the guard tried reaching for him, and Ashton was coming in from the side. I sidestepped around Marco, which Dominic had been anticipating, turning to meet me head-on, but as he swung, I stepped back, evaded, and stepped behind him, then pushed his body down.

I followed him, punching as he went so he hit the floor. He was getting it from front and back. He lost his air for a moment, and I rained down another punch, and another.

I didn't think I could stop. I knew I didn't want to.

When he ceased moving, Ashton and Marco pulled me off of him.

"Like that move, Dad?" I was breathing hard but barely noticing. I had no trace of him on me. Nothing. Not one hit, but he was the one bleeding. "It's one I learned from you, you fucking piece of shit."

Ashton went still. He'd known. He'd been there when I'd had the bruises on my arms. He'd seen them at recess, but he hadn't known the extent, and he'd never asked. He was getting a picture of it now.

It was the one thing he and I didn't talk about.

He was writhing around on the floor now, trying to get up. The guard kept him down. Dominic was still glaring at me, and I knew, I knew right there that if my father could kill me, he would.

My demeanor changed in that instant. The hate was so clear. I stepped back, feeling a calming blanket settling over my insides. I narrowed my eyes and asked as the elevator opened again, this time bringing Bobby, "You regret it, don't you?"

My father was barely paying attention to Bobby, who had stopped just inside the floor. Buddha was with him. They took in the room before going and hauling Dominic up to his feet. Each had a hand on his arm, and before they could take him out, he held his ground. "Regret what?" He raised his chin up.

"Not finishing the job one of those times when I was a kid? When you could've."

He knew what I meant, and his eyes flashed.

He got my meaning.

Bobby and Buddha tried taking him again, but he held them off, twisting around until they had to stop. He held his arms up, their hands on them, but he looked me dead in the eye. "Yes, son. I regret that."

Right.

My gut flared, but I stomped it down.

I would not let him do any more damage to me. He was done. He was so far done that I didn't want to ask what Stephano was going to do with him.

"We're taking him." Bobby gestured to the elevator.

I lifted my chin up, just barely, to acknowledge him.

They were gone soon after, and that's when Ashton grated out, "What the fuck was that about?"

I met his gaze, letting some of my anger deflate. As much as I could because we still weren't done. "What's between him and me is better left unsaid."

He kept watching me, intensely, but he nodded, a faint up-and-down motion.

Marco cleared his throat. "Right. Well, we have one more girl to take care of. It's your call, Tristian."

I already had my mind made up.

"We'll take her with us."

———

Ashton never argued with what I proposed to her and for her friend, who I promised that we could get from the hospital if she wanted.

The friend was collected. Ashton's family didn't protest. They had not notified Nemah about her, so as far as he knew, she was gone to Dominic West. Nemah could bring it up to Stephano, but he wouldn't because another silver lining about my uncle—he hated Nemah.

There was a strict order that if Nemah came into our territory, he'd be killed on sight. Made this even easier.

But it was the next day, the girls were taken to a hotel, and we left. Or we were supposed to leave. Ashton and I watched from our SUV across the road in another motel's parking lot.

We saw the group arrive, the ones I'd reached out to. A few females slipped into the room.

Within minutes, they were all leaving.

They were fast and efficient, and they were good at their job.

They'd help those girls disappear. That was the point of their entire program, but they were not friendly to Ashton or me. Not as long as we were tied to our families. But I'd still approached, explained the situation, and they'd agreed as long as we weren't around.

"If this gets back to either of our families . . . ," Ashton started.

I gave him a look. "It won't."

Stephano would conclude that I'd had both girls "taken care of," which was how the family business usually "took care of things." He'd be satisfied.

He gave me a nod, sighing. "You ever actually consider not going into the family business? We both have cousins who aren't involved. We could have that, you know. If we wanted it."

Jesus. If that wasn't the million-dollar question for both of us.

Stephano's only remaining son had turned his back to the family business, and my uncle leaned toward the male-oriented way of thinking. My sister didn't count and wasn't considered to step in and take over. It was me and me alone to keep everything going.

Way I viewed things was to *not* view things. That gave me ideas and options, and Stephano was my father in so many ways.

I couldn't have those ideas or options.

I just shook my head. "We'll cross that bridge when it comes, if it comes."

He glanced my way, studied me. "And if it comes sooner than you think?"

I just held his gaze. "Then we decide then."

He nodded. Like I knew he would.

That's how we were.

CHAPTER TWELVE

JESS

I liked to think that I hadn't thought about him, but that wasn't true. I had, and I was still trying to suppress it, but he was always there. Always in the background. I felt like the idea of him was haunting me. I felt him touching me again at random times on Monday. Tuesday. By Wednesday it wasn't going away.

If anything, it was worse.

I was heading to meet Kelly for lunch when I looked over.

A black SUV was there, parked on the side of the street, and I paused before opening the café's door.

The SUV's door opened.

I sucked in a breath of air because I was not expecting it, but he was there. And he was looking right at me.

Was he there for me?

But then a guy hurried around me and went right to the SUV. He hopped into the back seat. The door closed, and the SUV took off.

And me, I was left perplexed because what were the odds?

I headed inside, going to give my order at the counter, but I couldn't shake the look he'd given me.

Was his PI still following me?

That made me heated.

But how he looked at me, knowing I was there. There'd been no surprise, no look of recognition, and there would've been if he hadn't been expecting to see me.

He looked shut down. Angry.

There'd been a way his jaw had been locked in place. He had not been wanting to do whatever he was doing, or had done, or was going to do.

God.

I needed to forget this guy.

I didn't even know his name.

I needed a life. That's what I needed.

A life.

Or sex.

I'd forget him then.

———

"I was fired."

I almost choked on my coffee at Kelly's announcement. She said it as she slumped into the chair across from me. The café was bustling around us, but she had her food in hand, so she must've stopped at the counter before making her way to my table.

"Today?" I picked up my coffee. I had also grabbed my food first.

Kelly didn't answer right away, her petite shoulders rigid before she slumped down and began to unwrap her sandwich. "I was fired two weeks ago."

I almost dropped my cup before gaping at her. "Why didn't you say anything?"

Kelly was a fill-in at an agency. She got sent to places if they needed an assistant, so she never had steady paychecks. She always got by, but Kelly didn't have a big nest egg saved up.

"What can I do?"

She'd been chewing on her bottom lip, then let it pop out at my question. "Can you ask Anthony at Katya for a job?"

Katya was my second job, the one I needed to help pay extra bills. I said, "They only have shot girls on the weekend opening."

"It's something. Tips are *good* there."

"You sure?"

She went back to chewing her bottom lip. Kelly would be out and about with the customers, on the floor with them. Some of the customers at Katya could get handsy. Management was supposed to take care of them, but sometimes it didn't happen, and sometimes the girls didn't want to cause a fuss, so they endured. I didn't have to deal with it because I was behind the bar. Word had gotten around what I did after I'd called in a couple of parole violators. No one messed with me, but I hated that Kelly might not get that same treatment.

I nodded, resolving to have a word with Anthony besides just seeing if he'd hire her. "I'll text him right now."

She sat up, her face brightening. "Really?"

"Tip money helps with rent."

She shuddered, nodding. "You don't have to say that again. Sorry to put you in this spot. I'm a bit desperate."

I shook my head. "No spot that you're putting me in. If I can help, I'm helping." I sent off my text right after that.

Jess: You still looking for any extra girls to carry around the shot trays?

Anthony: Please tell me you know someone, and yes. Immediately. Tonight.

Jess: Pay?

Anthony: You know what they get paid. Tips are theirs, but it's the standard rate.

Jess: She's my roommate.

He didn't respond.
That would complicate things.

Anthony: I'll hire her, but you have to promise not to go batshit on a customer if the guys don't move fast enough for you.

I grinned.

Jess: I won't unless they're taking their sweet ass time.

Anthony: Fuck. Fine. She's a little thing, isn't she?

Jess: Yes.

Anthony: She can start today. 4:30 my office.

I lifted my gaze. "You got a job."

She squealed, coming around to throw her arms around my shoulders. "Thank you, thank you, thank you! I could just kiss you." She smacked her lips to my cheek and gave me another hug/shake before returning to her seat. Her cheeks were all flushed. "When do I start?"

I checked the time. "You got three hours."

"What?!"

CHAPTER THIRTEEN

TRACE

My father could barely breathe.

I was staring at Dominic West in a hospital bed. He'd been tubed, and he was unconscious. They'd had to put him in a medically induced coma because they were worried about possible brain trauma.

Ashton cursed next to me. "Jesus. Your uncle doesn't mess around."

I grunted. "No shit."

It'd been a couple days since seeing him at the hotel, since Ashton and I had taken the girls and given them a whole different option in life. But there'd been radio silence from my uncle. I was now seeing why.

I got the call from the hospital an hour ago.

My dad's body had been dumped in front of the ER. They'd said the security cameras weren't working, so they didn't know who dumped him off, which was a lie. My family owned the security guards at the hospital—it's why they'd chosen this hospital—and half the staff was aware of who we were.

It's why no police were called in for this assault, and no police would ever be called on any of our family members.

"Mr. West."

I looked over, seeing the head nurse coming my way. A younger nurse was next to her, a file in her hand and sexual interest in her eyes. The head nurse, Sloane, plucked the file from the younger nurse and gave her a sharp look. The younger one glared, but after a momentary stare-off, she lowered her head and turned away. Sloane started our way, but the younger nurse stopped and looked at us. She was first giving me a very open and sexual expression, but at seeing how *not* interested I was, she switched to Ashton, who snorted under his breath as she did.

We shared a look, both of us amused, before Sloane got to us.

"Gentlemen." She didn't balk at seeing Ashton by my side. I was aware that other hospitals liked to give information out only to direct family members, but Sloane had been around. She knew how it was between Ashton and me.

She fixed me a stern look, coming to stand on the other side of my father's bed.

Ashton went to close the door.

A steady beeping sound filled the room, along with the intubation machinery.

She nodded at my father. "You do not seem angry or surprised at finding your father in this manner."

I ignored that, barely blinking. "What's the damage?"

She glanced at me, her eyes flickering before she went back to the file. "You know about the possible brain damage. He took several hits to the back of his skull. The coma will be lifted in a day, but he has three fractured ribs. A broken wrist. His ankle looked smashed to pieces, so they did surgery to put as much of that back together as they could. His skin endured second-degree burns. The doctor did recommend plastic surgery, but the burns aren't extensive over a large section of skin. Ultimately it's either your father's choice or whoever is going to be paying his bills. Is that you?"

I pressed my mouth tight together. "Who's the doctor?" I held my hand out for the file.

She gave it to me. "You guys lucked out with a brand-new doc who is very curious about why no one on staff called the police."

I had started to open the file but lifted my gaze to her. "He's new and ambitious?"

"*She's* new and not a dummy."

She. New. Smart. That wasn't a good combination for us.

I shared a look with Ashton, who asked, "Her name?"

Sloane's eyebrows instantly pulled tight together, and she took a step back. "Why are you the one asking?"

Ashton repeated, "Name?"

She took another step back, her mouth firming.

I looked at the file and read aloud. "Dr. Sandquist. Nea."

Ashton had his phone out and nodded. "Got it." He turned and headed out.

Sloane was watching him go, worry lines showing around her mouth, adding to the bags already under her eyes. "She's a good doctor, a good person." Her eyes met mine again. They were somber, *very* somber. "Do not hurt her, whatever you just sent Ashton to do to her."

"We won't."

"I mean it, Trace." Her words were clipped, and she pivoted to face me directly. "I've taken care of every member of your family for thirty years. I respect you, enough to know what it means to be able to call you by that name, but do not cross me on this one. Not with this doctor. She's too good to be collateral."

I stared at her long and hard. The message was received, but my family was my family. That meant we'd do what we needed to do, and since I'd sent Ashton, I couldn't totally dictate how he'd handle her. He'd do what he always did. He'd wade in, suss out the situation, and proceed from there, with whatever avenue he felt would get the best results.

"No need to worry, Sloane. We'd never do anything that would come back on you," I said with a small smile and a cool tone.

Her face clouded over. "I'm not hearing reassurances here."

I looked back to my father. "Nor will you because you should know better than to threaten me or my family." I heard her soft intake of breath, and I ignored it. "Tell me what my father needs to heal from this so that I can make sure to get him out of Dr. Nea Sandquist's care before she does something stupid, like call the police."

Within three hours, my father was being discharged before the good Dr. Sandquist started her next shift. And after all that, I headed to my uncle because he said it was time for the second favor he needed from me.

This time, I brought Ashton, because while my uncle sometimes got visits from only me, he knew that Ashton and I were barely two separate people.

Both families were aware. Neither liked it.

CHAPTER FOURTEEN

JESS

Katya was filled to the brim, but that was normal. Friday night was always insane. They'd booked a DJ, so the crowd was especially hyped up. Neon lights flashing everywhere. Shot glasses glowing in the dark, being carried around the place.

They had ultraprivate boxes where people didn't know they existed unless they were in the club with the lights on, or they were in one of the boxes. Then they had entire private floors, and the high rollers went there. They got their own bartenders, their own dance girls, their own shot girls. Then there were the VIPs, and I had no clue what they got because I'd never been allowed up there. I liked Katya, for the most part. I knew there were parts of it that were shady, but so far I hadn't had anything happen smack in front of my face. The biggest issue was if a parolee came in, not knowing I had a second job here, and I had to notify their PO, just in case. I enjoyed it as much as they did.

"Your girl is doing good." One of the new bartenders came over—Justin.

I looked where he was looking and saw Kelly circling a booth with her tray. I'd been watching her, too, and he was right. She knew how to smile to engage the customer but step back and evade when necessary.

I was guessing Anthony had put an extra couple security guys around the floor she was working because there'd been two customers who'd ignored her rebuff and tried to grab her. The guys had moved in right away, and I mean, they were there even before Kelly could blink. They were fast tonight, not taking any bullshit.

"She's done this work before, but I'm protective."

He nodded.

He'd started working here a couple weekends ago. Anthony had asked me to train him one of the nights, but it wasn't necessary. He'd been a natural, so I wasn't surprised he'd been moved to Friday nights already. Trim but built with defined shoulders, chest, and arms. He had a quick grin and golden-brown curls on top that I'd witnessed more than a few girls sighing over, and he was nice. Plus funny. He was already a favorite over some of the other guys behind the counter. Customers knew where to go, who were the asses and who weren't. Justin was popular.

"I'm surprised you had time to come over here." I nodded at the customers waiting for him to get their drinks.

He flashed a grin my way. If I could've seen better from the lighting, it looked like he was blushing a little. Maybe? I couldn't tell. He leaned closer, quieting his voice but still loud so I could hear him. "I'm wondering if your girl is single?"

I stepped back, giving him another once-over, but more intentional this time.

He braced himself, taking a breath and holding it.

"You're single?"

His head lowered, some shyness coming over him. "I am." He nodded toward the girls behind him. "That's work. I never dip where I work, but . . ." His gaze went back to Kelly, and I saw it then. A full glaze came over him.

He was a goner for her.

And Kelly with how she was . . . I scowled at him. "You fuck her over, I will destroy you."

He jerked his gaze back to me, his eyes widening for a second. He blinked, a wariness edged in, but I still saw the determination shining through. "That's not the plan. I'm not that guy. I mean it."

I was going to regret this, but I nodded. "She's single."

That was it. That was all the opening I was giving him. No way was I going to let him know she was a romantic and tended to fall quickly. If he was worth his word, he'd figure that out and proceed with caution. Or the ultimate respect.

He dipped his head a little. "Thanks, Jess."

He was leaving as Anthony was zeroing in on us.

Our manager pushed around the customers waiting for me, frowning at me and Justin talking, but jerked his head to the side. When he added a lone finger wave, I knew he meant business. The funny thing about Anthony was that his outsides were all smooth and slick. Dark-black hair slicked back. His face was always manscaped to perfection. Smooth skin. Full lips. I swear he used a ChapStick a day. He was maybe five ten. One eighty. He kept himself trim. Silk shirts, half-unbuttoned. Soft trousers. Loafers. But his insides were stressed. He always seemed worked up and tight about something. I'd learned to half enjoy it.

I frowned but moved to the side so he could lean over better to talk to me.

"I need you in VIP tonight."

I leaned back to make sure I heard him right. "What?" I'd never been up there. I didn't even know where to go.

He nodded upstairs. "Don't say anything, just go in and stay behind the bar. These are VIP, so keep your mouth shut, smile, and don't act up."

I bristled because what the fuck did he mean by "act up"?

He let out a deep breath before counting to five. Not ten. Five. "These guys are important. My normal girls are gone, and I know these two." He glanced in Justin's direction before adding, "Do not fuck this up."

"I've been working for you for four years. When have I ever fucked up?"

His eyes were shining bright, fiercely. "I'm not talking about drinks."

Oh, snap. Not a fan of his right now, but I kept my mouth shut and listened when he told me where to go. I was assuming the VIP section was fully stocked, and when he stopped giving me instructions, I headed off. I gave Kelly a last cursory look, and she seemed fine. Justin had moved down a little, but he remained close enough to overhear I was being sent off, and he moved to help cover my area. "I'll watch her."

Normally I'd make a comment about how that's what I was afraid of, but not this time. Justin seemed sincere, and my gut was saying he was already in love, but there wasn't much I could do about anything, so I headed toward the locker area. I freshened up a bit, readjusted my uniform, which was a tight black top, and because I was in the bartender section, I was able to wear black pants. They looked dressy, but they felt like yoga pants.

Once I was done, I went off for the mysterious VIP section.

This one was on the sixth floor. I'd gone up as far as the fourth, but not the fifth or sixth.

Going to the only elevator that allowed entry for those floors, I saw the bouncer reach for his radio. A second later, Anthony's voice came over. "She's good. Sixth floor. Get her situated, Monty."

Monty. I half grinned, but seeing the wall on his face, I didn't feel like sharing that my last name was Montell and I'd been called Monty in grade school. This Monty didn't seem to care.

He hit the button. The elevator arrived, and he got on with me.

He had to put in a special code for the elevator. I memorized it, just in case.

When we got to the floor, he led the way.

It was a simple layout. Three doors. He pointed out the first to the right. "*Your* bathroom."

I nodded, noting the *your* emphasis.

The door on the left was labeled **STAIRS**, so that was self-explanatory.

The middle door opened to a large apartment-like floor. He motioned to the bar area, and I went right behind, starting to find where all the bottles were kept. There was a phone. I saw the instructions and knew I would use that to order more inventory. "I call down for bottle service?"

He nodded before moving through the place and going into the rooms. He came back, settling by the bar. "These guys are big, but they're respectable. If you want to fuck 'em, you can, but you don't have to. They aren't like that."

Jesus. Yeah. This place definitely had some shade. "I'm not like that, in *any* situation."

He barely nodded my way, watching for the door. "It's usually the case where the girls want them, not the other way, not with these guys, but you do you. I'm security for the floor, just in case."

In case of what?

———

We waited thirty minutes. Nothing.

Another thirty. Nothing.

Two hours later, an hour before the club was supposed to close, Monty's radio crackled to life.

I'd taken to sitting on the counter with my phone out, dwelling on the loss of tips. Monty was doing the same, and not a word was spoken between us. I didn't think Monty cared. I knew I didn't. He popped in his earpiece and nodded to me. "They're coming."

He went to the door and propped it open.

The elevator pinged its arrival. The doors slid open, and instead of laughter or shouting, which was the norm for this place, there was nothing.

A male came inside, looking at his phone before he gave me an absentminded look, but he did a double take, seeing me, and he ground to a halt.

I frowned, not knowing this guy, but he was gorgeous. Dark features. Black hair. Nearly black eyes. He was sleek and toned, and the air rippled around him, exuding he was dangerous and powerful. This guy was not one to mess around with, and I braced myself before all of his gaze was fixed on me. Those eyes sharpened, and a smirk showed before he half turned for the second guy coming in behind him.

"Someone fucked up," he said, addressing the other man before I saw who he was.

"What?"

I sucked in air, my whole body freezing, because . . .

I knew that voice. And as he came forward, stepping around his friend, I was pierced by those same eyes that had haunted me over the last week.

It was *him*.

And he was staring back at me in shock, but also some anger.

He was *not* happy to see me.

CHAPTER FIFTEEN

TRACE

I was staring at her, at who I'd been fucking obsessed with over the entire week, and I'd just resolved to shut everything down. But here she was, staring back at me, every bit as surprised as I was, and then her eyes cooled and she flinched, turning away.

Fuck.

That was me. All me.

I gave her that look, and I couldn't blame her. I was livid. Cody ran this club for us. He was supposed to be discreet in getting word to whoever was supposed to know that I did not want to cross paths with her, not yet.

And today of all days.

I needed one minute, one fucking minute, because I couldn't unhear what my uncle had said to me three hours earlier.

"How you handled your father's indiscretions was your test, and you aced it, my nephew. My son. Now, I need you to do more for this family."

"What do you need?"

"I need you to run the family business."

Ashton's question came back to me. *"You ever actually consider not going into the family business?"*

"We'll cross that bridge when it comes, if it comes."

"And if it comes sooner than you think?"

"Then we decide then."

Hearing those words from Stephano, I couldn't ignore the gut check I was enduring right now. I had *not* wanted to hear those words, at least not yet. I wanted time.

Helping out was one thing. Running the entire empire was a whole different thing.

I'd stared long and hard at my uncle. He placed a hand over his chest. "I'm sick, Tristian. There's another family trying to push in, from up in Maine. They want to come down into the city, and my health . . . it's bad. I don't trust anyone else to step into my shoes." He then said the last three words that were my kryptonite with him. I could never not do what he needed.

He'd said, "I need you."

Staring at her now, knowing who she was related to, knowing the first problem my uncle needed me to handle . . . I was torn, right here, right now.

My family or—no. That was crazy, but for a moment, one moment, I considered it. I had to, and I had to admit that I wanted her. It was still there, still buried deep inside, and the longer I stared at her, the more I knew what my uncle needed me to do, the more that need for her was burrowing deep inside of me.

God-*fucking*-dammit!

I growled, snapping, "Get out!"

CHAPTER SIXTEEN

JESS

My arms were shaking.

The look on his face, how he hated me.

"Get out!"

I left, not waiting for Monty to escort me down.

I was sick to my stomach. I couldn't—no. No! I would not cry, not over that asshole. Such a dick.

Fuck him. Fuck his friend. Fuck everything.

The elevator got to my floor, and I pushed past whoever was there. I didn't know who it was. I didn't care. I didn't even know where to go. Locker room? Leave? Back to my station.

Okay, calm down, Jess. You have people who curse at you all the time. One guy is nothing.

Right.

I was at work. He didn't want me, fine. I went back to my old station.

Justin saw me coming, and his eyes widened, but he moved aside, going back to his station.

I'd poured one beer before Anthony was at my station. "What the fuck did you do?"

I stilled myself, making sure I didn't throw the beer I just poured *at* him. Setting it down, giving the customer the price, I glared at Anthony. "I did nothing."

"Well, what the fuck happened? Monty said the guys came in, saw you, and went ballistic."

I winced, seeing the look of utter disdain on his face when he saw me and hearing it again. "I don't know what to tell you, Anthony." The customer paid, slipping an extra five for a tip, and I gave them a thankful smile because the customer was a female and she was glaring at Anthony for me. Girl power here. I took the money and began filling the second order. Anthony moved down, on the other side of my customer. He propped an arm on the counter. "I sent someone else up in your place, but I need to understand what happened or my ass is going to get reamed. It's not just your job at stake here."

I almost really did chuck my glass at him, but I tightened my grip, willed myself to think rationally before moving to grab the Captain. Pouring it, grabbing the mix for it, I said, "I know him."

"Who?"

"The guy. The one who told me to get out. I know him."

He was blinking, confused. "What?" He raked a hand through his hair. "You know him? Tristian West?!"

Tristian.

That was his name.

That was . . . Tristian . . . I liked his name.

That made it all the more horrifying.

Seriously.

I was stupid.

Mooning over his goddamn name? After what he just did to me? And now my job was in jeopardy?

"I guess."

"You guess?!"

I shot Anthony a look. "Why are you worked up about this so much? It was a mistake. I didn't know who was coming up there, and you didn't know my history with him."

"You don't get it." He cursed again, a second rake through his hair before he turned and went rigid. I caught the end of yet another curse before he straightened. "I have to fix this, somehow." He twisted to me. "What's your history with him?"

My entire body flooded with heat. "I am not telling you that."

"Why?"

"Because. I'm not."

He stilled before closing his eyes for a beat. "Jesus Christ. You fucked him?"

No way was I giving him that answer because it was *none of his business.* "It's *none* of your business. I didn't even know his name until you told me."

His eyes bugged out. I realized what I said and now what he was thinking of me, but I knew that was a wasted fight. He'd believe what he wanted to believe.

I began doing another drink—or finishing up because that customer was still waiting for the rest of his drinks. "Just don't send me up there again."

"You don't get it. But you'll find out." He tore off after that.

The customer watched him go before handing over his card for his payment. "Your boss is an ass."

I snorted. "Tell me about it."

———

Justin came over to check on me later.

I was fine, or that's what I told him.

Kelly came over, too, getting her shots refilled.

I could feel her worry because she knew something had happened, but she just came in and gave me a hug.

I looked up, seeing Anthony glaring our way from where he was talking to another guy that I'd never seen before. Whoever he was, Anthony was getting an earful.

I nudged Kelly. "You should get going."

She harrumphed, making it obvious her opinion on that matter, but picked up her tray and moved off.

I didn't miss the little look she sent Justin's way, or how he reciprocated.

The club closed. The lights went on. We needed to go through our inventory, close out our drawers, and I had cleaned my section when I made my way to the staff room.

Anthony stepped out of his office. "A word?"

His tone was nicer, but I saw the stress had taken a toll. His shirt was stretched out. Worry lines were sticking out around his eyes and mouth. He raised a hand, pinching his nose as I made my way to him and then past him inside.

He closed the door, but it was soft.

My stomach was in knots, and I didn't even know why. I mean, I knew why, but I didn't at the same time.

He motioned to the chair in front of me as he went to sit behind his desk. "Sit."

"No."

"Please." He leaned back, pinching his nose a second time. "Just, please sit."

He had a love seat in the corner, and I perched on the armrest, giving him a glare and then crossing my arms over my chest. "I did nothing wrong. If you're firing me, then—"

"I'm not." He held a hand up. "I'm sorry. I was further explained the situation, and the mess up wasn't on my end or yours, but it's been handled. I called you in because I wanted to apologize. Tristian West is a big deal here. The biggest that comes around, and I didn't handle any of this the right way. I sincerely apologize to you."

I was annoyed.

This wasn't supposed to be my stressful job. I had a day job for that, and I didn't need to put up with this bullshit.

"Get out!"

I flinched again, unable to not hear that or not see his face as he spewed that.

"I do need to ask." Anthony's eyes were heavy, resting on me. "What's your relationship with him?"

"I don't have one."

"But you said—"

"It's honestly nothing. We met a couple times, by accident, and the last time I told him to stay away from me. That's it."

His mouth dropped, and he jerked forward. "*You* told *him* to stay away from you?"

I rolled my eyes. It was close enough to what I said. "Why is that so shocking?"

"Because—" He shook his head. "Never mind. It's obvious you actually don't know him, and knowing that now, I think this will be fine. I'll keep you on the floor in the future and send someone else up instead."

Fine. Right.

I was still pissed by the whole experience.

I stood up. "Can I go? I'm tired, and I need to check on my roommate."

"Oh yeah."

I started for the door, but he called my name.

"What?" I asked.

"Kelly did really well tonight, but let her know that if she fucks the new bartender and it ends badly, I don't tolerate drama. One of them will be kicked out."

My lips thinned. I was guessing since I was getting this message at who would be getting the boot.

"You're an imbecile. See you tomorrow."

I left, not waiting around to see his reaction. I was one of his favorites because I didn't take shit, and tonight he'd made me take *his* shit. I was heading to the staff room to see if Kelly was still there. I'd left my phone in my locker, and she was able to leave earlier than me. Shot girls got to leave as soon as the bar closed. They didn't need to do the cleanup, and it took me a little longer to go through everything since Justin had been manning my section.

I wasn't shocked to see the locker room was empty when I went inside.

I grabbed my purse and pulled my phone out.

I was heading for the back parking lot when I heard Anthony call my name.

I stopped, but I didn't turn around.

Could this night get any worse?

"Jess."

I pivoted, my head back and my chin up.

He had a hand on his doorway, half stepping out into the hallway with a funny look on his face. "You got someone waiting for you in the back."

My nostrils flared. "The back where?"

"Out the back. The lot. The vehicle there is for you."

I frowned.

He gave me a nod. "See you tomorrow," he said before disappearing back in his office.

My phone buzzed, and I read the texts.

Kelly: Hey! Are you okay?

Kelly: I couldn't find you and Justin offered to walk me home. You usually have your car. Do you want me to stay?

Kelly: Someone said Anthony is talking to you. I'll wait.

Me: Are you still here?

Kelly: I'm with Justin. We're at his apartment. He lives super close. I wasn't sure how long you'd be. Hold on. I'm on my way back.

Me: No. It's fine. I'm not up for conversation anyways.

Kelly: You sure?

Me: Yeah. You going to hang with Justin for a while?

Kelly: Is that okay? I've got my coat on. Give me a few minutes and I'll be there.

Me: No. Stay. Hang with Justin. I'm heading home.

Kelly: Okay. By the way, I love this job!

My phone buzzed once more, but I was assuming it was Kelly saying goodbye or good night, so I put it back in my purse and pushed out the door. I'd taken one step, not sure how I felt knowing someone was waiting for me.

When the SUV door opened, I stopped because it was him.

Tristian West.

He nodded to the empty seat beside him. "Get in."

CHAPTER SEVENTEEN

TRACE

"I have a problem, and I need you to fix it for me. Can you do that for me?"

My uncle had started our second meeting with that question.

"I thought I've already shown you that I can handle a problem. I helped with my dad."

"Yeah, but you were motivated for that. Your father is your father. You and Ashton did well. I'm proud of you, and I heard about the new doc and how you maneuvered around her. That's not always an option, but it was smart this time."

I glanced at Ashton and knew he was pissed off by that, but he wouldn't say anything. I wouldn't have, either, if the roles were reversed. Both our families had a hierarchy. The heads were gods.

"What's the current problem, Uncle Steph?"

"Billy Garretson." He tossed a file down on the table between us, and I was staring at some guy.

Ashton went still beside me, and me, I turned into ice because no fucking way was that a coincidence. *"Who's this?"*

"He's a worker in upstate New York—there's a shipping facility we need access to, and he's the one who can get us in. He's been refusing, and I've been told that you've taken to his niece recently."

"Niece?"

"He's married to the niece's aunt, Sarah. She's a sister to Chelsea Montell."

Montell?!

I loved my uncle, I did, but right now I was envisioning myself taking a long and dirty knife and gutting him with it because that's what he was doing to me.

"Your reports are wrong. That's over, not that anything even started."

Uncle Steph had stared at me then, long and hard. His jaw clenched once before he sat back. "For some reason I have a feeling that won't be an issue. We've not moved on your new woman because of her father and the fact she's a parole officer, but you know her. We have an opening now. I want you to use her, do whatever you need with her to get her uncle on board. I need into that shipping facility, and you know what will happen if someone continues to stand in my way."

He had meant bodies. Lots and lots of dead bodies.

I was staring at her now as she slid into the seat beside me, closing the door. Her movements were jerky, stiff.

I wanted to go to Katya to get away from the family, but I wanted to go there because *she* was there. I wanted to watch her work, like I had the last weekend when she had no clue I was there, and mull over what I was going to do. But her supervisor sent her up instead of our normal bartender.

I had no idea why there was a change, but I walked in and saw her, and I was livid.

I'd wanted another day before I made my move. I needed that time to think of every option because that's what I did in my job as a hedge fund manager. You thought of every avenue, every angle, every direction the money might go, and then you decided which one to sell, which to buy, and when. It was a thrill if you did it right, and even if you didn't, you learned.

That time had been taken out of my hands, and I'd not reacted in the right way.

"You are a cop."

She watched me, not blinking, not looking away. She wasn't hiding. "I have not asked who you are. Ever think there's a reason for that? I've not looked you up or asked for a favor. I could. It's easy for me, but I haven't. I didn't go up there knowing you'd be there. I meant what I said at bowling. Stay away from me."

I almost smirked at her, because she meant every word, but her body didn't. "And yet you're in my vehicle."

"You said 'Get in.'"

"Since when do you do what you're told?"

"What do you want, West?"

So someone had told her who I was. "You know my name now."

"I was told Tristian West. I wasn't told anything else, and I'm going to be honest, I haven't decided if I'm going to do a search or not."

There was that, but it wouldn't matter within twenty-four hours. "Your father was killed when you were in high school, and your brother was convicted of the crime."

She reached for the door handle. "Stop the car."

"Your mother's a drunk. You're working two jobs to take care of her and your brother's debts."

She reached for the door, but I moved, reaching over her and grabbing it before it could open. Or I tried. She turned, grabbing my arm, twisting, and I was shoved away from her instead.

"Don't."

The car door was still open, but Pajn had pulled the vehicle over.

She didn't release my arm, just leaned in. "Do not move on me again. You did it once. I won't allow it a second time."

I pulled my arm free and moved, slower this time, but she didn't move back.

That brought us close, real close, and this was not what I had intended to happen. Having her so close, feeling her again, I was staring at her lips.

I knew how she tasted, and I wanted another touch.

I was moving in when she sucked in her breath and jerked out of the way. The door was still open, and she reached for it, but she didn't get out yet.

Pajn was waiting for my order on what to do, so right now, I was waiting for her.

"Why did you wait for me?"

"To apologize."

Her eyes clouded over, and she looked down. She didn't say anything else before she got out of the vehicle and shut the door.

"You want me to go after her?"

I shook my head. "Take me to my downtown office."

I needed to do some work of my own.

My uncle said they hadn't done anything about Billy Garretson because of his niece's job and her father. He hadn't expanded and I hadn't pushed because a part of me didn't want to know. I didn't want to fully wade into that world except for the random times I already had, helping with what my uncle needed me to do. But this was different. This was personal, and I was nearing a line where I needed to know all the angles before I proceeded any further.

For now, I'd do what I excelled at for my normal work.

Research.

CHAPTER EIGHTEEN

JESS

I was staring at a college photo of Tristian West and kicking myself.

After getting home last night, I pulled him up to see what I could find.

We'd grown up in the same neighborhood, but while I went to the public school, he went private, and it hadn't stopped there. Columbia for his first four years, then to Yale for his MBA. He was now a Wall Street guy.

I remembered joking to myself about how his shoes looked like a Wall Street guy attending a hockey game, because that's what he'd been.

And he owned Katya. Big shock there. The guy was my second boss. No wonder Anthony had been having a fit. Tristian, or Trace to his friends, owned it with his best friend, Ashton Walden, who'd attended all of the same schools as Tristian. Same high school. Columbia. While Tristian was at Yale, Ashton went with him, but he started his first business, something in cybersecurity. Tristian graduated, and both returned to New York.

And after getting a job on Wall Street, he and his friend Ashton started their first joint business and since then were operating a whole list of them.

Each was wealthy, but together, they were a whole other force.

There wasn't much on Tristian other than the obvious. He'd been in the system because he was arrested when he was sixteen on drug charges. He and Ashton were both arrested on the same day, but no charges were pressed. Their lawyers would've come in and made it go away. But the kicker, the real kick in your teeth about all of this, was his uncle.

Stephano West, head of the West Mafia family.

Goddamn.

Tristian West was the nephew and, according to my report, considered "like a son" to a Mafia boss. And I turned my phone over because that last text last night hadn't been Kelly.

Unknown: I would like to see you again. Here's my number.

"Morning!"

I was at the kitchen table and shut my laptop when the door opened and Kelly came in, but she wasn't alone. Justin trailed after her. He glanced my way, a sheepish look on his face as he put his hands in his jacket's front pockets.

The dude worked fast.

Kelly had showered, and she sailed over to me, then threw her arms around my neck and pressed her cheek to mine. I was still sitting, so she bent down, and I could smell Justin's shampoo. Head & Shoulders.

She squeezed my neck a little. "Hmmm. You smell so good."

I had to chuckle. When Kelly got laid, she thought everything was perfect and magical in these early days. "You're in a good mood."

I got up, grabbing my coffee mug because I needed a refill.

I caught the blush before Kelly grabbed her purse. "I need to change clothes. Be back!"

After pouring my coffee, I set the pot back. "You needing some of this?"

Justin chuckled. "God yes. Your friend is, uh, she's got stamina."

I gave him a look. "Don't go there. I love her, but I do not want the details."

He chuckled again, finding where we kept our mugs and moving so I could pour him the last of the coffee. I nodded to the cupboard. "Sugar there. Creamer in the fridge."

"Thanks." He glanced over his shoulder as I moved back to the table and lifted up my laptop once again. "What happened last night? I saw Anthony call you to his office."

I didn't need the reminder. "It's nothing."

He looked unconvinced.

"I mean it." I gestured toward Kelly's room. "You move fast."

That sheepish look came back over him, and he shuffled, moving around before settling back against the same counter. "I like her. A lot." He gave me a meaningful look.

"I saw how you looked at her last night. You're already half-gone on her."

His eyes got big, and he'd been taking a sip of coffee but half snorted on it. "Jesus. Don't tell her that, please."

My phone buzzed again.

I refuse to put his name in my phone: We need to talk.

God. This guy.

Me: BLOCK

I refuse to put his name in my phone: Now.

I blocked him.

I needed to forget meeting him, forget talking to him, forget touching him, forget his kisses. Forget how I felt with my body over his in his vehicle last night. All of it. Done.

The end.

My phone buzzed again, but this time it was my *other* boss.

Leo: I need you at your mother's house.

Those texts were never good.

———

Leo was standing on the front steps when I got there, and he did not look happy. He'd been smoking a cigarette, but at seeing me, he tossed it on the ground and put it out. He was in plain clothes, wearing an open jacket over jeans and a sweatshirt beneath. Leo was old school. If he wasn't working, he was at the neighborhood bar having a beer and watching whatever game was on the television. All the years I knew him, I'd never seen him drunk, so I always suspected he sipped one beer the whole time.

Some days, like today apparently, he was here checking on my mom.

I parked and walked over to the sidewalk. "What's wrong?"

I looked behind him. The door was shut, the curtains drawn closed. I wasn't hearing yelling or anything behind him.

One of his hands moved inside his jacket pocket, and he indicated the house. "You were here a few days ago?"

I frowned. "Monday. I stopped over. Why?"

"You go through her stash?"

Christ. We were dealing with this? "I found a new vodka bottle in her bathroom and watered it down."

"That's it?"

"Yeah. What's going on?"

"She's having a conniption, saying you emptied all of her bottles."

The irony of my mother throwing a tantrum to one parole officer because another parole officer watered down one of her stash was just . . . I was at a loss. "What sort of conniption? What's the damage?"

"I'm standing out here to greet you. That should tell you something."

For fuck's sake.

I walked up the stairs to face my mother.

"Be prepared. She . . . she went overboard today."

I skimmed another glance his way. He moved back a step, not giving me anything else. I tried the doorknob, found it was locked, so I pulled out my key and unlocked it. Opening it, I wasn't even going to focus on how she'd locked the door on Leo. It was Leo. He'd been best friends with my dad. He was family.

I stepped in, not hearing any movement, no sounds.

But the smell hit me next, and I almost bowled over. "Mom!"

I heard a lumbering footstep above, then a groan and a thump.

I took off, taking the stairs two at a time.

There was blood on the floor, and I rushed into her bedroom. More blood. A trail of it, leading to her as she was on the floor beside the bed. "Mom!" She was in her bathrobe, and I knelt down, avoiding the blood.

She let out a moan, her head moving a little.

"Mom. Mom."

"No." Another moan. She reached out, trying to push me away. "Go away. Don't want you here."

Her breath was rank. She'd been busy drinking.

I rolled her over, moving gently, and began searching for where the blood was coming from. Her vitals were good at first glance, but I grabbed her wrist, counting her pulse as I kept looking over her body.

"Oh my god—" Leo came in from the door, kneeling at my other side. "She—she wasn't like this when I stepped outside. She'd been drinking and she was angry, going on a rant about you. There's a bunch of plates downstairs on the floor. She must've stepped on them." He added the last bit as I ran a hand down her body, lifting up her foot and seeing the blood there. It was a massive cut, deep. "She'll need stitches."

"No. No stiches," she grumbled, before her head shot to the side, her body following, and she threw up.

Vomit landed just past me.

I jumped out of the way but cursed and went back to finish my assessment. She had cuts on both her feet and one on the palm of her hand. None of them looked self-inflicted, which was a relief on this shitty Saturday.

"Here." Leo must've left to grab some gauze. He knelt back down, the first aid kit in his other hand.

I took it, pressed it to her foot. She started to balk, but she was so drunk that a second later, she was passed out.

I hated dealing with drunk people, but it was always worse when it was your parent.

We worked in silence as I cleaned all of her cuts, disinfected them, and then bandaged each one. I wrapped both her feet and her hand, and as one unit, we both bent to pick her up and placed her on the bed.

I stepped back.

Her breathing was deep but ragged at the same time, and her bathrobe fell open. She was still in her pajamas. "She needs stitches."

Leo nodded, his phone in hand. "I know. I'll make a call."

A call.

Right.

Easier to handle this having them come here, then taking her in.

Leo was saying, "Yeah, yeah. Thank you, Ben. She's passed out, so the sooner the better."

He'd called one of the medics that he played poker with, which made sense. Ben could do the stitches, no problem, and Ben wouldn't say anything. He never did. We were a community in that way, but for a moment, I wished he would say something because this was not the first time Leo had called Ben over for something like this.

I knew it wouldn't be the last either.

He hung up and moved to the bed. "We need to put her in clothes. He can't see her like this." Meaning he didn't want Ben to see the vomit.

I put a hand on his arm, stopping him. "He can see her like this."

"Your mom would be horrified."

I nodded at her. "Obviously not because she's in this state. He's seen worse." I gave him a look, moving for the door. "We've all seen worse."

I went downstairs because while I couldn't do anything more to fix *that* mess, not unless I wanted to finance another trip to rehab, I went to find the mess that I could clean up. Rounding the corner for the dining room, I saw all the smashed plates on the ground.

My mom had been ambitious in her drunken fit. She'd cleaned out all the expensive dining sets she got from her mother-in-law. I started cleaning.

There might've been a joke there somewhere. I was too tired to find it.

———

Ben had come and gone.

My mom was sleeping it off. Her clothes had been changed and she was snuggled into her bed. Leo found me in the living room, a beer in hand and the game on the television.

He sighed, taking the second beer that I handed to him, and bypassed me for the lounge chair that my dad used to sit in. He sank down and put up his feet. "Score?"

"Twenty to seven."

"Fourth quarter. They need to get going, don't they?"

I ignored that because we were pretending we were both rooting for our city's team, but Leo was really a Rams fan and I was actually a Bengals fan. Neither team was playing today. "This was really all because I watered down one of her bottles?"

He shrugged, gripping his beer and taking a long drink. "Who knows. She mentioned a call from her sister."

"What?" My attention snapped to him. The game was forgotten. "My aunt?"

He looked up, dragging his gaze from the television before clueing in that this was a big deal. A real big deal. His eyes widened a little. "Yeah. She's got two sisters, right?"

"Which one was it?" She didn't care for the older one. My mom always griped she was spoiled, but the younger one was a whole different ordeal. They'd been close growing up until my aunt met her current husband and conversation had come to a halt. It wasn't a good situation. "She live up north or the one who lives in Alabama?"

"The one up north."

The younger one.

I sat up straighter. "Did she say anything? How'd the call go? What'd my aunt say?"

He was frowning at me, and I was clueing in here, too, because I was realizing it was the aunt that we didn't talk about. Leo was family, but I was guessing he didn't know about her.

"She didn't, just said she called and that was it. She started in about you right away, and I took my cues from there."

Fuck.

That'd been it?

Damn.

I'd have to come back and talk to my mom when she was sober and not wanting to hate me.

I reached up, fixing my hair before I sighed, needing to let it go. I couldn't do anything about it right now. "You staying?"

He was quiet before a long, "Yeah. I'll stay."

I stood, grabbing my coat.

"That's it? You're leaving?"

I turned back in the doorway and shrugged. "We both know how this goes. I don't know why you're choosing to stick around, but if you are, then I'm leaving. I have to work tonight anyways."

His whole face flinched, and he took a drag from his beer. "You shouldn't be working at that place. You need extra money, there's other places."

"What *do* you know about where I work?"

He'd brought this up before, but I never pushed. I always assumed it was because it was a nightclub and thought he wanted me to work at the local pub where he spent time, where others in our industry hung out. Now knowing what I knew, did he know too?

"Nothing, just . . . there's rumors about that place."

"About Tristian West?"

His face slackened, and I swear he paled just a little bit. "What do you know about that name?"

"Just that he grew up not far from here, and he owns Katya."

He was studying me. "He's some local hotshot, isn't he?"

I shrugged. "I guess, but he never crossed paths with me when we were kids. Don't feel it matters now."

Or did it?

But Leo shut down. I could tell in the resolved expression on his face. He wasn't going to say anything anymore, and I did have a shift to get to.

"Okay." I started for the door. "See you, old man. Get some sleep. Don't let my mom take advantage of you too much."

He chuckled. We both got the joke. He took care of her for my dad, and the few times he stayed, like tonight, when I came by the next morning, I found him passed out on the couch.

"Be safe out there, kiddo."

CHAPTER NINETEEN

TRACE

She looked tired.

I was watching her from one of the private boxes, one that had a view of the nightclub. I first came to work, thinking Katya would help clear out my mind, but eventually found myself migrating to where I could see her and she couldn't see me.

This wasn't going away, the pull to have her, to claim her, and my uncle's favor wouldn't stop either. There had to be a compromise, but there wasn't.

Tonight would be the final straw. If she didn't know who I was, she would, and she'd hate me. But family was family.

I'd do what I'd have to do.

A door opened behind me. The sounds of the club sounded clear and then muted.

I didn't move, knowing who it was, and a second later, Ashton came to stand beside me. He had a drink in hand. I looked to see him watching her as well. He took a sip of his drink, the ice rattling in the glass. "Are you going to be okay with this?"

No. "I'll have to be."

He glanced my way, studying me. I turned my attention back to her. It was her. It had always been her. Ever since I'd first seen her.

"Maybe she won't find out? Intel said they weren't close."

I shook my head. "I doubt it, but we'll deal with it."

"You sure?"

I gave him a look, a hard one. He knew the situation. We got an order.

He gave a nod, a wary look coming over him. "Let's do this then."

I took one last look at her, one lingering long look because everything was going to change.

CHAPTER TWENTY

JESS

It was another busy night, but I needed the distraction.

Kelly was working again; so was Justin. I'd not been back to the house, having gone straight to Katya from my mother's house, but I was guessing from the hooded looks each of them was giving the other that they'd spent the day together.

I wasn't sure how I felt about the two of them together, but I just hoped if and when they ended, that it was amicable and that Kelly wasn't the one who needed to quit here. But, knowing Kelly, knowing her entire history of relationships, they never ended well, and she *would* be the one who'd quit or get fired. Thinking on that, I waited until we had a small break between customers before going over to Justin.

He was filling a drink but paused, seeing me.

I stepped in, turning so my back was to the bar. "If you hurt her—" He turned to look at me squarely. I kept going: "—I'll do something to make you stand before a judge. You hear me? Do not fuck with her."

I didn't wait for a response as I returned to my section.

And Anthony was there, giving me a fixed look.

I frowned. "What?"

He had his arms crossed over his chest and slowly shook his head.

"What's going on?"

"I don't know what's going on between you and West, but I'm stating it here that I do not like it."

I frowned, my whole body tensing. "What are you talking about?"

A hard look entered his gaze. "I like you. You're tough. You don't take shit. Customers back off from you, and you show up every day. So here's the one time I'm giving you unsolicited advice that does not benefit me at all: *Walk*. Quit. Leave your shift right now and never come back here. Whatever dance you and West are doing will not end well. He has connections you will *not* like. Trust me."

A cold feeling replaced the tension.

He added, a grim look on his face, "Trust me on this one, Montell."

Justin moved over, eyeing the two of us. "You guys okay?"

Anthony's jaw clenched, giving him a hard look too. "We're good. This ain't none of your business." One last searing look my way. "When things go off, don't say I didn't warn you." With that, he stomped away. Justin was giving me an assessing look, drying his hands with a towel. "I'm aware I'm new here, new in your roommate's life, but I'm here. My brother's a cop—"

"A cop?"

A more guarded look came over his face, hardening it before he gave me a tight nod. "Detective Worthing. He's at the 116th."

I didn't know his brother, but the 116th was a good district. "I've known Anthony for a long time, that's all. History. I can take care of myself."

"Kelly told me what you do for a living. You gotta be tough to do that job."

I gave him a look. "I'm good."

But he didn't look convinced. He lifted his chin up, moving back to his section, and I caught the measured look he gave in the direction Anthony had gone. The rest of the night passed with less drama, which said a lot considering I saw two parolees violating their parole, right in front of me. One caught me looking, looked like he shit his pants, and took off. The other one came over and bellied up to my bar, thinking we'd be "friends" about this. The crowd around me enjoyed the stern warning I gave him, which went like this: "Get out of here. Sober up. Expect a call from your parole officer."

His chest puffed up the same time he was reaching over the bar for me. "Now, come on, you bi—"

Then he wasn't talking anymore because I was around the bar, his hand twisted behind his back, and I was marching him out of the club myself. The security guards saw me coming, saw the guy red in the face because even though he had a good seventy pounds on me, I was still handling him. They opened the door. I shoved the guy out, and when he started arguing, I was in his face. "Walk! I don't have time for this. Not tonight. Not here."

He came at me again, and this time he swung.

I ducked, grabbed him, twisted his arm, and pushed him to his knees. By the time that happened, a nearby patrol squad hit their lights. I knew the cops. They knew me. They arrested the guy, but he'd be out within an hour.

So yeah. I still considered Anthony's earlier warning the most drama of the night.

The rest of the night was me filling orders, getting hit on by a few guys and a couple girls, and also being called "bitch" six times because I didn't take someone's order fast enough. The whole time I was trying not to think about whether he was upstairs. If he was watching me. If someone else was sent up to serve him and his friend.

Then it was closing time.

I did the usual. Closed out my drawer, counted up the tips, cleaned my section, and went over the inventory list. Kelly came over, giggling and half all over Justin, who gave me a rueful look back.

"I'm heading to Justin's for the night. Want to come over? We can unwind with a drink?"

Tempting, because I was still wired. A drink wouldn't help this "wired" feeling in me. Only one thing would work it out of me.

"I'm going to head home."

Kelly's face got somber, and she came over to give me a hug. She said in my ear, "You okay? I saw Anthony at your bar earlier. It looked tense."

I hugged her back, giving an extra squeeze. "I'm good. Stay safe, all right?"

She was back to her giggling and sighing self as she drew back, but she rested her forehead to mine. "He's nice, huh?"

Some of the tension in me eased, just a little. Kelly sounded scared in that one question, but I nodded slowly against her forehead. "He does seem like a nice guy."

"Can you look him up for me?"

I barked out a laugh. "I don't need to. Anthony put him in the section next to mine—that says he's solid. Anthony wouldn't have done that if he had something I'd find in the system. My guess is that he's fallen a bit too quick for you."

She jerked her head back, her eyes wide. "He's fallen for me?"

Ooh. I winced. "I'm guessing." Maybe I shouldn't have shared?

But it didn't matter. Kelly was back to swooning, and the ever romantic in her was falling as well.

They took off after that, Justin giving me a wave as they left, his other arm around Kelly's shoulders.

Once I was done, I headed out, and it was the first time I checked my phone.

I saw the text when I was almost to my car.

Leo: Call me asap. Your aunt's call earlier was a big deal.

I didn't react, not outwardly, but inwardly, a whole ball of dread filled me. I had known earlier that it was a big deal, a really big deal, but I'd tried telling myself to leave it alone.

I called once I was inside my car.

He picked up on the first ring. "There's a situation."

I prepared myself, hardening. "What is it?"

"You know where your aunt lives?"

"My aunt? Yeah . . ."

"Can you go and get her?"

"What?" I bit out, alarm filling my chest. "What's happened?"

"A domestic situation happened. Your aunt is leaving him. Her and the kids. They're at a local shelter, but I talked to a guy I know up there, one I trust. Your uncle has a reputation, and he's not one to stay away from the shelter. Your aunt's best bet is to get out of town ASAP. I volunteered to go up, but your mom overheard and started howling about it. She's not receptive to taking care of your aunt here."

"Shit, Leo. You've been there all night long?"

His voice came out gruff. "I don't mind. Don't have much else going on today anyways."

Right. Because taking care of a drunk, especially the drunk of your best friend's wife, who wasn't quiet on the attitude side when she was liquored up, was totally something I'd be up for handling on my day off. But Leo asked.

"I know where she lives, but there's basically no relationship with her. I'll head up, see what I can do, though."

"You good to drive?"

"Wired for a fight, to be honest."

He chuckled, relaxing a little. "Let's hope it doesn't get to that."

I laughed, starting the engine and noting I'd need another tank of gas and a couple big drinks of straight caffeine. I had a two-hour drive ahead of me.

CHAPTER

TWENTY-ONE

TRACE

We arrived, and the plan had been to grab the uncle and take him somewhere else for our interrogation. That was until we walked in and found the house in shambles.

The plan changed.

The place was empty. Ashton walked through the house while I surveyed the primary bedroom. The wife's clothes were gone; an empty suitcase was thrown on the bed. There were more empty spaces in the closet. Spaces where other suitcases might've been but weren't anymore.

Ashton came in. "Kids' stuff is gone. Wife left him."

I nodded. "We wait. He'll be back."

"And if she's with him?"

I gave him a dry look. "She look like she'll be coming back?"

"Domestic fight." He was noting the holes in the wall, the shattered glass. "A lot of times they come back before finally leaving or getting dead."

"We stay and wait. This is a small town. If we start looking for him, it'll raise flags."

Ashton gave me a nod.

Demetri, one of my guards, came in as we were in the kitchen. He gestured outside. "They got a shed in the back. We can take him in there?" He pointed at the other door. "Or the basement. There's a room in the back that looks built for shit like this."

Demetri and Pajn. My two guards. They'd grown up with me, guys we knew from the neighborhood, guys that got into trouble with Ashton and me when we were teenagers.

"What do you mean it looks built for this shit?"

He gave me a long and hard look. "Come see for yourself, boss."

I followed him down, knowing Ashton was coming right behind.

He led us through a room that had chairs set up in the corner, facing the corner. A chalkboard was on the wall. There were no windows, no light shining in from outside. Cement flooring. We went through that room to another room, which was just as sparse. Another room that had canned foods lining the shelves and then to another room that opened from a small door that we all had to stoop to get through.

"Trace."

I turned, seeing where Ashton was gesturing. The door opened our way. A lock was on the outside of the door.

My blood went cold.

"Boss." Pajn indicated a post.

It had a chain wrapped around it. It was stained, and I knew the smell of dried blood. The post was drenched in it. At the base of the post was another stain from liquids, and I didn't think it was only blood that made that stain. It circled out from the post.

He kicked a bucket. "Smells like this is used for piss and shit."

"Goddamn," came from Ashton, under his breath.

I was taking it all in.

A whip was hanging on the wall.

A knife.

A cleaver.

More chains.

Manacles that looked like they were from the medieval era.

"Fuck." Ashton was staring at a pair of fuzzy handcuffs, and that was *more* than enough for me.

I growled, "We're doing it in here. Right. In. Here."

The guys were in agreement.

———

A pair of headlights flashed through the house as a truck slowed and turned into their driveway. Ashton and I were both waiting in the kitchen.

"He's coming." Demetri moved to the back of the door.

Pajn was on the other side.

They were big guys and could be mistaken for bodybuilders, but both were trained to handle themselves. They'd learned on the streets and moved like cats right now. Quiet and stealthy.

Ashton tapped the table to get my attention. He mouthed, "He alone?"

I leaned back, moving the curtain a slight centimeter. Billy Garretson was trudging toward the back door of the house. I nodded to Ashton and turned back, watching him coming.

His head was down. He didn't suspect anything.

We heard keys jangling.

A key inserted into the lock, turned. The door was pushed open.

"Fuck dammit—" He stepped in, and we were hit with a rank odor coming from him. He fumbled inside, reaching for the light switch, and he flipped the light. It should've turned on, but the fuses had been turned off in the basement. "What the hell?" He stepped all the way in, shut the door, and flipped the light switch up and down before growling. "Bitch. She blew a—" He turned, making a startled choking sound as he came face to face with Pajn.

"Hi." That was Pajn, and *punch*!

Pajn hadn't wasted time.

Ashton and I both stood, expecting a fight.

It didn't happen. Pajn hit him once, and the guy wavered on his feet before falling.

Pajn smothered a chuckle, stepping back and over the body. "The dude's out."

Both Pajn and Demetri knelt and picked up the body.

"Now you're going to have an ego about this, saying you're a cold-cocker," Demetri grumbled.

They lifted him together.

"Yeah, yeah. You can start now. Address me as Mr. Coldcocker from here on out." Pajn made a gagging sound. "This guy reeks. Did he shit his pants or something?"

"Who knows. That room downstairs smells like a sewer."

Pajn grunted in response to Demetri as they carried him downstairs.

I waited, giving them time to set him up down there.

"The information we got was that he was a religious nut." Ashton was looking around. "Not seeing any religious items in this house."

He was right. There were no crosses, no Bibles, no Bible verses anywhere. No rosaries, if those were a part of his religion. The walls were sparse, empty. The rooms each had the minimum of furniture. A couple chairs in the living room. The kitchen had only a small table, big enough to be a card table, and two chairs. The second chair was pulled back, sitting against the wall as if when he sat to eat, she sat there to wait on him.

The built-in shelves were empty as well.

I'd walked through the kids' rooms earlier, knowing they had three younger children. It was the same there. Bed mattresses on the floor. A pillow. A blanket, if even one. One of the closets had some children's books in the corner, a flashlight next to them.

"We won't be working with this man."

Ashton's head snapped to mine. "Your uncle is firm."

I shook my head, my gut flaring. "He deserves a slow and tortured death. We'll reach out to his supervisor, make sure whoever is put in his place will work for us instead. We'll handle it if we need to."

"And when this guy disappears? If someone starts asking questions?"

I gave him a very dark and long look. "You really think anyone is going to ask questions?"

"She might."

"Then she and I will have a conversation when that happens." I was going with my gut that if this guy disappeared, everyone would consider it a blessing.

Demetri called up from the bottom of the stairs. "He's ready."

Questioning or interrogating someone wasn't new to us, but Ashton was the one who looked forward to it. He thrived on the cruelty of it. Me, it wasn't my specialty, but this time was different.

With what I wanted to do to this man, this time I was just as excited.

CHAPTER
TWENTY-TWO

JESS

I wasn't ready, not by a long shot, when I saw my aunt. Sarah was a shadow of my mom, and my mom was already a shadow of herself, so that was saying a lot there. Then a little girl lifted up her head, and I was staring at a female version of my brother.

Same eyes. Same shape of eyes. Same coloring all over and the same almost-white hair color. My brother had a boyish look to him, at least he did when he wasn't trying to be fierce, and this girl had the same. It was in the cheeks—both had the same round cheeks.

I was struck speechless, my throat closing up before I took in the other two kids. A little boy playing with trucks in the corner and another girl, this one with frizzy red hair sticking out. All of the kids were taking me in, but they weren't scared. They weren't curious.

They were staring at me because I was one more stranger to them.

I pulled my gaze back to my aunt, and she was also watching me, waiting.

She was tiny, but those eyes were seventy years old.

"You look like your mother." Her words were soft.

I gave her a half grin. "Please don't say that again or I'll think you mean it."

A flare of something showed in her gaze, just briefly before it was gone just as quick. "She won't want us at her place." Her gaze trailed down to my hand, where I had placed it resting on my gun, under my shirt.

I hadn't realized I'd put it there and moved my hand back at my side. "I talked to a lady who runs this shelter on the way up. She's going to make some calls, find a shelter closer to the city."

She was noting the invitation wasn't for my place, and for the life of me, I couldn't tell if she liked hearing that or didn't. After a beat, she gave me a small nod before bending down and whispering something to the little girl who was wrapped around her legs, whispering it into her ear.

The little girl kept staring at me before her mom straightened again and gently nudged her on the back. "Go ahead, honey. Take your brother and sister too."

She broke away. Once all three were out of the room, my aunt ran a hand through her hair. "They don't know who you are. I figured it's easier on them not knowing, not unless we get situated, and we can go from there."

"Who do they think I am then?"

"They think I know a lady in New York who is connected to all the big police that can protect them. That's what I told them. And I need a favor. I mean, another one before we leave."

I frowned because for some reason, my gut took a nosedive at hearing that. "What's the favor?"

"I left something at the house. I can't leave without it."

I found myself resting my hand once again on my piece. My fingers slowly wrapping around the handle, but knowing it wasn't her that was making me feel this way. "What is it?"

"My kids' birth certificates and my own ID. I had everything packed in a run bag, but not those items. I was too worried they'd get lost if I left them out. They're in a safe that he doesn't know about."

Lovely.

I checked the time, but I couldn't call for any reinforcements, and I didn't know the cops here. Interdepartmental cooperation sometimes didn't come so easy.

I also wasn't sure if I wanted to come across my aunt's abuser or if I wanted to avoid him. But those items *were* needed. The longer she left them behind, the better chance he had to find them.

"Where's the safe?"

CHAPTER TWENTY-THREE

JESS

This was beyond a bad idea. The worst idea. Whatever was beyond worst.

I'd parked a block away, and I was maneuvering through the neighbors' backyards to the house. Her safe was in the basement. She'd given me the layout of the house, said where the asshole would be sleeping, or where she assumed he'd be sleeping.

"You should be able to slip in through a side window that goes into the basement. The screen is loose, and when you climb in, there's a footstool at the bottom for you. The safe is in the next room, but he won't be in the basement. He doesn't go down there unless . . ." She looked away, and I got an up-close-and-personal view of a bruise on her cheek.

Abusers normally didn't pick a specific room where they would only abuse, but going with what she wasn't saying, I was guessing some really bad stuff happened down there.

I took the key she gave me. "He'll be asleep?"

"He should be. I'm sure he was up all night driving around looking for us." She indicated the key in my hand. "That's for the safe. You won't need a key for the house. The window is unlocked, and no one would ever break into that house. All our neighbors know, you know." She looked down this time.

I knew. I was getting a real good view of the entire situation, and there was a special place in my belly that burned against assholes like her husband. Neighbors knew. The cops knew. I was now wondering what my mom knew as well.

When I turned to leave, she wouldn't release my arm.

She said, "I'm not letting you go into that house alone."

I frowned, holding up the key. "That's why you gave me this."

She was shaking her head. "I don't know you, but you're my niece. I'm coming with you."

A whole argument ensued because no way was I bringing an abused woman back to her abuser.

"I have a gun. I can protect myself."

Her head just kept shaking from side to side, going faster and faster. "I know how cops work, and you guys don't go in without backup, not if you can get help. I'll . . ." She was looking around, her eyes wild, panicked. "I'll stay in the car. How about that? I won't go in, but I would never forgive myself if something happened to you too."

So a compromise was made.

My aunt came, but she'd stay in the car. That's why I'd parked so far away.

I was tearing down an alley when I looked back to make sure she was doing as I said. After that, I ran a little bit lighter, hurrying forward.

The garage and back door were on the opposite side of the house from where I crept up.

No lights were on.

I listened but didn't hear anything, so at this point, I was hoping her information was correct.

I went to the window she identified, felt around, and found the screen was loose indeed. I took it off, gently laying it on the snow beside me. I pushed open the window how she told me. When it was open, there was enough room for a medium-size person to crawl there. I went in horizontally, holding on to the windowsill as my legs went down, feeling around for the footstool.

I found it, tested it out, but it was sturdy.

She was right, and also I didn't want to know how many times she'd needed to leave her own house this way.

The room was dark. I pulled out my flashlight, shining it on the floor as I edged to the door.

I opened it. Still dark. No sound, so I crossed to the wall she'd indicated.

I felt around, finding a notch in a little crevice, and I pulled it back. It lifted easily, and voilà, it wasn't a safe inside, but it was a box with the lid locked down. I fitted in the key, unlocked it, and aimed my flashlight inside the box.

I located their birth certificates and her ID, but there were some drawings the kids had done. I grabbed those, then looked through the rest. Bank statements. That was interesting . . . I wasn't sure what to make of that because they were addressed to him. I still took them. Some other documents, a letter, a piece of paper with a number scribbled on it. I took all of it, and the bottom was lined with cash.

I took that too.

I cleaned the box out, stuffing everything in my jacket. I locked it up, pocketed the key, and put it all away and moved the piece of wall back in place.

I was turning, planning on leaving, when a bloodcurdling scream ripped through the house.

I jumped and whipped around, drawing my gun.

A chill went down my spine. That wasn't upstairs, like she'd told me. It was from down in the basement, and by my guess, a few rooms away.

A second scream was right on its heels.

A third.

I was moving before I was thinking, opening the door and seeing a bunch of rooms in front of me.

More screams.

I heard yelling now, and I didn't pause because if that was him? If he found my aunt again? One of their kids? Or if he took someone else to torture in their place?

I wasn't going to answer my own questions, not until I knew, and then I would deal with whatever I was going to do.

It was coming from a back room, on the other side of a seriously small door.

The screams started up, and that sound was no longer human.

I wanted to kick down that door, go in there and start showing my teeth, but I refrained. Every cell in my body was begging to fight, but I had to stop, I had to think. One second.

It started again, and I ceased thinking.

I reared back and kicked the door open, and then I froze in place because the animal screaming wasn't an animal. I was taking an educated guess that that was my aunt's abuser, but while he was tied to a post, with liquids seeping out of him, it was another person in the room who I recognized.

A large guy was standing over my aunt's abuser, and there were two other people in the room.

I skipped over Ashton, my eyes finding and latching onto Tristian West, who was standing in the corner.

"What are you doing here?"

Tristian's eyes flashed, hard, and he came at me.

I stepped back, jerking my arm up, my gun right at him.

He stopped but indicated behind me.

I didn't move. Not at first.

God. What were they doing to him?

But then I lowered my gun, and Tristian reached over, touching my arm and guiding me back. I allowed it, or my body did because my body recognized his and it was having its own mind. I was seeing red; my body was heated.

He took me back to the room where the safe was.

He flipped on the lights.

He paid no attention to the room. His gaze was on me, pinning me down. "What are you doing here?"

My mouth fell down for a split second before I was pissed. "Are you kidding me?! That piece of shit in there is married to my aunt. What are *you* doing here? What are you doing to him?"

They were torturing that piece of shit. And I had walked in on it.

Now I was in this room, and I was putting my gun away? What the hell was I doing?

I started reaching for my phone.

I needed to call this in. It was out of my hands.

"No." He plucked my phone away from me, pocketing it.

"Give it back."

He glared. "No."

I growled before pulling my gun right back out. "Give it back now."

He eyed the gun, not fighting me, but he wasn't doing what I ordered. His eyes narrowed, and he leaned close. "No."

I growled again, this time more feral. "You are in so much shit that you won't be able to comprehend it—now give me my phone back."

He kept studying me, before a slow grin showed and a chuckle slid out. He moved back a step. "I don't think so." His eyebrows rose up, mocking me. "How are you going to explain yourself? You didn't walk in through the back door or front door. I'd know. I got a guy up there. You broke in. Now *I'm* wondering why *you're* here when *my* business with your uncle is none of *your* business."

"He's not my uncle. He's a piece of shit that abused my aunt."

"Huh. You mean the aunt that's not here?" His voice was grating on my nerves because he was fully taunting me, and I didn't understand why.

"Give me my phone." I moved closer, my gun now too close for both of our comforts, but he ignored it.

And right then, he dropped his act.

The amusement fled, and I got a glimpse at the very real and very blistering anger under the surface.

He lowered his head, his nostrils flaring. "This is why I didn't want you around me. This is why I should've forgotten you the second I found out you're a cop."

He began to move toward me. His chest touched my gun's muzzle, and I swallowed a curse before making a decision. I wasn't going to shoot him. He knew it. I knew it.

I holstered my gun, and then he was in my space, moving me back against the wall. He was breathing hard, staring down at me, and looking like he wanted to chew my head off, literally. But his tone came out soft, and all the more dangerous because of it. A whole new chill slithered down my spine. "For three years your uncle has been a pain in my family's ass, refusing to work with us. Did you know that?"

I didn't respond, too caught up in what else he was going to tell me, because I knew more was coming. I felt it, and I didn't know if I wanted to know or not. I did.

His hand slid up, touching my chest and slowly moving to my throat, then around to the back of my neck, cupping me there. He held his own head back, watching me from his fullest height. "Then I met you. I became *fucking* captivated by you, and somehow that shit got back to my uncle, and guess who my uncle thought I should move in on *now*? Fuck him for seeing an opportunity to capitalize on, and fuck *your* uncle for being the abusive weasel shit that comes out of his own asshole. Goddamn fuck *everyone* because now we're in a situation. So when I ask why you're here, you're going to tell me because you are now in this too."

A low growl was building in my throat, and I brought up my hands to shove him away.

They didn't, though. They rested on his chest, and at the touch, he sucked in some breath, closing his eyes a moment. When they opened, raw pain flared briefly. "You're not going to call the cops on me, and you know it. I'm sure there's a valid reason you came in here, but the real reason you came and the real reason you came into that room is because you were hoping to do something to your uncle, probably what we're doing."

I looked away. "You're torturing him."

I felt the distance closing, and then his forehead touched the side of my head, softly, before he whispered, "I'm killing him slowly, for you. Because he's hurt someone who shares your blood."

A surge of emotion surged through me, and I really didn't want to identify what that was. I ripped myself out of his arms and went to the opposite corner.

He went with me.

"Stop," I grated out.

"You and me, it's been there since the beginning. You've done a search on me by now. I'm not stupid. You know who I am, and you know who my family is."

"You're a Wall Street guy."

"I'm barely there lately."

God. This was all so bleak. Why did I feel I had a small opening that I could see out, but it was closing on me—and it was closing fast?

I dropped my voice. "What are you doing here? Really?"

He angled his head back, giving me another assessing look.

I met his gaze, steadily. "I need to know."

His eyebrows dipped down again, and he moved back a step, his head lowering. "We're here creating a job opening."

A low and swift curse came out of me.

"I shared. Now it's your turn."

I seared him with a look, stepping away from him. "That's none of your business." I took a step toward the room for the window when he moved just as quick, his hand grabbing mine. "What are—"

He was pulling me toward him, a whole different and intense look filling his eyes, when suddenly—*bang!*

We both took off running.

I pulled my gun.

From the stairs, another stampede of steps barreled down. It was Ashton and the other guard; they must've gone upstairs.

Tristian cursed, getting to the room first.

The door was open. I went in first, and Tristian ran to my side. He had an arm in front of me as if to guard me. I swore, holstering my gun immediately, and I started forward.

Tristian caught me, holding me back. "Stop—"

Ashton moved around, then stopped, cursing.

I twisted out of Tristian's hold and moved to the side.

Aunt Sarah looked at me, dropping a gun, and she took an unsteady step my way. The smoke was still coming from the barrel. "You didn't come back. I was worried, and then . . ." She looked back at her husband, whose head was hanging down. More blood seeping from him, but at this point, he was just one bloody mess. "I knew where he kept his gun."

Jesus. She shot him.

A cupboard was open behind her, and a section of the wall was opened.

"Get her out of here." Tristian pointed at her, and his guard swooped in. He bent down and lifted my aunt completely off her feet. He carried her out of the room. She wasn't struggling, a wide-eyed look on her face.

I started after them, but Tristian took my hand again, holding me in place. "She's in shock."

I pulled free. "I have to go with her."

I followed the guard up. There was another big guy there. He didn't look surprised to see me, but his eyebrows twitched at the sight of my aunt in his colleague's arms. "We killing both?"

The one holding my aunt stifled a laugh. "Doubt it. Boss wants in that one's pants."

Guard Two swung his gaze my way, giving me a perusal before whistling. "He's got morbid taste. She's a copper." He nodded to my aunt. "What are we doing with her?"

"I have a car around the block. I'll bring it around." I pulled out my keys, which were taken just as easily as he'd taken my phone. Tristian moved around me, once again gathering my hand in his as he tossed the keys to the first guard. "Deal with the body, and then drive her car back to the city."

The guy nodded and was gone in an instant.

"Stop! How many fucking times do I have to say that before you listen?!"

He ignored me, again, and drew me to him, moving me in front of his chest. He spoke over my head. "Take her aunt back to the city—"

"No." I ripped away, again. "She has kids." I skimmed over my aunt, but she wasn't here. Full shock had settled in.

All of the men stilled in the room.

"Where are her kids?"

I looked up, making sure he saw the resolve in me. "I am not telling you that, and you cannot steamroll over me for that. I have to go alone to get those kids and if I don't show up with my aunt, they will know something's happened."

Tristian was gauging whether I was telling the truth.

"I'll take her alone. I'm not letting those kids come into the vehicle and seeing another strange man inside. They're already scared. They're leaving him. That's why I'm here. I came to grab one of their toys before we headed back to the city."

Tristian's jaw clenched. His eyes were blazing. "You were going to sneak in alone? Thinking he was here?"

"You already guessed the reason why."

His eyes flashed once more before he exhaled loudly.

"Let her get 'em, but she can go back in one of our vehicles. We have her keys for her car. We also have the gun her aunt used to kill him. She's not going to snitch," Ashton said.

That's what he was worried about?

It was. I saw the speculation deep in Tristian's eyes.

He didn't look away from me, but he angled his head toward Ashton. "She's not particularly close to her aunt. My PI was thorough."

I wasn't giving anything away. I couldn't. This was some sort of standoff right now.

"They're family. She came up here after her job. Think on that, brother," Ashton said.

He continued to drill holes into my head before he sighed. "Fine." He nodded to the guard remaining, who was holding my aunt. "Help her get situated, then give her the keys to your SUV."

"Won't they question me when I pull up with an SUV instead of my car?"

"I doubt they even know what vehicle you drove here in, but Jess . . ."

Ashton gave us both one last lingering look before heading down to the basement.

Tristian stepped in close to me. I could feel his body heat. "Keep your phone on. I'll be calling with instructions. Unblock me." He handed me my phone, and I took it, giving him one last glare before leaving the house, this time going through the actual back door.

Nope. I was *not* going to ruminate over the shitpile I'd just stepped into.

My aunt. Trace.

None of it. This was a situation where I didn't want to think. If I did, I probably wouldn't like what went through my head.

CHAPTER

TWENTY-FOUR

TRACE

We watched from afar as Jess parked and went inside to get the children. It was a minute wait until the door burst open and a little girl sprinted for the SUV. The front door was opened. Jess's aunt got out and caught up to her kid, and they both moved into the back seat.

Ashton chuckled next to me. "Looks like Jess is chauffeur now."

Thirty seconds later, two more kids came out, each holding a bag awkwardly, half dragging on the ground. A boy had one arm inside his jacket and was struggling to get his arm through the other. I watched as Jess stopped him, knelt, and slowly and very patiently helped him get his other arm through the sleeve. Once the jacket was in place, she zipped him up and took the bag he'd been trying to carry. He didn't thank her but looked up briefly before taking off and climbing into the back door of the SUV. The last girl had red hair, and she was zipped up already, carrying two bags herself.

Jess glanced back, checking on her. The little girl stopped. Jess held a hand out to her, saying something, but the little girl's head lowered before she shook it from side to side. Jess looked at her for one second; then the girl darted around her, also clambering up into the back seat.

"Aren't there laws about child seats?"

I gave Ashton a look. "That's your concern this morning?"

He gave a shrug, half smirking. "Don't want her to get stopped."

"I have a feeling Jess will handle it if she does."

"Cops are assholes."

"Says the guy who's got how many on his family's payroll?"

"That's why I can say it. *I* know."

"Jess is a parole officer."

"There's a distinction there if you want to start considering it."

I narrowed my eyes. "What are you talking about?"

He continued to watch how Jess now had the reverse lights on and was backing out of the driveway onto the street. "I know where this is going. You know where it's going. So does she. Might make it easier if you stop thinking of her as a cop."

My stomach churned. "I do and that's when someone will get burned."

"You already got her. Her aunt murdered her abuser. Demetri is covering it up right now. We have the gun. We know where the body will be. Relax on her. She would've raised the alarm then and there if she was going to."

I gave his comments some thought.

"And if she doesn't play ball, we still have the brother card to pull."

That was enough. "Stop talking."

He snorted but complied.

We'd started following behind Jess when I called her.

A part of me didn't want her to answer. A part of me wanted her to drive straight to the nearest police station and everything would get handled from there, but I knew she wouldn't because it was too late. If she did that, they'd go to the house. Our cover-up job wouldn't be complete, and my family would be implicated. I knew what my uncle would do. But, and that was a big *but*, everything could be stopped. It'd be messy but doable, and somehow I'd try and make sure Jess would make it out alive. Her aunt wouldn't. I didn't know who else Stephano would kill, but not Jess. If that happened, Jess would still have her soul. She could still do her job and not be compromised, but there'd be no us.

Maybe there shouldn't be an us.

If I had anything good in me, I would walk away from her. I'd call her now, tell her to drive to the station, and we'd handle it from there.

I didn't do that because she was too deep in me. And I was selfish.

It was already too late for me. So why the hell was I even thinking about this?

When she turned onto the main road, I pulled out my phone and dialed.

She picked up. "Yeah?"

"Get off this road."

I was a little surprised when she put on her right blinker, slowing. She complied with everything I said, turning onto a smaller road.

There were houses around us. I added, "Keep going."

"How far?"

"Just keep going."

Once we were out of the town, past houses, and the road looked desolate, I told her to pull over.

We both did.

Ashton was out of the car in a heartbeat. He went up to her side, opened the door, and motioned for her to get out. She did. He gave my vehicle a nod, and slowly, reluctantly, she came toward my SUV. I got out and went around the front, giving her a nod to take my passenger seat. She did, giving the other SUV a lingering look as I got behind the wheel.

"Get in. Those kids don't know you either. They'll take cues from your aunt, and your aunt isn't dumb. She'll do as she's told."

She looked at me, her eyes flashing before her mouth flattened into a hard line, and she swung up into the SUV. She shut the door, yanking on it harder than was necessary.

My phone buzzed.

D: All good. Heading back now.

Me: Drive her car to the cleaners, then return it to her place.

D: Will do.

"What now?" She'd been watching me text.

Ashton's SUV was already gone.

I texted Ashton.

Me: Take them to the family safe house.

Ashton: She's saying they had a shelter lined up for them.

Me: I don't care.

Ashton: Ten-four, buddy. Might want to turn your phone off. Uncle Steph is going to want to know where the uncle is.

Me: I'll be in touch later today.

He knew what that meant, and after that, I powered down the phone, then headed off.

Once we got to the city, Jess and I were going to have a *way* more in-depth conversation.

I shifted the car into drive and started off. "You can sleep while I drive us back."

"What about my aunt?"

"We'll talk when we get there."

"Tristian—"

"Trace."

"What?"

"I hate the name Tristian. Call me Trace."

She didn't respond. I only heard her let out a soft sigh, but a few minutes later, she was sleeping. She must've needed it.

CHAPTER

TWENTY-FIVE

JESS

"Trace" took me to a downtown high-rise. I woke up as we pulled into a parking lot. When he got out of the SUV, I waited. I couldn't bring myself to move, not yet. The night's events kept replaying over in my head. Over and over again.

What my aunt did, which was understandable.

It was not understandable that I helped cover it up. I didn't report her, and that was on me. I was an accessory now.

My whole life would change from this day on. I knew it. I felt it. It was in the pit of my stomach, but as my body filled up with lead, there was a different sensation in me, and I couldn't place it. I didn't want to place it. It went against every moral value ingrained inside of me, why I became a parole officer.

I was so beyond fucked that I couldn't comprehend it, and I knew that I would start losing focus.

The days would blend. The lines were blurred now and would continue to be blurred. All this would keep happening, every step I took after I walked out of that house, until the day I would no longer rec-ognize myself, but still.

I lifted my head up and saw Trace watching me from outside the SUV. He'd stopped, but he hadn't said anything. He was just waiting for me, and there was a look of understanding there, like he knew exactly what was going on inside of me.

A part of me liked that. A part of me hated that.

I loathed it, and yet I needed it. All at the same time, and that didn't make me hate him, but it sure as hell made me despise myself.

The hard part of living in a world where it was either wrong or right was that you forgot that being human meant you were never only on one side of that equation. What did you do then? Apparently, what I did. You chose, and you tried to survive your choice.

With almost numb hands, a numb body, I unclipped my seat belt and got out.

Trace turned, and I followed.

He took me to an elevator.

When it arrived and we stepped inside, a voice came over the inter-com. "Good morning, Mr. West. Is there anything you'd like?"

Trace studied me before hitting a button. "No, thank you."

"Have a good rest of the day, Mr. West."

"You as well, Gervin."

It wasn't long before we arrived. I was no longer expecting *anything*, so I wasn't surprised when the elevators opened onto his apartment. It covered its own floor, with floor-to-ceiling glass walls that ran the entire apartment. He had a waterfall gradient island. A gas fireplace that was already running for him. His place looked like an industrial art gallery. It was chic, expensive, and manly, all at the same time.

"You slept the whole way back, but would you like a coffee? Or would you like to sleep more?"

I ignored him, walking past the living room and all the way to the wall. I could easily imagine that I was able to see the whole of

Manhattan, we were that high up. The water was visible on two sides of his place, but I looked straight down. The street was so far beneath us.

I lifted my hands, fingers spread out, and touched my palms to the glass.

If I pushed hard enough, would it shatter? Would I fall?

A better question, was that what I wanted?

My aunt killed a man.

"Your men, on your orders, hid a dead body today. They did it fast and easy, and it's very obvious they've done this before. You help with your family's business. Am I wrong?"

I hadn't arrested her. I hadn't called it in.

I looked, seeing his jaw clenched. "At times, yes," he clipped out.

"Illegal activities? That way of helping?"

Another jaw clench. "Not all the time."

Right.

"Doing what I do, life is right or wrong. You're either wrong, or you're right. There's no middle ground." I took a breath. "Having said that, I do not want to *ever* know about what you do for your family. I *cannot know*. Do you get me?"

His eyes were blazing at me. "You just asked."

I had.

I didn't care. Shit was swirling in my head. Impending doom and shame were right behind it, going through me, filling me up, and I wished for a second, just a second, that I would shatter that glass.

Just for one second.

"My dad is dead." I wasn't telling him anything he didn't know. "My brother was convicted for killing him. My mom's a drunk, and because of her illness, she's burned all her bridges with her family. That aunt is the first relative I've met in twenty years. I've had a few relationships during my life—most were just sexual. I'm twenty-nine years old, and during all of that serious shit, I loved being a parole officer. Which is surprising because it's almost a joke now. New mission statements, new focus so even if a parolee violates, he's given a new resource as a reward. Some rehabilitate. Most don't, but they're out there, and you can only hope they don't hurt someone before they violate enough to go back in. Even with all of that frustration, I still loved my job. I loved the community, my coworkers, but today, all of that could be taken from me. The integrity I had, that was taken." He hadn't moved an inch since I started talking. "I don't blame you, but I'm not an idiot. You guys were there for a reason. I'm aware my aunt's abuser worked at a large shipping facility. But I don't want to know why you were there, and I don't need to know the reason. There's no half-in and half-out. You're not half of a criminal. You are a criminal, and today, I became one too."

His eyes grew fierce, sparking from the emotion. He started for me. "I'm not going to speak about my family. The line is real fucking clear that you won't be told anything, nor would the fuck I want to include you on anything. Instead, I'm going to give you a choice. It's something you can offer to your aunt. We'll help her disappear. Her and the kids. We'll set them up in a new life, with money, assets. We'll get her a job. We'll make sure her family is healing and is starting to thrive before we pull our guys from watching her. I'm offering you that, for them, but also for you."

"Why?" I grated out, my throat feeling so dry that there could've been cracks inside.

"Because you're not the only one cursed here." He took another step toward me. "And despite your derision, I *still* want to fuck the shit out of you. And because of that, because I can't get you out of my head, *instead*, I'm trying to do something right for you."

"What are you expecting in return?"

"Nothing." He held both of his hands up, palms my way. "Jesus."

"His disappearance will be noted."

"It's already handled. I won't tell you the details, but we have a lot of people on our payroll."

"They'll look for her."

"No." His tone was so sure. "They really *won't*. It'll be assumed she vanished with reason. No one will look for her, not unless it's you."

A knot was in my throat, swelling up. "It's so easy for you to make entire lives disappear? Just like that?"

"It's not. It takes money, intelligence, and planning. A lot of planning. A lot of money. Your aunt is another sad story, but this time, she's going to disappear of her own volition, not at the hands of him. Not this time. That's all."

His phone beeped, and he read the text. "She's already decided. They'll be gone by tonight."

I sucked in my breath, rocking back by how much power was in that last statement.

An entire family, wiped out by his hands.

I started shaking my head, a sick panic beginning to fill me up. "What are we doing here?"

His eyes lowered, fierce. "You know what we're doing here."

Sex.

My body heated, instantly, but no. I shoved that down.

"No," I clipped out, shoving *everything* down. I was moving, going around him. "I'm leaving. This conversation is over."

"Jess."

He was going for my arm. I knew it and anticipated it, and a part of me wanted to let him touch me. Wanted to let him pull me in, because he could. The power he had over me was spiking all my blood in fear.

But I couldn't. So because of that, I moved out of his way. "After this, we are done. Do you hear me?"

I went to the elevator and pushed the button. When it opened, I stepped in. Staring straight ahead, not seeing him, not anymore, I hit the button for the main lobby.

I'd find my own way home.

CHAPTER
TWENTY-SIX

TRACE

It was a week later, and I was watching her.

I was *always* watching her, but I stayed away.

Still, I watched. I could do that much.

And as she was working, and I was standing in my private box, a conversation came back to haunt me.

"Was there collateral damage?"

Stephano had wanted to know more. He hadn't been satisfied with the initial report of what had happened with Jess's aunt and her abuser.

I had braced myself, steeling myself, and raised my chin up. "What do you need to know, Uncle?"

His eyes flickered just once before his own face hardened. "You killed the uncle?"

I didn't answer that. "My men buried his body. He's dead."

His jaw clenched. He knew I was playing word games, something I'd been doing more and more lately. Anger flared in his gaze before he smothered it. "The aunt?"

"They're gone. Ashton made his calls. She'd checked in with their local women's shelter earlier that day. We think she left him."

"Where's she now?"

"Disappeared. Probably hiding from him." I studied him. He wasn't happy still. I needed to give him a little more. "She'll never know that she doesn't need to hide. He's dead. He wouldn't help anyways. He was an abuser, and that would've made him a liability. He could've offered evidence on us if he'd ever been arrested for domestic assault. You know the kind. We have someone in his place who we can control. It's a win-win for everyone."

It was enough. I saw some of the suspicion ease from him, and he nodded.

I started to relax.

Until he spoke again. "We have a problem. The family wanting to push in is getting worse, and my health is still deteriorating. I need you to take over the family business."

I gritted my teeth. "When?"

There was silence. He was back to studying me. "I want you to be running everything within three months."

Three months. Three months before everything would change.

It wasn't enough time.

CHAPTER
TWENTY-SEVEN

JESS

I was watching my brother walk toward me on the other side of this plexiglass window. He'd trimmed down but bulked up in muscle, and his hair was gone. He'd shaved it all off. I looked for tattoos but didn't see any, and that ball in my belly unwound a little bit. Still, though. I saw our cousin, the one he'd never meet, and I doubted he'd ever know that she looked like him with the same round face, plush cheeks, and eyes maybe a little too close together.

They even had the same freckles.

Isaac had always been a little rough looking. He walked with a wide swagger, his head low and his shoulders out. If someone hadn't known him, they might've stereotyped him as a bully at first sight, or a thug, but then the next event always happened.

He'd smile. And when he did, everyone else smiled too. He had that effect, and he was so far the opposite of a thug that it made me tear up when I considered how he'd ended up here.

I loved him so much that my throat was swelling up, just like it did on the drive here and would on the drive home.

He flashed me a smile, taking his seat and pushing the intercom button. "Hey! You look good. I see you got your VO."

Visiting order.

I nodded, at the same time absorbing all of it because these days, I needed any moment of happiness I got. "Hey yourself. You're looking good."

He laughed, and his smile got wider. "You must've got the day off? Leo give you some ribbing?"

I only smiled, deciding not to tell him how Leo was almost a permanent fixture at our house because our mother was drinking every day, or how she never asked about our aunt, even though Leo told her one of the times she was sober that I'd gone to help out. Leo called the next day, asked how it went. I told him as much of the truth as I could, that she got on a bus and didn't tell me where she was going to end up.

He got it. He never asked again, and it was another thing Trace was correct about: how little they would look for my aunt.

God. Trace. It'd been a month since I'd seen him.

I ignored the emotion filling me at just remembering him. I didn't want to name that emotion.

"Tell me. What's new with you? Still working? Still working at that club? Kelly still single and hot as fuck?"

I informed him about Kelly. She was a lighter conversation to have.

"Still working. Still at the club."

He made a face. "I know someone in here who knows Anthony. He says that the owner has ties to—"

"I know."

He frowned, his eyebrows dipping down. "You know?"

I nodded, but slowly because this was opening Pandora's box. "I know."

"Why are you still working there?"

"Because." Because I liked Anthony. Because I'd worked there so long. Because . . . because if I left, then I'd have no contact with Trace, even though he'd followed my warning. I never saw him, but I swear, I *swear* that he was there and that he was watching me. I just never asked, and I never looked. It was a sick obsession at this point. "You know how it is. Work somewhere so long it becomes too familiar to leave. I know the workers. I like my supervisor, for the most part."

Isaac grunted. "That guy I was telling you about? The one who knows Anthony, he says he knows dirt on your supervisor. He's not the good guy you think he is."

I gave him a look. "Anthony? A good guy?" I raised an eyebrow.

He laughed, sitting back. His shoulders lowered, and he rolled forward again, his head bobbing up and down. "Yeah. Yeah. I know. You know him. I didn't tell that guy about you, though. Don't want it getting around—"

I hit the intercom. "Hey."

He stopped, looking up.

"I know." Everyone had relatives, but sometimes a guy just needed to look for something to target another guy, and finding out his sister worked on the other team could make him an easy target. "It's okay."

He went back to bobbing up and down again, a steady nodding movement, before he propped an elbow on the table and raked his hand over his head. "There's stuff coming down the pipeline in here, and it's got to do with, you know, your other boss's family. Anthony's boss. They put out an order of protection on me."

"They did what?"

He stopped, his eyes widening at my tone. "I thought you knew. It came out the day after I found out who your real bosses at the club were. I thought . . . Was I wrong?"

My stomach was twisted up in a knot again, one big motherfucker. The truth was that I had no idea.

Liar, liar. Pants on fire.

I cursed at my own inner voice calling me out.

You do too know. He said he'd help your aunt. He's helping your brother too.

"You okay, Jess?"

I realized I'd been sitting here, quiet, glaring at my brother while I was having an argument in my own head, against myself. "Yeah. Sorry. I'm fine. I don't know why they did that."

He looked over his shoulder, checking the inmates and their visitors next to us. No one was paying attention, and he leaned closer to the plexiglass. "You think it's about Dad? Because he was involved with them?"

My stomach rolled over, not wanting to hear about those days. I shook my head. "No. That was too long ago."

"But—"

"If that was the case, you would've been protected since your first day here. You haven't been, right?"

He shook his head. "No, just that one guard who looks out for me because of you."

I clipped my head in another fast nod, because that didn't need to be spoken out loud either. It was a corrections officer—or CO, as we referred to them. I knew him from taking the same parole officer training. He hadn't passed, and I had. We got close anyway because we were from the same neighborhood. I gave him a call when my brother ended up in this prison, and he'd asked if I could keep an eye out for his family. It was an easy "I'll scratch your back if you scratch mine" sort of situation. His wife was a sweetheart, and the only time I had to look out for them was when their little boy got into trouble at school. I gave him a sort of "scared straight" scenario, one that didn't break any rules. He met some parolees who never violated and remained on good terms with us, but their little boy hadn't known that fact when he met them.

"Fill me in. How are things with you?"

"I don't want to do that. You tell me about Ma, tell me about Kelly. She still ask about me?"

I laughed, but I told him. I left out the part about Justin and the part where Mom was herself.

When it was my time to leave, he stopped me. "Hey."

"Yeah?" My gut sharpened again, because that tone was serious.

"Quit working at that nightclub. They're protecting me for a reason, and I don't know it. That gives me a bad feeling."

My little brother, four years my junior, and he was worried about me. I reached out, unable to tell him what he wanted, and placed my hand against the plexiglass.

He hesitated but mirrored mine with his, and I gave him a smile. "Love you."

He dipped his head down in a jerking motion. "Love you too."

———

I couldn't stop hearing his words the entire drive back to the city, and that bad feeling he had—I got it too.

It only grew the closer I got, but it was Thursday. I'd taken the day off from work, and I didn't have a shift at Katya until tomorrow.

Instead of going home and hanging out with Justin and Kelly, I turned toward a place that I hadn't visited in a long time. Too long of a time.

I went to an art studio that I used to use, because once upon a time, before my dad died, my mom started drinking, my brother went to prison, I'd wanted to be an art student. The owner was my high school art teacher, and she gave me a key years ago, saying I could stop in and use her products anytime. I barely ever took her up on the offer, and the few times I had, I'd reimbursed her for the products.

That was a whole lifetime ago, but I was feeling the itch tonight.

CHAPTER

TWENTY-EIGHT

TRACE

I'd been keeping tabs on her, but this place was new. She'd deviated.

Ashton was the one who let me know where she was, and it'd not been in our PI's report, so I wanted to find out for myself what place this was—or *whose* place this was.

Sitting in my vehicle, parked on the street, I couldn't believe what I was seeing.

She was painting. It was an art studio, and it was set up so if an artist was in process, the windows were placed where people on the street could watch. It was set back and off the sidewalk so it wasn't totally visible to just anyone driving by. But if you were coming specifically for the studio itself, or if you were someone like me, you could sit and watch to your heart's content.

Her head was down. She had paint covering her hands, her arms, her shoulders. When she turned once, I saw more on her face. She didn't look outside. I didn't think she was even aware she was on display, but I was guessing there was music because her head kept swaying from side to side. She dipped her hand into the paint and turned to the canvas, going at it.

She painted with her hands. No brushes. No pencil. No charcoal. Just her hands, and the canvas was set to the side so I couldn't see the painting itself, but it was taller than her. She stood up on her tiptoes more than once to reach the highest parts of it, and it was set on the floor, so she bent down as well. She disappeared from sight for those moments. A cupboard or table blocked my view.

I wanted to see the painting, enough where I got out of the vehicle and approached the building.

I moved to the side, propped a shoulder against the wall, and turned so I had a view through to her. I still couldn't see what she was creating, but I could see her.

She was mesmerizing, moving in a rhythm where it was obvious she was in some sort of trance.

I stayed there even when the cold seeped through my jacket and into my bones, deep in my bones, but I still remained. It might've been hours. I didn't know until suddenly, the lights turned off, and I straightened, shaking from how cold it was. I started for my vehicle.

"Last time I saw you, I told you to leave me alone."

I turned slowly, thinking how her tone matched the weather. Fucking cold.

She was standing outside a back door, in the alley that my back was turned to. One of her feet had the door propped open. She was staring at me.

"You said we were done."

"What's the difference?" Her nostrils flared, because she knew there was a difference. "I told you another time to leave me alone too."

I started for her, going slow. "You said I should leave you alone."

Should.

I kept going. She wasn't shutting the door.

Should had a whole different connotation because she was right. I should've left her alone, but I hadn't, and I saw the yearning in her eyes. It was there. She hid it quick, but I still saw it.

I moved, knowing how much of an idiot I was being, but at this point, unless she shut the door in my face, I needed to touch her again.

Her eyes widened, seeing me coming at her, but she didn't move. She didn't dart inside, and I was fully aware of the line I was treading here.

Five feet.

She stayed.

Four.

She was still there.

Three.

I could almost touch her.

Two—she moved inside, but I caught the door.

"Tristian—" She backed up.

"Trace." I moved with her, taking in the room. A small light was on in the corner, enough so I could see my way inside. My hand went to her waist, propelling her backward.

Damn me to hell, but I needed this.

"Wha—" she started to say, her eyes so alive, and a new light had been lit in them.

She'd get angry. It was sparking in her, coming, and my god. I was a damned man because that's when I knew. Her spirit made my dick twitch. I groaned, my mouth taking hers, hoping she wasn't going to hit me with a hammer or some other weapon. I let her wrist go because if she did, I'd deserve it, but after a surprised gasp, after a moment where I swear my body sagged in relief at the mere touch of her, the fire swept through both of us.

It lit her, and she became alive. Her mouth opened under mine. The hammer dropped. Her hands were on me, pulling on the back of my head, and she was trying to clamber up.

Finally.

I lifted her at the same time she jumped.

She was yanking at my clothes as I angled my head, my tongue sweeping inside of her, needing to taste her that way, knowing it would be fucking heaven. It *was.*

I needed more.

She had my shirt halfway up my body, her hands exploring me in return, and I glanced once, making sure the door was shut. She had turned the light off. My god, I needed to have her. I didn't know if she'd let me taste her again.

I moved down her throat, tasting her as I went, and she arched her neck, her breasts pushed upward toward me. My hand moved down, pushing under her leggings, finding her thong and ignoring that it was even there, and then I found her, and my finger sank in.

Fucking. Goddamn. Heaven.

I hissed at how tight she was, and her legs wrapped tighter around my waist in reaction. She held still, panting in my ear as I worked a second finger inside of her. I went slow at first, drawing it out, and then deeper with each stroke, building pace and tempo.

I knew her. I knew this woman. I knew her body. I didn't know how, but I did. Other lifetimes maybe. I would've believed it if someone told me in that instant because it was like I'd already had lifetimes worshipping her body.

I kept working her, sliding in and out, my thumb moving over her clit. A nice slow circle rub and she was moaning in my arms, barely holding on. Her body fell backward, her head coming to rest against the wall behind, and her eyes opened a little bit, a haze over them as she gaped at me, but I needed more. I reached up with my other hand and tore her shirt apart. Her bra was shoved aside, and I sank my mouth over one of her tits. I needed this taste of her.

I needed to taste every inch of her, but I'd content myself with this touch, for now.

She shuddered in my arms, her hand coming up and clasping onto the back of my head as my teeth grazed over her nipple. My tongue moved around her. I sucked her in, caressing her, but I needed to be inside of her.

Now.

Yesterday.

A year ago.

Her breathing had picked up, she was only holding on to me, and I picked up the pace, feeling the start of her climax coming. It was a little rest, where her body paused for a split second, and she was moaning softly in my ear now. I lifted my head, finding her throat, and then lifting again and finding her mouth. My tongue moved in, claiming her as she went over the edge. Her entire body jerked against me, lifting up off the counter, and she screamed into my mouth.

I swallowed it, catching it and tasting that too.

Feeling her body calming, just enough, I moved back but reached for my wallet.

I held her gaze when I pulled out a condom. She was watching what I was doing, a dark lust coming over her eyes, and she bit her lip. Then she reached for the condom and tore open the wrapper.

I shoved my pants down, my boxer briefs with them, and she was reaching for me.

Goddamn.

I hissed at the touch of her hands circling my dick, and my head fell to her shoulder.

She was working me over, running her hand up and down, her thumb moving over my tip, but I groaned into her ear, "Enough. Put it on."

A slight chuckle rasped from her throat, but she smoothed the condom over me, using both her hands to smooth it down, and that was all the permission I needed from her. I grabbed her ass, hoisting her up and angling her down for the perfect access. I wasn't gentle, but she groaned, her eyes closing at how I was handling her, and I moved her legs aside, pushing them open wider, and then I was there.

I sank in, both of us molded to each other at the contact.

I'd been wrong before. This was heaven.

First it was her mouth. Then how she felt on my fingers, but this was the ultimate form of paradise.

I couldn't hold back any longer.

Her head snapped back, her eyes finding mine, and she growled, "Fuck me, you asshole."

I moved back and then thrust into her, glaring right back at her because I saw now that this was just as much needed on her end, but she wasn't happy about it.

Thrust after thrust, I pounded into her. I didn't look away, and neither did she.

She truly hated me, but there was the same starving look underneath, the one I felt for her too. Haunted. I'd used the word before because it was true. This goddamn fucking obsession was on both accounts, but I was here and I touched her, and she fell apart for me.

I'd do it every time I could. I made the vow to myself, here and now.

Moving forward, every time I could have her, I would.

She arched her back, her clothes had been torn off, and she was naked for my viewing pleasure. Paint covering her, covering me. I drowned in this view, burning into my brain, knowing I'd be envisioning her for the rest of my life.

She reared up, her feet finding the counter beneath her, and I adjusted, stepping back to keep us in contact, but she used the counter to push back against me. She was fucking me as greedily as I was thrusting inside of her.

I was tempted to halt, enjoy her riding me in this new way, but no. The need to dominate was real inside of me, at least with her, and I fell into her body, holding her up with a hand under her back, pushing inside of her over and over again.

Her whole body came apart when she crested, and I waited, holding off until she rode out the waves. Once she was down, I picked her back up, moved, and pushed her against a wall. Her back was to it, her legs wrapped tight around my back, and she was hugging me around my neck. Her front was fully against mine, and I could feel her breasts crushed against my chest. It was the best position. I loved how this one felt, and I groaned, nipping her throat as I pistoned into her, my hands holding both of her ass cheeks until I wanted to get my handprints tatted there.

My own climax ripped through me, and I groaned, feeling my release going through my body too.

It was then that I realized how truly fucked I was, because I would never get this with another woman. No one could make me taste heaven three different times.

I growled, knowing she would hate me after this, and feeling so damned frustrated at the same time because I understood. I got it. I just needed her more.

She let me hold her for another minute before her hands came up to my chest and she shoved me off of her. She dropped down, glaring at me, totally naked. I glanced around, not remembering pulling her leggings off, but she didn't care.

"What the fuck, Tristian?"

"Trace," I snapped back.

"What?"

I leaned over her. "I just rode you hard. Goddamn use the name I don't hate. To you, my name is Trace."

She backed off, just a little, both physically and emotionally. I saw her take a step back and felt the distance coming back between us. In another minute, I'd feel as if I'd never left my vehicle. She was putting the walls between us, and fast.

"What are you doing here, Trace?" Wariness flashed in her eyes before she began grabbing her clothes.

I righted my own, pulling my shirt back down and drawing up my boxer briefs and pants. My coat . . . I looked around for it, finding it tossed on the floor some distance away. Going, plucking it up, I held it and watched as she found her bra and began clipping it back on. She'd already grabbed her leggings and had them back on.

She lifted her head, a flash of irritation flaring at me from her gaze. "Are you going to answer me?"

She was rattled. It was the only reason why she wasn't thinking about where I had found her and why she wasn't demanding to know how I knew she'd be there.

I rolled my shoulders back, throwing up another distraction right now. "There's a development with your aunt. I thought you might want to know."

Concern flared next, and she straightened up from finishing dressing, the hand going through her hair falling back to her side. "What is it?"

"They're in Canada. She's been set up. A small house. Enough money to get her started. I've got her in touch with a program that helps women like her disappear from men like her husband."

"Okay . . ."

"The drawback is that once the program takes over, my family won't know where she is anymore. They're not particularly open to working with people like my family."

"So why did they?"

"I approached them, explained her situation. They were willing to step in for her but to hide her from us. Before we pull back, I need to know that's what you want."

"Yes." The word rushed out of her, her eyes lighting up. "Yes. That'd be amazing. What's the name of these people?"

"The 411 Network."

She stepped back from surprise. "They exist? I thought that was just myth or something."

I gave a hard nod. "They exist."

Relief softened her face; her shoulders slackened, too, and then a soft chuckle. "The irony of them hiding my aunt from your family."

"I'm to take that you approve of this?"

"Yes. I didn't know they existed, but I've heard of them. I've wished they would exist, and finding this out now, I feel a lot better. They truly will be hidden then." She frowned. "How were you able to approach them?"

My gut twisted. "I'd recently worked with them regarding two other individuals. It made them more amenable to me."

"Two others?"

"I can't tell you, and it's not because I don't want to. It has to do with my family."

She locked down as I said that, which I knew she would. That was the deal with us. She was law, and I was half and half. I feared the day I would become *mostly not*.

My whole body locked up as well because I heard what else she wasn't saying. *"They truly will be hidden then."* Even from me. She'd have no more ties to me.

"Thank you, Trace."

I looked up, surprised at the genuineness in her voice.

But her eyes were flashing hard again. "But I meant it. Stay away from me."

"You still work for me."

She had started to turn away but froze before turning back again. "You want me to quit?"

I snorted, shaking my head. "Right. Do *you* want to quit?"

I was calling her on it, because she wanted this fucking thing between us as much as I did. I, at least, was being honest about it. Maybe if we both gave in, this fucking need would leave.

Her eyes flashed, and she knew what I was calling her on.

"This." She motioned between the two of us. Her eyes hardening. "It has to stop. My job gives me purpose in life, and you're eroding that. I can't change what I've already done, but this can't happen again. It does and I'll quit Katya. I don't want to, but I will if I need to."

She was pulling out every intestine inside of me, one at a time, a slow tug each inch.

But fuck that. I wasn't going to say the words she wanted to hear.

I started to leave, but I needed to see one more thing.

I hit the light switch by the door, and the entire room lit up.

I saw the painting.

It was me.

CHAPTER

TWENTY-NINE

JESS

A week passed. No Trace. No mom drama. It was quiet, for the most part.

I liked it, but . . . something was missing.

Justin slept over on the weekends after our shifts at Katya. Kelly slept at his place during the week. And I'd started going from work to the gym to the studio.

When he'd seen that canvas of him, my heart had lodged itself in my throat. I'd never intended anyone to see it, but I needed to get him out of me. Doing the daily grind of my job hadn't done that. Keeping busy with Katya just made it worse, so yeah. I now had three more canvases of him sitting around the place, and all were in different textures, different colors. Each one had a different feel to it.

Fuck me, but this was annoying.

Maybe a one-night stand was the right option. Get under someone *else* to get Trace out of my system.

It was worth a try.

———

"Yo, Montell. Hold up."

It'd been two weeks since I'd last seen Trace. I was trying not to think about him—*nope*. I wasn't.

Hearing my name, I turned and saw another parole officer heading my way. Tall. Built like a thick cornerback. Pretty face. Blue eyes. Sandy-brown hair.

I gave a nod. "What's up?"

Officer Reyo was the newest PO added to the department. I'd worked with him on a few house visits, and he was a solid officer. Kept his mouth shut. Followed protocol.

"You doing house visits today?"

I nodded, frowning a little. "Yeah. My partner is supposed to go with me."

He shook his head, drawing up next to me and giving me a half grin. "Valerie called, asked if I could fill in?"

"What?" I started to pull my phone out because this had been planned since yesterday.

"She—uh—" He inclined his head, coughing, before taking a step closer to me. "She, uh, something came up. It was my day off, and she asked if I could cover her today."

I pulled up our texts, and there was nothing there about this. "What's going on?"

He opened his mouth, and I could literally see the bullshit starting to be delivered at my doorstep.

I cut him off. "No BS or I ain't going anywhere with you. You tell me what's going on right now."

His mouth was open, but he closed it as a rueful look came over him. Then he closed his eyes, and he gave a soft sigh. "Okay." His hand rose, rubbing over his head as he glanced around us and took another step closer, lowering his voice. "Look. She's sick, okay? We're thinking morning sickness or something—"

I reeled away from him, taking a full three steps back.

It was like he had grown three heads because this wasn't computing. "Val is pregnant?"

"Yeah." He motioned toward his mouth, looking around once more. He covered the distance again. "Can you, you know, keep it to yourself? It's all new, like, everything."

Like him and her.

"You knocked up my partner?"

His mouth hung open a second before he clamped it shut again. "Yeah. I mean, it wasn't planned, but—" He reared back, cringing. "Dammit. That's not what I meant. I, just, look." He held a hand up. "This is all coming out wrong. Is it okay that I come in Val's place for the house visits or not?"

"Oh. Yeah. Why didn't you just say that in the first place?"

I was fighting back a grin as I headed to my vehicle. I heard him choke back a groan.

I raised my hand up. "I'm driving, Officer Reyo."

He followed and sat in the passenger seat, and I waited until I was past the first block before starting. "So. You and Val, huh?"

His elbow was resting on the door, his hand up and lightly holding on to the overhead handle, but at my question, his hand dropped abruptly, and his head went back against the headrest. "Shit." He scrunched his face up before looking my way, with a whole lot of wariness. "I mean . . ." He let out a dramatic sigh. "I don't know what I meant, but yes. We're new. We're taking things . . . slow." He smoothed his hand out as he said the last word.

I laughed, yanking the wheel to the right. "Not that slow. She's preggos."

He grabbed onto the handle again and braced himself. "We're . . . today won't happen again. We're figuring it out."

I shot him another look. "You do know the officer you're bagging, right? If Val is sick and if she had to send you in her place today, guaranteed she's going to have everything figured out by the end of the day. You'll be lucky if you find out whether you're still having a kid or whether you'll be in that kid's life if she decides the other way. Val has never wanted kids, so I know she's dying a whole lot and probably planning your murder at the same time."

His face scrunched one more time, like he got a bad whiff of something rotten. My guess, it was the reality I was shoving down his throat. Reyo was young. Valerie was in her forties. She was more married to this job than I was.

I kept on. "How'd you guys even hook up?"

"Oh my god." He hung his head down, mumbling under his breath. "She told me you'd be like this."

I barked out a laugh, taking a hard left on the street and hitting the horn at the same time. But I wasn't done. "For real, Reyo. I want to know. How'd you two hook up?" I was throwing sideways looks his way, checking him out as he seemed to just be bracing for this line of questioning.

"Val doesn't date, or she doesn't date colleagues. That means . . . my guess, was she drunk? Was it a one-night thing?" It clicked. "That wedding three months ago! When Barkie and Papi got married. Val was tossing back tequila. You were eyeing her."

He glanced my way, his eyes widening a little. "You noticed?"

"Val's my partner. She's also the only other PO that hates Travis as much as I do. Travis got his ass handed to him earlier that day by our team leader. I was the one *handing* her the tequila. Yes, you're damn sure I noticed because she noticed. She asked if I thought it was a good idea to fuck you or not."

"What'd you say?"

"I told her fuck no."

His head fell back against the headrest again, and he shook his head slightly. "Of course."

I was enjoying this a bit too much. "I told her if she needed to scratch that itch, to head down to Wall Street and find one of those guys at one of the many stuck-up nightclubs they hang out at and—" I stopped because the irony was not lost on me.

It was painful as fuck too.

Reyo glanced my way. "And what?"

"And nothing," I clipped out.

CHAPTER THIRTY

JESS

"Oh my gosh! What happened to your eye?" Kelly took one look at me that night and screeched. She dragged me under our brightest light and tipped my head back, her hands not so gentle, and she started touching around the bruise just under my eye.

"Ouch." I moved back, already having had a first responder check me out. It was all protocol, along with the amount of paperwork I had to file when my parolee's sister wasn't feeling me after I gave a lengthy discussion that surprise home visits were a real thing between a parole officer and a parolee, especially one that had missed two office check-ins and two UAs, and that was after a positive UA. Urine analysis. This parolee was *beyond due* for a visit by me, and in my books, he should've been prepared for it. Her place of residence was the one he'd put on file, and since he was there, I needed to come and check the place out.

She took offense, and when two loud neighbors distracted me for a moment, she decided it was a good idea to punch me when I couldn't hit her back.

She was now in jail.

I held up a hand, putting my frozen bag of peas over my eye once more. "I'm good. Just, a stupid thing at work."

"Are you still going to your shift tonight?"

I would've shot her a look, but it would've been painful, so I tossed the bag of peas instead.

She caught it, her hand jerking up. She looked at it as if she didn't recognize what it was.

I frowned but moved over and took it back. "Yes. Dark lighting and makeup will be fine."

She stared at the peas in my hand before jerking her gaze upward. "Justin's going to freak when he sees your eye. He's protective of us both."

I let that slide off my back because Justin would probably make a comment. It was his way of showing he cared.

"Speaking of Justin, you two are getting serious?"

Kelly turned a shade of red before rotating in the kitchen and starting to grab items from the cupboards. "Yeah." Then she paused in midreach for a spatula before she rushed out, "Hemightvebroughtupthepossibilityoflivingtogether."

I turned fully around, my coffee in hand, and stared back at her. Hard.

I wouldn't have to wait long. A pigeon could stare her down, and Kelly would fold.

Suddenly, she threw down the spatula on the counter. It bounced, hit the side of the pan, and then bounced back onto the counter.

Kelly turned back around, a panicked look on her face. "I don't know what to do! He dropped the bomb on me two nights ago, and I've been hyperventilating about what this might mean. Could mean. Would mean! I mean, I have no idea. I have horrible taste in men. You seem to like him, but what if we're both wrong? What if my bad luck in men wore off onto you and—"

I set my coffee down and moved in front of her. If she didn't breathe, she was going to pass out. I went to her and touched her arms, cutting her off. "Breathe."

She did, her chest rising up, and she held it.

And held it.

And held it.

"Oh my god! Let it out!"

She did, choking and coughing at the end before she shook her head, a tear slipping from her eye. "I'm so scared, but I think I'm more scared about leaving you."

Somewhere inside of me was a marshmallow, and it was melting. I started to pull her in for a hug, but she misunderstood, and she rested her forehead to my shoulder, bending at a slightly awkward angle. I began patting her back, burping my overgrown adult baby. "It'll be okay. Justin's a good guy, and I'll be fine."

"You're not fine. You just never talk about it."

I stepped back, frowning once more. "What do you mean?"

She gave me a long look before sighing. She swung her hands around, and one connected with the spatula, and she snatched it up. I didn't think she was aware she was holding it and now swinging it around. "You're not okay. I can tell. You're never here unless Justin and I are here. You've not been to our Sunday bowling for three weeks. Justin took your place, and no one is happy about it."

"What?" My stomach started to sink, but to be honest, it'd been sinking since I'd met Trace.

Trace.

This was all him.

Or no. My family. Dad. Brother. Mom. Nope. This was me, my luck.

Kelly was right. I wasn't okay. "I think I'm cursed."

"Yes!" The spatula went up in the air before she lowered her arms. "Wait. What? No. You're not cursed. You're just . . . not happy." She scooted back. I didn't think she could get any closer to that counter than she was unless she started climbing up it. She took a deep breath, those big eyes of her watching me with an emotion I didn't like seeing. Fear.

"I'm worried about you. I'm worried about if I move—what will happen to you? Before, when it was just you and me, we had our thing, and I'm not trying to put guilt on you because I don't want you to take it the wrong way, but my job was to ground you. I did my job. I know your family stuff, but you were smiling, and we were hanging with friends. Since I met Justin, that's started to go away. I don't like that. If I move in with Justin, what will happen?" A tear slid down her other cheek. "Am I going to lose you completely?"

The award for shit friend goes to me.

"Hey." I grabbed the spatula before she impaled herself with it. Her eyes widened, and I was right. She had no idea she'd even grabbed it. I tossed it on the counter away from her before standing in front of her again. I gentled my tone. Kelly responded better to low and soothing sounds. "I am just going through something. It's got to do with my family, not you, and I don't want you to worry about me. I was fine when you were married, remember?"

Her head lifted up an inch. Her shoulders relaxed a little too. "That's right. You had that Latin lover, who was *muy* hot. Holy shit. I had to fan myself after I saw him every time."

I cracked a grin, remembering Eduardo. "He was very pretty to look at."

Her eyes bulged out, and she moved her head up and down in a dramatic nod. "Understatement of the year."

Smothering a laugh, I kept on. "Your happiness is your happiness. There's no contract or lease or deed on mine. Okay? You got me? If you want to move in with Justin, move in with Justin. I want you to be happy. If I found out that you didn't because of me, you know how that would make me feel. I'd feel horrible. Right?"

"Yeah." The ends of her mouth started to curve up.

"So if you want to move in with him, move in with him. I'm a big girl. I carry a gun around on a regular basis. I got a stick too. I'm kinda tough."

A little bit higher and she was grinning now. "You got a badge too."

I laughed. "I got a badge. You're right. And trust me, I'm not afraid to use it."

"That's right."

A few more pep talks like this, and she'd be cheering with the spatula in the air. Though I moved that back to the table because with Kelly, it could be turned into a weapon. I eyed her, tilting my head to the side. "You going to move in with your boyfriend, who I wholeheartedly approve of?"

A glow was starting to take over her face. She was low-key beaming at me, ducking her head in a bashful way. "You do, don't you? You've never approved of any of my guys."

"Justin's the real deal. He's a good guy, and I think if you move in with him, you'll be happy and will make babies."

She gasped. "You think?!" Her voice went up on a sharp hitch.

"I do." Kelly's dream was to be a mother. "I think Justin would be a great dad too."

"Oh my gosh! Oh my gosh!" She was shaking her hands in the air, more tears coming to her eyes, and she was trying to brush them away at the same time as searching for a new spatula to grab. I didn't think she was aware of any of this as well. "Babies. I didn't—I didn't dare let myself hope, you know? I've just been so scared. He is so great and ohmygoshbabiesohmygoshbabies."

Oh, boy. Round two, but I knew for Kelly, she was going to get the happily ever after she always dreamed about, so I waded in, cutting her short and just hugging her.

This was a good thing to celebrate.

———

I purposely got to my shift a little late, just minutes late because I wanted to avoid seeing peeps in the locker room. Kelly worked wonders on me for makeup, and I knew the lighting in Katya would cover the rest, so it shouldn't be a problem, but locker room fluorescent lighting wasn't the greatest. It exposed everything. And not that my bruise was a big deal. I'd had worse, much worse, but I didn't want to get another Kelly reaction from anyone.

Justin did give me a long look when I stepped behind my section.

I lifted my head up in one of those manly nods. It seemed to work between him and me. He stopped studying me, giving me one back, and we were off to work.

They had a new DJ, one whose name I even recognized. He'd been on a reality show too. Kelly had given me the info on the ride in, but my mind had been elsewhere. I'd realized today that it'd been too quiet on my mom's front. I'd been avoiding her because I didn't want to deal with questions about her sister, but I was now thinking maybe she was avoiding me, too, and that would never sit right with me.

I made a note to head her way tomorrow, whether she wanted me there or not.

But back to the DJ.

The club was busier than normal, and after the thirtieth girl was almost crushed against my bar, I'd had enough.

I headed over to Justin. "Can you cover me for a minute?"

"Yeah." He was distracted, finishing a drink, but glanced over his shoulder. He did a double take. "What happened to your face?"

Kelly must not have gotten to him yet, which wasn't surprising. I'd yet to see her for the first hour, which meant she was swallowed up by the crowd, working.

"It's nothing. Work thing."

"Here work thing?"

"PO work thing."

Understanding dawned, and he nodded. "Gotcha. Yeah. I'll keep an eye on your section. Where are you going?"

"A word with Anthony. This place is violating too many fire codes for me to ignore it."

"Good luck."

Yeah, yeah. I was noting his sarcasm, but this place was just *asking* for a fire marshal visit. I pushed through the crowd, seeing two of the bouncers outside of Anthony's office. "He in?"

They exchanged a look before one shifted forward, but he didn't seem too sure he wanted to do that. "Uh, boss is with the boss. He doesn't want to be interrupted."

Lovely. I was being sarcastic. "How long have they been in there?"

The two shared another look.

I didn't wait for them to figure out which would respond to me. I jerked a thumb behind me. "I don't have time for this. You see what's happening out there? Let me in there to talk to Anthony, or this place is going to get an official visit. It's out of control out there."

They did another look thing, and I was out of patience.

I shoved between them, opened the door, and pushed inside.

I didn't give a look at who else was in the office before twisting and locking it. Not that the two guys were going to try and fight me. They knew me. The charade was more for them so Anthony wouldn't be too pissed at how easy they let me in.

I looked around, and Anthony had an eyebrow raised; he was sitting behind his desk. "Really? I bet they just let you walk right past them."

Okay. So the show had been for nothing. I shrugged. "I have that kind of demeanor." I'd been preparing myself to see Trace in Anthony's office and was trying to avoid the pull to look at him, but it wasn't Trace. It was the other one, Ashton Walden, and he was eerily studying me.

I frowned. "What?"

Ashton's eyes narrowed. He pointed at me. "You got something on your face."

I started to reach up, thinking it was a bug or glitter, but realized he was referring to my bruise. "It's nothing."

His eyes cooled. "Right."

His head swung toward Anthony, who was watching our exchange with both of his eyebrows raised, and he was leaning as far back in his seat as he could get.

Ashton said, "You do what you feel is fit."

Then he started past me for the door.

I shifted aside, but when Ashton didn't open the door, I looked back at him.

He was staring smack at me, his eyes flat, his mouth in a line. "He's going to want to see that for himself."

The door opened, and he was gone after that.

I closed my eyes, just a second, and let the curse word slip in my mind. *Shit.*

"Okay." Anthony's chair squeaked as he stood up, and he held his hands in front of him in surrender. "I don't want to know. I don't want to know about whatever the fuck that was between you two, or why you obviously have a black eye. You're tough and threatening, and it's not my job to worry about you, so all that said, what are you doing in here?"

"To threaten you." I pointed outside. "You know how full it is out there? Your guys at the door aren't sticking with the capacity limit."

"We got a temporary permit for tonight. The DJ's a celebrity."

"Your temporary permit is bullshit. Scale the people back, or you don't want to know the consequences." I began reaching for the door.

"Or what? You're going to call us in?"

I stopped, my arms folding over my chest. I gave him a cool look. "You kidding me? I'd be shocked if there haven't already been one or two people who've already been trampled or near trampled. I've had to pull girls over the bar. It's too crowded out there. If the fire guys come here and see that I wasn't the one who called them, you bet your ass this will affect my other job. Get your shit together. I'm not playing."

I yanked open the door.

The two bouncers scattered, and I marched right back. No one got in my way, so I was guessing my irritation was clearing the way.

There was no change in the next fifteen minutes, but the fifteen after that, the bouncers were wading through the crowd and pulling people out. It was thinning, enough where I didn't need to be tense about seeing some of the fire guys I knew.

I went back to work, even spotting Kelly a few times.

Justin came over at one point. "I have no idea what you did, but I noted the timing. Thank you."

I grunted, jerking my chin up.

He flashed me a smile, with two thumbs up in a cheesy grin.

I almost missed our manly normal greeting, but it was easier to work now, so I was relaxed enough to give him a half grin back.

Anthony showed up not long after that, one of his eyebrows still raised. "Happy?"

I lost my half grin. "Yes."

He rolled his eyes but kept moving through the club.

I watched him go. He was checking everything over, and Justin shared a look with me after he moved past his section too. I was thinking it was the first time he'd seen Anthony actually walk through the club. My threat of people trampled must've rattled him.

Either way, the DJ was good, and the people weren't going to get crushed. I was content for the rest of the night. It was an hour later when I was getting low on vodka. The people who were supposed to help us keep stocked up must've fallen behind. I grabbed one of the bottles and raised it in the air to get Justin's attention. He looked and I shook it, showing that it was empty.

He gave me a nod, raising one thumb up this time.

I slipped out and headed for the back where we kept the extra stock. It was a bit of weaving through a hallway because I rarely came back here. The sounds of the club faded, and I came to the room and went inside.

It was dark.

Finding the light, I switched it on, and at that time, the door opened.

Trace shoved in.

"Wha—"

His hands were on me, and he snapped out, "Yes." He locked the door and barricaded it, but when I braced myself, thinking he was going to kiss me, his hands turned gentle, touching my face. He leaned over me, moving me more under the light so he could see me better. He went eerily still, his touch so soft that it was soothing, and he traced the edge of the bruise, before moving my head gently from side to side.

He was looking for more bruises, and he wasn't content with just my face. He moved me around, his touch still so gentle as he had me turn around in front of him, lifting my hair so he could inspect my neck. "I'm fine."

He stopped me in front of him when he was done, but he was focused back on the bruise. "Who?"

I flushed, starting to shake my head. I began to step back, but he stopped me, taking my hips and moving me closer to him. He leaned fully back against the door, opening his legs, and he fit me in between them.

I should leave the room or at least step back.

But dammit. My body was heating, and the swirls were grazing my insides. Those were his swirls, making me go crazy.

"Who touched you?"

I let out an irritated sound. "It was the sister of one of my guys. What are you going to do? Threaten her?"

"Who?" His eyes flashed, and his fingers held firmer to my hips, but his thumbs began rubbing back and forth, tunneling under my shirt. "I can find out."

I stilled.

Jesus. I knew they had people on their payroll. Knew from the trip up north, but hearing it said in front of me so easily sent chills down my spine.

"Are you protecting my brother?"

He stilled, even more than he had been.

My head reared back, just an inch, and I took him in. His face was guarded but not surprised. That was all I needed to know.

"Why are you protecting my brother?"

He let out a soft sigh, almost so soft that I didn't hear it. "He's someone you love. Can't we leave it at that?"

My heart flipped over, but damn. Damn! Seriously? He said that?

I was mad at him, but I was starting to forget why I was mad at him, and then I remembered—he made me a criminal.

I moved back, firmly.

When he tried holding me in place, I shoved back even more assertively. "Thank you."

I spotted the vodka I needed.

"For what?"

I grabbed two bottles and moved around him. "For reminding me why you can't touch me."

As I reached for the door, he stepped aside. "Jess."

I opened the door but gave him a searing look, or I hoped because my insides were a jumbled mess. He did that to me. Every time. Right and wrong, good and bad, he was fucking me up.

"You were hurt."

"I've been hurt before."

His eyebrows dipped low. "What does that mean?"

"Just . . ." I held a hand up and cursed when I heard my voice break. I couldn't finish what I needed to say.

My heart wasn't in it because he was here, and he was worried, and . . .

I left, feeling my heart breaking in a way that I never knew it could.

There were people in the hallway. I ignored them, not looking, and went right back to my section, and for the first real time, I started to consider if this was going to be my last night here.

Justin came over twenty minutes later, during a brief break. "You okay? You look stressed."

"Yeah." I'd been on autopilot since seeing Trace, and I even tried to give him a smile. I was faking. I knew it wouldn't match my eyes, and Justin saw through it, giving my shoulder a soft squeeze before going back to his section. "Hang in there, okay?"

I had no other option, but Anthony made a point of coming to tell me before closing that *he* wasn't here anymore, and it was then that I realized how I'd been half holding my breath all night long.

And I realized that I was disappointed.

CHAPTER

THIRTY-ONE

JESS

I had coffee in hand when I walked into my mother's house the next morning but smelled freshly brewed coffee and almost dropped the two I was carrying.

"Ma?" Was I in someone else's house?

"Hey, honey."

Jesus. I almost dropped my coffee again. My mom was on the couch, curled under a blanket, but she had washed her hair recently. It was shining. She was also dressed for the day in normal clothes, like a sweater, and as she stood to greet me, I saw she was in jeans. Tennis shoes. She took one of the coffees and kissed my cheek. "So sweet of you, Jess. You're a good daughter."

My mouth was on the floor when she headed for the kitchen.

"You want any breakfast, honey? Leo made pancakes earlier."

Footsteps sounded above me. The stairs creaked as Leo was coming down, pulling on a sweater. He looked like he'd just showered, too, and he was dressed in jeans. I looked; he also had sneakers on. "Jess!" He came down, opening his arms for a hug.

I hissed as he enveloped me against his chest. "What sorcery have you done? Whose soul did you sell to the devil?"

He froze just for a second before releasing me, stepping back. "Nothing like that." But he glanced to the kitchen and drew me to the door. "Outside?"

I knew it.

He went first, and as soon as the door was closed behind me, I pointed inside. "Who is that? That's not my mother."

"Jess." He sighed, sitting down on the front-porch swing.

"She called me 'honey.' My mom's not called me 'honey' since—" *Oh, dear god!* "Are you two fucking?"

"What?!" He shoved back up to his feet, the swing hitting against the house behind him. "No! Why are you saying that?"

"Because that's when she last called me honey. When she was getting laid. When Dad was alive. What is going *on*? You're over here all the time lately."

A resigned expression sobered him. "I'm not actually. You happen to come the very few times I've checked on your mom. You know my local hangout is Bear's Pub. A lot of our friends hang out there. It's easy for me to come over in between games."

"Um." I was in an alternate universe. "It's eight in the morning. There's no between games. You made pancakes this morning? *How* early? I'm early."

"You have been gone for a long time." He gentled his tone. "Your mom called me one night, out of the blue. I had nothing to do with it, but she suddenly wanted 'to get healthy' again. I have no idea what brought it on. I didn't ask. I never ask, not with this family. I support and I help. That's my job, what your dad would've wanted me to do, so I agreed. Four mornings a week, I come over, and we walk at six in the morning."

"At six?"

He nodded.

"In this neighborhood?" We weren't exactly in SoHo.

Another nod.

"The local gangs like to curse at me. That's our neighborhood."

A third nod, and a sigh. "I'm aware. I get the same curses. Why do you think I go with her? She said she's going to go with or without me. I go. And I let my gun show."

Jesus Christ. My mom was in a walking phase.

"I have to sit down." My head was starting to pound. "I'm getting PTSD from her mood changes. She hates me one visit, now I'm 'honey' and 'dear,' and she's walking. She looks sober."

"She's been sober, at least since this new health kick."

I gave him a look. "Every day?"

"Every day I've seen her, and we're walking four times a week. You know I'm here a lot on the weekends. She's been sober. I swear it."

"I can't. I just can't with this." I started to get up, needing to leave.

This was bringing bad déjà vu of other times she'd gotten on a health kick. It would keep on and on, and I'd start to think she'd be good and happy, and then I'd wake to text messages telling me how I was the daughter of Satan. How dare I exist? I was the reason my father was dead. I should've gone to prison instead of Isaac.

"I'm out."

I couldn't handle that whiplash. The PTSD was real.

"No. What? Stay."

"No. I know how this goes, and I'm not going to get sucker punched, not by my own mother. Not again."

I was starting for the stairs.

"Jess! Come on. Stay for breakfast. Just . . . stay. Please."

I continued down the stairs. "Nope. Good luck. Though, she doesn't abuse *you* when she starts drinking again. I'm sorry she keeps calling you, but you keep coming, and I don't get it. My own dad wouldn't have been as patient as you're being with her, but cool. Have fun with this new Chelsea Montell. Enjoy it as long as it lasts, because it will end. And when it does, she's a bitch."

"You never told me how it went with your aunt."

I was at my car, and I reached for the handle but paused. I looked at him across the top of my vehicle. Forget the aunt. "Good luck with her. You're going to need it."

I got in and pulled away.

I had an entire day before my shift. That meant downtime for me to think or, worse yet, *feel* things. I went down the list of my options.

Bar. There's always a game somewhere. That meant drinking.

I was lying to myself.

The studio? No. That also meant feeling, and I didn't want to feel.

The gym? I could do the gym. My mind was made up, and I was at a red light when my phone started ringing.

Kelly calling.

"What's up?"

"Where are you?"

I recognized this voice of Kelly's. Something happened or she got an idea in her head, and she was on a mission. I'd learned in the past that if I could, I tried to always be around for whatever Kelly got into when she sounded like this. It was usually epic entertainment. Sometimes I felt guilty because Kelly was like my own real-life reality show playing out in front of me, but then I hushed that feeling and enjoyed whatever was going to happen.

"Leaving my mom's. What's up?"

"Justin's cousin called and invited him to a whole-day party at this mansion. You in?"

"We work tonight."

"We'll be back in time. I promise. Justin said he could drive. Please, please, please. We have not hung out in forever, and I know, I know. I'm partly at fault because I'm at Justin's so much, but Jess, what about if I move out? This could be like our last hurrah or something."

True. Also, Kelly was fun, and it was a perfect day for some Kelly funness.

I couldn't believe I was doing this. "Where's this place, and who is throwing the party?"

"It's Justin's cousin's boss. Who I don't really know, but he said she works for some bigwig exec, and there would probably be famous athletes at this party." She lowered her voice. "I'm going to be honest, I'm really going because I want out of the city for a little bit. It's early. We can get there in time for a decent afternoon, and this mansion is supposed to be epic. Who wouldn't want to go?!"

Me. But . . . Kelly.

"Fine."

She squealed. "*Oh my gosh! This is the bestest thing ever!* We'll pick you up in thirty."

"Wait—"

She ended the call.

I'd just be getting to our place in that time frame, but screw it. I hit the accelerator and gave the middle finger to the two kids dealing pot at the end of my mom's block when I drove by.

CHAPTER
THIRTY-TWO

JESS

The party was at an estate, not a mansion. We drove in and went past Ferraris, Rolls-Royces, and more than a few BMWs, and a helicopter was parked in the back . . . by the other helicopter. I leaned forward from the back seat. "*Who* are these people?"

Kelly giggled in the front passenger seat.

Justin glanced up in the rearview mirror, driving. "I should've explained that half of my family are cops, or a similar position like yourself, and the other half is in business. One side of that family is in the oil business."

"Which are you?"

"I'm the black sheep. I have a business degree, and I'm an entrepreneur during the week and a bartender at night."

I grunted, leaning back and taking in the scenery. This was not my world, that was for sure. "And let me guess, bartending is paying the bills."

"For now." He looked up, meeting my gaze in the mirror again. "I've got some things in the works, but I'm not in any hurry." He gave Kelly a fond look. "I'm enjoying my life right now."

She gave another giggle, and this one I knew by heart. It was the one that was a mix between sigh-I've-found-my-Prince-Charming and I'm-a-total-and-complete-goner-even-if-he-turns-out-to-be-a-dud-somehow. I had no idea Justin was this connected, and when we parked, I walked next to Kelly. "You knew about this side of him?"

Justin was ahead of us, leading the way as a woman was coming out from a large white barnlike structure to greet him.

"He told me recently."

"How recently?"

"Last night, when he officially asked me to move in with him." She was biting her lip, gauging my response.

Well . . . okay then. My chest was a little tight. "And you said?"

She took a deep breath, still eyeing me. "I told him yes. That we talked about it, you and me, and you were fine with it. You are, right? I mean . . ." She gazed around, her eyes big and wistful. "Look at this, Jess. When he first asked me out, I just thought he was a cute bartender. This is like a dream come true."

"Kelly!" Justin was waving, standing by the woman, who I now recognized as a model. Her face had been up on Times Square for an entire month.

She squealed before waving back. "We're coming!" Dragging me with her, or trying, she hissed under her breath, "That's his cousin. Vivianna Harper. It's her boss that owns this place, but she works with the rest of their family. I don't know how. Investor maybe?" She hurried the rest right as we drew within earshot. A wide smile took place, and she let me go, extending her hand to the woman.

Justin did the introductions.

Mine was a "hey" grunt, and when Justin was about to say what I did for a living, I interrupted. "I bartend at Katya too."

"Oh!" Vivianna perked up. "I didn't know that was the place you were working at, Justin." Her hand rested on his arm, but she turned to me. "I know the owners."

Oh—a myriad of curses swept through me. I wasn't thinking them, feeling them, saying them. I *was* them. I was embodying a whole litany of curses.

Justin's cough sounded forced.

I grated out, "You don't say?"

"Oh yes! And they're here—" Cue a repeat of my cursing episode. She kept on, having no clue. "Or one of them. I know there's two owners, but I know Ashton. I've only heard of Tristian, but Ashton and I used to model back in the day, during college. We kinda bonded because we were both going against our family wishes, you know. Doing our own thing for a while, but then he went out to Cali for a few years. We recently reconnected. What a wonderful surprise. Justin"—she turned to him—"I bet he has no idea you're my cousin."

This seemed like a great idea.

I needed to take lessons from myself. If I thought it was a great idea, do the opposite. I should've stayed for breakfast and borne through a morning of Healthy Chelsea Montell. It would've been better than this.

"Come on. Justin, you probably know most everyone here . . ." She faltered, seeing Justin's arm curving around Kelly's waist. She blinked a few times before another smile came over her, this one softer, gentler. "Who's this?"

He'd already done introductions, so his head inclined toward Kelly. "This is my girlfriend."

A whole new wondrous look came over Vivianna. She blinked a few more times, her eyes darting to Kelly's hands before lifting back to Justin. "This is serious then?"

His arm tightened around Kelly. "It is. She's moving in with me."

"Oh." Another few blinks before she swallowed, her neck stretching from the motion. "So this isn't a random or casual stop-in, huh?"

"It's not, no."

Kelly shot me a look, biting her lip all over again.

Viv's disdain was thick as she glared at Kelly, then to Justin. "You drove all the way here to drop *this* on our lap?" Her tone turned clipped, and her hand gestured to Kelly when she said *this*.

Gone were the niceties.

Justin's arm moved from behind Kelly. He took a step forward as Kelly moved back a step, her head lowering as she gave me another fleeting look.

Oh, fuck. I was hoping I was reading my best friend right because she wanted a breather from this sudden weird interaction. I cleared my throat. "So, huh, Viv. Where'd you say our boss was? Maybe we could get the rest of the night off."

She seemed dazed, so it was a pause before she responded. "Wait. Tonight?"

I nodded.

She looked to Justin and Kelly for affirmation. Justin said, "We're all supposed to work tonight."

She shifted back on her heels, her very high heels, and why was she wearing heels? She was a model. Good grief. That wasn't jealousy on my part. Nope. It's not like longer legs would've helped me in my life at all.

"Viv—" Justin started.

I finished, "Hey! Vivianne."

She was glaring at Justin but drew in a sharp breath before her head snapped in my direction. Her eyes were sparkling from irritation. "It's Vivianna."

"Right." I laughed. "You should probably know what my day job is. I'm a parole officer, so I'm really hoping that you don't have any parolees in there, and if you do, they can't be drinking or doing drugs. I mean, I know some parolees are allowed alcohol, but that's pretty rare, so if I see it, I gotta report it."

Her eyes were blinking rapidly. "Excuse me? What?"

"Yeah." I kept on, sounding casual. "Normally in situations like this, on my day off, I don't like to cause waves, but you know, you're being a bitch to my best friend, so that ship sailed. Like"—I whistled, the sound before a bomb drops—"so *far* sailed that you can't even see the yacht thing of whatever was happening before. And also, you're pissing me off."

"Oh, good god, Jess." Justin dropped his head, muttering under his breath.

Viv's eyes were latched to me, glaring. I was fairly certain she'd tell us to leave, or that's what I was hoping for. "You're a parole officer."

"Yep. Excuse my demeanor. If I wasn't pissed right now, I might give you two thumbs up. But when you started referring to my best friend as 'this,' that made me more in the mood where I can show you the teeth that I do still have."

"You're out of your jurisdiction."

"It doesn't quite work like that. Parole officer. There are some differences, but the main one is that I can't give you a ticket, so you're safe to speed in front of me." I was smiling as I said every word, still sounding casual, like I'd just finished giving her a weather report.

"Too bad Justin didn't take you to his other side of the family. You would've fit right in."

"Well, that would've defeated the purpose of 'getting away for the day.' You know."

She glared at me before including Kelly and then moving to Justin. "I see you actually haven't changed that much, Justin. Still slumming." She turned on her heel but said over her shoulder as she began to leave, "You can show yourself around, thank you."

Justin's mouth was hanging open, but a choked laugh ripped out of him. He laced his hands together, raised them up, and cupped the back of his head. "I can't believe that just happened." He was taking me in, his eyes wide. "All of that and you know the real reason she left is to make sure no drugs are visible. My cousin can handle a catfight, that's not a problem for her, but good call on the little threat." He started laughing as he reached for Kelly, then pulled her to him and buried his head into her neck and shoulder. "Please don't leave me because a part of my family are rich assholes. I try not to associate with them."

Kelly wound her arms around his neck, hanging on to him as well, a little laugh slipping from her.

He lifted his head, his hands dropping to her waist but holding her against him. "But fair warning that the rest of my family are just as bad. I wanted to drop the bomb on them that you exist, but knowing Viv, she'll be on the phone and calling what relatives aren't here to get here ASAP."

Kelly's laugh dried up. "Really?"

He nodded, more somber now. "It'll be fine, though. The only one I really want to introduce you to is my aunt. She's everything this side of my family isn't. Kind. She's a big reason I am who I am. I lived with her for most of my life."

"Really?" she whispered.

"I only care about her. I swear. I'm not a part of all the family bullshit, and I don't have to kiss ass because I'm not dependent on them for money. Drives them all crazy."

Kelly was back to swooning. "Then I absolutely cannot wait to meet this aunt of yours."

Justin's gaze grew dark, and he was starting to lower his head right as I clued in on what was about to happen. I turned, coughing, and gestured toward the main house. "Yeah. I'm, uh—going there."

They were still kissing when I got to the barn.

CHAPTER

THIRTY-THREE

JESS

There were rich people everywhere.

I knew they were because they had the rich-people speak. The "oh haw-haw" or the "Insert name, dawrrrling, how are youuuu?" or the "lovely" and "gracious me" and the laughs. Fake and forced and uppity. I knew my rich people, and I was surrounded by them.

That's why I stuck to the food table and the bar.

I was on my second martini—don't judge if I was pretending to be a rich folk today, but the martinis were *good*—when I heard next to me, "Officer Montell. I was informed of your arrival, but didn't believe it. The same birdy told me you drove here with two other of my employees."

Aw, crap.

Ashton Walden was at the end of the table, his head cocked to the side, and his eyes narrowed.

I tried to get a beat on what he was thinking or feeling, but I got nothing. Maybe curiosity? He didn't seem perturbed that I was here, and I didn't want to believe he was amused I was here either.

"Please tell me your other half is not present today."

Now he was amused. I could tell as he tried hiding a quick grin. "At this rate it seems like he's more like your other half."

"You know what I mean."

"I do, yes." He glanced behind us, and I saw Vivianna watching us with avid interest. He came forward and took my elbow in his hand in a light grasp. He moved in close, speaking to the bartender. "A bourbon, please." He eyed my drink. "Is that your first martini?"

I tipped my head back, drank the rest, and slid the glass on the counter. "Soon to be my third, hopefully."

The bartender was eyeing us as he filled our drinks.

Ashton moved back a step, dropping his hand, and he turned to face me directly. "You are not striking me how Trace speaks of you."

"How does he speak of me?"

"He's never said you're funny."

"I take offense to that. I have a dry humor. It's like wine. It appreciates."

Ashton hid another grin before taking his bourbon from the bartender. "I'm learning. And I'm finding you oddly amusing."

"It's that wine humor. You must have class."

He choked on another chuckle as he fished out a twenty and put it in the tip jar. "I'm sure I do." His head lifted and he moved back, standing with his back to the bar but still beside me. "What'd you say to Viv earlier?"

The martini was slid across to me, and I took it, giving him a smile. "That tip was from me."

"Thank you, Miss."

Ashton turned again, giving me a wry look before putting another twenty in the jar. "I'll take it from Trace later."

"I'm sure you will."

I was smiling and drinking, all casual and cool looking on the outside, but on the inside I was freaking out. What the hell was I doing here? This was a lesson to me. Stop hanging out with new people. Stop thinking an adventure was a good idea. Stick to what you knew, and maybe life wouldn't get handed to you backward on a spike. And I was still hoping the latter wouldn't happen, but knowing my luck, I doubted it.

Ashton indicated forward with his head. "Come with me. Tell me about your interaction with Viv. It looked very entertaining."

That was another rich-person word. *Very.* They liked their "verys."

We moved to the side, going through the barn to the back end. I glanced his way. "You were watching?"

"I was having a conversation on the side patio of the house before the barn. I saw your arrival. The birdy who informed me was myself. I informed myself."

"Do you have appreciating humor too?"

He laughed, stepping out first to a back patio area. Beyond was a myriad of walking paths made of cobblestone. A large fountain was in the middle. Beyond was a horse pasture fenced in by white posts. I glimpsed a tennis court to the side.

Why was there not a pool here as well? Perhaps on the other side of the estate?

I was being sarcastic.

"I'm waiting, Officer Montell."

Right. He wanted the 411. "It wasn't much of anything. She insulted my friend, and I didn't like that. I informed her of my profession and that I had a penchant for reporting whenever I saw drugs around. That was all, really."

Ashton stopped, his head reared back as he was giving me another assessing look. We were in the middle of one of those cobblestone walkways, making our way around the fountain. I was hoping we'd keep going and I could see what kind of pool these people had. My guess was that it would be epic.

"Viv insulted Kelly?"

I frowned. The jokes were less appealing. "You're aware of my friend's name?"

He flashed me a look. "Of course I am. Trace is my best friend. I was the one who hired the PI for you."

My stomach dropped. "That means . . ."

"That means I got the files too. I'm quite aware your roommate and best friend, who is probably going to not be your roommate soon, is also my employee. I'm aware of her name too." He tilted his head to the side. "I'm aware of Justin's family connections. I had him placed next to you also because of his other family's occupation. I thought you'd both bond with each other."

Right. I was swallowing bark here. "I wasn't aware you are that active with Katya's employees."

"Trace handles the money. I handle our businesses."

"And your families?" Guess I *was* going there. I needed to double down. "You're both on retainer for your families? Is that how it works? You do your legit work during the day and act as your family's bitches at night? Is that what you guys were doing at my aunt's—"

"Careful. I won't be like Trace, and I doubt you're wearing a wire. Right?"

"I'm asking about your families."

"Our families are none of your business." His tone matched mine, becoming serious.

I bristled. "Does *Viv* know what business your family is in?"

"If you think Viv's family doesn't have connections as well, you're not the jaded PO that I'm assuming my best friend is banging."

I started for him but caught myself.

He stepped back, his eyes flashing. One of his hands lifted, but his head moved again, going the other way. "I struck a nerve? Or maybe you haven't screwed yet."

"I'm thinking that's none of your business."

"Trace isn't just my best friend. He's my brother. He's more family to me than my real family, so yes, a certain parole officer who is leading him around and toying with his emotions most definitely is part of my business. In every sense of the word." His eyes chilled. "Amusing as this conversation has been, I need to impress upon you not to fuck with my best friend anymore. I don't enjoy him suffering."

Well, holy fuck.

I took a step back. "Are you kidding me? He's in my business, in my family's business, finding me when I'm doing art, and I haven't done a painting in goddamn years. But *I'm* fucking with *him*? Who the fuck do you think *you* are?"

He smirked. "I'm fairly certain you know exactly who I am."

"You might want to be careful who you're threatening here."

"Because you're a PO?"

"Because while you think you know me, at the end of the day, you have no idea who I actually am." I lowered my voice.

So did he. "Get out of my face, while I'm not feeling murderous right now."

I reacted without thinking. That was a threat and, tossing my drink, my hand went for my weapon. I always wore it, or at least most of the time. At the same time, someone screamed, and suddenly someone else was at our side. A hand closed over mine, and goddamn, I knew whose hand that was.

Trace pressed in, keeping my weapon where it was, and he spoke fast. "I don't know what the fuck you two just got into, but it's over. Ashton, walk."

"Tra—"

"Walk!" He didn't wait. Moving so he was blocking my view from his best friend, his eyes drilled into mine. "I'm going to let go of your hand, and I'm going to back up and give you space. Don't shoot me."

He did as he said, his hands in the air a little bit.

I breathed in, reeling that Trace was here.

My hand was tingling.

He stopped two steps back. "You okay?"

I looked away, swallowing over a lump in my throat. "He threatened me."

"He tends to do that." He took a step toward me.

I shook my head, moving backward myself.

He stopped. "Okay, okay. I'm not coming any farther, but I suggest we get out of here or move where we don't have so many eyes on us. People know us here, and there will be talk. I'd like to head off any talk before I get a phone call from my uncle. You hear me?"

He was right.

Goddamn, he was right.

I was still half reeling from what had almost happened.

As if sensing it was okay, Trace moved in. He touched my arm, lightly, and began steering me away. "What happened between you two?"

"He told me to get out of his face while he wasn't feeling murderous. That's a threat."

He cursed under his breath. "Yeah, well, that's Ashton."

"You can't say something like that to someone like me."

"I'm thinking he's realizing that, too, right about now." He let go of my arm but tapped the back of my hand. He jerked his head toward a sidewalk going around the other side of the house. "Who are you here with?"

"My roommate and her boyfriend."

"Come on." He was leading the way until we cleared the side of the house and pulled out his keys, going toward the vehicles.

I stopped. "What? No."

He stopped too. "Jess, you need to listen to me. You should not be here. There are people here who have connections to my family that we don't want them to know about you. The more you're here, the more you'll get on their radar. I know you have threatened and pleaded with me enough to leave you alone, but I'm being totally up front here. I can't, *not here*. You cannot be here."

"Kelly. Justin."

"Justin is protected. And while she's with him, so is she. You're not, and I'm not talking about your safety. I'm talking about my uncle asking questions about you, and then about your aunt, and then her husband. Are you following where I'm going?"

My chest felt like it was caving into me, but damn. Yeah. I was following.

I clipped my head to the vehicles. "Which one is yours?"

He led the way to an SUV, and as he got into the driver's seat, I got into the passenger side. I was pulling my phone out as he started the engine.

"Who are you calling?"

Kelly picked up just as he was asking. I raised my voice, trying to talk over him. "Hey!"

He grimaced but pushed down the accelerator as we sped off.

"Where are you?" Kelly dropped her voice to a whisper. "Okay, can I tell you how freaked I am right now? Justin is amazing and all, but this family of his is terrifying. They're terrifying. I did this already with my ex, and you see how that ended up. He cheated on me with seventeen women. I mean, yeah. My ex doesn't have the family connections that Justin does, but they were still well off, and they had expectations. I don't like families that have expectations. I'm a no-expectation girlfriend from now on, or I'd like to be, but ugh. Jess. It's Justin! Why does he have to be so amazing? Also, where are you? They have free martinis here, and they're free! Did I already say that they're free? I've had two already. I'm going to be drunk before Justin gets around to introducing me to his aunt, and then what'll happen after that? She'll not be impressed. I'm sloppy and sad when I drink martinis. Where are you?!"

"Um." That was a lot to digest. I shared a look with Trace, who I was seeing was on his phone too. "I'm—uh—I got a call, and I have to head back to the city."

"What?! What's wrong? You need to leave? I can grab Justin."

"No, no, no. I'm, uh, I'm already leaving. I got a car and I'm going back." So, lying. Me. To my best friend in the whole world.

I was going to hell.

"You got a car?"

"Someone came in with an Uber, and I grabbed it when they were leaving. It worked out perfectly."

"I guess that makes sense."

"Yeah. So. I'll see you later then?"

"I think Justin really is going to ask our boss if we can have the night off, so it might not be till tomorrow. Please tell me you're going bowling on Sunday? You've missed too much. They're missing you."

The whole concave sensation in my chest was happening again, this time from guilt. "I'll be there. You'll be with Justin until then?" I sensed Trace watching me and knew he'd overheard the last part of my conversation.

"I don't know what's going to happen after, so yeah. Just in case. If anything we'll go back to his place. We have a lot to talk about."

I softened my voice. "Are you going to be okay?"

She sighed. "I think so. It's just scary. Falling for someone always is."

"Yeah." I glanced at Trace, pain slicing through my insides. "Whether we want it to happen or not."

We said our goodbyes and hung up.

"Your friend is okay?"

I pressed my lips together first before answering. "They're going to ask Ashton for the night off from work."

Trace snorted. "He'll give it to them. He'll get a kick out of it if they ask him in front of Viv."

"You know Viv?"

"I know of Viv. She's been after Ashton since college. He'll enjoy the show of it. I'm betting that your friend Justin won't be working at Katya long anyways, and I'm guessing he won't want his girl working there if he isn't."

I tensed. "Why are you saying that?"

"Because he'll have figured out by the end of the night, if he hasn't already, that Ashton gave him the job because of his family connections, and also because he saw us leave together."

"What?"

He frowned at me. "He's aware of who we are, who our family is. It's why he's working there. His brother put him up to it. He's eyes on us. Or I'm guessing that's the situation. He can work, get paid, get his tips, meet a nice girl, and if he happens to hear something or see something, he'll pass it along. But nothing like where he's going to search out for something to report. Your friend is too smart for that, and his brother wouldn't want to needlessly endanger Justin. And also they don't really think they'll get anything, or there's no way his brother would sign off on letting your friend work in one of my businesses."

I was feeling gut punched but pissed at how I hadn't figured any of that out, and I should've.

"He told me his brother was a detective too."

Trace glanced at me. "You've been distracted."

Still. I was disappointed with myself. I should've known. "He saw us leave together?"

"He did, but Ashton is the only one who knows anything, and he won't say a word."

"Kelly knows."

"What?"

"She saw you at Easter Lanes. I told her about the hockey stairway guy and let it slip that it was you. If she saw you, she knows. She might say something."

We drove for a bit in silence.

"My guess is that she didn't see or she would've said something on the phone, and Justin won't bring it up. Who would when he's hoping to introduce his new girlfriend to his family? Guys like Justin don't say anything unless they have to."

He was right. Justin would wait, ask me about the situation. He'd feel me out first before deciding how to handle it. I nodded, settling back into the seat. "I'll make something up, cover."

"I think that's smart."

That was all sorted out, and so now I had at least an hour to sit in the same vehicle with Trace.

The understanding was dawning on me as I looked at him, and he met my look before needing to watch the street. A whole hour or more depending on traffic.

This would be fine.

All fine.

My body wouldn't react to him.

I wouldn't think about kissing, or touching, or . . . yeah. It would be all good.

Why wasn't I believing in myself?

"Viv said you weren't there when we arrived. When did you come?"

He grimaced before answering. "I had a family thing not far away. Ashton texted when he saw you show up, and I considered not coming. I thought about respecting your wishes, but I'm glad I didn't."

I closed my eyes. "Why did you decide to come?"

He didn't answer at first.

He didn't answer in the next minute, or the next five.

Ten.

It was a full thirty minutes later. His voice was hoarse when he finally answered. "Because when it comes to you, I have absolutely no *fucking* control over myself."

I wished I hadn't asked.

But I was glad I had.

CHAPTER

THIRTY-FOUR

TRACE

I was walking into my downtown office when my phone started ringing.

"Hello, Mr. West." The doorman gave me a nod, opening the door for me. I was pulling my phone out, ready and needing a full day in the office, when I saw who was calling.

Uncle Steph calling.

I stopped a few feet inside. The front desk receptionist was waiting for me. She always had a greeting for us as we came in, and I'd been rarely coming in during normal hours. I'd been working remotely, but I wanted a normal day in the office. I wanted to talk to my colleagues, hear the bullshit stories about how much money they'd traded the day before. Half was bullshit. Half was testing if we'd heard anything. Half was just connecting to each other. Most of the guys who did this job lived for it. They drank, ate, shit stocks, but some were like me. They did the deep dive research, and when one of us was found, we'd always get "visitors" dropping by to "shoot the shit" or wanting to grab a drink.

But if my uncle was calling, I knew none of that would happen.

"Mr. West?"

I held a hand up to the receptionist but didn't move any closer. I knew. I just knew—work or family.

She stood from her desk, still watching me, and after a moment, she frowned just slightly. Stepping out from the desk, she smoothed down her skirt and shirt and began to cross the lobby toward me. A few other guys were coming in, going around me.

"Hey, buddy! Long time no see."

"What's up? Two o'clock lunch?"

"Tristian, my man! Drinks on me tonight. You in?"

I didn't answer them as my phone fell silent, and suppressing a curse, I moved to the side and hit the call-back button.

"Mr. West?"

I held a hand up. "One minute, please."

She coughed just as my uncle answered. "My nephew! My boy. How are you?"

"Mr. West." She raised her voice, inclining her head toward me.

I frowned, saying into the phone, "One second, Uncle Steph." Pressing the phone to my chest, I raised an eyebrow at her. "Yes?"

"You have a visitor."

"A visitor?"

She gave me a tight nod. "In your office. She was *very* insistent."

"She?"

"Yes, she. She informed me that you share blood, and her name is Remmi."

This day went from bleak to even bleaker, but I could see the evidence of Remmi. She liked to lay a path of destruction wherever she went, and it made sense now why the receptionist came out to tell me of her presence.

I grimaced. "If she threatened you in any way, I apologize on her behalf."

The receptionist gave a tight nod and an even tighter but grim smile before heading back for her desk.

I lifted the phone back up, saying, "I'm usually happy for a call from you, Uncle, but I've been informed of a disaster waiting in my office for me."

He began chuckling. "I heard, but listen. I need you to come around today."

"When?"

"Earlier than later. We need to revisit our talk we had a while ago, about my health and what that might mean for you. And about other matters too."

Fuck. Fuck. Fuck! I was very aware my uncle's line was tapped. FBI continuously listened in, and because of that, we had a code. A very serious code we used on certain phone lines, but he just broadcasted to whoever was listening in that they needed to start looking my way.

Why? Why would he do that?

There was a reason. I loved my uncle, but there was a reason for everything he did.

"I need to deal with Remmi, and then I'll come around."

"Let's do lunch. I'll cook."

"Sounds great." It didn't sound great.

We hung up, and when I got to my office, I was in a mood.

For one moment, I stopped, and I was back in the car with Jess on Saturday.

That drive to her place was a bubble. A brief moment in time where we were in between who she was and who I was, and we were able to connect for a shared purpose. I felt like I'd been given a gift because she wasn't tense with me. It was like she gave herself permission during that drive to be herself, and it'd been the best car ride I'd ever been on.

We laughed. We talked. We were friends, and when I drove to her place, she was quiet for a long time. She didn't leave the car, so I pulled over on the street. She had an hour to get to work, and I offered her a ride. I'd been expecting her to say no, and I think she was going to, but after a moment's hesitation, she accepted. While she went upstairs to dress, I waited in the car. It was her request. She came back fifteen minutes later, but when I started to put the car into drive, she stopped me.

"Can we not? This is . . ." She looked out the window and swallowed her words before looking back to me. Such sad eyes. "Can we stay a little longer like this?"

We did. There was no conversation this time.

But a moment, a pocket of time, it was just the two of us.

I wanted that back so badly right now.

"What are you doing?"

My office door was opened, and Remmi stood in the doorway, an air of irritation swimming around her. Her dark eyes were heavily made up. She was wearing black leather pants and a black sweater that wrapped tightly around her body, and she had on those hoop earrings she always wore during college. I didn't know why I was cataloging any of this. Maybe for extra time. Because I knew I'd be going from one fight to another fight right after this. They might not look like fights. They might not sound like fights, but they were. There was a push-pull dynamic going on under the surface. Remmi would want something. I would probably not want to give it, the same with Uncle Steph, but in his instance, I always gave it.

I gave it because I had to, and I had never wanted to see what would happen if I didn't do what Uncle Steph wanted. Looking at Remmi right now, I don't know the reason, but today was the very first day I was starting to question *when* that day would happen.

"Hello, sister."

CHAPTER
THIRTY-FIVE
JESS

I was lying in bed Monday night, wired from the day but trying to will my body to sleep, when my phone buzzed.

Trace: Did you unblock me yet?

Trace: Also, I know you did but the circumstances weren't great so I'm pretending that this is the first time you unblocked me. Hi.

I stifled a grin, because he was right.

Me: I did.

It'd been nice seeing him on Saturday. The car ride back to the city was even nicer.

That wall I'd built against him took a hit on Saturday. A crack formed, and a piece crumbled on Sunday, and another today for the mere fact that I missed him.

It was just texting, I was telling myself.

Only texting.

My chest tightened. I knew I was lying to myself, but my resolve was starting to weaken.

Me: Why are you texting tonight?

Trace: Because I had a shitty day and a rumor got to me that your roommate moved out?

I frowned.

Me: How did you hear that?

Trace: It was a big deal at the party on Saturday. Viv told Ashton, and Ashton just told me. You okay?

Me: She's not moved yet, but it almost doesn't feel different. She's gone during the night at his place anyways. I'll have less furniture.

Trace: It's a big change, right?

Me: It is. It'll be fine. Kelly's still my best friend. That won't change. Why was your day shitty?

Trace: Family.

Me: Don't want to talk about it?

Trace: I did. Family. That word alone signifies shitty.

I barked out a laugh before covering my mouth.

Me: I understand that mantra.

Trace: See. I knew texting you would be a good idea. I feel understood.

Me: I'm glad you feel understood.

Trace: I want to ask you what you're wearing right now, but I'm assuming that'll be pushing this . . .

I groaned because now my body was heating up.

Me: I've got a gun.

Trace: You're saying that's all you're wearing? Your gun? That's hot.

Stifling another laugh, I heaved a deep breath because this was going from a bad idea to an even worse idea.

Me: That's not what I meant, but I'm going to sleep. Good night. I'm sorry your day was shitty.

Trace: You made my night better.

Trace: Can I text tomorrow night?

I responded the next morning.

Me: Yes.

CHAPTER
THIRTY-SIX
JESS

It was three nights later when my phone lit up. I grabbed it, not looking at the screen, because let's be honest—I was hoping it was Trace.

"Hello?" I was in bed, trying to fall asleep, or that's another lie I was telling myself. I was in bed, but I was hoping for another night of texts.

"Why are you alive? Why didn't I abort you when I could?"

I heard the slurring, the hissing, and knew I'd messed up.

My body went cold. I didn't move, not at first.

My heart began pounding, thumping hard in my chest and eardrums.

This was it. The healthy phase had stopped earlier than I'd anticipated.

"When you sober up, give me a call to apologize."

I ended the call, and I hovered over hitting the block button.

I couldn't. God, but I wanted to. I really wanted to. It'd be so easy. Life would be easier.

But she was my mother.

Mom calling.

I declined. I sat up, drawing my knees up to my chest, and I just held the phone.

I knew I shouldn't. This was so dumb of me. Literal self-punishment, but it came alive again. The screen lit up; the phone started shaking.

Mom calling.

I declined again.

And again.

And again.

Then the texts started.

Mom: I wish Isaac was out here with me not you. I HATE YOU.

Mom: If I could've killed you, I would've. You SHOULDA DIED instead of your father.

Mom: Y not one of my miscarriages.

Mom: Ur fat. Ur stupid. Ur worthless. No man will love you. Ur the reason why I'm alone.

My phone kept going, so I hit her texts, then muted the alerts. If I wasn't going to block her this way, it was pointless to do anything else. She'd be going until she passed out.

I texted Leo.

Me: You at home?

He didn't respond, so I was guessing he was asleep. Weekday nights he went to bed after the local news.

I called someone else. Besides Leo, he was another of my mom's friends who helped take care of her sometimes. Bear Rivera. He owned the local bar that Leo and so many of our colleagues hung out at, so I knew the two conversed at times over who would check in on my mother. But while Leo had been friends with my dad, Bear never talked about any good times with him. I asked one time about their history, and Bear told me he went to high school with both of my parents, but he and my mom had been friends.

He picked up, the sounds of his bar telling me he was still at work. "Jessie girl! How are you?"

"Bear. Hey. Could you do me a favor?"

"Sure. What's going on?" His voice dipped, going serious.

"My mom's on a rampage tonight. Mind checking on her after you close up? I know it's a little out of the way, but—"

"Don't say another word. You know I'll check on her. No worries there, little Jessie girl. I'll give you a text when I get over there."

Bear was witness to some of the times my mom had lit into me. We never spoke about it, because it was what it was. My options were to care from a distance or let her go. I couldn't let her go; maybe that was my downfall.

Maybe that was my pattern. Not letting go of people who would only hurt me.

"Thank you, Bear. I mean it."

"No thanks needed. Been taking care of your mom before anyone else. No problem for me, and you, honey, you get some sleep tonight. I know you gotta kick some ass in the morning. Put your mom's shit out of your mind."

We hung up, and I tried to fall asleep.

It was fifty-three minutes later when my phone lit up again.

Bear: All good. She's passed out. Looks like she just went on a bender, no damage done to herself or the house. You sleep tight now.

I sighed, and I should've felt relieved. I didn't. I just felt hollow.

Thirty minutes later, I flipped over in bed and cursed, reaching for the phone.

Fuck this. Fuck my mother. Fuck everyone.

I was using that as an excuse because I found myself pulling up Trace's name and hitting *call* before I let myself think about what I was doing.

Rin—

I stopped it, and then I powered down my phone before I did something seriously stupid.

What was I doing?

I wanted him to text, like he had the last few nights.

I'd thought it was him. I'd been so happy, grabbing the phone, but it hadn't been. It was her, and now she was in, past my walls, and her loathing was coating my insides.

Goddamn.

Goddamn it all.

I woke to twenty-three texts from my mom, the last ten minutes before Bear might've checked on her. I didn't read the words, just looked at the time stamps. And there was one text from Trace.

Trace: Sorry I didn't text last night. I saw you called. Are you okay?

That was it from him, but still, going to work, I focused on his one text and tried to forget the twenty-three from my mom.

CHAPTER
THIRTY-SEVEN

JESS

I was doing home visits with my partner today.

I waited until after the first stop before bringing it up. "So, you and Reyo, huh?"

Val had been taking a sip of coffee, and I was noting that it was her only very small purchase of caffeine for the day. I knew her daily habits, but since finding out about the bun in her oven, I was paying extra attention. Val knew I knew. I knew she knew that I knew, so I'd given her time to adjust.

I was done giving her time to adjust.

She choked on her coffee, almost spitting it out before she swallowed, and glared at me. "You did that on purpose."

I gave her a shit-eating grin, taking a cool and casual sip of my coffee. "You bet I did. Perfect timing on my part too. I'd give myself a four point five out of five."

"We're not doing this." She was trying to be all assertive, putting her coffee back in the cup holder in her car before starting the engine.

I waited until we were in traffic. Less chance she'd punch the gas or hit the brakes when we were merging. "So you're keeping it?"

"You're not going to stop, are you?"

"I've asked two questions."

She made a growling sound as she flicked on the turn signal and zoomed into the other lane. "You better not have said anything to Leo. I'm aware you two are like family, but he's my team leader too."

My grin wiped clean. "That means you're thinking of not keeping it?"

I wasn't referring to the baby as "the baby" out of respect for my partner. Val was all or nothing, so the fact that I even knew about the little beanpole said she was keeping it. She'd probably decided in the back of her mind the second she'd suspected, but Val needed time to come to grips with her decision. It was how she handled everything in her life. Having a kid tended to change things for us, and I wasn't meaning with our jobs. I'd watched other females have kids. They became human. I didn't think Val was ready to be human.

Another frustrated growl as she hit the steering wheel with the palm of her hand before settling down. She grumbled, "I don't know, okay? I just want to keep it quiet for a while. I'm cool with you knowing. You can keep your mouth shut, but Jesus. Can you imagine if someone else found out? Travis?" She shuddered. "Just fuck me like a trucker, why don't you? It'd be all over the office in two minutes. He'd do a fucking TikTok about it."

"Tell me about Reyo instead."

She rolled her eyes, another grumble leaving her. "What's there to say?"

"You two got it on that night at the wedding?"

She got quiet. "Yeah."

"He must have stamina."

She snorted, a slow smile lifting on her face. "Fuck you. You know he does if I went back."

I grinned back. "He seems like a good partner."

She glanced at me when I used that word but sighed. "He is. He's like a young eager beaver. Fucking cute with his little dimples in his cheeks too."

I was *not* touching that one because I'd witnessed the guy smiling. He did not have dimples in the only set of cheeks I wanted to see on him.

"Oh, Jesus. Fuck me twisted. Are you seeing what I'm seeing?"

I was. There were two guys walking on the sidewalk, walking within distance of a school, and one of those guys wasn't supposed to be within a certain distance of any school. She veered over and pulled into the parking lot just ahead of them, and then we were out of the car. One of those parolees was hers, and he was a sex offender.

"Mr. Bartram, why are you within walking distance of that elementary school just a block away?"

"Oh, hey, Officer Hartman."

Our day had officially started.

CHAPTER

THIRTY-EIGHT

TRACE

I was in the back of my SUV, parked a block from my uncle's place, since that meeting he'd wanted the other day was happening now. I wasn't able to push it off anymore, but I was here and it was nighttime and I'd not heard from Jess all day. She'd called last night but hung up.

That's when the back door opened and a body slid inside, real quick-like and stealthy.

I started to reach for my own gun when her face turned my way, and I expelled a ragged breath.

"Jess."

Jess was in all black. I was assuming for camouflage since it was dark. She'd gotten the jump on the guys, and my privacy divider was still in place.

"Mr. West?" That was Demetri. He was the driver tonight.

Pajn was out of the car, and as he opened her door from the outside, I was pressing the intercom button.

Jess had her gun out. It wasn't pointed at Pajn, but it was out.

She was feeling on edge, vulnerable.

I spoke into the intercom. "It's fine." I let go of the intercom button, giving a nod to Pajn, who eased back and returned to the front seat.

Jess shot me a dark look before reaching and pulling her door shut.

"We're beyond that." I looked down at her gun, which was still drawn. "Also, I know guns. Your safety is on."

Her eyes narrowed, but she holstered her weapon.

"Why'd you call last night?"

Her jaw tightened.

I tensed, waiting . . .

A sigh from her. "Why does it matter?"

I made sure my tone was soft. "It matters to me. You matter to me."

I didn't know why she sought me out. I'm sure there was a reason, but she didn't look ready to confess to it. Instead, I was going my route.

"Why'd you call, Jess?"

Her head lowered, but she didn't turn to me. She remained facing the door. "It's family, right? That's our code for 'shitty situations.'"

She was giving me something.

I wanted more. I needed more.

I asked, "What happened?"

"Just . . . my mom being her usual bitch self. She called."

Right. Some of my tension shifted to sympathy. A slice of pain went through me. "When you looked me up, did the file have what happened with my own mother?"

She half turned my way, stopped, thought about it, and her head turned the rest of the way.

I felt better, seeing her eyes on me. I felt even better seeing there was no condemnation there. Just curiosity. "She killed herself. I was in California at the time, but my sister was here. She was a freshman in high school, and it messed her up."

"Why'd she do it?"

"She didn't leave a note, but my guess—my dad fucked up enough, and she'd just had it? He's a piece of work, if your report didn't have that either."

"It did about your dad, not about your mom. Or your sister."

"Remmi. She won't talk about those days. No one will, so I don't really know myself what happened. I knew my mom was torn down by my father. Every year, every month, every day. She was a shell of herself by the end, and not in a good way. She was bitter, angry. I got my fair share of phone calls taking her anger out on me. I can't imagine what Remmi went through."

"Are you sharing that thinking I'll feel even more of a connection to you?"

"I'm saying that I have some awareness of how shitty it is to get woken up to a phone call from a mother abusing her child. That's all."

She didn't reply, only staring hard at me until I felt a shift in the air.

A wall split open for me.

"My mom's mistake was choosing my dad, but if she hadn't, then my brother wouldn't have been born and . . . I can't fault her for that. What happens after is whatever happens after."

"She had you too."

Her head lifted again, her jaw firmed. She reached for the door handle. "Yeah, well. Maybe that was her other mistake." She opened the door and was gone, not bothering to shut the door.

I got out, looking up and down both sidewalks, but she was truly gone. A ghost.

"Your uncle just called. He wants to know where we are." Demetri had gotten out behind me, going to shut her door.

I nodded, resignation taking place in me. "Tell him we're coming now."

I got back inside, readying for this meeting, but I did not miss what just happened. Something that had changed the game.

Jess had come to *me*.

CHAPTER THIRTY-NINE

JESS

Kelly was off.

The moving had started this week. Most of her stuff was gone. Her clothes went on Tuesday. Her kitchen items, her photos went on Wednesday. Her bed and couch went yesterday. She didn't have much else at the place. But considering they were doing the move, I thought she'd talk more with me than she had. She'd been quiet all week. It had me wondering if Justin had said something about seeing me with Trace. Either way, I was working at Katya and keeping my eye on him in the section next to me.

So far, he was normal. He gave a chin lift to me in greeting and came over, shooting some small talk bullshit before the first wave of customers came in. We had some breathing room today, but that'd only last for one more hour, and it would be customer after customer after that.

Maybe that was why he came over ten minutes later, leaning with his back to the counter, watching me work. "So . . . can we talk?"

Here it was.

I gave him a small nod. "Sure. Here?"

"Yeah. I mean." He gestured behind him and toward his section. "Both of us can't leave."

I knew so I kept working, casting him a sideways look. "This about last weekend?"

"Um." He drew in a breath, raking his hand through his hair. He stood up but moved closer to me. "Listen, I know who you left with."

Right. This was the talk. For a brief moment, I'd hoped it was about him taking my roommate from me.

I was still eyeing him, still working. "Yeah?"

"I'm aware of who he is, you know. Our families . . . there's a connection there, and I figured out what Viv did. She never told me, but she used me to try and get in with Walden."

"Right. Okay." I was still waiting for the other shoe to drop.

"My, uh, brother, you know what he does."

I stopped taking orders and straightened up.

So did Justin, putting a little bit of distance between us, but not much. He indicated farther back so the customers couldn't overhear. I went, and he dropped his voice, his head bending toward mine. "I don't know the reason why a West would be giving you a ride back to the city, or why you lied to Kelly about it, but I can only imagine, and I'm hoping I'm getting all of that wrong. I did talk to my brother more about West and Walden. Look, all cards on the table? I mentioned this job to him, and he said if I happened to overhear anything, let him know. That was it. I'm not here snitching for him. I don't want you thinking that."

It was more alarming that he was explaining he wasn't a snitch to me.

"Look, what I'm trying to say is that I don't have a good feeling here anymore. Tonight's my last night. So's Kelly's. I had a long talk with her about who the owners were, but I kept it quiet about who your ride was with last Saturday, though I'm not sure why I should keep that quiet. Since you're the one who lied, and since you've always been up and up,

I'm assuming you had your reasons. My brother told me that there's another family trying to move in on New York. That means they're going against our bosses, both of them. I don't know the specifics of how involved our owners are with their families, but I know they are involved. That's enough to worry me. I want you to resign with us. All of us can go somewhere else. Kelly would love that. She's been upset all week, thinking about leaving you behind. It's double since she's moving out and now quitting here. I know someone at Octavia. They can put in a good word for us—"

"Octavia's owners aren't active in New York, but don't think for a second they aren't connected either."

He stopped talking, startled by my statement. "You serious?"

I nodded. "I'm guessing your brother didn't tell you about that place."

"Shit. No." He shook his head, raking his hand over his head one more time. "It doesn't matter. We're resigning. Come with us."

God.

I should. I needed to.

Common sense dictated I do exactly as he said, but . . . even now I wanted to look up where his private box was. I wanted to check my phone, see if he'd sent me a text. I couldn't stop replaying being in the car with him.

My throat felt stripped raw as I patted Justin on the arm. "I'm a sucker for what's familiar. It's my downfall. I've stayed this long; I'm going to stick it out. I like working at Katya, but it means a lot that you want me to go with you."

Regret tightened his face, his mouth pressing in a firm line. "Are you sure?"

I dipped my head down. "I'll be okay, Justin." I indicated Kelly, who was watching us from a level above. "You take care of her. All right?"

He drew in a deep breath, resignation settling over his shoulders. He raised his head up, but he didn't look at Kelly. He kept watching me. "I can't change your mind?"

I gave a small shake of my head.

He nodded, giving in. "Okay. Come on. Give me a hug."

I didn't object as he drew me in, and he squeezed me tight. "Be safe. I don't know why you were in the car with him, but please be safe. Be smart."

I couldn't promise on the smart part, but I hugged him back. "I'll watch my back. Don't worry."

He stepped back, letting me go. "You've become family, so I'll worry."

I gave him a crooked grin. "Guessing that means what I think it means."

He grinned back, a half one. "I love her. A lot."

"Also guessing that's what was behind our trip last weekend."

"My aunt loved her. I wanted her to meet Kelly before I proposed, but I have the ring."

"Give me a heads-up when you do, okay? I want to make sure I'm by my phone."

He snorted, starting to back away and go to his section. "Uh. You're going to be there, and I'm going to be needing your help in planning the whole thing."

That was total BS, but I liked that he was pretending he needed my help. "I told her you were good people from the very beginning, you know."

He flashed me one last grin. "I know."

He turned to his customers, and I did the same, but I couldn't shake the feeling that tonight was the first ending before a whole lot of other endings. I didn't know what the others were, and the dread sitting firm in my gut didn't know either.

———

I checked my phone on my break and saw the text there waiting for me.

Trace: Want a ride back to your place after work?

Me: I have my own car here.

He'd sent his text an hour ago, but he responded right away.

Trace: So maybe I could get a ride instead? Or you can leave your car for the night. We have a secure parking spot. You can park it there.

Trace: Anthony said Justin stopped by his office earlier.

So he knew.

My heart was heavy, and I clicked out of his messages, spotting there were thirteen more texts from my mother. I hit them, wanting to make sure nothing was wrong, and, spotting the first words of her most recent text were *you bitch*, I clicked out of them.

I responded, knowing I was making a mistake.

I was going to make it anyway.

Me: I'd like a ride.

———

Kelly came over at the end of her shift. "Justin said he talked to you."

I was still packed with customers, so I didn't stop working. "Yeah. I'm staying."

She nodded, her eyes sad. "I can't change your mind?"

There it was. I gave her a grin, seeing she'd been quiet because of the change. I finished this guy's order and went over to her to give her a hug. She wrapped her arms tight around me, hugging me fiercely. "We need to do more than Easter Lanes on Sunday."

I pulled back. "We'll do so much more than Sunday bowling."

She flicked a hand at her eye, blinking away what had been there. "Why do I feel like this is permanent this time?"

"Because hopefully it is." I saw that Justin was half watching us as he kept doing orders. I flashed him a smile, and he gave me a nod back. "Your path is with him. We were great roommates and better friends. You bet your ass I'm not letting go of our friendship. I need it. You balance all the other bullshit in my life."

"I worry about you."

Oh. That was making my chest hurt. I pulled her in for one more hug. "Text me tomorrow, and let's set up the next time we get together. We'll do a weekly thing."

"You promise?"

I was nodding when I heard behind me, "I *cannot fucking believe* this."

Kelly's response was immediate, twisting around. She'd handled her fair share of female fights in the past, so she was the first to snap back: "Can we help you, *ma'am?*"

Ma'am. I almost started laughing. This chick, whoever she was, was obviously younger than us. And smart, because she registered Kelly's insult. The young woman had straight dark hair, model-like long legs. She was dressed in high-waisted skintight jean leggings. A black corset crop top. Hoop earrings that I thought had gone out of style when I was in college, but they looked good on her. Her makeup was on point, too, but the sneer directed at me was taking away from everything else.

"I know who you are." She slapped a hand on the bar, her long red nails distracting even me. Also, those looked painful in a fight, for her. I'd go right for them.

"Excuse me?"

Kelly started to move in front of me, but I held her back. "I got this."

Justin was looking over, and I waved for him to take her. He gave me a nod, and as I moved toward the woman-child, I saw Justin moving Kelly away. I could handle this. I didn't need to worry about my best friend getting a nail in her eyeball.

"Ma'am." I was using my PO voice. It came out loud and assertive as fuck, and it had an effect on everyone around me. They all sat up and sat back.

I gave her the hard eyes too. Those worked wonders on most offenders. "If you have a problem with me, state it. But I'm going to warn you that if you make any more aggressive moves toward me, we're going to have a completely different type of conversation."

"Oh yeah?" Her sneer had faltered when I first started speaking, but it came back. She folded her arms over her chest. "What kind of conversation would that be?"

"You'll find out. Now. What's your problem with me?" The level of hatred in her eyes was next level. It was like I'd personally destroyed her childhood, or wait. Maybe I had. "You know anyone in prison?" Better question, was I part of the team that put them in there or back in there? That would make more sense.

"No. Well, yes, but that's not why I'm going to have your job tonight."

"You want my job, ma'am?"

She flushed, some confusion chipping away at the loathing. "What? No! God. Who are you?"

"I believe that's the question here. Who am I to you, and why do you have a problem with me."

"Are you kidding me? You don't know who I am?" She slapped a hand back down and leaned over, doing her best to intimidate me. She was tall enough—it might've worked on someone who hadn't gotten cursed out by every which word, and that was just this afternoon.

"Ma'am. If you do not state your business for being here, you will need to leave."

She barked out an ugly laugh, standing back again. Those arms crossed over her chest. "That's hilarious, especially considering the fact that my brother owns this place."

Wh—oh. Oh no.

Recognition hit me, and Trace's earlier conversation filtered back to me.

He'd talked about his sister.

Shitty situation. Family.

"Who's your brother?"

"Tristian West, but it doesn't really matter because Ashton's just as much of a brother figure to me too." She was loving telling me this, drawing it out with a smug smirk. "Trust me, bitch. You're going to regret stepping into this place. I'll have your job by the end of the night, and then I'm going to come after that whore of a mother too. I'm going to make it my mission to put you and your slut of a mother out on the streets."

This was Trace's sister. Who knew my mom somehow.

Well. If we were showing all of our cards, I reached up and drew the chain from around my neck until my badge came up. I took it off and put it on the counter, ignoring the effect it had on the customers around us. I cared only about her reaction, and the shock that was quickly veiled and shoved down was what I needed to see. She had no clue who I actually was. She came in all emotion and no plan.

"Let's see you try to make me homeless. And while you're at it, why don't you educate me on how you know my mother? Because that's news to me."

I glanced over her shoulder, seeing Ashton coming toward us. I couldn't get a read on him, but as he passed Justin's section, I saw Kelly giving me a discreet thumbs-up.

The woman-child drew back, giving me a more assessing look, but anything she said was cut off because Ashton was in my section. She turned to him. "Ash—what are you doing?!"

Her voice rose up in a screech as he took her arm, a hold just under her elbow, and he gave a slight jerk of his head. "Excuse us." He began to lead her away, like a parent removing a child who was throwing a temper tantrum.

"Ashton! What are you doing?! Do you know who that is?!"

They went a little more distance, past Justin and Kelly, and by then the music drowned her out.

I continued watching them go, because what the *hell* was that about?

"This real?" One of the customers was inspecting my badge, and I grabbed it, put it back around my neck, slipped it inside my shirt.

I ignored that question. "What do you need to drink?"

———

It was after closing, and I was cleaning my bar when Ashton came back.

I straightened, the washrag in my hand. "What was that about?"

His eyes narrowed. "You honestly don't know?"

"No." I was done with this. After tossing my rag into the sink, I moved toward him until I was standing a few feet away. I crossed my arms over my chest. "She called my mother a whore and a slut and said she wants to make us homeless. We're past games right now. What was that about?"

First things first. I wanted to know.

Ashton was going to tell me. I knew it. I was banking on it.

He stared at me, long and hard, and I was aware of the attention we were getting from the other workers because it was not often our owners came down to the floor after we'd closed, or at all. Like I said before, I'd worked here for how long and had had no clue who really owned the bar. That spoke volumes.

"Your mother had an affair with Dominic West. It was before your father died, and no, Trace has no idea, but he will after tonight. He was told just moments ago. *Your* mother was the reason *their* mother killed herself. She found out about the affair." He moved closer. "It's the reason your father stopped working for Trace's."

Jesus.

I was rocked.

I was wheeling.

My mother . . . their mother.

I kept hearing Trace's words earlier today.

The coincidence was too much, but . . . my father had worked for his. I was never told the specifics. I was kept out of it on purpose, my mother saying on more than one occasion that I didn't need to bother with that "stuff." That's what she said. Stuff.

But she had affairs. I knew she did, and so did he. My father.

He was in that world before he died.

It could be true. It could all be true.

"For what it's worth, Dominic is a piece of shit. I'm told your mother is cut from the same cloth. My advice? Stop fighting and just fuck Trace. It's getting old, this whole torture episode the both of you have going on." He drew back, his face firming again. "Remmi won't bother you again, and we took the liberty of moving your car into the secured spot. Your ride is waiting outside when you're done."

I was still reeling from the mother/father thing, but right. Okay. Back to business as usual.

Trace was waiting for me, because I had texted him earlier, agreeing to the ride home.

"Jess."

I drew upright, focusing back on Ashton. He was waiting.

"Yes?"

"I don't care what kind of badge you're carrying. You need to be aware of what I'll do if you hurt him. If you hurt my best friend, I will kill you."

With that said, he smiled, waved, and left.

Right. Okay.

Trace: Are you coming?

CHAPTER FORTY

TRACE

I was in the back lot, waiting.

It'd been thirty minutes.

"Should we go?"

I checked my phone. She'd not responded to my last text, asking if she was coming out. "Let's wait."

We waited another twenty before the back door opened and she came out. She stopped, seeing my vehicle, and put her hands in her pockets. She stared at the door. My windows were tinted, but she was looking right at me, as if she could see me.

God.

She was hurting.

Everything in me wanted to open the door and go to her. I wanted to hold her.

I wanted her to come into the vehicle.

I wanted to give her a ride home. I wanted to give her a ride home every night.

I wanted it all, but it was happening.

She was letting me in, slowly, so slowly, but it was still happening.

Now Remmi—I couldn't think about that. Not yet.

I just wanted Jess.

I was starting to will her to come, and the door opened.

She slid in, like the other night.

She didn't turn to me, just stared straight ahead, and then she closed her eyes.

She slumped forward.

"Jess?"

She jerked back up and twisted to me. "Why aren't you saying anything?"

Holy—women. The whiplash. I had to blink a little bit. "About what?"

"About our parents. My mom! Your mom. Trace . . ." A deep sob choked out. She was frowning, shaking her head. "Is it true? Please, tell me it's not. My mom—God."

I opened my mouth, closed it, and frowned. Then I went with the truth. "I have no idea, but this is what I'm going to say: my mother was sick long before my father had an affair. If he had one with your mother, I wouldn't be surprised. I don't know your mother's stance on fidelity, but my dad didn't have one. Still doesn't. He screws strippers, secretaries, assistants, cooks. Your father worked with mine. I do not know the relationship, but I will after tonight. I was in college when that happened. What I can tell you is that my mother did not kill herself because of your mother."

"Ashton said it. He stated that your mother killed herself because of my mother. He said it like it was fact."

"He was telling you the reason in Remmi's eyes, not the truth."

"How do you know that?"

My lips twitched because how could I explain my best friend to her? "Because he's my best friend. He said it that way to you for two reasons. One, because that's what Remmi thinks, and the second is a dig at you. You're a cop." I put it more simply. "You are the enemy."

"Why are you so calm about this? If this is true, it's huge."

My lips twitched again. "Because I know my dad. I know my mom. I've read files on *your* mom, and I've seen her picture. She's a good-looking woman. It's not out of the realm of possibility that your mom and my dad crossed paths, and I can see why my father would be attracted to your mother. She's a beautiful woman, still is, and I'm rather obsessed with her daughter. You do have some resemblance to your mom."

She groaned. "You're saying you and your dad have similar tastes in women?"

I was trying not to laugh, but this was the only connection I would admit to regarding my father. "You are stunning. Your mother is beautiful. I'm just saying I couldn't fault him for being attracted to your mother, if that was the case. Anything else, no. I have learned long ago to separate myself from my father's transgressions with women, gambling, anything. He's a disappointment as a person and even more so as a father. If my sister wants to put her anger on you, she's mistaken to do that, and she'll be handled, but also, that tells me she's not reached the level of disillusionment that I have with him."

"You're being very . . . forthright about this all."

My lips thinned because this was an easy choice. "He's a father by blood, but that's it. I have more emotion about a trash can than I do about him."

Her eyes were shining, but I didn't think it was from happiness. An unshed emotion was there. I got a glimpse before she turned her head away again.

She murmured, "I should go."

"Stay." I said it quietly.

"Why, Trace?" Her voice broke, hitching on an emotion. "We are literally getting every roadblock thrust in front of us, and where are we? Still here. Still in this vehicle together. We are insane. This is the definition."

Probably. "A ride, Jess. That's it. I would like to give you a ride home, and if you want, I'll bring you back to get your car tomorrow."

"But why?" she whispered, her head bending down.

"I just want to spend time with you. That's all. A ride . . . it's extended time with you in a closed-off shelter from the rest of the world. I get you for this little escape, and I'll take it every fucking day if you'll give it to me."

She turned to me, tears in her eyes, and her lips parted. She blinked, still staring at me, but something cleared in her gaze, and she nodded.

Relief broke free in my chest.

I leaned back in my chair, settling in. "We can go."

The SUV started forward as Jess moved, her arm falling to rest in the seat between us. It grazed mine, and looking down, I saw her hand was half turned toward mine. I glanced up, seeing she was watching me, and as a small smile toyed at her lips, I lifted my hand and took hers.

I held her hand the entire drive to her place.

When we parked, she stared at me long and hard. She took her keys. "Thank you for the ride."

"Could I give you a ride tomorrow to get your car?"

She paused, but before she got out, she nodded.

I would get to hold her hand again.

CHAPTER

FORTY-ONE

JESS

My alarm went off at six. I smacked it and rolled to my back, slightly panting.

A sex dream.

How old was I? All because he held my hand, and the next morning he held my hand when we went to get my car?

What had I been thinking about, agreeing to that?

I knew. I hadn't wanted to be strong for one fucking night.

I'd wanted a ride home, but it wasn't even that. I'd wanted it to be him giving me a ride home. How stupid could I be?

My phone buzzed, and I grabbed it.

Val: Drinks after gun training. You in? Little Micky is transferring. They want to do a send-off the right way.

God, yes. This was perfect. A night with our colleagues.

Me: Fuck. Yes. Where are we drinking?

Val: Bear's Pub.

Oh. Fuck no. That was Bear's bar, and I wasn't saying *fuck no* because it was his place, but, well . . . because it was his place. There'd be conversation done between him and me, and it would center on my mother, and thinking back on Trace's sister's revelation, I was filled up with the need to *not* see or deal with or talk to my mom. She hadn't been blowing up my phone since Saturday, so why would I want to seek more of her out? Still. I groaned as I texted back.

Me: Sounds good. Time?

Val: Who the fuck knows. Whenever everyone finishes their shifts.

Me: Why are you going? You can't drink.

Val: I can smell it. I can pretend. Don't take this shit from me. I need it.

Me: Is Officer Reyo going to be in attendance?

Val: Fuck off. See you at training.

Right. I laughed but then groaned again.

That sex dream was still with me. What was wrong with me? Oh, right. I had horrible, horrible taste in men, but Trace wasn't horrible. He was amazing. What his family did, what he sometimes helped with . . . I needed to stop thinking about it.

I'd need a hard workout this morning.

———

Bear was behind the counter when I walked in.

In a way, he resembled his pub. He was shorter, around five six, but he was built like a literal tank. He kept his head bald and clean, the same way he kept his bar clean. His pub was small, closed in by bricks on the inside and out. He'd kept the old building's charm when he'd done renovations. He was ex-military, and when he'd come back home, bought this place, the word had gotten around. Veterans, cops, firefighters, paramedics, and sometimes hospital staff showed up too.

Bear saw me and gave me a slight chin lift. I returned it but bypassed him for the table I spotted Val already had claimed. We were far in the back, and knowing Val, she would've had a private word with Bear to only bring her nonalcoholic beer. Bear being Bear, he'd probably comp her drinks.

That was just Bear.

"Officer Montell." Val wasn't alone at the table. Brian Wittel was there, and judging from the very *not* subtlety of Val wiggling her eyebrows, this was a date setup.

I slid onto my stool and gave him a nod and small smile back. "Officer Wittel."

I liked Brian. We'd hooked up in the past. He was a good cop, kept himself trim, and he kept his mouth shut. Whenever he was on a scene for one of my guys, I knew I didn't need to worry anything extra would pop off. He was as professional as professional came for us. Plus, he was easy on the eyes. Handsome. He had dark features, and he was good in bed. The past with us had been clean, no messiness. We'd hooked up with the understanding if the other wanted another go, just send a text. No strings. Nothing else. Val knew about the hookup, and I was guessing this was payback for me messing with her about her Officer Young Stud.

I glanced around and didn't see him. "Where's Little Romeo?"

Brian started laughing while Val growled at me. "Shut up. Shut up! Shut up! Okay?"

I frowned. "Sore spot? You guys break up already?"

She hissed under her breath, half rising out of her chair and leaning over the table to me. She pretended to give me a whack on the face. "That's still under wraps." Her eyes darted to Brian. "Except Brian knows, but no one else. Okay? Got it?"

I laughed as Bear showed up at our table, sliding a pint in front of me. "I was figuring Brian knew but wasn't totally sure. Hence the code name Little Romeo."

She gave me a withering glare. "Brian knows because he caught us leaving my apartment building."

Brian laughed. "Perks of living in the same building."

I turned to Bear. "Thank you."

He gave a small nod. "Been a while since you came in, but figured you'd want what you usually drank." Bear knew I'd drink anything he brought over. That was respect for him, but his gaze skirted the table before landing back on me. He gave a slight nod toward the corner and dropped his voice. "A word in private?"

All laughing went by the wayside. I slid off my stool.

"Sure." I shared a look with Val before I followed him to the back corner. He led the way through into his kitchen, and he didn't stop. The cook was in the back, and he raised a knife in the air. "Heya, little Jessie!"

"Hi, Tony. Food smells delicious tonight."

"Always, but especially for you tonight now that I know you're out there."

I grinned back before going into Bear's office.

He stepped back and waited to shut his door.

I moved to the side. He had two windows with the curtains both drawn, a desk, a chair, and a love seat, which was pushed up against the wall. The love seat was covered with files and papers, and Bear didn't sit, so that told me this was going to be fast or uncomfortable.

Either way, I tightened up my resolve and waited, getting prepared for whatever he was going to send my way.

"This about my mom?"

He shook his head, a sad look flashing for a moment. Disappointment was next, and that was a gut punch. Bear nodded and then shook his head. "Yes and no. She was a mess when I went over there."

I shifted back on my feet. "What kind of a mess?"

"She was passed out when I got in, but she woke when I was leaving. She started in, swearing at you, swearing at me until she realized who I was. She stopped with me, but not you. The things she said, they alarmed me, Jessie."

I lined my insides with steel, not letting anything in.

He said, shaking his head, "It's not right, Jess. Not what she said, not what I just saw you do. You walled yourself off, and I'm getting that it's a coping mechanism. I know enough psych to know the reason for that, but it ain't right."

"I don't know what you expect me to do about it? You've been around enough. You know how she feels about me. I check on her, but I try and stay away as much as I can. She's a drunk. Sometimes she's worse than other times."

"I'm not saying you should do more."

He was talking gentle with me. I could feel his pity, and I hated that.

He added, a gruff drop in his voice, "I'm saying maybe you should step back completely. Your mama, things in the past shaped how she is today. It ain't your fault. No one thinks that, even her, but she's angry. It's turning her bitter and hard. She'll get worse." He looked away, and it was then I clued in that he was nervous for this talk. His Adam's apple bobbed up and down once before he looked back to me. "I had a talk with Leo one night. He said he's worried about you. Can feel something's going on."

I gritted my teeth. "He say my work performance is slipping?"

"No. Your work is up to usual standards, which is high. You've always been a good worker. That ain't the issue, but we get feelings in this business. You know it. I got 'em when I was overseas, but so does Leo. Something's off with you. We think it's time you step back from checking in on your ma. Totally back off. Let us step in. We'll take over."

They thought it was my mom bothering me.

A wave of relief and guilt hit me all at the same time.

"What are you proposing?" My voice cracked.

"Stop worrying about her. Leo and me, we'll check in on her every day. I ain't married, and neither is he. We're old bachelors, know this is how it'll be for us for the rest of our life. We got some extra time carved in our daily. He and I both care about her. I been taking care of your mama since we were in sixth grade. This ain't no different, but you'll just know I'm watching over her. You step back. Stop worrying about her, and do your thing. We got her. We'll have your back on this."

The thought of not worrying about her? Because she weighed on me. Every day. I gave up a long time ago trying to get her to stay sober, but I got her to stop going out. She drank at home. She was a danger *only* to herself that way, but even in that way, there was only so much I could do.

She hated me, blamed me for everything wrong in her life.

Maybe it was for the best.

I jerked my head in a stiff nod. "Fine."

His eyes closed, and his shoulders slumped down. "We'll let you know when we need you with her, but it'll be a while. We're going to try and work on her, get her into a sober house or something. We're not just going to check on her—we're going to try and help her."

Right. Because that's not what I'd been doing. They'd do better.

That burned. But, fuck.

I was blinking back stupid annoying tears, and my throat was rubbing up against a knife in there, but it was what it was.

They'd help her. They'd do what I never could.

My voice was rough when I grated out, "Thank you, Bear. I appreciate it."

"She—"

I was gone before I could hear any more. I needed to leave.

I raised a hand as I sailed through the kitchen. "Great night, Tony!"

He said something in return, a jovial greeting, but I didn't hear. There was a pounding in my ears as I went back to the main area and found my table. I'd left my coat there.

Val was asking me something, but I couldn't hear her either.

There was a wall of emotion stuck between me and everyone else, and their voices were all muted.

I said something. Again, no clue what it was, but I made sure to scan all of their faces. The guys who didn't know me gave a grin and nod my way. Only Val wasn't buying it. And Brian. His gaze was clear, watching me intently, and his eyebrows dipped just slightly together.

I gave a wave, put down some cash for my share, and started to leave.

I was out of the door, halfway through the parking lot, before I realized someone had followed me.

"Jess—hey! Jess." A hand touched my arm, and I whirled around, my arm up to block them, when I saw it was Brian.

He put his hands up in surrender, stepping back, but he zipped up his jacket. Stuffing his hands in his pockets, he raised his chin up to me. "What's going on with you?"

I looked past him to the door. "Val coming after me too?"

He frowned but shook his head. "She saw I was coming, so she stayed. What'd Bear want? What's going on?"

I shifted on my feet, feeling a restlessness inside of me.

Maybe I should tell him. Brian was a good guy, but dammit. There was a distant understanding between us, and that was the key word. Distant.

No. I couldn't share. That'd be wrong. He and I didn't do emotional shit like that, but I was giving him a different sort of eyeing now. The one-night stand I'd been intending to do but had been too chicken to follow through with. Brian. I could use him for that.

I started to reach for him before I realized I'd made my decision.

I took hold of his jacket, pulling him to me, when his head jerked to the side. He didn't move except for his hand snaking out and grabbing hold of mine, now on his jacket. He just held me there, giving me that intense stare, and then he moved in a flash.

His body hit mine, and his lips were on mine, and I was being pushed back against the truck behind us.

Yes. Yes. Yes!

Heat surged up in me, but then no. No. No.

A foreign and alien feeling came over me.

I knew his lips. My body started to respond to them, but another rejection surged up in me.

This wasn't the mouth I wanted on mine, the body against mine.

I tried kissing him harder, forcing it. He responded by gripping the back of my head, his mouth opening over mine, and his tongue slipped in.

No!

I moved him back, my mouth hanging open, because what had I just done? Why? Why not him?

He was a better fit for me.

I could keep going with this life how I wanted with him.

But my body was shaking, and a coldness invaded me.

"What's wrong?" He was panting a little bit. "I thought that's what you wanted."

Yes, but not him.

I felt hollow once again, and I was starting to think I'd always be hollow.

"It was, but . . . I'm a mess right now. I gotta go home." I waved a hand toward him. "Before I do something I'll regret."

He flinched before stepping back again. "Didn't think we were like that, but okay. I can take a hint." He began walking back to the bar. "Take care of yourself, Jess."

I started after him. "Brian—"

He ignored me, the door slamming shut behind him.

Goddamn. I was making a mess of everything around me.

My phone buzzed then.

Trace: Where are you?

I closed my eyes, because just a text had my body warming all the way back up. Him. It was him for me, and my body had chosen, and I was so screwed.

But I responded, giving in once again.

I was sliding toward those gates of hell.

I was starting to welcome the heat of being wrong.

Me: Heading to my place now.

CHAPTER

FORTY-TWO

TRACE

Me: Are you sleeping?

My phone buzzed when the elevators opened for my floor.

Jess: No.

Me: Where exactly are you?

Jess: In bed, just not asleep.

I went to the bar, poured a whiskey, and took it with me to the bathroom. After turning the shower on, I stepped back and began taking my clothes off.

Me: I want you naked.

I began stroking myself, waiting for her, envisioning her lying there, considering it.

Jess: I can't do this with you.

Me: Take your clothes off and wet your lips, baby. Now.

Jess: These texts could be evidence.

Me: I'm hard already and I'm getting harder. Do it. Now.

Head back, eyes closed, I kept going, imagining her right now, seeing her sliding her pants down, her underwear next.

Jess: I'm naked.

Me: Are you under your covers?

Jess: You want me to be?

Me: No. I want the open air to touch you. Suck on your fingers, baby. Put one inside of you.

Jess: I have one in me.

Me: Play with yourself. Push in, move it around. Make some room, and then put a second finger in you.

Me: Are you doing it? Tell me.

Jess: I am. I'm fucking myself with them.

Me: Keep going.

Me: Harder.

Me: Push all the way in, as far as you can. Arch your back. Lift your hips up for better access. Do it for me.

Jess: I am. It feels so good.

Me: Keep going. Harder now. A little rougher.

My hand was a fucking vacuum over my dick. Holy fuck. I was seeing everything she was doing, but it was at my commands. She was following my orders.

Jess: I'm feeling weird doing this.

Me: Don't. It's you and me. You keep going or I'm driving over and doing it myself.

I groaned as I kept pace with her. My head was down, my heart was racing. Jesus. The thought of her touching herself, thinking of me as she did that, was going to make me blow early.

I had to pause, squeezing harder to hold off.

The urge to go over there and do what I threatened was raging inside of me. Why couldn't I drive over there? Why couldn't I lay claim to her body all over again? She'd let me. One touch and she folded, but it was the same for me. One thought of her and I wanted to brand her from the inside out so she only felt me for the rest of her life.

Jess: I'm going to come. It's coming.

Me: One second. Let me catch up. I want to go when you go. Can you do that for me?

Jess: I'm waiting. Hurry up!

I grinned, chuckling.

Me: One more stroke, baby. For me.

Jess: Okay. Going . . .

Me: Are you coming?

Jess: Yes!

Two more jerks of my own and I was blowing. I let it out, finishing with a few more strokes to get everything, and then I leaned back against the counter.

Me: Did you come?

Jess: Yes. You?

Me: I did. How are you feeling now?

Jess: Weird.

I grinned.

Me: Seems to be the theme tonight?

Jess: Just hard doing this with you but without you. And to type one handed. I tried kissing someone tonight, forcing you out of my mind.

I hit dial, and she picked up a second later, breathless. "Hello?"

"You did what?" I growled.

"It didn't work." She sounded drowsy and sad at the same time. "He wasn't you. You've ruined me for men. You don't get it."

I quieted. "What don't I get?"

"You and me, if we do this . . . everything changes for me. Everything."

Yeah. I was getting that. "The alternative is to go mad because that's where I'm at, Jess. Are you?"

She didn't answer.

I didn't push her, but it felt right to be standing bare-ass naked in my bathroom, the shower on and waiting for me, listening to her breathe through my phone. I was in no hurry to put an end to this.

"I choose you, and I'll lose everything else."

"It doesn't have to be like that."

"It does, and you know it. It is how it is, so the question should actually be for you: Are *you* okay knowing what it'll cost *me* to have *you?*"

She hung up after, and it took me a long time before I pulled the phone away from my ear.

A long time.

CHAPTER

FORTY-THREE

JESS

Weird things happened over the next week.

One, Trace stayed away from me. No contact. No texts. No calls. Anthony made a point to share that "he" wasn't in the building and wouldn't be during my shifts. The other thing: my parolees were perfect. They were almost gentlemen to me. The women weren't. They still wanted to claw my eyeballs out, but the men: one accidentally shut his door in my face and was so apologetic afterward that I'd had enough.

I shoved into his apartment, the door banging shut behind me.

"Hey!"

I yelled through the door, "Give me one second, Officer Hartman!"

"What?"

"One second. Please."

I could hear her grumbling. "Really fucking weird, but okay. One second. That's all."

"Uh, Officer Montell, I don't want any trouble." He was backing up, his hands in the air. He was a giant of a man, easily outweighing me by two hundred pounds, and he was pure muscle. And his attitude was a total changer because he'd recently come out of prison, and he'd not been one to take advantage of the many resources that were available to him on the inside. Sometimes that was an indicator how cooperative they'd be with us on the outside. This guy did nothing and had had an attitude every time I'd met with him since.

"What the fuck gives? You are my seventh parolee with a magical attitude change about me? What? Christmas Past come to visit you all? I want to know what's going on and why."

He took me in and frowned. His whole face twisted up in confusion before he dropped his hands. "You serious? You don't know?"

"No. You're going to fill me in."

His eyes bulged out, and he was starting to look for an exit route. "Now!"

He jumped at my bark. "Word's out on you. You're protected."

I lowered my head, my eyes trained steadily on him. "What does that mean?"

"West Mafia. They put it out there not to touch you. You're considered theirs."

"Theirs? Explain that."

His head inclined back, and he was giving me a once-over but not in a sexual way, in a way suggesting he wasn't recognizing who was standing in front of him. "What are you talking about? You know what that means. It means you're in their pocket, or you're fucking one of them." He took a step to the side, eyeing his own patio door. "Gotta admit, I never saw that coming from someone like you. Thought you were all straight and narrow, that sort of shit."

I was going to murder Trace.

"I am," I snarled. "I don't know why the fuck this order is out, but it's wrong."

He lowered his arms, his head still inclined all the way back. "Wait. You're saying they're doing this to jam you up?" He relaxed and whistled under his breath. "Can't believe they be doing that to you. You're known as a tough bitch. I was warned about you but figured I'm likely to still do what I'm likely to do. Though, this new order came through, and the West Mafia are tight with the Waldens, and I don't want any of that trouble. You feel me?"

I was seeing red. I was feeling red.

I was *only literally red.*

Taking out my set, I gestured to his bathroom. "You missed your UA. We're doing it now."

"What? Here?!" His voice went up a notch.

"Here, and get over your shit because I'm not letting you fuck this up. Now, start envisioning you pissing waterfalls while I bring my partner in here to help witness this, and you ain't going to say shit about what you just told me. You put the word out that the order is wrong on me."

"I ain't spreading nothing on you regarding the Wests. That's your battle."

I growled, but pointed toward his bathroom. "Go."

He did as I let Val in, and after we collected his UA, she asked once we left his building, "You going to fill me in on what that was about?"

"Nope. Better you don't know."

"Wait." We'd gotten to my car, and she stopped me from opening the door. She lowered her voice. "I've noticed what's going on too. You know it'd be easy for me to ask around, find out for myself. It's better if you tell me."

She was right, but dammit, I couldn't bring myself to say the words. Once I did, she'd know. Awareness would be raised, and she'd start asking other questions.

"It's better if I know. You know that. I can help keep a lid on it, whatever it is. If Travis finds out? You know what he'll do."

"He won't find out because trust me, the parolees don't want to talk about it themselves."

"That makes it even more urgent you fill me in. I'm your partner. Come on, Jess."

A rage and a helpless feeling were being ripped up through my feet at a breakneck speed. I would regret this. I knew it, but he'd done this to me.

"The West Mafia has put out a decree. I'm protected."

She drew in a sharp breath.

"By them."

"You serious?" she hissed, her head falling all the way to the side.

"Yes."

"Why would they do that? Wait. Your dad used to be connected to them back in the day. This from back then or recent?"

I gave her a hard look, not wanting to lie any more than I had. "I intend to find out."

"Okay. What do you want from me?"

"Just have my back if you hear anything about me."

"I can do that." She looked at the car. "You're going to find out right now, aren't you?"

"I'm going to start. You should not be with me when I do this."

"You don't want backup?"

"One of us getting dirtied up is enough. I don't want this shit to spread to you."

She gave a nod and stepped back, taking the sealed UA from me. "Hey, Jess."

I opened the door, looking back at her before getting inside.

Her gaze was hard on me. "Just be smart, whatever you're going to do."

Smart? I'd try. Anything else, I couldn't promise.

I indicated the UA. "Can you turn that in for me?"

"I will. I'll call for a ride."

"You sure?"

"I'm sure. Go handle this shit before it spreads any more."

"Thank you, Val."

Another sober nod from her. "Just remember what I said. Be smart."

She was right. When I murdered Trace, I'd have to be *very smart* about where I hid his body.

CHAPTER

FORTY-FOUR

TRACE

"Mr. West, an Officer Montell is here to see you. She's saying she doesn't need an appointment."

I frowned, not expecting this greeting when my phone had rung from the building's front desk.

"Let her up."

"Will do, Mr. West."

I exited out of the portfolios that I'd been studying when the elevator pinged her arrival. The front desk staff would've notified my assistant, who indicated my office for Jess, as she saw me through the glass walls we had in this building. Normally I didn't mind being surrounded by glass walls. It'd been a trendy thing when they'd first designed this place. Everyone wanted to see what everyone else was doing. It cut down on any stupid shady shit, too, which I always thought was the real reason behind the design. Everyone had coverings for their computers, so privacy was still maintained, but getting the warning burn from Jess's glare had me cursing the see-through walls right now.

Still, when she came inside and once that door shut behind her, I hit a button, and we were soundproofed now. The windows clouded over. We were still visible, but our facial expressions would be blurred.

She came in, stopping just inside so almost the entire room was between us. Her hand was on her hip, where I knew she kept her weapon.

I stood up from my desk. "What's going on?"

"You put out an order of protection on me? With the West Mafia stamp of approval?"

What?!

That would condemn her. It was the exact opposite of what I wanted for her. "I didn't, Jess."

"You did!" She started for me but slammed on her brakes. Her body ricocheted back from the force. "Do you have any idea what that does for me?"

"Yes. I do! I would *never* do that to you. Not that I wouldn't want to, but I wouldn't. Jess." This was the worst-case scenario. I'd done so much to keep my mind off of her. "What you said to me, the last time we talked, it's true. I wouldn't want that for you. I wouldn't want to do that to you. I've been staying away."

"Then who the fuck put the order out on me? I look like—"

"I know what you look like. I *know*. I would never do that to you."

Her eyes were sparking fire, and every inch of her body was rigid. She was ready to fight.

I brought out a burner phone and dialed Ashton's number, the phone reserved exactly for these conversations. When he answered, I put him on speaker. "Just so you know, you're on speakerphone. I'm in my office with Jess."

He was quiet. "Well. Didn't expect *this* call, though maybe I should've, considering you're using one of these phones. What can I do for you both?"

"Jess just informed me that an order of protection was put on her, on behalf of the West family."

He started laughing, which turned into a coughing fit as he tried to settle himself. "Sorry. I—just—what the fuck?!"

I relaxed at hearing that. He hadn't done it on my behalf, and I sat down, lounging back in my chair. "Who would've done this, Ashton?"

He cursed. "You're asking me? It's your family."

I cast the phone a look. "You know exactly why I'm asking you. Who do you think did this?"

Jess was still rigid, her head back and her eyes closed. Her chest was barely moving, and her hands were digging into her hips, but I noted that her right hand was not by her weapon anymore.

"I honestly don't know, but . . . can you take me off speaker?"

Jess's eyes opened. She had a guarded expression over her face, but she didn't object as I took my phone and took him off speaker.

Standing, I went to the window, my phone to my ear. My back was to Jess. "What are you thinking?"

"You did that so she could hear my reaction, right? Make sure she believed it wasn't you?"

"Yeah."

He exhaled over the phone. "Don't fucking do that again."

"I won't, but who are you thinking did this? You know what this means for her."

"Yeah. She's marked on the streets. No wonder she showed up at your office."

"Ashton," I growled. He had a better feel for the streets than I did. That was his area of expertise. "Who did this?"

"Only someone considered family could've sent this out. Myself, since I speak for your family on your behalf a lot or . . . your uncle or your father. The question would be, Why would either of them do this? Your father doesn't know about her, and your uncle wouldn't want to push you like this. He likes that you might have a relationship with her. He wanted to use it earlier before you removed her blood from the equation."

"That wouldn't make sense. He'd use it for later, not now."

"Exactly."

Which pointed at one other member of the family, one who *would* want to hurt Jess.

"Trace." Guessing by how low Ashton's voice just got, I was guessing he was there too.

"You're thinking who I'm thinking?"

He swore, still low. "I thought I had her handled. I took her back to Vegas. She was supposed to stay put."

"She can make phone calls from Vegas."

"I know, but—" More curses from him. "This means that she got someone asking questions about Jess. That is not good for you, brother."

"I'm aware." Every cell in my body was on alert. My sister in my business was most definitely not good. She was erratic and unpredictable, and she had no idea who she was going to blow up.

"I'll put out the word that Jess Montell is not ours. It was the wrong call, but ears are pricked, and eyes will start watching."

Which meant it was incredibly stupid for Jess to be remaining in my employ, and in this office itself. Not unless things were going to drastically take a turn. I'd seen her face when she'd barged in here. This was her worst nightmare.

"I'm fully aware of that too." I turned, starting to include her when I said, "Your employment will—"

I stopped because she wasn't there.

The door was open. The elevator door was just sliding shut.

Jess was gone.

"Ashton."

"Yeah?"

I had a distinctly bad feeling starting in me. "Find my sister."

"To warn her off?"

"No." I was moving because I knew what Jess was going to do. She'd been pushed too far this time. She had one thing left in her life, and that was her career. She was going to snap. "To protect her. From Jess."

"Oh, shit. Will do."

We hung up, and I grabbed everything. "If I have any meetings today, cancel them. Cancel them for the week." I breezed past my assistant, heading for my private elevator. Once I got to the parking floor, Pajn had a finger to his ear. He saw me coming and straightened up. "Got the call you were heading out. What's going on, boss?"

"Call my sister."

He started to reach for his phone but stopped. A funny look on his face. "Boss?"

"Your phone. I'm guessing she won't pick up for me or Ashton, but she will for one of you two. She'll be too curious not to answer."

The gravity of the situation hit him, and he brought up my sister on his contacts, hit dial, and handed me the phone. After one ring, she picked up.

"Pajn? Is Trace okay?"

"No," I ground out into the phone, indicating for Pajn to get behind the wheel. I took the phone to the back seat and lowered the privacy divider. Demetri was in the passenger seat, looking between both of us but keeping quiet. "Where the fuck are you, Remmi?"

She didn't answer right away, but then her voice was shaking when she did. "You sound angry at me, Trace. Why are you angry? I don't like when you're mad at me."

"Then you completely blew that out of the water because I'm livid with you. Where the fuck are you? You're supposed to be back in Vegas. I'm guessing you're not there."

I couldn't get Jess's face out of my mind, how pale she'd been coming into my office.

How she left without a word to me.

"You're scaring me, T."

"You should be scared. You fucked with the wrong cop."

She inhaled sharply. "How do you know about that?" Her voice went shrill. "And why do you care about her?!"

Jesus Christ. It *was* her.

I pulled out my burner, sending a text to Ashton.

Me: It was her.

He replied back right away.

Ashton: Word is out to correct what Remmi did. My contacts say they'll spread it out, but some damage is done. Will have to spin this somehow to protect Jess. You want me to handle your sister?

Me: No. I got her.

Ashton: Don't murder your own blood.

I pointedly did not respond to that one, barking into the phone, "Tell me where the fuck you are! Now, Remmi!"

She cried out, half screaming, "Okay, okay! I'm at your club."

"You're where?"

"At Katya. I'm here to threaten her. Doesn't she work tonight?"

It was the following Tuesday, but that meant Remmi was guessing, and it also meant that Anthony was not being cooperative with her. "Is Anthony there?"

"He just went into the hallway to take a call. I think it was Ashton."

"You stay put."

Her voice came out trembling. "Why am I scared right now? She's a cop. She shouldn't be working here anyways. What did I do wrong here?"

"Stay put, shut up, and don't do anything stupid. You got me?"

"Yeah." She was sobbing, her voice hiccuping. "Trace, what did I do wrong, though? I don't know what I did wrong."

I swallowed a curse because fuck me for not making sure she'd been handled the right way before. Switching to my burner, I dialed Ashton.

He answered after the first ring. "She's at Katya."

"I just got off the phone with her. What did you tell her when she saw Jess at Katya the first time?"

"I drove her to the airport, put her on a plane for Vegas, and told her to forget that woman ever existed. I told her not to mess with Jess, and if she did, she'd be messing with family matters."

"She say anything back? You used Jess's name?"

"I didn't use Jess's name. That'd be throwing gasoline on the fire, and no, Remmi got quiet. She started crying, but she got on the plane. I *watched* her get on the plane, and I watched the plane take off."

"Which meant she flew to Vegas, pissed and stewing, and probably turned around and got on a plane right back here."

"Yeah," he ground out. "I thought I handled it. Remmi is—"

"She's my sister. I should've handled her, not you."

"We handle each other's families for the other all the time. Sometimes Remmi listens to me when she won't hear you. We both know that. Your sister is just unpredictable. Who could've guessed she'd do something this extreme?"

"Find my father. Her going after Jess in the first place is suspect. If she'd been stewing about Jess's mother since our mother died, we would've heard about it."

"What are you thinking?"

"I'm thinking someone's putting shit in her head, someone who has reason to be angry at me."

"That fucker, if he did that."

"We handed him over to Uncle Steph. We cleaned up after him. I'm guessing he wasn't too appreciative of how we handled his situation."

"He should've been. That prick is too entitled. If you're right and he did this, what the fuck are you going to do? Because he's fucking with family business, and your family business is my family business. I can't predict what Stephano will do, but I can tell you how my uncles will handle him. Especially since they've been treating him with kid gloves over the years because of you and me."

My dad was dead if he'd plotted to hurt us, found out about Jess, and gone from there. That meant finding Remmi. Manipulating her, filling her head with whatever fucking lies he'd filled her head with, and now this was the end result. Jess was put on blast with her career.

He did all that, and that meant he knew about me and Jess.

My tone went real low. "He did this, I'll kill him myself."

I didn't care what the consequences were.

CHAPTER

FORTY-FIVE

JESS

"Val." I called her as soon as I was on the elevator, as soon as I'd heard who was behind it. I was beyond the point of controlling myself. This little woman-child, blowing up my entire life? Goddamn their fucking family genes. I was done.

"Hey." She sounded guarded. "Where are you?"

"Remmi West. That's who put out the order."

"What?" She laughed. "The Mafia princess. Doesn't she reside in Vegas half the time? Why would she do that to you? She's gotta know how that makes you look."

"She knows. She's got some crazy idea that our parents had an affair and that's why her mom took her own life."

"Whoa."

The elevator doors opened, and I stepped out, ignoring anyone in my path and heading right for my state car. "Exactly."

"What are you going to do?"

"I need to know where she is." I was in the car and hit the speaker volume so it switched to the car phone.

"You want me to find her?"

"I want to find her before anyone finds her."

"What are you going to do?"

I expelled a ragged breath, pulling into traffic. "I have no idea right now. Arrest her?"

"She'll deny everything. And for what?"

"Putting my life in danger? Falsifying a report?"

She laughed, but it was cut off shortly. "I can't tell if you're being serious, but she did the order on the streets. Nothing's official. And no one will testify against a West. You know that. Let's run by option B."

"I'm going to kick her ass."

"I can stand behind that one."

I would've laughed if I wasn't so serious. "Val, I mean it. I want to find her first. Can you ask your cousin? He works in the organized crime unit."

"And when he asks me why?"

"I'm betting that he'll know exactly the reason when you ask, but when you have that conversation, can you please hold off judgment before hearing me out?"

There was a moment of silence before she asked, her tone dropping as she did. "Why are you asking for that now?"

"Because when you ask him, he's going to turn the tables and ask what my relationship with Trace West is."

"And why would he ask that?" Her pitch went up a notch.

"Because he's an itch that I've not been able to fully scratch and get him out from under my skin."

"Oh, no. *Jess.*"

I hit my turn signal and headed for the interstate. "You know I work at Katya on two of my nights off."

"Yeah, for extra cash. What does that have to do with Trace West?"

"He's one of the owners."

She sucked in a harsh breath. "Who's the other owner?"

"Ashton Walden."

"Are you kidding me?! Walden? You know that family owns cops, like a lot of them."

"I know. If it means anything, I didn't know who the owners were until a couple months ago."

"You've been there for three years. How did you not know?"

"Because the owners came up as a standard LLC."

"That place has always been a little shady."

"What nightclub isn't?"

"Yeah. That's true." She groaned. "I'm going to bypass the awkward conversation with my cousin because knowing him, he'll just wait and corner me at our next family holiday anyways. He likes the live-and-in-person interrogation. I'm texting him."

"You're going to send off his radar."

"You're not saying anything we don't already know. You don't have to narrate the stupidity of this to me, but I'm still doing it. You're going to be my daughter's godmother one day."

I almost hit the brakes, almost. "You're keeping her? And *her*?"

"I don't know if it's a her or him, but I'm envisioning a her, and you knew I was keeping her the day I missed work and sent Reyo instead."

I did. I knew my partner. "You'll make a great mother."

"Yeah, yeah." We both heard her phone beep, and she let out a sigh. "She's in Katya right now, and apparently she's been on the phone with a burner number they're trying to trace fast. So my guess is that big brother Trace found her. You're off to the races to get her first."

I had what I needed, and I hit the turn signal because this was my exit. "Thank you, Val."

"Hey."

"Yeah?"

"You rough her up, how will they retaliate?"

"You're asking the wrong question. They should be hoping that I *only* rough her up."

She groaned again. "Just be safe."

She'd been telling me earlier to be smart. My partner knew me, knew we were long past that.

"I'll try." I disconnected the call and sped up because I *did* know one thing.

I was getting to Remmi West first.

CHAPTER

FORTY-SIX

TRACE

Anthony was in a frenzy. He met me at Katya's front door, looking eighty instead of his near forty years. The guards were with him. Something was already in the works.

"She's a good person. She's a great bartender, and I consider her a friend."

I stopped in my tracks. "What are you talking about?"

He didn't answer, just stepped aside.

Ashton was coming out of a door. "Trace. Back here."

That didn't sound good, and Anthony's jaw was firm as he looked away, pointedly walking out of the room. Ashton didn't look much different, but he nodded toward the door. "She beat you here."

I cursed. "When did you get here?"

"Ten minutes after she did. We need to ask how she found Remmi so fast, because she shouldn't have."

I sailed past him but gave him a look. "Are you joking? With her resources?"

He flicked his eyes up to the ceiling, raking a hand over his head. "Then we're all sorts of fucked if she called in favors."

"We're way beyond that."

I shoved through the door; it led to another back section and another set of closed doors. Some of Ashton's men were trying to get in, which said a lot because Ashton didn't usually bring his guys. He preferred to travel alone or use my guards, but he'd kept all Katya staff out of this section. That was smart.

Tim turned around, seeing us coming. "She's barred the door, and we're hearing hits going on. We don't know what she's doing in there."

Jesus. This had gone from bad to worse, and now it was epically worse. If my sister was harmed, I wasn't sure what I would do. Remmi was blood. Jess . . .

"Move aside, guys. Let him try."

I pounded on the door. "Let me in, Jess."

Nothing.

Thumps. Or what could be *slapping* sounded.

But there was nothing else. No cries. No screams. No yelling.

Something wasn't right here.

"You have feeds in there?"

"No." But Ashton sidled up next to me, an iPad in hand, and he hit a button. "But watch that."

It was the security feeds showing Jess walking inside. She was moving calmly but with purpose, and when she hit the hallway leading to Anthony's office, Remmi stepped out. She saw Jess and froze, and suddenly Jess rushed her. She grabbed her, twisted her arm behind her, placed another hand on the back of Remmi's shoulders, and she marched her right through the next set of doors.

The feed switched to the room where we were in, showing no one in the vicinity as Jess guided Remmi through the doors that were now barricaded. No one put up a fight, even Remmi. It was all done with utmost professional efficiency.

"Rewind it."

Ashton did, and I studied my sister's face, noting how she just looked surprised. She wasn't crying or wincing from pain. Just shocked.

That eased some of my concern.

Ashton had been rewatching with me. "She's good. No one even knew they were in there until I showed up looking for her."

"There's feeds from the back of that room?"

"Back of that room goes nowhere . . ." He stopped talking as a strange look came over him. "But it leads to a basement that we've never utilized."

"Let me guess. There's no feeds down there either."

He grunted. "I can't believe we never thought of that."

"But I *can* believe she did. Also, why the fuck do we have a basement that we don't use?"

He shrugged. "It's New York. It's probably bricked up from the Prohibition days."

We shared a look because *why* weren't we using that again? "I highly doubt she's interrogating or whatever she's doing to her in the basement. If they're down there, there's an exit."

"You're talking like she's taking your sister hostage. This is Jess Montell. We know her day job. She's going to do whatever she needs to do, and then she'll cut her losses. She won't prolong this."

Which alarmed me even more. I looked around, seeing an exit door. "Come on."

"Where are you going?"

"Have your guys blow that door down." I had my phone out, sending off a text to tell Demetri and Pajn to come in and block the other set of doors so no staff could get in. This was the definition of where we didn't want our Mafia business to cross over into our non-Mafia business. Any staff saw anything, and that would happen. I wasn't including Anthony because he took off when we showed up. He knew the deal.

As soon as that text was sent and it buzzed back that they had gotten it, I was through the exit door.

Ashton was right behind me, stepping out into the side alley where some of the staff kept their vehicles, those who did drive to work.

"What are we doing?"

I was looking around. "I don't know, but I can't stay in there. I can't do nothing."

Ashton grunted, moving to walk beside me as we went to the back of the building. "You're looking for an entrance to our own basement, the one we didn't know we had."

"Exactly." Though I hadn't formulated it into an actual thought, but yes. That's what I was doing. Or what we were doing.

The back of our building ended with the side exit door where we'd stepped out, but there was another parking area in the rear. The farthest door leading here was one that most of the staff took, from the main hallway. I had waited here on the night I'd given Jess a ride home. She'd used this door, but there had to be another entrance. Why go into that room?

"Hey." Ashton had rounded to the other side of our alley, on the complete opposite side of our building. He stood just above a set of small storm doors. They looked like they were leading into the other building, not ours. He indicated them. "I've looked at all the blueprints for our neighbors, and these weren't on them. I just never looked hard enough."

I swore. "You're honestly suggesting we should try and open them and go down into a potential basement that we have no idea actually leads to Katya?"

His head went back, and he started to lift his arms. "Well, when you put it like that—"

"We're doing it."

I said that at the same time he finished with, "—hell yes."

We shared a grin, but then reality hit me. "What the fuck are we doing?"

He jumped down, bracing on either side of the doors, and flashed me a grin, his entire face lit up way too much for what we were about to do. "We're exploring. Call us the New York Goonies." He bent down, took hold of one of the doors, and hoisted it up.

It wouldn't go, but there was a little opening.

I dropped down, braced myself, and grabbed the other door. Together, we lifted them, seeing they both had to open at the same time.

After that, total and creepy darkness.

"I can literally hear the rats scampering."

"Let's just hope there's no New York alligators we don't know about."

"You know people probably have snakes as pets, snakes that got away through their toilets."

I suppressed a shudder. "You could be a serial killer. You're that kind of sick and disturbing."

He barked out a laugh but pulled out a flashlight and handed it over to me. "Here."

"You just keep these on you? For days when you might have to explore a creepy basement?"

Another flash of a grin as he pulled out a second flashlight and put it in his mouth, then reached for something else. It was his gun, and he switched his hands, positioning the flashlight over the gun so he was holding both together. He dropped his voice. "I have flashlights on me because you never know what the hell we have to do for our families. Also, you lead."

"Always gotta be prepared, huh." But I was stalling, and I knew it was time.

I aimed my flashlight down, seeing it was a set of crude carved-out stairs that led down into this tunnel/basement.

I suppressed a shiver and started down.

It didn't occur to me until Ashton was fully behind me that he should've been the one going ahead. He had the gun.

I told him, "You better have that thing aimed down."

"Of course, in case I need to kill any New York alligators."

"Dumbass."

"Uh, I'm the smart one. I got you to lead the way."

That was true. *I* was the dumbass.

CHAPTER

FORTY-SEVEN

JESS

"Where are we?"

"We're in a basement room underneath your brother's nightclub."

Remmi shivered, looking around her. Not that I blamed her. The room had all sorts of ick factor to it, but I'd found it a year ago when I'd been looking for lost inventory, hoping to come upon a surprise pile. I found the door that led down here and got adventurous one day, actually exploring. It was obvious no one from the club knew about it. The spiderwebs had been on another plane, they were that big.

But for all intents and purposes, I summarized so she wouldn't freak out. "We're directly beneath Anthony's office."

"Oh." Her eyes got big, but they'd been big since I'd shown up.

I barricaded the one set of doors and turned on a fan, hoping it would stall anyone coming through.

"Are you going to hurt me?"

I squatted not far from her but definitely out of range of touching. Or lunging. I wasn't totally trusting myself. "Do I need to?"

"This is a criminal offense, you know. You're holding me against my will."

I kept quiet on that front but did say, "This coming from the girl who put it out among the criminals that I was 'protected' by the West family Mafia? You kidding me? Orders of protection in the criminal world have a whole lot different definition than in the justice system."

"Not really, not if you think about it. It's the same thing—stay away—but it's against everyone except the person. You know? The other in the justice system is a restraining order against one person, not everyone. The one I did makes more sense, and a lot more effective too."

She was talking freely and without fear. And that pissed me off. I felt like reminding her: "I have a gun, and we both know you won't use the justice system against me, so instead of talking about that, why don't you explain to me who put it in your head that my mother was the reason for your mother's suicide?"

She stiffened, hunched down in a chair. "Don't talk about my mother."

"Your mother's the reason we're here, because news flash, I had no idea your pops and my mom hooked up. I have a feeling I might've known that if that had happened, you know, since I'm a PO and all."

It was dark in the room—my flashlight was the only light—but I could still see her glaring my way.

"I didn't know until recently. My dad told me, and I think he's a better source than you."

I didn't like hearing that, because . . . was it true?

I was still squatting but moved a little closer to her. "He told you recently?"

"Yeah. Why?" she snapped at me. "This is what we're doing down here? You're just going to interrogate me? I thought you were going to beat me up or something."

I admitted, "I'm still thinking about it."

She gasped.

"Haven't made up my mind."

She began whimpering just slightly, and I didn't buy it, but she was putting in good effort. "My father will kill you for this."

"Doubtful." I stood up because I needed to pace. I needed to think. "I have a feeling if your dad could get my death sanctioned, he wouldn't have had to resort to filling his daughter's head with decades-old bullshit."

"Then my brother," she clipped out.

"I doubt that too. For doing something as reckless as you did, you weren't smart about it. You didn't suss out the real relationships going on. If you had, you might've stopped to wonder why Ashton took you away and didn't fire me. Did you think about that? Did you ask yourself why your father was bringing up your mother's suicide to you recently? I might be going out on a limb, but I don't think a family suicide is fodder for normal conversation."

She sniffled, adjusting on her seat. "I have no idea what 'fodder' means."

"The context is that it's not an everyday fucking conversation. You talk to your dad often?"

She didn't answer.

I didn't expect her to, because that didn't fit the profile. I wasn't a profiler, but I had enough psychology under my belt to know the reputation of her father wasn't one of a great father. If he had been, if there was something to this beyond what I was starting to feel was total manipulation, then Trace would've reacted.

He hadn't. There had been no reaction at all.

"I brought this up to your brother, you know."

Her sniffling quieted, and she raised her head up.

I met her gaze, what I could see from the flashlight. "He didn't blink once. He shrugged it off. Does that make you wonder again? You have a good relationship with your dad? You trust him? Or you trust your brother? It seems the two different reactions might say something by itself."

She looked away, her nose turning up before her mouth did a weird motion. "I didn't talk to Trace about our mom. He hated her, so why would he care about this?"

"What about Ashton? He'd have the wherewithal to speak on your brother's behalf. How'd he react when you told him why you were threatening me?"

She didn't answer.

I took a step toward her, raising my voice. "What'd he say?!"

"He didn't. He took me to the airport, booked me a flight to Vegas, and told me to stop talking about shit I didn't know anything about."

Fuck's sake. Right there. She said that, and there wasn't one ounce of remorse in her tone. The whimpering was fake. I stepped back and heard my own voice. It matched what I was feeling on the inside. Cold. "You don't even believe it."

"What?" More alarmed this time. Less of the pretending to be scared.

I frowned, going with my gut here. "You have no emotion now. You're not scared. You've not once tried to leave or asked to leave. You're faking it. And you're almost bored. You struggled against a yawn five sentences ago." I was right. I knew it, and I moved to the side, trying to make her feel unbalanced, more than what she should've been, but she wasn't scared. That was glaringly obvious to me. "Why did you put the order out against me? You wanted to blow up my career, because that's all those kind of orders do to people in my career field." Another step, my head cocked all the way to the side, still exploring where my gut was taking me. "I gotta think that takes a lot of balls, doing what you did."

Her eyes narrowed. "What are you talking about?"

"Laying claim to a parole officer on the streets. You'd know what kind of shit that leads to for me. My colleagues thinking I'm dirty. Them thinking I'm either snitching or fucking someone in your family."

Her eyes went to slits, and she went eerily still.

Her lips parted.

"People die from orders of protection like the one you put out there. I'm here trying to piece it together, scrambling because I don't want to die, and I don't want to kill someone to defend myself. That's what that shit does. You getting that now?"

A real gasp sounded. This one quiet and in the back of her throat, like she didn't know she'd even made the sound herself. She wasn't looking at me. She was staring off.

"Who suggested to you to do what you did?"

Her mouth opened again, wider, before she clamped it shut and shot me a withering look. "I ain't saying shit. You can go to hell for what your mother did to mine." She raised her chin up. "I hope you die, cop slut. Then maybe your mom will hurt an ounce of what she put me through. You deserve all the hell that's coming to you."

The door suddenly shoved open from behind me.

I barely reacted, while Remmi screamed before jumping up and squealing. She took off running, going past me.

"That's enough." Trace's voice filled the room, echoing around me.

"Trace!"

I didn't watch, instead hearing some shuffling and, from her, "What the hell, T?"

His own coldness barely resonated with me. "Go with Ashton."

"But—what?! Trace!"

"Let's go." Ashton's own tone was clipped as well, no patience there either.

We could hear them moving away. She kept demanding to know what was going on, if Ashton was mad at her, why would he be? She was the victim. What the hell? A lot of "what the hells."

After they left, I spoke. "I never restrained her. Not once. I told her to come with me, and she did. If she had asked to leave, I wouldn't have stopped her."

"You think I give a shit about that? I love my sister, but right now I don't like her. She's been given a pass on a lot of things because of how she was affected by our mom's suicide. I'm seeing that didn't do her any favors, and trust me, she'll be learning a steep lesson. One, not to trust my father."

I turned now, flinching as I saw him gazing at me with a softness.

I didn't want that look from him.

I didn't want his pity.

I rolled my shoulders back, raising my head up. "Your father's a threat. He knows you care for me, and he pitched her against me to hurt me, to hurt you."

"I know." His barely restrained fury told me he'd pieced it all together as well.

"You heard?"

"I was turning it over in my head when we were on an exploration through hallways and basement stairs that I never want to see again in my life. Do you know what creatures are down here?"

"Right now?" For some reason I could only think about the worst that we'd done, what we'd helped cover up. Because what made us so different from his sister, or his father? Even his uncle. "Two people who could be convicted of accessory to murder."

I moved past him. He reached out. "Jess."

I moved my arm away, continuing out of the room. "Don't. Just, don't. Not this time."

CHAPTER

FORTY-EIGHT

JESS

Knock, knock.

The knocking was soft and cautious. That was my first indicator of who was on the other side, but I checked to make sure. It was Trace.

I sighed, opening the door and stepping back so he could come inside. "You waited a whole day. I'm impressed." I closed the door, hit the locks, and checked my phone. It was off. It'd been off since I got home, which was after I'd had to inform Leo what had gone on. He needed a heads-up because I didn't know what was being said on the streets anymore.

"It's been put out that the order was wrong."

"How'd you get that done? Once things are out, they're out."

"Ashton did it. He has his ways."

I shook my head, moving to the kitchen. "The damage was done. My team leader knows. My partner. Organized crime got a heads-up."

His gaze sharpened as he was watching me in the kitchen. "Organized crime?"

"How do you think I found where your sister was?"

His mouth tightened. "You think that was smart?"

"No, Trace! No, but what do you expect me to do? For you to cover it up? Hide her from me?"

"You think I'd do that? To you?"

"Yes. She's blood. At the end of the day, you're always going to pick blood. Even if it's not good for you, you pick who was there in the beginning." My voice cut out. Visions of my mom blasted me, the night Bear had told me I could step back, that he'd handle it from there.

I was losing it. "I've lost everything. Everything. The only thing I had left is my career. You're threatening to take that away. You don't get it—"

"I do get it! What do you think I'm trying to do? I stayed away from you. I *have* stayed away, or I've tried, but this last time, I was gone. I was out from you. Ashton was going to take care of the club on the nights you're there, but we see how that worked out." He sounded so frustrated. "I physically ache every goddamn fucking day for you, but you're right. I am toxic for you, so I tried to stay away, but not tonight. I have to be here. I—if there's any questions where my loyalty lies, you took my sister hostage. Didn't matter if she wasn't aware of it or not, but you did, and I'm here. *I'm here, Jess.*"

I was a fucking dichotomy.

Hard. Soft.

Angry. Hurting.

Jaded and wanting to have hope?

It was him. "You're messing with my mind."

"I'm not trying to, I swear to god. I'm just as messed up."

But I was back in the studio, that night when he'd shown up.

How he'd touched me.

Kissed me.

I could feel him against me again. His hands on me. Tasting me. When he lifted me up on the counter, when he filled me.

I was remembering every moment between us, and my body was heating again.

I wanted him, but I couldn't have him. *What the hell do I do, then?*

I had to quit. Soon. Yes. Decision made. I'd have to quit working at the club, and I was beyond needing to do that. I'd been ridiculously stupid for not leaving, but then that would be it. No Trace. There'd be no reason after that.

I took him in, seeing his hair was mussed. Bags under his eyes, but he was here, and he was watching me back, and I just wanted him again.

One last night? Could I stop after tonight?

I didn't have the willpower to walk from him, not yet. But I would. I had to, or I'd be ruined.

I gazed around, trying to remember what I'd been doing before he showed up. "Do you—uh, do you want something to drink?"

He came up behind me. I could feel his body heat. "Hey." Always so gentle with me. "Look at me."

I shook my head, pulling away. "I can't. I do and I'll lose it."

"You want me to go?"

I should've. "No," I whispered instead.

There. That was that. I guess I decided.

I didn't say anything else, going down the hallway to my room. He followed me and stood in the doorway as I moved around my room. He watched me change out of my clothes and pull on a sleeping tank and my underwear. I didn't sleep in anything else. I moved into the bathroom to wash up, and when I came back, he wasn't in the doorway.

A light went off in my apartment. Another. And another. He was turning all the lights off. I heard him check the door, and then he was coming back. He saw me waiting for him and paused in the doorway, reaching out. The hallway light was turned off, and he came inside, a soft sigh leaving his mouth.

We didn't speak.

I don't know why. Maybe because there was nothing to be said. Or we'd said it all so much, but we were still not doing what we knew we needed to do, and what do you say about that? Nothing. The body was choosing, and I could not make myself kick him out. I was aching inside, my chest literally hurting from the thought.

He moved past me, his hand touching my hip, grazing over my back, as he went into the bathroom.

He closed the door, and I stood there, listening to him, liking the sound of him in my bathroom. Liking this feeling of waiting for him, knowing he wasn't leaving tonight.

I slid into bed, under the covers, when he was coming out.

He stopped, gazing down at me.

I rolled to my back, just watching him in return.

His eyes narrowed before they closed, and he seemed to come to some decision.

He began undressing, putting his clothes on the chair by my bed. When he reached for his boxer briefs, he paused, taking me in again, and then leaving them before he reached to turn off the light on the nightstand. The covers lifted. The bed dipped, and he slid in beside me.

We moved to each other, his arms sliding around me and pulling me to him.

I ran a hand down his arm, his side, to his boxers, and I slid a finger underneath the waistband. "These are staying on?"

He skimmed a hand down my arm and to my waist, returning the favor. "When these come off, mine will follow."

I lay back, seeing him rise up over me, resting on an arm beside me. Lights off, but I could still see him from the moonlight filtering through my curtains. It gave him a whole shadowed look.

One last night? I considered it, my body heating as I felt him all over again.

I couldn't stop then.

"Just sleep." He settled down beside me, one of his arms over my stomach, cupping my hip.

I whispered, "Okay."

Slowly, muscle after muscle began relaxing. Settling down, and soon my eyelids were heavy too.

He was gone in the morning.

———

I went to work the next day, expecting the shit to hit the fan. It didn't.

Leo gave me an intense, appraising look in our morning meeting but didn't say anything.

Val and I had a day of home visits planned. We needed to finish the ones we hadn't gotten to yesterday, and even she was quiet, or more than normal. We talked. She did not ask what happened, but I was back at work, and throughout the day, the first few visits followed suit like yesterday.

Our last one was when we were told to shove our sticks up our asses if there was enough room beside our own dicks.

Val started laughing. So did I. I never thought I'd be as relieved to be told to go fuck myself as I was right then.

We were coming back inside our office building when Travis walked by me.

If anything was going to be said, it'd be by him. He still hated me.

Val paused. So did I.

Travis kept going but shot both of us a weird look. "Montell, I never have any hopes for you, but Hartman, what's with the constipated look? Officer Reyo plugging you up too much at night? Can't take a shit now?"

She wheeled around. "I can't believe you just said that to me."

He stopped, frowning. "What?"

I hit her arm, pushing her forward. "Ignore him."

"Fuck you, Travis." She twisted around me. "Keep pissing off your coworkers. A great philosophy in our line of work. I'm sure that'll work out for you."

"Not that I care much about you, since you're close to Officer Montell here."

"What is your problem with me, Travis?"

His eyes slid beyond me but came back, and he smirked. "Nothing. I just don't like dirty law enforcement."

I stiffened but then looked behind me. Leo was there, frowning at us. I wanted to do a few things to Travis that would make me dirty, but I couldn't. Val was fuming, glaring at Travis. She looked ready to go find him, too, so I moved and guided her into the hallway.

I glanced back, saw he was regarding us with narrowed eyes. "You're a piece of shit, Travis. I hope you keep insulting everyone. You really will fuck yourself at the end of the day then. Have fun while you're doing it."

I kept moving Val ahead of me. If I didn't, I was going to go myself and do something I'd regret.

"What?" Val slapped my hand away.

"He doesn't know."

"What are you talking about? He just said—"

"He was confused when you reacted. He wasn't expecting that. He was joking or trying to throw out something and see if it would stick."

She realized what I was saying and tipped her head back, a low growl rumbling out from her throat. "Jesus. And look at me, I basically confirmed if he had suspicions." Her face tightened. "He's usually riding your ass—now it's my turn?"

I pressed my lips together tight. "Trust me, if you got it today, that means he's saving something up for me."

"I didn't ask today, since, you know, you showed up, but are you okay?"

I moved my head up and down, once. "I'm fine. I'm hoping it'll blow over."

I was really, really hoping for that to happen, but my gut knew. It wouldn't.

———

He showed up that night, a soft knock like the last time.

I let him in.

I couldn't not anymore.

———

Thursday night.

We had a hard day at work, and Trace came over.

I couldn't talk about my day. I didn't want him to talk about his, but he held me again.

He was gone in the morning, and I wasn't going to think anymore.

———

I went to my shift at Katya, and I could feel him there.

He was watching me. I didn't know where he was, but I knew he was there.

I went home after my shift, and ten minutes later . . .

Knock, knock.

I let him in.

He was gone once again when I woke up, but today was Saturday. I had nothing to do today.

I didn't know how to handle a day of nothing.

CHAPTER

FORTY-NINE

TRACE

This was meeting number eight.

My uncle had started falling into the same pattern. I came in. There was small talk. He inquired about my sister, then he asked how my work was going. I answered everything, waiting for the real reason he'd asked to meet me. He'd get to it, and the last few times, it'd been the same request or warning. I considered it a forewarning of sorts. His health was bad. He needed me to take over the family business.

The time remaining was dwindling. I had a couple weeks to go.

Of course this was never expressed in a way where he was asking me to do it. He was telling me he wanted me to do it. It was an old classic Uncle Stephano way of where he paved the road with his intentions first, and then when it was clear, he marched right on through.

This meeting was different.

I noticed that immediately when his men stood up straight when I exited my vehicle. Before, they lounged. They nodded. They might have given a wave; sometimes they did nothing, and that was because I didn't care for my uncle's men. They only knew violence and used violence to get whatever they wanted.

This time, there was fear in their eyes.

"Tristian." Stephano's head guy, Bobby, gave me a respectful nod, opened the door, and led the way inside. We bypassed the kitchen, where my uncle preferred to do his meetings, and he took me down to the basement, into the back television room, where Stephano was on a back couch. "Tristian is here."

"Ah. I see." My uncle stood up and came over.

His hands went to my arms, and he leaned in. A kiss to my left cheek. A kiss to my right, and then he gave me another clasp on both arms, a smile before he stepped back. He blinked a few times before he turned away.

"What's going on, Uncle Stephano?"

He cleared his throat, shaking his head. "We can get to that. Sit, sit, sit. Bobby, get us some drinks. I'm feeling wine tonight. The best red we have."

Bobby gave a nod before glancing my way, a lingering look, and then he left.

I frowned. What was going on? "I'd rather we cut to the chase here. We've had enough of these meetings over the last two weeks, Uncle Stephano."

"What? Oh. Yeah. Uh." He waved to the couch he'd just stood from. "Sit. Have a seat. Relax a little. All in due time."

I sat, not wanting to, but I sat.

He moved to the back, where he kept a table. There was a pile of papers, and he shifted through some before his phone buzzed. "Yeah?" He grew quiet. "Yes. I do. Yes. Thank you."

My own phone buzzed.

Ashton: At Katya. The old roommate is here, talking with Jess.

Me: Thanks for letting me know.

Ashton: Want me to pass on any messages? She's alone.

Me: I'll come by after this meeting.

Ashton: Want to guess why the old roommate showed up? I'm hoping they're going to start bowling again.

Me: ?

Ashton: I like bowling. Your girl hasn't gone for a while.

Me: You like bowling or you like who owns the bowling alley?

Ashton: Is there a difference?

Me: Where is this coming from? Have you been watching their group of friends Sunday nights?

Ashton: Maybe.

Me: Ashton.

Ashton: I checked in a couple times, just keeping abreast even though your girl wasn't there.

Me: Did the owner recognize you?

Ashton: No.

"Here you go." Bobby brought a wine bottle, two glasses, and a corkscrew into the room. After placing everything on the table closest to where I was sitting, he opened the bottle and began pouring. "Tristian." He handed one to me, then filled the other.

I took it but only held it. No way was I going to drink from mine before my uncle drank from his. We were family, but we were still Mafia. Everything about this meeting was setting off my alarms.

"Thank you, Bobby."

"You want me to . . . ?" He gestured to the door, and Uncle Stephano nodded.

"Yeah, yeah. Close it. Leave us alone. I need privacy with my nephew now."

"Okay." Bobby shared another look with me before he left, shutting the door behind him.

"Uncle Stephano—"

He stopped me, a hand in the air, and gestured to the door. "Make sure they've all gone."

What? That was news to me. "Is there something I should be made aware of about your men?"

"What?" He continued to watch the door, listening, and once we heard a thump upstairs, he relaxed. "Ah. Good. All good." He moved his glass toward me. "You can never be too sure. Now. How are you? Tell me, how is my favorite nephew doing? Still making all that money with your job and your businesses?"

Now we were falling back into old patterns. I relaxed, just slightly, but scooting forward, I put my wine back on the table in front of me and rested my arms on my knees. "Uncle Stephano, you know I'm doing well. Everything is well for me."

"Yeah?" He sat down in one of the deeper chairs, facing me. "And the woman? Are you still seeing that copper? Montell."

"She's a parole officer, and yes. Things are . . . fragile between us."

His eyebrows shot up. "Fragile? What does that mean?"

"It means we're slow, but I'm still seeing her, or trying to. She's basically the enemy—you know that."

"I do. Yes. But you did good with her uncle, or the new guy who replaced him. He turned out to be a good employee for us. We moved a lot of shipments through that warehouse thanks to him. It was a good call what you did."

"Yeah. Thanks."

He noticed my wine, and his eyes sharpened. Leaning forward, he motioned toward it. "Wine not good?"

"It is. I already took a sip."

"You did? Good, good."

He was thinking. And because I was able to almost see him thinking, that meant a lot of things to me. He was tired. He was distracted. He was . . . frenzied? Was this all because of his health? It was a general rule of mine not to lie to my uncle, ever, but I tried to tell him as little as I could. Being vague tended to appease him. He used to like to feel in control, but now my uncle was not coming off as being in control. With him, what he could do, that made him extra dangerous.

"Uncle Stephano." Calm. Quiet. I needed to ease into this.

"Hmm? Yes?"

"What's going on? Why did you want to meet tonight?"

He stopped thinking and focused on me. Only me.

I knew my uncle was dangerous, though I'd never actually feared him. But right now was the closest I'd gotten to being scared of him. He was making me nervous. "Uncle Stephano?"

"Our problems have escalated."

"Which ones?"

"Some of our shipments aren't arriving. Getting lost. Stolen. And there's other skirmishes. More and more businesses are starting to refuse to pay us. Some of our other more unsavory businesses are taking a hit too." He began waving a hand in the air. "One or two, they're fine.

Normal. We can handle those, and we do, but we're getting hit on all sides, and it's got me thinking. You know?"

"Sure." I wasn't going to like where he was going with this. I knew it.

"And I think, what's new going on? And then I think, this all started when you started banging that copper."

Oh, Jesus.

"It's not Jess."

"But she's a Montell. You know what happened with the other Montell? Her daddy. He was a little piece of shriveled dick. The smallest I'd ever seen, but he didn't want others to know, so he liked to overcompensate. Is that the word? Walked big. Talked loud. That sort of stuff, but he was a moron." His hand kept going, round and round. "A total idiot, but he was in with the crew. We let him do some things for us, bust some heads, then your daddy. You know about this?"

None of this was sitting right with me. I shook my head. "I've not heard the exact story, no."

"Yeah, yeah. Okay." He drank half his wine in one gulp, and that hand started up again. "I'll tell you. You sit. Relax. Want more wine? I can get Bobby to bring another bottle."

"I'm good, Uncle Stephano. I'd like to hear the story."

"Oh! Oh, oh, right. Your woman, huh? You want to hear about her daddy?" He tossed back more wine before standing and pouring the rest into his glass. His movements were unsteady as he moved back, until he could sink back down. As he did, the wine sloshed over the rim of his glass. He didn't notice. "Okay. Where was I? Oh, right. Your daddy and her daddy worked together, but they didn't like each other. Dominic had gotten his dick into your woman's mother. She's a good-looking woman too. I still see her sometimes. She's started walking on our street, and she makes sure to wave to the guys when she does. You know why she's doing that, right?" He laughed, his eyebrows wiggling a little.

"She's asking for some visitors, but don't worry. I'd not do that to you, not when you're plowing the daughter." He laughed, loud and long.

There was something wrong with Uncle Stephano.

I hadn't put stock into it when he'd first started talking about his health, but this wasn't him. He didn't act like this. He was reserved, cautious. Smart. He was being like his brother right now, like my father. His men's reactions were making more sense.

"What happened with Jess's father?"

"Oh yeah. I forgot. Yeah, yeah. There was a fight. You see, her daddy wanted more power in our family. He wanted to climb the ladder, and he staged a coup against your father. But blood is blood. You feel me? He came to me about it, told me everything your father was doing, and I'm saying everything. The whores, the cops he was blackmailing. He had his fingers everywhere, and her daddy knew about it all. He gave me a proposition. He'd take out your dad if he'd get his job. Said he could take your dad's position and do it better." He began laughing, his shoulders shaking. "And you know the funny thing? I bet he could've. He wasn't a stupid idiot. He was half-smart most of the time. The other half was dumb because what'd he think? That I'd choose him, an outsider, over my own blood?"

I was bracing myself. "What happened to him?"

"I had him killed. That's what happened."

"You did?" My tone was sharp. Everything in me was on high alert. Her brother had been convicted for their father's death.

"I mean, we set it up, but we didn't do it. The kid did. He just needed proper motivation, but yeah. We got the son to kill the father, and now it's almost karma that you're banging the daughter. Funny how that all works out, huh? Especially when Dominic made sure you were never here. He never wanted you to run into the girl, said you'd fall for her. She was a looker even back then, but we put out word not to touch her. That was a promise to the father, that she'd be left alone. But you see, I can't fulfill that promise if she's the one singing on us?"

"She's not," I ground out.

Good fucking Christ.

I started to stand up. "Why am I here? Tonight?"

"What do you mean?"

I took out my phone.

Me: I want a guy on Jess at all times. I think my uncle might do something against her.

He was staring at my phone, and he pointed at it with his wineglass. "What'd you do there? Just now. You sent a text off? To who?"

"To Ashton."

He nodded, easing back into his chair. "That's good because you're here for two reasons. One, I need to know if the woman you're banging is turning evidence on us, and if she's not, then we got a whole other problem on our hands."

"It's not Jess. I've had men on her and a tracker on her. It's not her."

The wino lunacy charade was gone, and my uncle was back in power. He was clear and alert, and he was studying me like I was his enemy. He nodded, slower this time, and he spoke, his voice all serious. "Let's hope it's not your woman because if it is, then I'm going to have to take out her family. Can't get rid of another one and let the other two stew."

"It's not her, so who's the other choice?"

He stared at me, long and hard. "The other choice is that family from Maine. They could be behind everything."

"What do you want me to do?"

He stood up from his chair, taking a sip of his wine before moving back to the table. He lingered, staring at something before he put his wine down. He picked up a folder and brought it over. "You handled your father. You handled the uncle situation. Now." He nodded to the folder as I opened it. A picture stared back at me, and I knew who this

273

person was. "That's the ringleader for the Maine family. I've told you about them. Worthing Mafia is what they're being called, but you know one of their cousins. He used to work for you."

Justin Worthing.

I picked up the picture. "Are you serious with this?"

"I am. He's got a brother on the force, a Detective Worthing. They're using him to move in on us, and they're going to keep coming."

"What do you want me to do about this?"

"I want you to handle it." He moved back, sipping his wine. "Handle it how you've handled all the other situations I've sent your way. You'll have to rope Ashton in on it because his family runs the cops in town. Worthings are moving in on their territory too."

He was asking me to "handle" more people.

"You might want to ask the reason why you had a Worthing at your club, too, while you're at it."

"Excuse me?"

"You had a Worthing working for you. Don't think I didn't consider that maybe you were the one plotting against me?"

He had better not be threatening me. "Are you fucking kidding me?"

Now he went eerily still, and there was a whole layer of ice filling the room around us.

"Why the hell would I plot against you when you've been telling me that you want me to take over for you?" There was a storm in his eyes. I saw it, checked it, and it only kept growing.

My uncle was a problem.

The man who had been the one going to my sports games. *He* was the father to me. My birthdays. He was the one who kept my picture on his fridge. He was there for me. When his son left, I was at his side. When his other one died, I'd helped plan the funeral. He was a mess. His wife left him years ago, and she was gone gone. Like vanished gone. The story had been that she'd had enough of him and took off, not wanting anything to do with this family. I'd never questioned it, but now, had he done this to them? Threatened to turn on them?

Or worse, had he turned on them?

I was staring at my uncle, wondering if I was just seeing him for the first time.

A smile broke out over his face, and he started laughing. "I got you! I got you, didn't I?" He came over, clapping me on the shoulder, but his hand holding that wine was still so steady.

"Uncle."

"Yeah?" He was still laughing. "Why aren't you laughing? It was a joke. I was trying to ease the tension. I know I came down hard about your girl, and then about your employee, but one never knows." He motioned to his back. "A lot of people want to put knives in my back."

"You just threatened me. You threatened *family*."

I was still holding myself steady, watching everything he did. Listening to every word he said, every inflection of tone. All of it was being burned into my brain because this day changed everything moving forward. He showed me the card that he could turn on me. I'd be stupid not to believe he would.

"It was nothing. You're my nephew. I'd never do anything to you." He moved in, clasping the back of my neck, and rested his forehead to mine. "I love my nephew. He's the only one loyal to me. I'd be a fool to lose him. I'd be a fool to lose you. It was a joke, Tristian. Please forgive me. It was a bad joke."

It wasn't a joke. It was a test. He'd wanted to see how I'd react.

I stepped back from him, but I didn't say anything. I didn't know what to say.

He faltered, frowning. "Trace?"

I took another step back, and another. Still not saying anything.

"Trace? I was joking."

"You weren't," I grated out. "I've never done anything to you to make you believe you couldn't trust me. Never. I handed my father over to you, and I saw what you did to him. Now this?" I motioned to him. "Justin Worthing is not a part of his family's business. I can't speak to the rest of his family, but I know he is not. And he's not one of my employees anymore."

Stephano raised his chin up, slowly. "His woman is currently in your nightclub, talking to your woman. You can see that I do have cause for concern considering that your woman hasn't chosen sides yet. She's still working for the other side."

"Excuse me?"

He had eyes in my club. In my club! I wasn't surprised about the reporting on Justin, or even about Jess. I half expected it, but the questioning me, and now this? Current reports right now.

"I was *just* told myself that she's there. How did you know?"

I began looking around.

He'd gone to his table. He was looking at papers.

Bobby had brought the wine in—that's when I'd received the texts from Ashton. I went over his movements after that text.

He'd been in his chair. He was drinking. Testing me. Challenging me in a way. Then he stood, went to his table, and he paused there.

I began to turn toward the table, moving to it.

"What are you doing?" His voice sharpened.

I held up my phone. "You don't have eyes at my club, not current ones. But I do, and I was *just* notified. That means . . ."

"Trace! Don't go over there."

I ignored him, starting to read the papers.

They were files. Stocks. Others were numbers that he had scribbled down. Photos.

"Stop, Trace. I mean it," he barked.

I moved aside one of the papers, and I saw a phone. I hit the screen; it was my wallpaper. I picked it up and turned back. "Unlock it."

"Nephew." He lowered his head, trying to go soft with me.

"Unlock it. *Now.*" I tossed it at him.

He caught it, barely, crushing it to his chest with his arm. Giving me an annoyed look, the ends of his mouth pinched in, he moved his thumb over the screen and tossed it back. I went straight to changing the passcode, putting in the numbers I just saw him use and entered my own before I went through the phone.

It was mine. Everything was mine.

He'd made a duplicate phone of mine.

I checked my texts, seeing Ashton's recent one there.

Seeing my sexts with Jess.

I turned, a cold rage starting in my stomach, and it was growing fast and fiercely. "What else do you have on me?"

"Nephew—"

"What else?!"

He jerked. Swallowing. He finished his wine—thank god for that—and put the glass on the table beside him. Then he held up his hands, both of them. "Now, listen. Trace . . ."

"You have one phone; you could have others. I don't enjoy my privacy being invaded." Which was hypocritical of me because I had invaded Jess's over and over again. I got it. I was getting it. But right now, I was dealing with this fire.

I just hadn't decided if I was going to add gas or smother it.

"Tell me. Now."

His head went back, and his Adam's apple bobbed up and down. He had a resigned set to his shoulders. "I can tell that this meeting went sideways. I didn't mean for any of this to happen, and that's on me. I just needed to know. Your woman, you care for her. A lot. I can tell, and she's in the law. I had to know, Tristian. I had to take precautions. Can't you see that?"

"You cloned my phone. I'm not seeing anything right now."

"You launched an investigation into me."

"What are you talking about?"

"I know you did. I have computer guys. They set up alerts, and they notified me that you were mousing around. You did it a while ago, on a Friday night. I even know where you were, at your place downtown. That fancy high-rise you own. I couldn't believe it when they said your computer was the IP address that was looking into my finances. Thought it was a joke, but then you got more serious with the cop, and what was I supposed to do? Huh? You're the only family I got."

"Maybe there's a reason."

His whole face shuddered before he reared back, snarling. "Stop being an ungrateful little bit—"

I was gone.

I couldn't hit my uncle. If I did, I wouldn't stop. The other choice I had was to leave.

He stopped but shouted as I was out the door and headed for the stairs, "Where are you going? Trace?!"

I shoved through the stair door and was going to the front door. "Trace?"

I stopped, seeing Bobby standing in the front living room. It was set up as my uncle's meeting room when he didn't want someone any farther into the house. He rarely used it because most of his business was done in the kitchen or at his warehouse two streets over.

"Don't talk to me." I was going for the door.

"Trace, stop."

I opened the door.

"Trace." He hurried forward, and then something was being shoved into my hand. "Read it."

I closed my hand around whatever he gave me and was out the door.

Demetri saw me coming, hurried from the front, and opened my back door.

I got in and called Ashton. "Wipe everything. We need new phones. New computers. Everything."

Demetri was getting back inside but heard me and looked at me through the rearview mirror.

"What happened?" Ashton said.

"My uncle's been spying on us, and that *seriously* pisses me off. Wipe everything."

"On it."

I unraveled the piece of paper Bobby had put in my hand.

Your mother is alive. He doesn't know.

CHAPTER FIFTY

JESS

He didn't come.

I left work, thinking we'd follow our routine of the last few nights. I didn't like admitting that I'd come to expect him, but ten minutes after I was home, there was no knock.

I waited up an hour; still no knocking.

My phone flashed next to me, lighting up the room, and I rolled over to grab it.

Trace: Don't contact me on this phone. Not safe. Tell you later.

I jerked upright, my heart already starting to pound. I wanted to call, text him, see what was going on, but he'd said his phone wasn't safe.

I hit the floor, already moving before I'd fully formed my plan. It didn't matter because I was already going.

Clothes were on in a flash. Socks. Shoes.

I had my coat fastened, my keys in hand, when I opened the front door and stopped.

"Kelly!"

She was shivering, her eye makeup running down her face. Snowflakes were still on her eyelashes, and she held up a hand, her coat completely swamping her. "Hi."

"What are you . . . come in. Come on."

She did, a bit tentative at first, but once she was through the door, she collapsed. Her shoulders fell. Her knees crumpled, and a sob left her. "Oh—hey! Hey." I caught her, helping her to one of the chairs by our kitchen table, and as soon as she felt the chair, she bowled over. More sobs erupted from her. Her forehead went completely to the table.

I shut the door, locked it, and went over. "Hey. Hey." I scooted into the chair next to her. She'd not been like this at Katya. I'd caught some yearning when she'd looked around, but I'd thought she missed working with me. That was it. "What is this? What happened?"

She lifted her head on another choking sob, her face completely wrecked. She grabbed for my wrist. "Can I stay here tonight? Please?"

"Of course. But, tell me what's wrong. Please. You're my best friend, Kelly. I need to know."

She started shaking her head. "I can't tell you. I—I just can't. I want to stay here. One night and then I'll figure it out. Yeah. I'll figure it out then."

"Wait." I knelt at her feet, one of my knees on the floor. "Kelly, what's going on? I'm worried. Please tell me what's going on."

"I can't. I really can't. I, just, want to sleep here for the night. Is that okay?"

"Uh—" I was about to try and push her again, but my phone buzzed then.

Unknown: I'm downstairs. Can I come up?

I stood up, texting back. Kelly was watching me, her sobs quieting a little bit.

Me: Who is this?

Unknown: Trace. New phone. Explain later. Can I come up?

Me: Kelly is here.

"Um." Two crises were happening at once. "Kelly, can I—I need to run down to the door for this. I'll be right back—"

"No, it's totally fine." She stood up, her chair scraping over the floor. She was hugging herself and looking around. "I need to go to the bathroom anyway and get ready for bed. Can I, uh—my bed isn't here. I can sleep on the couch. I know where everything is."

"No. Wait. I'll be right back."

"Take your time, okay?" She'd started down the hallway to her old bathroom. I hadn't touched hers since she left. Her voice was suddenly better, calmer. "I mean it. I'm going to shower and clean up. I'm a mess." She motioned for the door. "Whatever or whoever that is, don't rush back on my account."

I opened my mouth, but I wasn't sure what I was going to say.

She was gone, the door closing behind her, and I could hear the fan turn on. The shower was next.

Unknown: You want me to go?

Me: No. I'm coming down.

———

When I got downstairs, Trace was there, and he nodded toward his SUV.

I stepped out through the door, leading the way, and as I got inside, he came with me.

"Demetri, can you give us some privacy?"

"Will do." He stepped outside right away, then went over and took point by the door. He lit a cigarette, and Trace's hand went to the small of my back as he hit the divider so no one could see in from the front of the vehicle either.

I touched his arm, my hand rounding. I was half holding on to him for him and half for me. "Hey."

"Hey." His smile was gentle. He moved in, cupping both sides of my face and bending to rest his forehead to mine. A brief second there, then his lips dipped, grazing over mine before coming back, more demanding. His body settled into mine, and I felt his tension leave his body. He continued kissing me, his tongue sweeping inside.

Heat lit inside of me, beginning to pulsate through my veins.

He did that. Always.

He groaned, pulling back, breathing unsteadily. "God. I could hold you forever."

My hands raised to his arms. I pushed him back a little, leaning my head to get a better look at him. "What is going on? New phone. It's not safe?"

His eyes got serious, and the softness left him. A wall came down before he pulled all the way back from me. My hands dropped to the seat between us. A chill came through the vehicle. I fought against shivering but couldn't hold it.

He looked up as if he could see my apartment. "Why is Kelly here?"

"I don't know, but hey." I touched the side of his face, turning him back to me. "What's going on?"

His face was closed off again. "I can't tell you. It's family stuff."

My hand fell away. "Oh."

He looked back up. "Is there something wrong with her and Justin? Did she say something?"

"No." Why did he care about that? "They probably just had a fight. It's Kelly. She gets like this. Emotional. They'll fight, and I'm sure even

283

by tonight, she'll head back again. This is normal relationship stuff for her. She feels deeply."

"Yeah. Maybe."

"Family stuff? For you? That's why you got a new phone?"

He focused back on me, seeing me again. His whole face sharpened, and he leaned forward, touching the side of my face. His hand cupped me there. His thumb trailed lightly over the corner of my mouth, and he angled his head, his eyes growing dark. Lust filled them. His thumb rested over my bottom lip, pulling it down. He shuddered, his hand falling away from me. "I need to stay away from you for a while, for your safety."

A shiver went down my spine. "This is business related?"

Of course it was. I was foolish to hope it was something else, something normal like . . . I didn't know. A divorce, which didn't make sense, but along those lines. Something normal people struggled with, but it wasn't. It was another reminder I was on one side, and he was on the other.

"Don't do that. I can feel you pulling away."

I laid my head against the seat, gazing at him. I felt the distance. It was cold, but I was used to it. It was lonely too. "It's how it's supposed to be, right? You doing Mafia stuff. Me doing law stuff."

His eyes were smoldering dark, lingering on my mouth. A growl left him.

His mouth was on mine, the heat there and climbing. I felt it. It was consuming me. Maybe it was because this was the last night before who knew how long until I saw him again. A night? Two? A month? If ever? That was in the realm of possibility, and I had a crying best friend upstairs who was probably done showering, but the ache had burrowed all the way into my chest, deep in there. It was in the pocket by my heart, and I couldn't bring myself to pull away from him.

His mouth was on mine.

Need. Want. Desire.

Lust.

It wrapped around my body, making me feel alive, warming me up, and I couldn't hold it back. I needed him, just him. Nothing else.

He picked me up, and I was climbing onto his lap, not thinking, not paying attention to anything else.

My hand tunneled through his hair as his swept down my body, pulling my hips against his, and we stilled from the contact.

God.

That felt so good. Too fucking good.

I began moving over him as his hands went to my hips, then to my ass. He gripped me, moving me with him. I tipped my head back, my mouth meeting him, his tongue moving against mine. One of his hands went up, catching my hair, and he tugged my head back. I made a guttural sound as his mouth began moving down my throat, tasting me. Licking me.

His hand let go of my hair, falling back to my pants, and he moved inside, finding my underwear.

I hissed at the touch because it felt so damn good.

His other hand splayed out, grasping my ass.

He pulled back, nipping at my throat. "Sit up."

I did, lifting up, and he moved my underwear aside, taking position, finding my entrance.

Together, as one, I lowered as his fingers slid up, his back hand guiding me.

His mouth landed on mine as I began riding him, slow, steady. My hips rolled forward, moving into a good rhythm. His thumb rubbed over my clit, pressing in slowly, a delicious circle, and I gasped, the sensations swirling through me. They were wrapping around every organ in me, in my spine, crawling up me. The pleasure was unbearable. Almost. I cried out, my hips pumping harder over him.

His mouth caught my cry, swallowing it, and then he pulled me down, sinking me harder over his fingers, and my whole body jerked.

I exploded over him.

The waves erupted through me. They were almost violent in their power. My whole body was shuddering, quaking in the aftermath, until I melted into him.

He held me, his other hand smoothing up and down my back in a calming, comforting motion.

I didn't want to move. My whole body was a pile, no bones.

He never urged me to move. He just kept caressing me, holding me.

I might've fallen asleep. Or not. I didn't know. Time had ceased in this little sanctuary we took.

He pressed a kiss to my forehead, his free hand tracing some of my hair aside, tucking it behind my ear. "I want to say things to you right now, but I can't. I don't dare, but . . . just believe in me. That's all I can say. When it's safer . . ." He let his last statement hang between us, and as much as I hated to hear it, as much as it let in the cold again, I knew he said it for a reason.

I pulled back, nodding. I began to climb off of him, but he caught me again. He pressed a hard kiss to my mouth before letting me go. "I'll be in touch. I promise."

I wasn't my job right now. I was a woman. Maybe that was my eternal struggle. Between what I did and who I was—but I let everything fall away as I stared at him right before opening the door. There were words I wanted to say, things I felt but couldn't say, and because of that, because of what we both did, I let them go unsaid.

I opened the door, stepped out, and walked inside.

I didn't look back, and I didn't once break down.

Not until I was inside.

Not until I saw that Kelly was sleeping soundly on the couch.

Then I went to my room. Closed the door softly. Went to my bathroom.

Turned my shower on, and there, I fell.

CHAPTER

FIFTY-ONE

JESS

March passed.
He wasn't in touch.

CHAPTER

FIFTY-TWO

JESS

April passed.

I tried calling. All his lines were disconnected.

CHAPTER

FIFTY-THREE

JESS

May.

I would've blocked him if I had a number to block.
I didn't.

CHAPTER

FIFTY-FOUR

JESS

Well, fuck Trace.

It'd been three months and no word, and my life was calm. Quiet. Steady. Val was entertainment every day through morning sickness, and she was starting to gain weight. She'd skipped her family's Easter, so there'd been no word from her cousin. Also, Kelly and Justin got over whatever hitch they'd had.

I was a regular fixture on Sundays at Easter Lanes again.

Bear and Leo both checked in with me, and my mom was doing good. Course, I didn't believe a word they said, but it was what it was. I wasn't getting cursed over the phone on a weekly basis.

I was almost glowing.

Work was the same. Same people going on parole. Most hating me. Travis was still a dick.

Yep. Familiarity was good. Boring. Boring was good.

Boring.

Blah.

Bleh.

Fuck Trace.

"Did you see this?" A newspaper was dropped on the table in front of me as Kelly slid into the chair across from me.

See. We were these friends, meeting for lunch again. Not boring. Steady. Stable.

I was becoming a somewhat healthy individual.

"What is this?"

"Page three. Also, I need to grab a hero before Mrs. Kappaleweitz gets the last good bread. You're going down today, Mrs. Kappaleweitz. Down." She was off, shoving through the crowd toward the counter. We weren't in a normal diner. I needed some excitement. The deli on Seventy-Fifth was all about loud customers and orders being yelled out, and some days there was a shoving match. One could only hope for the shoving match.

I turned to page 3, wanting to know what Kelly wanted me to see.

New Mafia Head?

The headline was large and in bold print, along with a picture of Trace and Ashton underneath.

Holy shit!

I jerked forward, skimming over the article. It said there had been a major shake-up in both the West and Walden Mafia families. New heads were thought to be stepping up, as there'd been recent shootings at a warehouse, listed to be controlled by the West family.

A full workup was done about Trace. They were using his first name of Tristian, so they didn't know about his name preference. They talked about his schooling, his work on Wall Street. He'd been on the crew team when he was at Yale. Why was I not surprised?

There were more pictures of him leaving another nightclub. With a woman by him.

Another image, another woman.

After the third woman, I flipped the paper over.

Fuck. Him.

A headache was forming behind my forehead.

This was good news. He was obviously moving on. He'd chosen when I couldn't, and good. Great. Wonderful. Just, fuck him to the highest mountain and ram an ice pick up his ass.

"Can you believe that?" Kelly was back, her hero in hand, and she gestured to the paper.

"What'd you do? Kill Mrs. Kappaleweitz? That was record time."

"Oh." She grinned, taking a big bite out of her hero, and waved it over her shoulder to the counter. "Me and Sal are best buds now. I told him about some pigeons I'm feeding from Justin's patio, and he had set aside my hero for me. I don't need to worry about Mrs. Kappaleweitz anymore."

"Who's Sal?"

"The guy who owns the place. He's got a soft spot for pigeons. I forgot I had a whole conversation with him last week when we were here. He said he knew to start my hero when you came in. Said he recognized the 'scary badge lady.'" She was snickering but leaned back. An older lady was going past our table, and Kelly took a giant bite of her hero before waving at the lady, who harrumphed on her way out of the deli.

I was guessing that was Mrs. Kappaleweitz.

Kelly leaned forward again. "We're coming here every Thursday. I'm going to take pictures of the pigeons and show Sal next week. He'll melt over them. He told me he has a pigeon video channel on YouTube. I'm so subscribing to it." She frowned at the newspaper. "Oh, right. I forgot. You're still at Katya?"

I nodded.

She got quiet before gesturing to the paper. "You think that stuff is true?"

My throat was burning. My chest felt like a closed fist was being pressed down on it, rubbing forcefully up and down to slowly break my sternum. But I shrugged. "I don't know."

"Says the one guy who works on Wall Street. You think that's going to hurt him? Says he's a big guy down there too."

"It'll probably help him, actually."

She grunted. "Yeah. Funny how that works sometimes. You haven't seen them at Katya?"

"Not for a long time."

I'd never told Kelly that the door visitor had been him the night she'd come over sobbing about Justin. She'd never told me what their fight had been about. It was a night she wanted to avoid talking about, so it'd been easy not to tell her.

"I can't believe the hockey hallway guy had been our boss the whole time. That's wild, right? And the other guy—Justin's family knows him. Can you believe that? It's all crazy. You couldn't make this up."

I frowned. "What do you mean about the other guy?"

"The other boss guy. Ashton. He was at the party that day, and Justin's cousin was all over him. I guess she actually asked him about Justin. It's why he was hired at Katya."

"When did you find all this out?"

"That night. When I came over." She took a big bite of her hero and looked up at me. She stopped chewing, holding my gaze, and then sat back and swallowed everything. One big swallow. I saw it go down her throat. "I never told you any of that, huh?"

"No. You did not." Since she'd brought that night up . . . "Was that why you were crying?"

She opened her mouth, stared at me blankly, and closed it. "Um. What's the question again?"

"What else did Justin tell you that night?"

She began looking around.

"Kelly." I leaned forward, a hand on the paper. "What else did Justin tell you that night?"

She shook her head, her eyes clouding over. She hunched forward, her head lowering, and her voice got quieter. "I can't tell you. I want to. I really do, but I can't, and it's nothing to do with me or Justin. But Justin's family . . . he's got a big family, it turns out. Big and pushy. He told me the real reason we quit Katya. Not because his cousin got him the job, though I think that was part of it. He really doesn't like Vivianna, but he said the two owners are into some shady business dealings, and he couldn't tell me any more because of you. He didn't want to put me and you into a bad spot. So, yeah. I kept quiet about it. You mad?"

Was I mad? Jesus.

I was more mad at seeing those women with Trace. Different woman every night, it seemed.

I shook my head. "I'm not mad."

"But." Her head dipped even farther down, her eyes still on me. Her chin would be grazing the table if she hunched any more. "I knew your bosses were shady, and I never told you. That's shitty of me."

Now I really felt like a shitty friend. "I already knew."

"You knew?!" She sat back up.

"But you don't work there anymore . . ." I was lying to cover my ass. I'd made a conscious decision not to tell Kelly when she was working there. Yep. Shitty. Me.

"Guess you have a point, but what about you? You're still there after all this time?"

She was right. Trace had *clearly* moved on.

It was time I did as well.

CHAPTER

FIFTY-FIVE

TRACE

Ashton: She put in her two weeks.

I knew instantly who "*she*" was and *where* she would've put her two weeks in.

I'd stayed away for so long, needing to get a handle on the family business. My uncle knew about her. My father as well. Remmi. There'd been a concerted effort to put them all off her trail. I went on dates so many fucking nights in a row, and all of them had left me cold. Every one of them.

All of that was for her, so she was safe, but she remained at Katya. That gave me hope that she hadn't moved on yet.

She was moving on now.

My phone rang right after. *Ashton calling.*

I answered, putting it on speaker since I was in my downtown office.

"That article came out today," he said as a greeting.

"I saw."

"There were pictures of you with different women."

"I also saw that."

"That means she still cares."

"What's the point of this call? You're not saying anything that's helpful."

He laughed. "The attention's been diverted. You could probably go and see her. It's been months."

See her? God, yes. Every fiber of my being wanted to see her, but it was pointless. "This shit's not going away."

"We've cleaned everything. Businesses. Phones. Computers. New security systems. We have men now on our relatives. We have the upper hand now. Remmi is in Vegas and quiet. If there's a time to go see your woman, it's now."

"She is still working for the other side."

"We all have our crosses to bear."

"Shut the fuck up."

He laughed again. "Go and see her. You're becoming a grouch to be around. You could do with getting laid again. Remember how that used to feel? And then after, we can move on Bobby finally."

Right. Bobby with his note saying that my mother was alive. My mother. Jesus. *If* she was alive? What Pandora's box would that open?

We'd had to wait this long before reaching out. Suspicion and alarms were high with Uncle Stephano. I didn't dare connect with Bobby about her, but Ashton was right. The last three times I'd seen my uncle, he'd acted like nothing had changed. There'd been no altercation with him. He was back to bringing up his health, me taking over for him, but there was no more mention of his timeline. All in all, nothing and everything seemed to have changed.

This shit was now my nightmare.

"Go see her. We'll talk about it after."

We hung up, and I checked in with a new security detail specifically for her. They were hired the same day we'd had her tracker taken off. It was at their request, stating the tracker would be found before they were spotted. They were specialized enough and trained specifically to handle law enforcement agencies, so we'd removed her tracker.

When it came to Jess, I wasn't messing around, whether she knew it or not. She could hate me, as long as she was alive to hate me.

Me: Where is she?

Team Leader 1: At a studio.

His second text was the coordinates.

CHAPTER

FIFTY-SIX

JESS

The lights were off except for one lamp in the corner. I had dark folksy music going, and I was drinking. Fine. I needed a break from my life, so here I was. Painting again. Feeling shit. Bring on the feels.

No rules, regulations here. No suppressed emotions. No box I'd have to be stuffed into.

No roommate. No thoughts about Trace or our last times together.

Me and paint and vodka and my feelings.

Fuck my feelings, but I needed this shit out of me. This was always the best way. Who needed therapy? Talk therapy my ass. This was quicker, cheaper, and way more cathartic.

And as I stepped back, black paint dripping from my hands, I stared up at the canvas.

Apparently fuck me, too, because it was a huge stormscape. But at least I had painted Trace's images out of me. Now all I wanted to paint were storms, over and over again, because they were coming. I could feel them. They were just on the horizon, and I wasn't talking about weather storms. I was talking life storms.

I shouldn't have been feeling this. My life was boring. It was so fucking clean that there was no drama. Squeaky clean. Maybe I was missing the storms. Maybe that's what I was feeling . . . or hell.

I missed Trace.

God.

I hated him. I missed him. I wanted him here, but I hated him too.

"That's beautiful."

Oh, hell to the no.

I turned, my whole body seizing because it was Trace. He was here, looking damn good too. "Get out."

Damn my voice. That came out as a rasp.

Dressed in a suit. His wide shoulders. Trim waist. Those cheekbones. His chiseled jawline. He looked tired, with mussed hair, but it always made him look better.

Goddamn *him*.

"Jess," he murmured, his voice low. Also raspy.

My heart squeezed, and damn even that.

"Get out."

"Jess."

"It's been three months and nothing. You asked for time, and I get it. Family stuff. Your family stuff isn't typical, but there were no calls. Your numbers were gone. I've moved on." I was lying, through my freaking teeth. Even seeing him had every nerve ending on high alert.

"I know you're lying."

"You're lying."

He paused, frowning. Then, a small laugh left him. "We're in kindergarten?"

"You're in kindergarten." So stupid. I didn't care.

I turned back to the canvas, and that storm wasn't dark enough. There wasn't enough texture on it. I was tempted to dip my hand into the entire paint can and start flinging it on the canvas. Over and over again. I wanted it covered in black paint.

He sighed. "You're quitting the nightclub."

I had my back turned to him. "I'm quitting you. You're just attached to the nightclub, so I'm leaving."

"I couldn't contact you."

"I don't care." Still going with the childish theme here.

"Yes, you do. Jess, my father knew about you. My uncle. My sister. You were becoming a target. I couldn't have that. Especially if we're going into a war."

I turned back now. "A war?" I remembered the article. "They said there were shots fired at your warehouse."

He nodded, looking grim. "There's a family pushing in. That's another reason I stayed away."

I got that. I did. Logically, I got all of it. It made sense, and my god, it's what we had both been trying to do for so long.

Logic went out the window when the heart was involved.

The dangers aside, I couldn't get the pictures of those women out of my head.

My heart was back to feeling squeezed.

Why the women?

"Did you touch them?"

"Who?"

"Those women."

"No. I didn't even want to. It was all for image." He stepped up behind me, so close that I could feel his body heat.

"Jess." His voice dropped low, raspy.

"What?" I didn't turn around. God. I wanted to . . .

"Why do you paint? Why do you come here and do this?"

"I'm not a parole officer in here. I'm not Chelsea Montell's daughter or my brother's sister in here. I'm no one. Painting takes it all away, and it lets me breathe." My heart was pounding. "I paint because I have to, and when I wasn't—I can never return to that again. I'm not naturally an artist, but I think that somewhere deep down in my soul, I am. Painting is helping bring that part of me back."

I wanted to close my eyes, lean my head back.

I wanted to rest against him, let him hold me. The ache was so strong, so fierce, but I couldn't. We were back there, all over again. The same woes and feelings. All angst and drama and yearning.

The same hurt, but I just wanted to touch him.

He dropped his voice and his head. I felt his lips almost grazing my shoulder. "I want to talk to you about it. I'd love to be able to do that, but I can't. You know who I am and what I do, and there's no getting around it. Even if I wanted to leave that world, there are steps I have to take in order to do that."

He was right. All of it.

Why did I feel more alive in the last few minutes he was here than the three months he was gone? And why did I feel the pain that came with him too?

"You know . . ." I stepped away from him, going to the canvas. Dipping my hand down, I started working, and I spoke at the same time. "I was overseeing this supervised visitation one time. A guy, one of my parolees, he was seeing his kids. I had to be there, but they had a therapist there too. I think about that therapist sometimes, what he said."

"What'd he say?" He sounded farther away.

I kept painting. "He said that sometimes people get addicted to crisis. They grow up in it, and that's what they know. And if somehow they find their life is going good, somehow they'll do things to bring drama back into their lives. I wonder if that's you and me." I paused, glancing over my shoulder to him. He was staring back with hooded eyes.

My mouth went dry, but I focused on the painting once more. Or I tried. He got in there again. In my head. Under my skin. I could feel him, and my movements changed too. I wasn't so choppy in what I was creating. My movements were slow, tender. Cautious, but sensual at the same time.

"You're talking about self-sabotage."

"Maybe. I don't know. Subconscious for sure. I think that's you, but it's more. It's how I grew up with my family. I've started remembering moments growing up. Like, my dad was a cheater, and I didn't remember that until the other day. My mom and dad were fighting one time when I was in my room. I went and overheard. They were talking about a woman in the neighborhood. And my mom used to drink when I was little. I thought she only started when my dad died, but that's not true. She started drinking again. And my brother." I hadn't visited Isaac, either, for so long. I almost forgot about him. How horrible of a sister was I? He was in prison, and I forgot for a full week. Then it was two weeks. "He took drugs, even when he was a kid. It's weird, remembering these things now. I knew it was happening back then, but somehow I'd forgotten. My brother was sober when he went to prison, so I've been operating on that narrative this whole time. He was sober, but that's not the truth. He took a lot of drugs in high school. I was in college when it happened, when he—you know. My dad. When it all fell apart, or that's how I think of it." I stopped painting as more memories were rushing in, old pain right with them. "I used to blame myself. I think I blamed myself so much that it became a part of me, like in my foundation as a person. Funny how I started realizing that stuff, you know?"

"You blamed yourself for your dad dying?"

Oh yeah. My throat choked up. There was the old searing pain I used to always feel. It burrowed deep, settling up right next to where my heart was.

"I was in college, thinking about going for something else. Art therapy. I wanted to work with at-risk youth, but then my dad died. My brother went to prison because of it, and it all changed. I guess. Like, if I'd been there, none of that would've happened." Another realization hit me hard. "My mom blames me, and I've always let her. I blamed myself too. That's why I've—" Why I let her say the things she said to me. Jesus. I believed her, so I accepted it. I expelled a deep breath. "Starting to know why some people can't handle silence. Because they hear what's in their head. That's fucked up."

"I think it makes perfect sense."

I looked. His hands were in his pockets, and his head was leaning against the wall. His eyes flashed, meeting mine, and his head moved forward, but he didn't step away from the wall. He stayed there, half lounging but now more focused on me.

"These three months, I learned more."

"About?"

"About me. About you."

His mouth parted, and his eyes went flat. "Yeah? What'd you learn?"

"That I could quit you, if I had to. It'd take a long time, way longer than three months. Maybe a year, maybe more, but I could do it. Everything else is fine in my life. My mom, she's not my problem anymore. My brother is getting by. My job too. I got friends. I got a good career, one that some days I feel like I make a difference. It's small, but that one time a parolee gets it is worth all the others that don't. I got people who care about me, so I'd be okay without you."

He pushed off from the wall, coming toward me. Slow. His eyes were dark, a glint of danger from them. "That's funny."

"How so?" I was holding myself steady, not backing up as he got into my space, crowding me.

His hands went to my waist, slipping under my shirt, and he began moving me back. To the wall. The canvas was right next to us.

I had paint on my hands. He didn't care as he just stared down into me.

"How's that funny?" I had a slight hitch in my breath. I didn't like that. I felt like it was showing how I was totally lying to him and to myself.

Or maybe I wasn't.

Maybe I actually could've quit him. Probably. Everyone had to move on, no matter how much time would pass, but there'd be damages. Haunts. Yeah. I could move on from him, but I'd be scarred. I didn't want to share that part.

"I told you to wait. I told you I'd need time and everything I was doing was to make it safe for you."

"You said it, but you were trying to push me away, and you know that too."

He continued watching me. I continued feeling him inside of me. He knew I was right like I knew he meant what he said, but conversations weren't always about what was said. They were about what was being said under the surface too.

"Maybe."

I pulled my gaze away, focusing on his chest and how it was moving in a slow rhythm. "Yeah. You couldn't stay away because I put in my two weeks today."

He didn't respond. That's okay. I knew the truth.

He broke first because I was going to make the last move to actually break away. If any of that made sense. But that was all gone now because he was here and he was touching me, and my body was heating up because the second he spoke, I knew what was going to happen.

I tipped my head back, seeing him studying my mouth. "Are we done messing around now?"

His eyes pulled up, meeting my gaze, and whatever he read in me, he cursed at seeing it. "Jesus Christ." But he bent, his hands went under my ass, and he lifted me up to him.

This was what I knew would happen.

He was here. He was in.

His mouth found mine.

All that nonsense, and this was the one thing that was crystal clear for us.

I could quit him, but I wasn't going to.

CHAPTER

FIFTY-SEVEN

TRACE

I took her home that night and stayed.

I came back the next night.

The night after.

Then we switched things up, and she began sleeping at my place.

The night after *that*.

And after again.

We were both so screwed, but I couldn't stay away.

I was done fighting.

CHAPTER

FIFTY-EIGHT

JESS

It was a new day, a new dawn, a new era.

Just kidding.

I was back at another New York Stallions hockey game, but things had changed. I wasn't *only* here with Kelly. Justin was also with us. I'd evolved where the hockey stairway guy was now my secret boyfriend, and Kelly's not-secret boyfriend was attending the game with us. Evolution. Right? I didn't think that could be applied in this situation, but I was past caring about that too.

Also, I was going to be thirty next week. I *liked* thinking of Trace as my boyfriend. Made me feel young and fresh. Hip. That's the word.

I was happy. And I shouldn't be, but I gave in. Trace and me were Trace and me. I wouldn't be going home to my apartment alone tonight. Who knew? I had all sorts of opportunities. Trace might meet me there, or snap, I might even go to his place. Because that was *also* an option.

I had a life. Well, I had a life before . . . actually, I had a pretty active life. Lots of friends, though half of that group was our bowling friends, but I had Leo. Val.

I didn't know why I was going on about what I was going on about. "You seem good."

There. That was it.

Kelly just went for beer, and Justin moved over to sit in her seat.

He was grinning at me, so I grinned back. "Thanks. I *am* good. You, too, by the way. You and Kelly seem happy."

His grin deepened. "We are. There was some drama with my family, but we got through it."

"The night she showed up at my place."

"Yeah. That night." He gave a tentative smile. "Thanks for, uh, not engaging."

"Engaging?"

"Some friends like to jump on the bandwagon of 'Oh, what'd he do? What an asshole.' That sort of thing. You didn't do that. Thank you."

I shrugged. "Sure, but that'd be stupid. Thanks for not telling her about the car ride I took with Trace."

"Don't know anything about that or why you would refer to your boss as Trace."

Right.

"Okay!" Kelly was back, falling into Justin's emptied seat. "Guess who I ran into at the concessions? Molly. Can you believe it? She came for the game."

"What?"

"Yeah!" Her smile was so wide. She was beaming. "She's sitting on the other side, but Molly's cousin is filling in at Easter Lanes for her."

"Who's she with?"

"She came alone. Said she got the ticket as a gift last minute and couldn't miss this. Molly never gets out, so I was thinking we could go dancing after. Maybe at Octavia? Right, Jess?"

Dancing at Octavia? I was in. That sounded like fun.

———

Octavia was one of the "in" nightclubs to go to, but it was in a shitty neighborhood. I was pretty sure we'd gone past two groups of guys trying to jack cars when we parked, and as we had to walk past them to get to the nightclub, I took out my badge and made sure it was in plain view.

Two of the guys started toward us, saw my badge, and backtracked. They were gone from sight by the time we walked past, and once we got to the club, I called to see if a squad could swing through here.

"Okay. That was kinda cool." Justin had a sheepish look on his face, his head ducking a little.

I tucked my badge back under my shirt once we were going past the bouncers. They gave us both a nod. One said, "Worthing."

Justin started at that, his eyes narrowing, before he touched my back and urged me ahead of him.

What was that about?

But then we were inside, into the same darkness as always, and he showed me his phone's screen.

Molly: Grabbed a booth table in the far east corner.

I nodded back. The music was louder than normal. The place was jam packed. Justin maneuvered us through the crowd. A few times a hand tried to grab both of us, but he either blocked them or I did.

When we neared the booth, he stopped dead in his tracks.

I hit into him, but he didn't notice. His back was completely rigid, and moving around him, I saw that Kelly and Molly weren't alone. Two other guys were with them.

I moved closer to get a better look.

Kelly was talking to them, her hands in the air, big bright smiles. She was acting like she'd known them forever. Molly had edged away from both, giving them space. The one guy was tuned in to Kelly while the second one was listening but giving Molly some looks.

They were good looking. Built. Big. Wide shoulders. All muscles. Tight white shirts, so they were really standing out when the neon lights flashed around the dance floor. Square jawlines. They were either personal trainers or criminals. As I moved ahead, the main guy spotted me, and his eyes narrowed.

His gaze was pinned to me, and I reached up, touching the chain where my badge was hanging from. A hardened look flashed in his gaze.

I didn't know his name, but he was a criminal.

Justin moved around me, and I looked up, catching a glimpse of his face. His face was in stone. I'd never seen such fury on Justin's face. I caught his arm. "Who are those guys?"

He spotted my chain and grabbed it, then tucked it under my shirt before realizing he'd touched me. "Sorry. Just—I need a favor from you tonight?"

"What is it?"

"I kept quiet about you and Tristian West. I need you to do the same about your bosses and about what you do for a living."

So my gut was right. "Who are those guys to you?"

"Family, and not the family I want you to meet."

He started to go forward, but I stepped in front once more. "Who are they in connection to Kelly?"

"She met them at that party you left. They came later, and since she moved in, they've come around a few times. They're . . . she doesn't know they're not good guys, okay? I haven't gotten around to telling her everything."

"You need to."

His eyes flashed. "Right. As soon as you do."

I didn't answer.

He scoffed, moving around me. "That's what I thought. Listen, it's not permanent. Okay? Either Kelly and I are going to move or . . . I don't know. I haven't figured it out yet."

I felt my phone buzzing and pulled it out. The screen was lit up. *Trace calling.*

I hit the button to send a text in response.

Me: At Octavia with friends. I can't hear you if I answered

Trace: Get somewhere you can hear me. Now. I mean it, Jess.

I frowned, but seeing that no one was looking my way, I slipped out until I found a back hallway. The music was a little more muted; then I found an unlocked door, and even better. It was a maintenance closet, but I'd be able to hear him.

I called him back.

"Why are you at Octavia?"

I frowned. "It's a thing called 'night out with friends.' You ever heard of it?"

He growled from across the phone, "Who are you there with?"

"Kelly. Justin. A friend from bowling." I kept frowning because I'd been to Octavia before. Trace knew this, and as far as I knew, there was no beef between him and the owner. "What's going on? Why are you being like this?"

"I'm getting reports that you're there with others."

Wait. "Reports? What are you talking about?"

He bit out another growl. "Listen to me, where are you right now?"

"I'm in a closet so I could talk to you."

"Stay there. Ashton's closer than me. He's on his way to you."

"Ashton? *What* is going on?"

"It's too much to explain. I've been trying to keep you out of it because of your job, but you're in danger."

"I am?" I reached for the door. "If I am, then Kelly is. My other friends."

"No. They aren't. *You* are."

"That makes no sense. I'm going." I was already out the door and hanging up.

"Wait! Je—" I heard that much and paused, but if Kelly or Molly or Justin were in danger, I had to go. It was who I was, what I did.

I was shoving back through the crowd when I spotted them at the booth.

Molly was in a far corner, half hiding behind Kelly.

Justin was standing in front of Kelly, but his stance was different. Half protecting, half shielding, but trying not to appear he was doing any of that at the same time. It was confusing, and the two guys were standing side by side. Hands in their pockets. One guy was all in, talking to Justin. Laughing, but his eyes kept darting to Kelly behind him.

The other guy was standing there, but his attention was fully on Molly. A suggestive sneer was in place, and she was trying to pretend she wasn't noticing, but she was noticing.

I started forward until I felt a hand on my arm. "Wha—" I started to swing on whoever was restraining me, but saw it was Ashton and pulled my arm free at the last second. "Do not ever grab me like that again."

He didn't care. He had turned his back to the booth, and was in front of me, herding me backward. "You need to listen to me. You are officially past the 'messing around' phase. If you're with Trace, you have to decide, because those two guys back there are not friendly with us. They find out about you, they won't hesitate to kill. They'll do anything to hurt us. Do you hear me?"

"Wait." I'd let him move me back, farther out of eyesight, but put on the brakes. I noticed three other guys going around us, both descending on the booth. I went to try and watch, but Ashton went with me, blocking me. I shoved away from him. "I have a gun on me. Don't think I won't use it if I'm feeling in danger."

"I'm aware," he lashed back, his eyes blazing. "You've been cleared to enter here with your weapon."

"Cleared? By who?"

"By us. We're on friendly terms with Cole Mauricio. This is his club, and his staff is very aware of who you are. They're the ones who alerted us about who else is here with you."

"Wait." Jesus. I couldn't keep up. "Who are you talking about?"

"The Mauricio family."

"I know who Cole Mauricio is. His family is not active here. They're active in Chicago."

"No, they're not, but they still have business here, and this *is* our area. We've had an understanding with them for a very long time, but they do not have an understanding with the Worthing family."

Worthing.

I moved back another full step.

Justin Worthing.

"What are you talking about?"

"This," he ground out. "This is why you and Trace need to stop messing around. You're either with him or you're not. None of this in-between bullshit. If you're not, you need to get the fuck out of our lives. Your friend back there is related to the family that's trying to move in on our territory. The gunshots that article talked about? It was from them."

"Wait a minute." What did this all mean? Panic was rising in me. Kelly. Justin. "Justin's involved?"

"No. We vetted Justin before we hired him. Or I did. Trace approved. Justin is innocent, caught between family members he's related to. That's all. We didn't realize the Worthing family would move into our city."

"What side of his family is Mafia? I thought he had a wealthy side and a blue side?"

"There are members of the wealthy side that are in the business."

"The side you're friends with?"

"No, but yes. They have distant cousins in the business. I wasn't fully aware of how powerful they'd grown until the party. They showed up when I was there, and it didn't go well. Trace was already gone, or it would've been bad. Very bad."

"Justin's brother is a detective."

"We're aware."

"Is he involved?"

Ashton didn't answer that, and that was an answer by itself.

"I thought you had cops on your payroll."

"We do, and the longer you stand here talking to me, the higher the probability that your name will get on a list that you do not want it to be on. So." His eyes flashed again, and he leaned in. "To further save everyone's energy and potential lives, you need to choose. Either be with Trace—and I mean it, let it be known—or leave him the fuck alone. You got me?"

I understood, but I was concerned about other matters right now. I moved to the side, looking for our booth and finding everyone's attention *right on us*. Guess we hadn't moved far enough out of their eyesight.

Kelly's eyebrows were pulled in, the ends of her mouth turned down.

Molly's eyes were big, bulging out, and she looked ready to start walking our way. Justin had a hand on her arm, his other arm blocking Kelly too.

Muttering a curse, Ashton let out a savage growl and was heading right for them.

I was right behind him.

The two guys moved forward, looking like they were going to meet Ashton, but seeing me next to him, they eased back a step.

Ashton let out a small laugh before turning his gaze to Justin, then to his hand on Molly's arm. "Hands off. Now."

Justin released her, his eyebrows shooting up.

Molly jerked to the side a few steps, her other hand coming up to rub where Justin had been holding her, but she didn't look in pain. Her own eyebrows were bunched together, her gaze jumping from Ashton, to Justin, to Ashton, to me, and back to Ashton. One of the guys I'd noticed moving in with Ashton earlier stepped up to her, touching her other arm lightly. He bent down, saying something to her, and with a small nod and another look toward Ashton, who was watching the whole thing, she headed off with the guy.

What the hell was that?

But Kelly had moved forward. "What's going on? Jess, where'd you go?"

"She—" Ashton started, but a hand was on my arm, from the other side, but this time, I recognized that hand.

I glanced up, seeing Trace's gaze skim over me. He had the same hard look on his face that Ashton did, and he eased me back behind him. "Go with my men."

"But—"

"Please." He indicated the same guy who had pulled Molly from the group. She was handed off to a different guy, and this guy was coming back for me.

Suit guy. I pegged him as security, noting the bulge on his side from the holstered gun.

I made my choice. I moved forward. "No, Trace."

"Jess." His jaw clenched.

"No. Not while Kelly is here."

He touched my arm, pulling me back away again. Kelly's head stretched at an angle, trying to see us, but Ashton and the security guy stepped in, fully blocking her.

Trace's hand moved to my waist, and he stepped in, the front of his body grazing mine. "Please. So I don't worry about you."

"I'm armed."

"I'm aware, but I am trying to save you from making a decision you might not want to make."

Ashton's warning. I had to choose. It registered then what Trace was doing. He was still trying to hide me from the other guys, but he didn't understand. The decision was done.

I touched his chest. "She's my best friend. She's my only sister. I'm not leaving."

His eyes were a whole storm, and he clipped his head. "Fine, but you're mine. I won't pretend otherwise."

I nodded, my whole body suddenly feeling heavy. "I get it. I do."

I was choosing him. Be damned or not, I couldn't hide anymore.

Let the cards fall where they fall.

CHAPTER

FIFTY-NINE

TRACE

Penn and Crispin Worthing.

Both major dickheads.

Ashton saw me coming, so he stepped back. I moved forward, taking point. "Gentlemen."

Crispin was the leader of the two, and he stepped forward, cracking his knuckles slowly. "West. This ain't your club."

"No, but unlike your family, my family has an understanding with the owners."

They shared a look at that information.

Justin stepped ahead, one arm held out toward his cousins and the other toward me. "We're just here having fun. That's all."

I ignored him, staring at Crispin. "Leave, Worthing. Now."

He started to tilt his chin up, but then his eyes went to the side of me.

I knew Jess was there, felt her. They were taking her in, but they were also noting my other men who had come with me. I'd added to my detail by another fifteen guys.

"You are here alone."

He bounced his chin up. "How do you know that?"

All bravado. A typical fucking Worthing—I was starting to notice their trademarks. They were hotheads, led by a hothead uncle who'd come over from Sicily thinking he could make a name for his family here and not respecting that the territories had been drawn up decades ago.

"Leave, Worthing, and we won't kill you tonight."

I felt Jess's instant tension.

She chose. I'd asked her to leave, but she'd made her choice. She was at my side.

Crispin smirked. "You got a copper next to you, unless she's on your take."

I didn't comment, stepping forward. "Leave while you can walk." At my order, my men moved forward. This time, Crispin stepped back. I could feel his reluctance, but he growled as he hit his cousin on the arm and jerked his head toward the exit door.

When they started to reach for Justin, Ashton stepped up. "He stays."

"Excuse us?" Penn started forward, but Crispin blocked him.

Ashton pointed at Justin. "Him, we won't kill. You two, we will. Leave while you can."

I heard Jess groaning behind me and reached back, touching her arm. She quieted, but as soon as those two left, she was around me in a second. Kelly began sobbing. Justin looked torn, not sure whether to care for his woman or to head us off. Jess took the decision out of his hands, enveloping her old roommate in her arms and leading her away. I watched, seeing my men directing them out of here.

I relaxed once I saw Jess was listening to them. Kelly's head was buried into Jess's neck, her arms wrapped around her.

Justin started snarling as soon as his cousins were gone and as soon as Jess had his woman out of earshot. "What the hell? What the *hell* was *that*?"

Ashton smirked before snorting. "It's called organized crime. Sometimes we have turf wars. You should google it before you end up dead, Worthing."

He strode off, looking as if he was whistling.

We were getting attention, but Justin turned my way this time.

"You threatened my family's lives."

Yeah. Okay. I stepped closer so he could hear me clearly. "Jess chose tonight. I chose tonight. I think if you don't choose, you'll end up dead, and let me be *very* clear: it won't be by our hands." I let that sink in before adding, "You have a night. You have a connection to my woman that I can't ignore. If you choose their side, you better leave fucking town. Are you getting me?"

He swallowed and raised his chin up. "You are putting me in an impossible situation."

"Tough. That's this business. Choose or die. If you don't choose, you will die, and I will not let you be the swinging door where my woman could get hurt."

"She's a cop."

I'd started to leave but turned back. "No one is invincible."

———

Ashton was waiting for me in the back hallway. He fell in step with me. "The first team is waiting for you. The second team is waiting for Worthing to hurry his ass up. They'll take him and his woman home, and if you want them to stick around and sit on their place, they'll do that too."

"What about Easter?"

"She's with team three, who already took her home."

I gave him a look. "She's pretty far removed from this whole situation. She should be safe."

"It doesn't matter. My family owns her father, so she's my problem."

"And Jess?"

"She's waiting in your car because she's with team one."

She was . . . I let that sink in, and I couldn't deny that her waiting in my vehicle, with my guys, was making me feel a certain way. "Where are you going after this?"

"I need to check on a few things, but I'll head to my uncles'. Worthings were here. They're escalating, and we will need to make a move sooner than later."

Which meant that he and I needed to make our own decisions because even though a certain news article had come out saying we were the new heads, it wasn't the case. We'd been dancing over the line ourselves. Choosing this life had a whole sense of finality, and I wasn't sure if I was ready to choose that finality. Not yet, but soon. Neither of us could push it off much longer.

My phone began ringing.

Ashton had started to leave but halted.

Unknown calling.

I showed him the screen, then moved farther down so we had privacy. He followed as I answered.

"Who is this?"

"This is Tristian West, nephew of Stephano West? Son of Dominic West? I presume I'm conversing with that person?"

"Who are you?"

"This is Nicolai Worthing. I've just been informed that you met my cousins Crispin and Penn."

Ashton raised an eyebrow and stuffed his hands in his pockets, getting comfortable.

"Interesting names in your family."

Nicolai barked out a laugh. "Yeah, well, I can say Tristian and Stephano probably follow in the same family tradition. You're Greek? Am I getting that correct?"

"What do you want, Nicolai Worthing?"

"Hmm. Yes. Straight to business. I have heard you are not like your uncle. That's a refreshing surprise. Your uncle, he could tell stories for hours before getting to the point."

"And your point for this phone call is . . . ? I am still waiting."

"I feel I may have a surprising proposition for you."

Ashton snorted, not caring if he was heard or not.

"Am I to presume that is Ashton Walden in the background? His grandmother is from Argentina?"

Ashton's eyes cooled. He leaned forward as I extended the phone toward him, and he spoke into it. "My family lineage is none of your business. How about that?"

"On the contrary, I feel that those of us who are in this business are in it because of our grandparents or the grandparents of our grandparents. Everything has history and lineage."

I pulled the phone back to me. "And your family does not have the history that ours does."

"No. You're correct. We're relatively new, but I have a great respect for those—"

"What's your *point*, Worthing? You're making me regret letting your cousins return to you, alive and intact."

"Yes. See. That's why I'm reaching out to you for this proposition. I've learned that you and Ashton both have your own businesses. Legal businesses. You are both thriving in your own fields. I've seen his records myself, and your uncle *is* dying. He has brain cancer, and if my sources are correct, he was first told about the possibility the very day he first told you he was having medical problems. Now, I'm sure there's a reason he has waffled back and forth. Denial. Negotiation. Anger. These are all common stages for grief when given the sentence that he was given. Am I correct in what has been reported to me?"

Who the fuck was this guy's source? My uncle's medical records?

"What is your goddamn proposition? I'm to assume you are the new head of your family?"

"Yes. And to the point. As always, you remain true to your reputation. My proposal to you is this: When your uncle dies, let me take over the handling of all the family business. You, in turn, will be in charge of my money. You can invest it how you see fit. You can remain in your very legal businesses—which I can't help but wonder if that will help your woman as well, considering her career choice—but you're in charge of the money.

"The name in your city, and it is *your* city, will remain the West Mafia, because you will be handling all of the financials. I love your city. You have beautiful hospitals and doctors here, but think of us as a franchise. We're coming in, taking over handling the actual work, but everything flows upward to where you would be: at the top. And with your blessing, we will work hand in hand alongside the Walden family because unlike yourself, the Walden uncles have no interest in stepping away from the business, as is their right. They've fought long and hard for their place in your city, but you, as I'm hoping one day I might consider a friend, have interests that lie along the legal world.

"What say you, Mr. Tristian West? Would you like some time to consider the offer? Time to also do your own research? Because while your initial instinct is to turn my offer down, I *truly* hope you do not do that. I also hope you do not judge me based on your meeting with my two cousins, who, though I love them, are imbecile human beings. They are very much considered the 'brawn' of our family genes, whereas I myself inherited the looks, some brawn, and the brains.

"Also." His voice went serious. "I went to Cambridge, and I'm hoping that when you look into me, you'll see the similarities between yourself and myself. Both raised to succeed in the civil world, but both with family that has pulled us into their world. It's certainly a plight that we find ourselves in, isn't it?"

Ashton's eyes were narrowed, his head down, as he listened to the call. When Nicolai was done speaking, he raised his head, but I couldn't get a read on what he was thinking.

"I'll take your proposal into consideration."

"It's been my pleasure, Tristian West. Until we meet in person."

I ended the call. "What do you think?"

"I think"—he was still eyeing the phone—"that you will do what you will do. You'll research. You'll get all your answers, and then you will gamble based upon that research of where you want to put your money, like the good Wall Street best friend I know."

I grunted because he was right. Though it *was* a tempting offer.

"He said brain cancer."

Ashton's face went somber. "He did. That would explain a few things."

It would indeed.

CHAPTER SIXTY

JESS

I was on the phone with Kelly when Trace walked into his place.

I'd been waiting with his team, but something had happened, and they'd driven me without him. As soon as I'd walked inside, Kelly had called, and for the last hour I'd been talking her down.

"I gotta go, Kelly. I'll talk to you later."

She was sobbing and hiccuped on a sniffle. "Okay. Be safe, please."

"You too." I was watching Trace steadily as he came in, taking his suit jacket off, then taking out two guns that I had no idea he'd taken to carrying. He put one in the drawer, and he took the other to a side wall, where he moved a photo aside, and I saw him open a safe for it.

"When did you start with those?"

"The day my uncle threatened you."

That got my attention. "What?"

"It was the last day I saw you too. Outside your apartment."

Oh. Right.

"He threatened me that night?"

"Make you feel better, he threatened everyone I cared about that night, but yeah. He made it abundantly clear that he knew about you.

It's why I stayed away as long as I could." He closed the safe and came toward me, raking a hand through his hair. "Want a drink?"

"What happened tonight?"

"I'm going to get a drink." He came over, stopped, pressed a kiss to my forehead, but moved beyond me to the liquor cabinet. There was a tingle left from his touch and his hand as he touched my waist, grazing it around me before dropping it back to his side. "Is Kelly okay? You were on the phone with her?"

"She wants to know about you and me, more specifically when you and me became you and me."

He gave me a grin. It was a tired grin, but still a grin. There was a huge boulder of tension in my gut, but a small piece of it chipped away at that look from him. Not everything was totally fucked up.

"Justin came clean with everything about his family, but he also told her about you and Ashton. So, yeah. There's that."

"Kelly is freaked."

I affirmed with a nod, moving over to him as he poured some bourbon in a glass and held it over to me. I took it. "Kelly is freaked."

He took a sip of his own, watching me over the top of his glass as he did. "I got an offer tonight."

I took a sip, raising my eyebrow. "Sounds interesting."

"I'm guessing Nicolai Worthing is related to Justin somehow. He called, said his cousins were imbeciles."

"Makes me like him."

He ignored me. "And he offered a sort of franchise proposition. He moves in, takes over everything, while I run the money. The West family still controls everything at the top, but I'm not involved with the dirty business."

"Except the money part."

"There's that. Yes. That part."

I pointed at myself, raising my other eyebrow. "And you're telling me? An officer of the law, more so in regard to parolees, but still. It's in my wheelhouse, and you know, there's the issue where I'm not dirty. I just like fucking you."

He grinned.

I grinned back. "Why are you sharing this new player with me?"

He swirled the last of his bourbon around the glass before letting out a small sigh. "I wanted to be straight with you. Assumed you would have questions, and I don't want to start this relationship off with lies. I'm sure little lies will come into play later, but not yet. And because while he was giving me this offer, I realized something."

"What's that?"

He had a look in his eyes, a gleam. It was a light, and he was still grinning at me, in a very delicious way, but while that was making my heart speed up, the look in his eyes was adding to it. He was happy, and that made me happy, and in our present situation, I wasn't sure either of us should be happy.

But he was, and that made me, so I was going to accept it.

"I realized tonight that when you chose me, it made me want to choose you back."

My eyebrows dipped down. "Huh?"

The grin was gone. He put his glass down on the counter, reached, and put mine next to it. Then he started forward, coming and placing his hands on my waist. "I realized tonight that I am in love with you."

He picked me up before I could react, and I squealed as he did. My legs locked around his waist. My hands went to his shoulders, but I leaned back to see his face. "What?"

"Yeah." He turned serious, his voice dipping down into a whisper. His gaze scanned over my face, going to my mouth, lingering, and then moving to my eyes. A whole new look was coming from him. Sincerity, but also a light. It was a new light. Like a bulb was turned on inside of him. He began walking, carrying me backward. "I didn't realize that after the call. I realized that when you stood next to me when we were facing off against those guys, but then the call came, and while I have no interest in accepting this guy's offer, I did realize something else."

"What's that?" I settled back, my hands connecting behind his neck.

His hands went to my ass, but I scooted back enough so I could bounce in place. It was odd, a position that I'd never been in before unless as a child, but I liked it. Felt carefree. Fun. Trace grinned at me almost ruefully as he cupped my ass cheeks, helping me bounce. "I want out."

I paused midbounce. "Out? From . . . ?"

"From the family business."

I went still. Tensing. "You mean . . . ?" My heart slammed up in my throat.

He nodded, slowly, intensely. "I want out. My uncle is dying, and when he dies, I'm going to make the business die with him."

"Are you serious?"

"I am."

"But Ashton?"

We were in the bedroom by now. He didn't move to turn the light on, and when we came in here, all the other lights would turn off. They were on motion detectors. His windows were slanted so that no one could see in unless he pushed a special button to let them see, but he never had. We could see out; they couldn't see in. He took me to the bed and moved so I was standing on it. Then, his hands went to my pants, and he began to undress me, sliding my zipper down. "Ashton is my brother. He'll either go with me or he won't, but he'll still support me. It was an understanding we've always had with each other. If one wanted out, the other would be fine with it. Our brotherhood was and is always first."

He slid my pants down, his hands trailing along with them. My skin was lit from sensations from that touch.

He reached up to pull down my panties. I lifted a foot, then the other. He tossed my pants and underwear aside. His hands ran up my legs, the back of each of them, going to cover my ass. He palmed me and moved me forward, his head tipping back so he could see me from the lights turned on outside. Streetlamps. Other buildings. The moon, what we could see. Even a few ships were out there, but they were background light, letting me see his face fully.

"Do you love me?"

His voice thickened as he asked, and he moved a hand around me. Coming to my stomach. Sliding up, moving my shirt with it as it went until he rested it between my breasts. He leaned in. He moved my bra down, and his mouth covered one of my nipples, his tongue sweeping around. He moved, finding my other breast as he pulled my shirt and bra off, probably tossing them alongside my other clothes.

I was fully naked in front of him, but he tipped his head back once more. His eyes finding mine. "Do you?"

I couldn't answer, not because I didn't know or didn't want to, because as he asked, his hand moved around to cup me. His thumb pressed over my clit, starting to move in a slow and sensual motion, and at the same time, two of his fingers moved up inside of me.

I jerked up from the motion, my breath hitching in my throat.

"Hmmm, Jess?" He grazed the insides of my breasts, moving his head. His jaw rubbed against me, and he was lowering me to the bed, his fingers still moving inside of me. In, holding, and back out with a twist. His thumb continued moving over me, pressing in. So slow. Achingly slow.

"You've not answered. Do you love me?" But his fingers pulled out. Both of his hands went to my hips, and he lifted me up. A pillow was brought underneath me. He positioned me so he had complete access to me. Then his mouth dipped in, and I gasped, my hands grabbing onto his head, his hair, as his tongue replaced his fingers.

He feasted on me, and I couldn't speak. I could barely breathe.

I was panting and writing in place as he continued to explore me. He took his time, his very languid and delicious time, until he lifted his head back up. He met my eyes, looking down my body to where I was watching him. He smiled. "Do you love me, Jess?"

I was melting into a pile of sensations, pleasure.

"Yes." I breathed out my answer, and he gave me a blinding smile before his head moved back.

I couldn't speak for the rest of the night.

———

I woke later, much later. The clock said it was six in the morning—6:43, to be exact. Trace's arm was nestled under my breasts. He was molded up behind me, one of his legs pushed in through mine. His head was burrowed into my neck and shoulders, but that hadn't woken me up.

What had?

I saw my phone on the stand next to the bed, and the red light was blinking.

I had a message.

Glancing back, not wanting to wake him, I moved gently to disentangle myself. He let me go, but not all the way. His head moved down so it was pressed into my back. His arm wrapped around my waist, and his leg moved higher up between mine.

He could press up a little more, and I'd be waking him up for a whole different need.

But, reaching over, I was able to grab my phone.

After opening it, I keyed in my code and saw the first message.

Bear: Don't be alarmed. Your mom is stable, but when you get this, you should come down to the hospital. Chelsea overdosed tonight.

CHAPTER

SIXTY-ONE

JESS

I shoved through the doors, flashed my badge, and bypassed the front desk.

Trace was on my heels. I hadn't cared he was coming. He'd tried to ask, to make sure on the scramble to get dressed and get here, but I'd barely reacted.

My mom. Get to my mom. That was my only concern, and now we were here, and I was racing down the hallway toward where she'd be kept. I'd been here enough times that the staff knew me by name.

I skidded to a halt, seeing one of the senior-most nurses on staff. She held up a hand. "Whoa there, Je—" She stopped, seeing who was coming right behind me. Her head straightened up, and she stood a little taller. "Fancy seeing you here." Her eyes darted to me and back again. "And with law enforcement."

Trace's hand came to the small of my back as he stepped to my side. "How's her mother, Sloane?"

She didn't answer at first, her eyes falling down to where he was touching me and back up again, then to me before slowing sliding once more to him. "No disrespect, Trace, but I have to say that I'm not approving of this situation."

His hand pressed harder to me, and the side of his body pressed against mine. I could feel his tension. "Why don't you save the judgment and tell us how her mother is?"

"She's alive." Her tone gentled, and she took a step back before turning and indicating we should follow her. "Call came in from the ambulance, so we were ready. Patrick was with her, and he had the bottle of what she ingested too." She moved to a room and pulled back the curtain, and a startled cry left me before I could clamp down on my emotions.

My mom was in bed. She was intubated, her skin with an unhealthy pallor.

She looked so small, like she could've been sixteen.

Trace stepped up even closer, holding me upright before my knees firmed. I gave him a nod before pushing off and approaching the bed. Her hand was peeking out from the blanket. I looked, but no one else was here. "Where—"

"Pat must've stepped out. He was here earlier."

Pat was Bear's first name. Or Patrick. I forgot some people preferred to use that name. Never made sense to me.

I nodded, suddenly so fucking tired. "He called, said she was stable."

"She is. She was. She'll be just fine. They administered Narcan. She's just sleeping it off now. She'll be sore when she wakes, but you know the drill."

Because I'd seen this before with parolees. Too many times to count.

I moved to the chair by the bed and took my mom's hand in mine, and I laid my forehead next to it. If I could've crawled in bed with her, I would've, but only while she was like this. The second she woke, I had no doubt it'd be back to the norm. Hateful words and loathing feelings. Blame all around. Same old, same old.

But right now, she looked vulnerable and peaceful.

My heart constricted. What did that say about me that I wished she could look like this a little longer before her fighting spirit lit her alive once again?

"You have got to be kidding me?"

A new voice, a new arrival. One that wasn't happy.

I lifted my head—everything in me was so heavy—and I saw Leo standing with two coffees in hand. He was glaring at Trace before jerking his gaze to find me, then my mother. His gaze softened just a tad before going back to Trace and hardening all over again. "Get the fuck out of here, West. I won't give you another chance, or the handcuffs are getting pulled out."

"He's with me, Leo."

My boss, mentor, and second dad swung his gaze my way. The soft look was gone. He barreled in, sweeping past Trace and Sloane, and put one of the coffees on the nightstand. He went to my mom's other side before turning and facing back at them. "Get out. Now."

Trace ignored him, looking to me. "You need anything?"

I scanned the room, taking in everyone's stances. Sloane seemed caught, which didn't make sense to me, but my mom was here. She was sleeping. I was okay right now.

I said as much to him, still holding her hand. "Gonna stay a bit." I gestured to Leo. "Have a talk."

His eyes lifted to Leo, who was barely keeping it together. He was huffing. "If I had a fucking shovel with me, you'd already be dead, West. Get out of here. I say it one more time, and I don't care whose gun gets drawn. You feel me?"

Trace took him in before his eyes shifted to me. "Call me if you need something. I mean it. Anything."

I nodded, and his eyes darkened.

I wanted him to come over, press a kiss to me or at least smooth a hand back over my hair, but he didn't. Not yet. And judging by his reluctance, he wanted to do the same, but it was too soon. I watched Leo as Trace left and heard Sloane comment, quietly, "That one never ceases to amaze me. Okay, folks. Jess. Leo. I'm on staff today, so I'm here if you need anything. In the meantime, I'll tell the doc you both are here and wanting an update."

No sooner had she left before I heard from across the bed, "You screwing the Mafia now?"

"Way to not judge and wait for a time to do some proper questioning. Good call, Leo. I'm *real* inclined to explain my bedmate to you now."

"You better explain. I'm your boss."

"And my mom is lying in a hospital bed from an overdose while you and Bear told me I was 'off the hook.'"

"She's an alcoholic."

"Exactly. An alcoholic. Not a drug addict. She overdosed, Leo. What the fuck is that about?"

The curtains slid back, and this time, the voice I'd been expecting spoke up. "Oh, whoa. Whoa. Whoa! I could hear you two halfway down the hallway." Bear came in, a bag of food in hand. He took me in, took in my hand holding my mom's, and took in Leo before coming around to my side. He put the bag on the other stand, came up, and gave me a half hug. Smoothing a hand down my head, he leaned down and gave me a kiss to the forehead. "Hey, kiddo. How are you holding up?"

Leo made an exasperated sound, sitting back and shaking his head. He pinched his fingers at the bridge of his nose. "You have no idea who came in here with her."

I reached up, catching Bear's hand and giving it a small squeeze, but I wouldn't let go of my mom's with my other one. "I'm tired but okay as long as she's going to pull through."

He nodded, a sad smile pulling at the ends of his mouth. "I bet." He shot Leo a hard look over my head. "And I can imagine because I saw him coming out of here. We had a word."

I tensed, tipping my head back. "You had a word with Tristian West?"

He met my gaze, arching an eyebrow up. "I had a word with Trace West. I remember him from the neighborhood. He's not the man his uncle or pops were. I know that much." He was looking around before he headed back to the curtain. "I'll be back. Going to get myself a chair. You two better not kill each other until I get back." He pointed at both of us before slipping out.

"Trace?" Leo snapped at me. "I wasn't surprised you used the name, but Bear too? Maybe I need to get on a nickname basis with the future head of the West Mafia family. Or is he currently the head, according to a recent news article?"

Bear's lack of reaction didn't surprise me. He was smart and kind. He was also patient before he made up his mind about something. Leo's quick reaction also didn't surprise me. I would've reacted the same, but it was what it was. I made my choice tonight. I'd known what I was deciding, and I'd meant it when I'd decided to let the cards fall how they were going to fall.

But right now, in this room, Trace and I weren't the pressing matter.

I sat back in my chair, not letting go of my mom's hand. "Tell me what happened."

———

It was a little later when Bear came back, a chair in hand.

He sat just as soon as the doctor came in too.

We were all updated.

My mom had overdosed on painkillers, and while they believed she'd make a full recovery, a social worker would be assessing her.

He gave us all a hard look. "This was a suicide attempt. Let's be very clear on that. She will be moved over to the psych unit once she's stable. If you're not on board with her mental health team, then she could do this again. I was told the nurses overheard an argument in here already. My advice? Get on the same team regarding Mrs. Montell, and then do what you need to do to get her on board. The more cooperative she is with her mental health team, the better results you can expect. Now. Let's hope Mrs. Montell wakes up with a renewed outlook on life, but considering the looks each of you has, I'm guessing that likelihood is slim. Good luck, Officers."

He left and left a pregnant pause of silence in his wake.

Leo let out a sigh, returning to his chair and taking the second coffee with him. "I told her what happened, Bear."

"Goddamn," Bear roared. "Why'd you do that? I told her we had this covered."

Leo rolled his eyes, but I was the one who got in Bear's face.

"You were kind to me minutes ago, but now I know the real reason, and do not think for a second that you're off the hook."

Roles switched real quick because Leo informed me that they hadn't been checking on my mother like they'd let me believe. They'd given her an ultimatum after she'd fallen off the wagon once again, which I knew she would do, because she'd been doing it for half of my life.

Bear held up his hands, a frustrated sound escaping him. "We— she doesn't listen to reason. We tried. We did. She—she's not going to change until she hits rock bottom."

"So you thought to speed it up by abandoning her? What'd you do? Get my phone and block her from my own phone so she couldn't contact me? You know she would've since you both weren't taking her calls."

I was reeling, my mind whirling over what they'd just shared they'd done.

It wasn't drugs. It was a suicide attempt.

334

My mother . . . what had I done? I'd let them take over for me. I'd *let* them. I hadn't fought—I'd abandoned her.

It took me a little bit before I clued in that neither answered me. I looked at them. Both weren't looking at me either.

"What?" I ground out.

Bear firmly wouldn't meet my gaze, but Leo did, and for the first time I saw a softening from him. "We didn't block her from your phone, Jess."

He didn't finish saying the rest of the statement.

My knees gave out, and I reached out for the bed, and I fell into the chair behind me.

My mom had never called me. She hadn't tried. She'd, just . . .

CHAPTER SIXTY-TWO

JESS

Time stood still but also sped up after that. It was a weird mind fuck.

When my mom woke up, she wanted nothing to do with me. She did not have a new outlook on life. The doc's wishes didn't come true, but she went into the psychiatry unit, and I was told that Bear and Leo would take it from here. *Again.*

I didn't have a good outlook on that, either, but while she was getting taken care of, I had other items to handle. Mainly, Leo and Kelly.

The difference between those two was that I didn't know I had a Kelly matter to handle. She informed me of this later in the week, asking me for a sit-down. I'd not told her about my mother yet. And when I got there, I didn't feel this meeting was going to be a good one.

"Justin and I had a big come-to-Jesus meeting and . . ."

Oh, boy. I hated the ". . ."; those silences were brutal, I'd come to learn.

I readied myself because at this point, who the hell knew what else was coming down the pipeline.

Her hands were on the table, her hero in a bag next to her. That should've been my first clue. That the hero was bagged. That was a whole different level of preparing. Not where she would eat it here or eat it on the way out. That's how Kelly usually did it. This said she was going to take it somewhere *else* to eat it. That was a *whole different* thing there.

"Justin feels that it could be dangerous for us, him and me, to be in the middle of what is going on between our old bosses or—your—yeah. Mr. West and Justin's family."

My mouth went dry. "Really?"

Yeah. I should've known. The hero was bagged.

"Really."

I frowned, but okay. Time to pull my head out of my mom's stuff and into my best friend's head. It made sense what she was doing. Being around me was sometimes dangerous too.

"I think that's a good idea."

She stared at me, blinking a few times. Her hand grabbed for her bagged hero, and she pulled it in front of her, like it was a shield. A hero shield. From me. "Really?"

I frowned. "Yeah. I mean, Justin's not in with that side of the family. Am I right?"

"You're right. Yes." She jerked forward, her head moving up and down at a fast pace. "He's not. And his brother, with being a detective. He just feels like he's being pulled in all directions, and I get it. I do. I mean, I love you. You know I do, but I think he's going to be my future. You know how that goes."

A tear slipped free, falling down. A second one went too.

I didn't think she realized they were there.

Reaching forward, I took the hand that wasn't gripping the hero and held it in mine. I squeezed it once. "I get it, Kel. I do."

More tears.

She was going to be sobbing soon.

She sniffled. "You do?"

"I do. I've got my own battles to handle right now. I don't expect you to get pulled into the middle, and my god, you know I'd want you to be safe."

The sobbing got worse. "I feel like the worst friend. You've been there for me through so much stuff, and now this. Now you got a fine man, and *girl*." She paused in her sobbing and held a hand out. "That man is *fine*. Holy shit, he's fine. And you were at his side, but Justin. I—he said it's dangerous, and you're always telling me everything is dangerous, so I kinda figure maybe I should listen this time. Do you hate me? Please don't hate me. I'm hating myself."

I moved over, pulling my chair next to her.

People were whispering about us. I knew we had a few minutes before Sal came over to check on his Pigeon Lover Best Friend. She sent me his videos from YouTube every time he posted a new one. I had to admit the pigeons were cute when you put inspirational music in the background. I was cheering for one that I was pretty sure shit on my head two days ago.

"It's going to be fine. Everything will be fine."

I was firmly blocking out the mess from my mother because I had no idea how to fix that or what I even could do.

Be strong. Keep going. Kick ass if need be. That was my motto in life. Paint when you need to fall apart.

I gave Kelly a tight hug and held her. She let go of the hero—that told me she meant business—and grasped my arm.

"I love you. I'll always love you. We're sisters, and right now, there's some dangerous business going on between families and our men. Be safe. You know I always want that for you."

She was nodding, but I could feel some tears falling to my arm. "I know. I know. I have this feeling like I'm supposed to ask you something, check in with you about something, but I can't think what it is. Are you okay?" She pulled away, turning to face me more directly.

Kelly was doing the right thing now. I wasn't going to say anything about my mother to get in the way, so I shook my head. "Nope. Not a thing. One more hug, honey."

"Oooh. You used the term of endearment. It's been my dream for you to call me honey."

I laughed, doing as I said. Hugging. But now I was the one choking back tears, so I stood, gave her a firm kiss on her forehead. I was finding I had a thing about foreheads and gently squeezed her shoulder. "Love you. When you get engaged, call me."

"Agh! I'm going to fall apart all over again."

"Not that." Kelly wasn't going to be able to leave first, despite the bagged hero. I knew my friend. Her gut was telling her to stay put, so I went first. One last touch on her shoulder, a smile from me, and I headed out.

"Bye, Officer Montell." Sal waved a loaf of bread in the air.

I pointed at him as I bypassed the counter. "Give my regards to the pigeons, and make a second hero for my friend. I think she crushed the hell out of the first."

"We were watching. We're going to start calling them emotional support heroes."

I barked out a laugh as my insides were being sliced in half, but it was what it was.

I had a feeling this was only the first of the Trace/Jess fallout.

———

I was right. It just took two weeks for it to happen.

———

"You're suspended."

"What?" My mouth was on the floor. I started to look down for it, see if I could find it.

I knew there'd be a meeting with Leo, but I hadn't expected this. At least, not without a warning or a talking-to. I came in and sat, and he opened with that.

He shook his head, putting his radio on the table. "I don't have time to get into this with you, but you're in a sexual relationship with someone who has known connections—and very strong connections—to an organized crime family. We have a code of ethics. You cannot work here as long as you're in his bed."

A part of me expected this. I just hoped for a little longer before it happened, but wow. I knew the cards would fall.

"You have nothing to say? You're just going to take the suspension?"

"I . . ." Damn. I couldn't speak. My throat was burning. "He's getting out."

He laughed and snorted at the same time. "Right."

"He is."

He shoved upward, his chair squeaking from the ferocity of the movement, and slammed one hand on his desk. "He's the prince of that fucking family! What are you doing, Jess? I raised you better."

"You didn't raise me. No one did!"

"Bullshit." Another pound on the desk, but he jabbed a finger at me in the air. "Bullshit. I raised you. I stepped in when your father died. I'm helping take care of your mother right now! Don't give this BS that I didn't raise you. I'm raising your whole family. Your brother will be released, and guess whose couch he's going to end up on? Mine!"

"He's getting out—"

His voice overrode mine. "He's not getting out! He's going to take over." He motioned to the phone. "I just got a call from organized crime. They were inquiring if I had a PO undercover in the West family syndicate. An undercover PO, all the brainless, witless bullshit *that* would be. Are you kidding me? Are you *kidding* me?!"

His voice rose an octave with each statement he was yelling, but there was nothing I could say.

Chain of command. You took it. I was taking it.

"I gave you two weeks. You showed up at your mother's almost-dead bedside. I thought you'd wake up. You haven't woken up. I'm getting reports that you go to his place every night. That he brings you coffee in the mornings. You're going out to eat with him. It was bad enough when you were working for him, but there was no known relationship. I got heat then too. Did you know that?"

I was stunned, but maybe I shouldn't have been. "You did?"

"Yes. Organized crime. They were up my ass. They wanted to use you, but I said no. I *kept saying no.* That it was a legit second job. You were shouldering your brother's debts and your mother's. Plus yours. Another person in your place, and they'd be looking at being dirty long before now. Not before you started sleeping dirty, but now. God! Now, I gotta suspend your ass. Without pay! You need to wake your ass up. Leave this guy, and when you come back, we'll start going over damage control, because don't think for a second this ain't getting out. It's already out."

"Leo—"

"I don't want to hear it. Honestly. Get the fuck out of my office. I want your gun, your badge, and the keys to your car."

"Leo—"

"Gun. Now. Badge second. Keys. Or do I need to pull in a second witness for this?"

Goddamn.

This was a punch. I, just, fuck.

I pulled out my keys. "I have things still inside."

"That's fine. Badge and gun."

My throat was burning. My chest was searing from the inside out, but it was what it was.

I took out my gun, placed it down. My badge was next.

"You better not put Travis on my guys."

"I will put whoever I want on your guys. You know you have no say." He shook his head. "Goddamn, Jess. I never thought you. Never in my whole life. Not you."

I was blinking back tears, but no way in hell would those things fall.

Forcing out a choked sound, I cleared my throat and went for the door, but just before leaving, I asked, "How is she?"

Another soft expelling of air. "She is dealing."

"Is she in a place? A hospital? Clinic? I truly have no idea what I did so wrong to her, but I need to know that much. You know I've always tried to take care of her."

"I know." He made a torn sound, and I couldn't begin to identify how that came out, but it was torn. All I knew. "She's at the mental hospital, and she's in therapy. Intense therapy. They're doing the whole dual thing, whatever that it is. Where they treat all the shits that happen together. I don't know those psych terms, but you know what I'm talking about."

I knew, and another day I might've laughed at how helpless his explanation was, but that was Leo. He was old school in ways. "I'd like to see her, when that might be able to open. I'd appreciate it."

He started nodding, then went to shake his head, and he paused, turning all the way away. "Another guy, Jess. There are other guys. Love *them*. Fall for *them*. Don't give up your career for this one. He ain't good—or wait until he's *actually* out."

That was the heartache of it all.

I'd already made my choice.

"Let me know about my mom."

I left, not seeing anyone who was in the hallway. They were there, but I wasn't paying attention to them. I just needed to go, but a loud *crash, thud* sounded behind me.

I paused, hearing Leo roar, "Goddammit!"

"Jess." Val was calling my name, coming after me down the hallway.

I held up a hand. "Better this way. Stay back."

"Jess! Come on."

I kept going.

Head down. One foot in front of the other.

I left that way.

CHAPTER

SIXTY-THREE

TRACE

Anthony: Jess just asked to pick up more shifts this week. What do you want me to do?

I frowned, reading his text as Ashton and I were heading to one of our warehouses.

"What is it?"

I showed him the screen before texting him back.

Me: She's a normal employee. Think she'd be pissed you're asking me how to handle it.

Ashton had leaned over and read what I'd responded. He snorted, taking my phone out of my hands, and he scrolled through it before hitting a button, putting it to his ear.

"Why are you asking for more shifts at my nightclub?"

Jesus. He called Jess. On my phone.

"I'm here with him, but you got me. Yeah." A pause. "Anthony wanted to know our thoughts. You should be happy to know that your man said you're a normal employee, you should be treated as such. He passed the buck back to Anthony, but I'm curious. I have it on good authority that your evenings are usually filled up, by you know, you getting fil—"

I plucked the phone from him and settled back. "Don't shoot my best friend. I inherited him as a moron."

"It's fine."

It wasn't fine. Her voice was restrained. That was never fine.

I lowered my voice. "What's wrong?"

"I'm taking time off from work for a bit. Could use the hours."

"What do you mean when you say you're taking time?"

"Oh, damn," Ashton said under his breath.

I ignored him. "Jess. What's going on?"

"I don't want to talk about it."

"Now I'm worried."

She sighed into the phone. "Look, could you do me a favor and tell Anthony to put me on every night?"

"What about me?"

She half laughed, half did her own snort into the phone. "You are busy doing what I don't want to know you're doing, but I know you're busy. I'm a workaholic, Trace, and my full-time gig just got put on hold for a bit. I'm going to go crazy if I actually have time on my hands."

That was not good, not about her not knowing how to handle downtime but about the job. "I'm sorry, Jess. I know you loved doing what you did."

"Yeah. Well. I just need to be busy right now. Mom and all."

"I'll let him know. He'll fill your schedule."

"Thank you. And, um, when are you coming back tonight?"

"Since you'll be working, I might be later than I'd intended."

"Maybe you can swing by and give me a ride from Katya?"

"That sounds very domestic. I'm looking forward to it."

"Me too."

I wished Ashton wasn't in the vehicle with me but also wished I wasn't in this vehicle heading an hour out of the city. "You want me to come back? Ashton can handle this. It's not imperative that I'm in attendance."

"Hey!" Ashton gave me a dark look.

I ignored him, waiting for her response.

"I think working is the best thing for me right now. I'll see you when you get back."

She hung up, and I stared at the phone for a second.

"What? No goodbyes? No 'I love you' yet?"

"Shut up."

"Man," Ashton grumbled. "If you two don't move faster, you'll be dead like the dinosaurs."

"What the fuck does that mean?"

"Means you're going fast. I was being a dipshit."

"When are you not."

"When I'm—"

"It was not a question. I wasn't asking."

"I'm aware, but please. Let me answer anyway. I enjoy that shit."

Ashton aside, that wasn't good. Jess and I were still learning about each other, but I knew she needed to be busy. She'd never not been busy since I'd met her. She did not understand how people slept in on their day off. It wasn't that she wasn't aware of what it meant. It was that she literally couldn't comprehend why people would do that.

She hadn't iced me out. She'd shared about the work, but I knew better.

"Job, huh? She's not fired?"

We knew this would happen, though Jess and I had not sat down and talked about how to handle this when it did happen.

"I'm guessing. She said she was taking time off. That's code for—"

"Getting fired."

"Or suspended?"

Ashton thought about it. "She was probably suspended. So the firing will happen later when they realize she's still going to be at your place every night."

"If that happens."

My gut was churning. I knew it would happen, but I didn't like hearing about it, and I didn't know how to process how she was handling it. She shared, but she also didn't share. Would she share later? Was she one to talk about her feelings? I couldn't see Jess being that type of woman. I hadn't known her to be that type of woman. She moved. She kept busy. That's how she handled life.

"You love her, right?"

That question was a shock. "Yeah. Why?"

He had pulled his own phone out and was scrolling through it. "She's not a woman that's fickle. She knew what she was doing when she chose you. She said the actual words. Whatever this is, you don't need to be spooked by it." He paused in his scrolling, looking at me. "She's one of the toughest women I know. The literal definition of ride or die. This, her job, is going to be nothing for you guys. You'll figure it out. You don't need to worry about her. She's got it handled until you pick her up tonight. She asked for you to do that. That's her telling you she'll need you, but it won't be till tonight. Till after you both do your jobs. She might be annoying as fuck for what career she likes to do, but you, my brother, got a good one."

I grinned. "There you go. Being annoying and a dumbass, telling me nothing that I don't already know."

He smirked back.

He knew I appreciated it.

Anthony: She just picked up shifts for every single night except Sunday. Do not shoot me. She informed me that's what she wanted and you told me to treat her like a normal employee. I'd be stupid not to take up her offer, but I also enjoy having a job so don't shoot the messenger.

Anthony: Please.

CHAPTER
SIXTY-FOUR

JESS

It was a different staff on weeknights. Felt weird, but Anthony put me at my normal section. I had seniority over the other bartender, who'd been sending me nasty looks the whole shift. She was disturbed by it all. I wasn't, and most of the other bar staff shared how bothered she was that I didn't care.

The other thing I noted was that she didn't keep her inventory updated. I was low on five bottles of liquor that should never be low. I'd already done the trip back for a refill on Patrón, but I'd have to go again. We were barely hitting eleven at night. I had three full hours left and would need a full stock of vodka. I sent Anthony a text, letting him know where I'd be for a few minutes.

Anthony: On my way to cover.

I had to laugh. He should offer just to go and get it, but Anthony wasn't that type of manager. He'd man the bar until I got back. That was the type he was.

That was the third thing that felt off—no Justin, not that there'd been a Justin to cover me for a while.

It was me. I was off. The whole thing was off.

When I saw Anthony heading my way, I held up a hand in a wave and headed to the back room. As soon as I got there, I went in and was grabbing my third bottle when the door opened again.

"Hey." I started to come out from the back where I was when I saw who'd come in.

He looked like Justin. Same height. Same hair, but his body was more defined. He worked out, and he was looking at me with dead eyes. Cop eyes.

I didn't need to see the badge to know this was Detective Worthing. "Why are you here?"

He clipped his head in a small nod. "Good. You know who I am." He took a step closer.

I was searching him for where he kept his piece. His shirt was tucked in and was smooth where it shouldn't have been smooth. The back? A shoulder holster under his shirt? His badge was hidden too.

"I'm here as a professional courtesy."

That didn't sound good. "I got suspended today."

"I'm aware. Birdy told me, but you're still one of us as far as I'm concerned."

"So why are you here?" I didn't usually need to ask twice, not for this kind of "professional courtesy."

"I got moved to organized crime. They're doing a raid on your boy. All of his places. His downtown apartment. His office. Warehouses the West family own. We're raiding here too."

Jesus. They were doing a full-gut renovation.

I began to put the booze back. "When?"

"One hour from now."

One hour. "Why are you telling me?"

"My little brother swears you're clean, but the guy who's sharing your bed isn't. I want to know what side you're on. If you let him know, we'll know. You don't, and I'll share with *your* boss. You got me?"

No, but I nodded to him anyway.

He began to back up to the door, watching me watching him. Neither of us was showing emotions. No surprise. No panic. Nothing. Stone-cold indifference. Then he blinked and reached for the door. "One hour. If I were you, I'd not be here."

Which would make me look suspicious to everyone. They'd do their jobs and would find out I was supposed to be working. If I wasn't at that counter, both sides would notice. I was fucked no matter what I did. But there'd be questions no matter what.

Be here when my colleagues raided where I worked? Or leave?

Funny thing was, I didn't need to mull over if I was going to warn Trace or not. His family business was his family business. Not mine. He knew the deal between us. Now I'd have to learn if I could trust him to remember the deal or not.

I texted Anthony.

Me: Heading out. Something came up. Cover me please.

Anthony: What?! What the hell? Call me. You better tell me your mother—oh shit. Never mind. I'm remembering. Hope everything is okay. Keep me updated.

Yeah. I wouldn't.

CHAPTER

SIXTY-FIVE

JESS

I ran through my options.

I wanted security cameras on me so people would know I wasn't up to anything shady. That meant public transportation. That meant an alibi, but I didn't want to go anywhere that might get raided. I was taking a big risk here, but I'd always been adamant that while I loved Trace, which was still new to me, I did not and would not love his job. So the raids were happening, and I wasn't getting involved, though interesting timing on Leo's behalf of when he suspended me. All that said, I wouldn't have an alibi if I went to my own place either. Staying alone somewhere and no one could vouch for me.

"Not that I don't love the surprise of you coming in here not on a Sunday night, but I'm a little concerned. You're drinking here, and you've not texted Kelly to join you."

I'd gone to Easter Lanes. Molly Easter, who was so removed from anything and so pure, was going to vouch for me.

Molly had bit her lip in the adorable way she did, heaved a sigh, and filled my first beer.

It was a beer night for me. I was on my sixth for the night.

She just slid a seventh to me when I noted a stillness that came over Molly.

She was looking behind me.

I turned, my whole gut clenching up, because I knew whoever it was wouldn't be good.

Ashton stood there. His gaze was fierce and filled with such loathing that I was burned from the inside out. He had two guys with him, and I was taking them in because they weren't the normal guys that I'd grown accustomed to around Trace. These guys were military.

All three were staring me down until Ashton strode forward.

"Don't!" Molly yelled as he began to reach for me.

He paused, but I knew my luck had timed out. I'd been betting that they wouldn't come for me until four in the morning. Maybe five. That meant Trace had probably been the one hauled down to the police station, and Ashton was already released from questioning.

"Don't get involved," he growled at her, in a savage hiss. Then his hand closed down over my shoulder, and he was hauling me off the barstool. "If you get any ideas, those guys are ex-rangers. So *don't*."

I was nodding. "Spotted that already."

He paused, narrowing his eyes at me, before he made another low growl and dragged me with him.

"Where are you taking her?" Molly shouted from behind. She looked ready to launch herself over the bar, a bat in hand. "Hey!"

Ashton shoved me forward as the other two guys took me, and he remained behind, but I heard him before the door closed. "Stay out of this."

The streets were quiet, calm, as they put me into the back of an SUV.

It was an odd feeling. It felt like the other shoe was about to drop. I just didn't know what shoe it was.

CHAPTER

SIXTY-SIX

JESS

They hauled me off to somewhere outside of the city.

Ashton kept glancing at me on the way. "Why are you so quiet?"

"Drunk. Also, what are you going to do?"

"They raided our warehouses tonight. Anthony sent word that after you went to restock, you took off, and it didn't take long to find the security footage or to identify Detective Worthing."

"Again. What are you going to do?"

"You knew an hour before the raids went off."

"And you're here super fast, so obviously they didn't get a whole lot."

He bit off a growl, reaching for me and yanking me toward him. "You knew. You could've warned him!"

I grabbed his hand on my shirt but yelled right back because the drunkenness was starting to fade. I was starting to get pissed. "And why would I? I'm a PO!"

"You're with Trace."

"Yes, I'm with Trace. I am not with what he does for a living or what his family does. I'll *never* sign off on that."

"Then you can't be with him, because he is who his family is."

"Please." But I was done with him grabbing hold of my shirt. I twisted his hand, shoving him off of me, and I glared. "Don't fucking manhandle me again, or you'll find out my other basic training, asshole."

The two ex-military guys were in the front seat. We were in the back, and the one in the passenger seat turned back to us. "You need help?"

I huffed. "Not a chance."

Ashton's response was more muted. "We're good. We'll wait until we get there."

I rolled my eyes, but I wasn't going to ask. He'd want me to do that, and he'd take pleasure in not telling me.

But, dammit. I wanted to know other things. "Is he okay?"

"Like you care."

"I do care, but I am not a criminal. Nor will I become one."

"You got a heads-up about the raids, and you did nothing."

"I had to make a choice. I can love Trace and not what he does for a living."

"Except when you could've stopped him from going to prison."

I shot him a look. "Come on. You're professionals. Your families have been doing this for decades. I'm betting that anything found in the raids isn't going to be anything that'll put Trace away. And again, you are here. That means if you were hauled in for questioning, you're out. That means they aren't looking at you. They're going only at Trace, and I am, again, highly doubtful they'd find anything on Trace."

"Yeah? Why's that?"

"Because it's Trace. He's smart."

"And I'm not?"

"You're both—" Why was I doing this? "Never mind. Interrogate me whenever we get where we're going."

We fell into silence, driving more north until they turned into a driveway that led to a small log cabin. The place was isolated and in the middle of woods. In this context, this was creepy as fuck. In a different set of circumstances, this could've been a romantic getaway. Either way, when we parked and I was led inside, I had the thought, *Here we go.*

Ashton took me to a back room, shoved me inside, motioning for the bathroom. "Wash up. Shower. Do whatever. Toss your clothes in the hallway and put on new ones."

They were going to wash out any wire I might've had on me.

It shouldn't be a surprise that's what their suspicion was, but it stung for some reason. Still. I did as he instructed. I had nothing to hide, and twenty minutes later, I headed back downstairs with a sweatshirt, sweatpants, and cozy socks on.

No one was in the kitchen. The living room. I checked outside and spotted another vehicle, along with two other guys who were also ex-military. They looked it, both taking me in taking them in, but they didn't move my way.

Okay then.

I went back inside, and this time, one of the guys was coming up from the basement. He saw me and whistled. "She's here."

"Bring her down." That was Ashton.

He gave me a nod, jerking his head toward the stairs. "This way."

I didn't move, eyeing the stairs.

I hadn't been scared going with Ashton in the beginning or riding with them out of the city, but now a whole different form of trepidation was filling me up. I didn't like basements.

Dead bodies tended to accumulate in basements.

I didn't want to be the dead body this time.

"He's not going to kill you."

"Yeah?" I shot the guy a look. "You're well versed in situations like these?"

"Unfortunately, yes. This is an interrogation with padded hand-cuffs. If that helps?"

It didn't. Going at me soft didn't mean the end wouldn't result in the way I feared.

"Is Trace here?"

"You really think he would let him come?"

I gave this guy another look because he was feeling *super* comfortable in his responses, but his expression was bland. Neutral.

Ashton had come up the stairs. "Come on. Sooner this is done, sooner we can move on to more pressing matters."

The dread just lined all of my organs, moving down my legs, into my toes, up through my chest. It went down my arms, my hands, my fingers, and it was circling up to my shoulders. There was no good feeling anymore, but I moved forward, my legs feeling like lead.

I stopped when I saw the room and began backing up. "Nope. This is not going to happen."

Ashton's hand came to my arm as he stepped to my side. The other guy took my other arm, and I was dragged/lifted to a single chair in the middle of the entire basement. The walls, the floors, the ceiling were all covered in plastic.

"Jesus Christ, Ashton. Are you serious?"

They shoved me down and held my arms as the third guy zip-tied me to the chair. My ankles were zipped next.

I should've fought. I was 98 percent sure that I wouldn't have been able to overpower them, but I should've tried. I just followed orders, sat down, and let them tie me up. But I knew why.

Hope.

In the back of my mind, I thought that if I fought them, that would immediately put me into the enemy category. Ashton might not even interrogate me. They'd kill me or simply let me go, but inform Trace that I had . . . I didn't even know. I had no idea what they thought right now. This was as much my interrogation as theirs.

I had to remember that.

But damn. I still should've fought.

"You're going to kill me, Ashton? This is a bit of an overreaction because I didn't give you a little bit of warning for the raids."

He came to stand in front of me, and it was like I'd never seen the real Ashton. Slowly, as he watched me, I saw a layer of him strip away. There were no more grins. No dark teasing. No smirks. No kindness. No patience. (Not that I saw much of those, but they'd been there when he interacted with Trace.) All that was gone.

In his place was someone who liked cruelty.

I saw the dark delight. Ashton just let some evil into the basement, and that evil was him.

"You're going to torture me."

"You're not here because you didn't tell us about a raid. That was the excuse. You're here because we have a mole, and it's my job to find out if it's you."

Then he started.

CHAPTER

SIXTY-SEVEN

JESS

I was carried out hours later. They took me upstairs, tossed me on one of the beds, and left. I knew without checking that the window was bolted shut and the door was locked. There was a bathroom I could use, but I was shivering, and my insides were twisted inside out.

He'd not touched me, but the questions and the tone Ashton had used.

If he could've killed me, he would've.

I would never forget the look on his face before they threw a sheet over my head, tipped me back, and poured water down my throat.

"Are you working for anyone in the Worthing family?"

"Have you installed listening devices on Trace's phone or anywhere on his property?"

"What information did you tell your team leader about us?"

"Are you working with the police in gathering evidence against Trace?"

"Did you give our locations to any member of the government? Were you taken in for any questioning regarding us?"

He asked the questions over and over again. Everything. Anything. For hours, in between times when they would waterboard me. Experiencing almost drowning over and over again had an effect on a person. I'd aged twenty years over the last three hours.

Or the last few hours.

I had no idea what time it was, but it was starting to get light out. I was guessing it was six in the morning. Maybe five.

I touched my nails, felt how cold they were from my own touch.

"Are you planning on turning evidence on Trace?"

"Are you helping to build a case against him?"

"Did you agree to work undercover against the West family?"

They checked my pulse every time they asked.

They waterboarded me.

They stopped, asked me questions. Checked my pulse again.

They repeated it over and *over* again until I realized what they had done.

I was conditioned so that if they asked a question I knew would get me in trouble, my pulse would jump at the thought of the waterboarding. It took a long time, but it was effective. I had nothing to hide, but if I had, I wouldn't have been able to hold it back.

———

I might've fallen asleep.

I must've because I woke as I was under the covers, curled on my side in a fetal position, and when I heard the door creak open, I almost pissed the bed. I was terrified but too terrified to leave this bed to relieve myself.

If Ashton hadn't hated me before, it wouldn't matter now. I hated him.

He'd reduced me to the six-year-old I used to be, and he'd become my father.

I gritted my teeth, tasting my own tears, and fuck him. Fuck them.

I didn't move, hearing whoever came toward the bed.

They didn't touch the bed. They didn't touch me, but it was Ashton. "Leave Trace alone. After this, when you go back, don't see him. Don't call him. Don't show up anywhere he'll be. You're fired from the nightclub."

God.

He was gutting me alive. That's how it felt.

"Trace has no idea about any of this, and he won't because you're not going to tell him. You proved tonight that you can't separate him from what he does." He turned, going for the door. The floor creaked underneath him until I heard his pause again. "You're not the snitch, but you're not far from one either."

I held my breath, my heart pounding against my sternum, until he went all the way downstairs.

I could hear conversation beneath me.

There were voices from outside.

Then, more voices outside, and a door shut beneath me. It was loud enough to shake the house.

I didn't dare move. I couldn't. Not yet.

A car started.

Car doors were opened, then shut.

Tires moved over gravel.

Then silence.

Nothing.

I bolted for the bathroom, falling into the shower as my bladder released at the same time I vomited, emptying out everything that was inside of me. Including me.

CHAPTER

SIXTY-EIGHT

JESS

A month later

My phone started ringing as I was balancing a box in my arms, stepping onto the front porch.

Molly came over, pulled my phone out of my back pocket, and showed me the screen.

Trace calling.

"Ignore it."

She hit *decline*, put the phone back in my pocket, and opened the door for me.

Of all the places I was moving into, yeah. I couldn't begin to explain it.

"That's like the third call he's made just today, and I've only been around you for an hour."

I gave her a look, taking my box into my mom's kitchen.

Yes. My mom's house. The joke was on me, in so many ways.

She looked around the house, noting the musty smell. "Your mom's where again?"

I hesitated as I put the box on the table and turned right around, heading back for more.

She followed me, taking one of the lighter boxes. "She's in rehab," I said as I went back up the sidewalk and into the house.

"You're moving in to take care of the place. Also, I knew about the rehab, but you hadn't officially told me, so you know, being considerate here."

I flashed her a grin and indicated she could put the box on the floor. I put mine down, and we were heading right back. Only about thirty trips left to go. Or sixty-nine trips. I was trying not to count.

"Yeah, well, she's not here, and I can't afford my rent anymore, not on my own. So here I am. Moving in here and hoping my mother doesn't kick me out when she finds out."

She grunted. "No shit. My dad did that to me one time, pulled a shotgun on me and everything. Saturday-morning breakfast has never been the same between us."

I shot her a look because . . . what? But also, I was hoping she'd talk more about that. It would save me from sharing the sadness and pathetic-ness that had taken my life's place. Like being suspended, being fired, being interrogated, being tortured, having your best friend take a safety break from you, and the latest, having no money, so you needed to be an adult and read the writing on the wall. Meaning, I needed to do something about my living expenses, or I'd be in serious trouble in a few months from now.

I really was praying my mom wouldn't kick me out. She'd banned me from the hospital, and then she went away to a clinic and was now at a rehab treatment place. I was told she was becoming a whole new person, but I'd have to just trust and pray for a somewhat not as bitter and abusive mother when she came home.

So, yeah. There was that. And I'd not even gotten into how Ashton's last visit with me made an impact and I was fully avoiding Trace.

He called. I declined.

He texted. I deleted it.

He showed up at my apartment, and I moved. He was the other reason I was moving, and I was sure he had a guy following me. I noticed someone the other day, so I'd have to do something to that guy to scare the living shit out of him. Until then, I was hoping he wouldn't show up here. I didn't think he would. Leo still came over to check on the place.

Leo, who didn't know I'd made an executive decision and was moving in. I figured I still had the right since she'd never changed the locks. Bear told me that I could work at his place if I needed extra cash, but considering half his customers were my friends, who I was sure knew all about who I'd been screwing, I wasn't that desperate. Yet.

I was holding out some pride.

But Molly was the only friend I was in contact with. I wouldn't let Val anywhere near me. Didn't want anything coming back to her and causing her a hassle with her career, and sometimes that could happen. I also hadn't reached out to Kelly. I'd agreed with her and Justin when she'd said they were going to stay away.

I figured when I got sorted, I would reach out. I was so far from being sorted, but Molly had offered me a temporary job. I was considering it. Who'd turn down a bartending job at a bowling alley?

We finished two hours later. My calves needed to be stretched, while Molly had done a great job of holding the door for me every time.

"Okay." She pulled me in for a hug. "Let me know if you need anything. Let me know when I can hire you, or to be more honest, when I can fire Sebastian. Bad move on my part hoping I was secretly hiring the Snowy Soldier guy since he kinda looks like the guy, but yeah. Super lazy and I've learned my lesson. I'll only hire friends or people who actually have bartending experience. I'll see you later." She gave me a two-finger salute, heading out.

"Thank you again!"

Another wave from her as she headed for the street and then to where she'd parked.

I had the rental truck for the night, but I looked around, going through the house.

It was empty, with a lot of shit inside. My mom's shit, but shit nonetheless. There were piles of dust. The carpets needed to be cleaned. Mold was probably in the walls or on her food. I knew I'd probably be wading through empty liquor bottles for the next week, but why was I getting choked up?

Also, that step was never fixed. What had Bear and Leo been doing this whole time?

Not wanting to deal with *these* feelings, I went in search for booze. Ten minutes later, I was heading back out to the rental truck with a full wine bottle in hand.

I was going to do what I'd been doing for the entire last month: paint and drink.

———

Two days later Kelly called me.

CHAPTER

SIXTY-NINE

TRACE

Jess: I want to meet.

I'd been to her studio.

I'd seen every painting she made. Saw every new one the next time I walked through.

I'd been to her apartment. Walked through when she wasn't there.

It was really fucking obvious she wanted nothing to do with me.

Shit hit the fan.

My uncle was calling, demanding to know what was happening. Who was talking to the FBI, to NYPD, to whoever else because it was a whole joint task force by the time the raid happened. And Ashton, the shit he pulled.

"You did what?" I must've heard Ashton wrong, what he did, what he did to Jess.

A wall slammed down over his face, and he raised his chin up. "You heard me. I did what I had to do. We had to know if it was her—"

"It wasn't! I told you it wasn't."

"I had to know." His jaw tightened.

His goddamn jaw. The jaw I was going to break. The jaw that he'd have to have surgery to put back in place. "You fucking did not do that to her."

"I did, Trace. I'd do it again too. I had to know!"

"No! You didn't believe me."

"I did it FOR YOU!"

"Bullshit."

"NO! No, Trace. No. We have to know. This life, we have to know. Anyone can turn on us, and you know it. Anyone. Even the women we love. They're the ones who'll do it first. I did it for you." His eyes were blazing. He meant every word he said, but he took my woman.

I turned, facing him directly, and I reached up. My coat was taken off first.

Ashton's eyes flickered now. He cursed, lowering his head, but he faced me too.

He took Jess. He had her tied to a chair.

Ashton was studying me. His eyes were lidded. He knew what was coming.

I no longer cared what was in his head, because he tortured the woman I loved.

"If anyone should've been the one to question her, it should've been me."

He closed his eyes, his head low, and a savage curse slipped from him.

I raised an eyebrow. Yeah. He'd fucked up, and he was getting it now.

"My woman. My interrogation."

"You wouldn't—"

"Don't tell me what I wouldn't have done. There are always ways to do it without needing to make HER FEEL LIKE SHE'S DROWNING!"

I was done with words.

I knew exactly what he'd done, and he'd pay.

They'd all pay, but Jess was gone.

No calls. No texts. She was gone from the club.

Now she was gone from her apartment.

She came here, to her mother's house, the mother who had spewed hate toward her. I didn't know who the hell the woman I loved was surrounding herself with, but they were not her friends. They were not her allies.

Leo Aguila.

Patrick Rivera, a.k.a. Bear.

They lied. They said one thing to her face and did the opposite.

Then Kelly. She made sense. Justin made sense, but they were both caught while the fight hadn't paused between the Worthing family and mine. It escalated because Jess wasn't the mole. Someone else was. I just needed to find out who.

But Jess. She was almost a sick obsession by now, and here I was, walking through her mother's basement because this was where she had moved her canvases. The studio she was using was being torn down. I saw the notice to the tenant myself.

I stopped at the latest canvas, seeing that this was a new one. She hadn't painted this two days ago.

I crouched down, studying it.

It'd been me. Then storm landscapes. Now she was painting herself. This latest one was her as a child. She was in the corner, arms wrapped around her legs. The shadows were large, threatening, looming over her. Two male shadows were outside the window. The door was open an inch, the light shining in, and there, right where the doorknob should've been, was a hand instead.

Who was that? What were they going to do? Comfort her? Terrorize her?

Harm her?

I had an irrational need to know what happened on that night, find out who put her cowering in the corner, and tear them apart.

I'd been having that feeling a lot lately.

Click, squeak.

The sound of a gun cocking and a step protesting under someone's weight told me the jig was up.

Jess's voice trailed down from the stairs. "Do not move. I've called the co—oh." She came down three steps, squatting enough to see me. "Wha—you're in my basement?!"

I cocked an eyebrow. "You texted earlier. Said you wanted to meet."

"Not in my own house."

"Your mother's."

She came down the last few steps, putting her gun away. "Are you kidding me?"

"No." Fine. She wanted to fight. So did I!

I needed it because this last month was bullshit.

I got in her face. "Where were you?"

"Wha—" She faltered, stepping back. "I'm having the locks changed. And what are you talking about?"

"The raid. Where were you?"

"Did Ashton not tell you?"

"I know what he did, and believe me, I am not happy about that, either, but during the raid, where were you?"

"I was tipped off."

"I know."

"Then why are you asking?"

Christ. I wanted to fuck her.

I wanted to grab her, turn her around, press her against the post, and sink my dick inside of her until I didn't come out until next week. Instead, I lowered my head so I was three inches from her, and I asked it again. "Where the fuck were you?"

"I couldn't tip you off. I am in law enforcement."

"Where were you?!" I was roaring.

She didn't flinch. She didn't care. She stood taller.

She raised her voice. "I was at Easter Lanes!"

"Why?!"

"Because I was hiding. Okay?! Is that what you wanted to hear? I was hiding because I wanted to make sure you knew I wasn't choosing them, but I also wasn't choosing you. I'm in law enforcement. It's my moral code. That's who I am at my core. I can't not be me."

"Bullshit."

"Excuse me?"

"Bullshit. It's not ingrained in your moral fiber of being. If it was, there'd be no you and me. You would've tried arresting me once you found out who I was. You never considered that."

"I did."

"Being a parole officer is what helps you make sense of the world. I get it. I do. Your dad was a criminal. Your mom was an abusive drunk. Your brother was an addict and is in prison. You went against the grain because you had to. It gave you some semblance of control, but don't tell me you're someone you're not. I know you. I've been inside of you."

She drew in a ragged breath, but she was hearing me. She was looking away, but she was listening.

"And before you get almighty with me, let me remind you that I don't care. You could be a federal judge, and I would try to move heaven and hell so I could be at your side, but you know where you were that night? *Not* at *my* side."

She flinched, grimacing. "Trace." She began to reach out for me.

I stepped back. "I don't care that you didn't tip me off. You know I'm smarter than that, but what I do care is that you hid when someone was doing a whole lot to pull the ground out from underneath me. You weren't there to either help, support, or to be the one slapping the cuffs on me. I don't care what role it is. I just want you. I love you. That has not changed for me. I'm goddamn obsessed with you."

"Stop!" She was crying. Tears were falling down her face. She didn't move to wipe them away. Her hand started shaking. "I'm sorry. I didn't know that's how you felt. Next time—"

I bit out a laugh, and it sounded ugly even to my ears. "Next time. There's not going to be a next time because I'm going to find who's leaking my information to the police, and I'm going to extinguish them. That's what I'm going to do whether you're by my side or not."

Her eyes closed a brief second, and when they opened, I saw how stricken she was. Haunted.

Fuck.

Something in me snapped.

I reached for her, almost blind about it because my god, she was mine, and she wasn't in my arms, and this wasn't how it was supposed to be. I touched her arm and waited. Would she push me away? She gasped, her hand finding mine, and we held still for one second. One moment. Her eyes were on me, mine on her, and I saw the burning desperation in her right before she launched herself at me.

Her mouth on mine.

God. I could breathe her in again.

I could feel her again. Taste her.

We were fast, rough. Frenzied.

Hands on each other. Touching everywhere. Mouths. Tongues. I ripped her pants down at the same time she was undoing mine, then reaching inside for me. She found me and wrapped her hand around my dick. I stilled, because that felt so good. So right. She began stroking me.

I groaned, resting my head to her shoulder as she kept going.

Her other hand clapped the back of my head, holding me in place. Her legs lifted up, going around my waist. I caught her, moving, putting her on something, anything. I had no idea what. A table? It held our weight, so I didn't care.

"Baby," I rasped, lifting my head and looking into her.

Her eyes were blind, glazed over. She was beyond talking.

I reached for her, sliding a finger in, and she moaned, her head falling back.

A second finger.

I loved how tight she was, and I worked her. In and out.

She paused, savoring what I was doing to her, but I needed inside of her. It'd been too long.

I moved, pulling her pants the rest of the way off, shoving mine down, and I lined up. I held still for one second, looked at her. She was watching me, biting her lip, and her eyes were dark, melting. The slightest of nods from her, and I slid inside.

Pushing.

I paused once I was deep, and we both started trembling.

I had to move. Had to.

Thrusting in, I began moving. She rolled her hips with me.

This was a moment in time that was a dichotomy. Slow and loving, but also frantic and rough. I kept moving in her, and she was clenching around me, her legs tightening their hold on my waist. As soon as I felt her body begin shaking, her own release, I let out a growl and began slamming into her.

She clutched at my shoulders, but she was pulling me to her. Her legs holding firm, and once her release had moved through her, she began meeting me, helping me.

God.

Please.

Damn.

I growled as my release pounded through me, and I held her, riding out the rest of the waves. I could still feel hers, too; her body was doing this little jerking movement. She lay fully out on the table, and I rose up when I could, looking down at her.

I couldn't speak, but I touched the side of her mouth, where she'd been biting down.

Her chest rose, and she closed her eyes at the touch. A new tenderness came through me, one that was new to me even with Jess. Pulling out of her, I turned and saw her painting. It was propped in the corner, just in line of eyesight.

A little girl was in the corner. "What happened there? That night?"

A door was opening, showing the light shining on her. In the corner of the painting, an arm was opening that door.

The floor just rolled out from under my feet. I couldn't look away from that painting.

"What?" Her voice dropped to a whisper.

"That's you. I know that's a memory. I know that night occurred. What happened after whoever that is came into your room?"

"I—" She choked off again. "I don't remember."

"What do you mean?"

She shook her head. "I've been painting in the last month, and I'm starting to have these memories come back to me. This one, I don't know what happens, but I know there were two bad men outside my house. And I remember that something happened that night, something bad."

The desire to murder whoever that was in her painting was fresh, rising up in me. It was swirling with all the other shit inside of me. Some of that was anger at her, but anger at myself too. "You've shut me out." I dropped my voice.

"I was trying to do the right thing. Ashton—"

"I do not give one fuck what Ashton said to you. He's my best friend. I'll always love him, but right now I could twist his head off of his neck. He took you away from me."

She jerked, her head flaring back.

It was that look again. The haunted look.

I'd put it there, but it wasn't just me.

"Trust me, I am not okay with what he did."

Her eyebrows moved together. A faint frown pulled at her mouth. "What'd you do?"

"I put *him* in the hospital."

"What?"

"He's out by now, but he was in there for a few days. We had words, and the words weren't enough, so we went up a notch. He's quite aware that if he ever fucks with my relationship again, there'll be permanent damages."

"Jesus, Trace. A punch would've sufficed."

"No." The same rage from that day came back, and it was the lethal kind. "It wouldn't have. I'm sorry for what he did."

The haunted look was there, but it shifted a little, looking more hollow. She ran a hand over her face. "That's why I wanted to meet. Or kinda why I wanted to meet. Kelly called today. She said something happened. Justin is terrified of his family. She couldn't get into it with me over the phone, but she said it's not safe to meet. She was adamant that they've not done anything against you, and I believe her. I'd know. Kelly's a lot of things, but she's not a liar. She's a horrible liar. She hiccups when she's trying to cover something up."

Hiccuping when you lie. That's a tell that's funny at times. Another day and I would've grinned at that. Not today.

I was beyond exhausted today.

"What do you need from me?" At her look, I clarified. "You didn't call to get back together. Your best friend called. You need something from me?"

"Kelly asked if I knew someone who could help her and Justin hide? Leave town and basically disappear. She asked me, but the only person I know who could do that is . . ." Her hand spread out, indicating me. "If they need to disappear, I can only guess that something bad happened with his family. She wouldn't call me if they needed to hide from you. They'd just go, probably to Mexico. You mentioned the 411 Network. Do you know someone that could help Kelly and Justin?"

"They don't typically hide people from this situation. It's where the person is getting abused." She started to open her mouth. "But I'll reach out. I have a different reputation from my uncle. They've worked with me already."

She expelled some air she'd been holding back. "Thank you. I mean that."

And the reason for the meeting had been unearthed.

The next part was me leaving.

"It's creepy that you're in my basement."

I smiled now because she'd just opened up a whole other conversation. Which gave me time. I could stay a little longer.

"I don't care."

She was looking around, frowning. "I just put these down here. How'd you know . . . ?" She gasped, whirling back on me. "You do have a guy watching me, don't you? I thought I was going crazy, but you *do*. Don't you?"

"I've always had someone watching you."

"Trace," she started.

"It's what we do in my world. I worry about you. I want to protect you. Don't ask me to pull him from you. Not again. Not after what Ashton did to you. I can't do it. I *won't* do it. I'll never stop worrying about you. It's what you do when you love someone."

"Trace," she whispered.

She drew in a breath, but the emotions were there. Wetness was shimmering just on her eyes, slipping, pooling on her lower eyelids. She closed her eyes, and some of the tears were pushed out. They tracked down her cheeks. "I hate crying. Hate it."

I reached for her, praying she wouldn't step back.

I needed to touch her.

My hand grazed her face, and she sucked in her breath, but she didn't push me away. She stepped toward me, opening those eyes, and I saw the pain. I saw the plea, too, and that was all I needed.

I moved in as she was reaching for me.

I needed her, but she needed me just as much.

We were both addicted.

CHAPTER SEVENTY

JESS

Six in the morning and I couldn't sleep.

The sun was peeking through the curtain in my bedroom. My old bedroom. I had softball trophies on a shelf. A few basketball ones. Volleyball. You name it, I played it. And my sports teams' photos. They'd been framed and hung on the wall, along with some pictures of my friends and me.

Trace rolled over in bed, his arm coming down to rest on my waist, and he moved in, kissing my shoulder. "You okay?"

No. Yes.

I put my hand on his and entwined our fingers. "I have no idea."

He tensed, raising his head. Studying me.

"Hey." He lifted himself so he was resting on his side, looking down on me, and I rolled my head on my pillow, taking him in. His hand, still with mine, flattened on my stomach. I shifted my hand so his palm was on my tummy while my fingers were still locked with his.

"What's going on?" he asked.

I reached over, grabbed my phone, and showed him the text. "I got this an hour ago."

Bear: Your mom is coming home today. She'd like to see you. Maybe come around the house tonight?

"He doesn't know you're already here?"

I shrugged, lifting my shoulder up on the bed. "I'm guessing not. Not surprised. This place wasn't being taken care of by anyone."

He gave me the phone back, his palm beginning to rub over my stomach. "She's your mother. She went through months of treatment. For someone to stay that long, that means she chose to stay. I think it'll be fine."

He didn't know my mother. "She hates me, and I don't know why. Unless she really is mad that I went into law enforcement and Isaac is in prison, if she blames me for that."

"It'll be fine."

"How do you know? I mean, really. How do you know that? You don't. You have no idea if it'll be okay or not." I needed to move. "I'm sorry. I'm just on edge."

I needed to be busy. Do something. I couldn't sit here and dwell.

I couldn't sit here and *feel*.

I pushed up, swinging my legs over the side of the bed.

Trace sat up with me. "What are you doing?"

I shook my head, standing. I grabbed for a sweater and pulled it on. "I have no idea. Shower? Then coffee? Then I'm going to clean every damn room in this house until they show up, I guess."

I padded barefoot to the bathroom, pulling the curtain back and starting the water.

I couldn't wait for it to get warm.

I couldn't wait for anything.

I peed. Washed my hands. Brushed my teeth. And looked around, waiting for that water to warm up. There were no towels. Jesus. Where'd all the towels go?

But the shower was still going. Was it ready?

I exhaled a deep breath. I needed to get my stuff together.

"Hey." Trace had come up behind me. He placed a hand on my back, and it soothed me, just through that touch. Some of his calmness seeped in. He leaned around me, tested the water, and moved the knob until it was a good temperature. As he waited, he stayed behind me, moving in so his body was touching mine.

I breathed him in, needing some of whatever he had that seemed to center me.

"Okay." His voice was husky. "It's ready."

I nodded before taking my clothes off, but I was moving slower now. More languid. The need to "escape" wasn't overtaking me so much. Trace helped me remove my tank top and my underwear, and as I stepped into the shower, his eyes were laughing.

I didn't pull the curtain closed, stepping under the water spray.

He leaned against the wall, folding his arms, and he watched me as I showered.

As I wet my hair. Shampooed my hair.

His gaze dipped low, moving up and down my body as I began rinsing the shampoo out, then applying some conditioner. After that, body wash, but he stepped in with me. His hands covered mine as I began to move the washcloth over my body, the body wash seeping out in bubbles.

No words were shared.

My whole body heated up, but I was still soothed at the same time. I'd missed this from him.

I hadn't realized that he did this to me. He made me feel okay. Protected. Loved. Just by being around me. I'd never gotten this from anyone before, and knew I wouldn't again.

It was Trace for me. I wasn't the type to open my heart for the next guy. There'd be no next guy. Trace got in, and that was an act of god by itself. As he began washing me, I reached for his boxer briefs and tugged them down. They dropped to the floor of the shower. He stepped out of them, but then his hands were circling me.

I was reaching for him.

His mouth found mine, and a few minutes later, he was pressing me against the wall and sliding inside of me. He held me as he pumped up into me. I held him back, our mouths tasting each other.

My mom would bitch about the water bill, but it was worth it.

Trace was worth it.

CHAPTER

SEVENTY-ONE

JESS

The whole house was clean. I'd gone through every room. Every shelf. Items were cleaned out, expired items were emptied, and the containers went into a recycling bin. Trace helped me. His shirt was wet from sweat by that afternoon, clinging to his very muscular and *very* ripped back, and I was starting to lose motivation about what we were doing.

Remembering the feel of him in the shower this morning, last night.

God. It was worse than it was before. I was just starting to feel how much I loved him, but it was full blazing by that evening. He helped with everything. Not one word bitching about it. He didn't ask for anything. He saw what I was doing and moved to assist me.

"Don't you have big bad Mafia stuff to do today?" I asked at one point, sitting back on my heels, my knees on the floor. I'd taken to scrubbing the kitchen floor because the grime between the tiles wasn't coming out. He'd come to the doorway, seen what I was doing, and dropped down to use a washcloth on the other side of the kitchen.

He spared me a glance. "If you think I'm going to leave you when you're terrified about seeing your mother again, you really have no clue what love means to me." He paused. "It means being at your side in days like these."

"If Ashton needed you—"

"I'm here. Stop trying to decide if you like me being here or if you want to chase me off. I'm not going to get scared off."

My insides were all wobbly and bunched together. I gave him a shaky smile, reaching for my washcloth again. "I'm a bit of a mess."

"I would be too. It's fine. You can be a mess today."

My smile wasn't as wobbly. "Thank you."

His eyes softened before he nodded. "I know you're going to be pissed if you don't scrub every inch of these tiles, so let's get it done. Then we can move onto another impossible task before your mom shows up. I'm hoping we can clean up later too. Maybe another shower?" His eyebrows went up, and he flashed me a half grin.

We got back to work.

CHAPTER

SEVENTY-TWO

JESS

Headlights flashed through the house as a car turned into the driveway.

Jesus.

Fuck.

Christ.

I jumped up from where Trace had pulled me down to the couch, on his lap. Or more accurately, I *leaped* off of him. What were we doing?

Right. The house. Was everything okay? Cleaned?

It was. The place was sparkling, it was so clean. All the blankets were folded and put in the blanket basket she had in the corner. We'd cleaned out all of the empty booze bottles, and I meant all of them. There were a ton. Trace told me he'd scheduled a recycling and trash pickup specially for everything we'd sorted through today.

The house looked like it'd been given half of a renovation, it was that much of a change.

And dammit, I was almost shaking.

I could see her coming up the driveway. Bear was behind her, bringing her bags.

She'd gained weight. I turned to Trace, wondering if he saw that too. That was usually a good sign, weight gain. The skin would glow too. But he was watching me instead, and the love shining from him took my breath away.

I forgot, for just a moment, where we were. What was happening. It was him and me, and me feeling how he felt about me.

My lips parted, my whole body feeling like it was glowing instead, but then I heard the front porch squeak under someone's weight.

They were coming in.

It was a matter of seconds now.

The key went into the lock.

I heard her say something to Bear but couldn't make it out. The pounding in my ears muted everything else out, but the door was swinging open.

I moved to the middle of the living room, smoothed my hands down my pants. They were sweating.

She came inside and stopped. Her mouth parted as she took in the house. Her gaze went up, around, and slowly, so slowly, she found me.

"Hi." I started to move forward but jerked back because that was too much.

I didn't want to scare her off.

"Hi." She was blinking. There was no reaction on her face. She glanced around, seeing Trace and stopping there. "Hi."

He stepped up beside me, a hand coming to the small of my back. "Hello."

Bear moved forward, seeing us, but going and putting the bags down by the stairs. His gaze sharpened on me but fell to where Trace's hand was, and his Adam's apple bobbed up and down. "See you got my text." He gave the house a scan. "Assuming you did this? Must've worked all day at it."

"Trace helped."

"Oh." From my mom, but sounding just surprised. No judgment. Bear's gaze hardened. He didn't comment.

"Pat." My mom touched his biceps. "I think I need some time with my daughter. Is that okay?"

"You want me to stay but give you space?" The words were directed to my mom, but his gaze hadn't moved from Trace.

"No. I'm okay. I think Trace would be willing to take my bags to my room?"

"Of course."

Bear glared at him as he went over, picked the bags up, and took them upstairs.

"Chelsea—" Bear started.

"No." Her hand was still on his arm, but she was focused on me.

I swallowed over a knot in my throat. I'd not seen that look from her in years, not since I was little. It was my mom, and I had no idea how to process that. Anger surged up, but that was weird. I pushed that down. She frowned a little. "I'm good, Patrick. You've been kind to come and get me. Bring me back all the way here, but I need some time with my daughter."

"Chelsea."

"Bear." She was firm this time. "I'm good."

He opened his mouth, but she flashed him a look, and he closed it. He glanced my way. "Time off seems to suit you, Jessie girl. You look good. You and your mama both look good." He came over, hugged me, and said to my ear, "He does anything, you let me know. Okay? I don't care who he controls. No one messes with my family."

I hugged him back. "Thank you, Bear." I wasn't going to focus on the rest because there were some bad feelings between me and him, specifically from me at him as he'd pushed me out, then given my mom an ultimatum. Then again, maybe it had worked? She wasn't cursing at me, looking for some booze, and kicking me out. Or she wasn't doing any of those yet.

Time would tell if anything had actually changed.

He left, and then it was my momma and me. My mom. Mother. What the fuck did I call her now? I had no idea.

I settled with "Chelsea."

Sadness flashed in her gaze before she lowered her head. Sighing. "I deserve that, I guess. No. I do. I know I do."

Panic seized me. "What?"

She lifted her head up, that "mom" look back in effect.

I didn't like that look. Felt wrong. Like she was seeing me with the wrong clothes. Made my skin feel like it hadn't settled right on my body.

"You cleaned the house?"

I nodded. "With Trace's help, like I said."

Her eyes grew distant, and she nodded. "I'm getting that." She began to look around before barking out a laugh. "God. Look at us. You're acting like you got caught stealing money for school lunch, and here I am, nervous like I'm going on my first date. I'd offer you something to drink, but I don't know what's in my own kitchen."

I jerked forward again. "We cleaned everything out."

Her eyes narrowed.

"You just got out of rehab, Mom."

Another sad smile from her. "I was thinking tea or water. It's good you cleaned everything out."

"Oh." My god. I was making this so much worse than it needed to be. "I'm staying here."

"What?"

"I—" *Such* a mess. "I—I got suspended without pay. And I lost my job at the nightclub. I'm trying to be smart, thinking ahead, trying to keep what little bit of money I have saved up. You weren't here. I didn't know when you'd be coming back. I hope—Jesus. I hope you don't kick me out."

"You did all this because you need a place to stay?"

What? "No! I did all this because I was terrified you'd come here, be pissed I moved myself in, and we'd go back to you hating me. I, just, if you don't want me here, tell me. I'll figure something else out. I can't be the reason you start drinking again."

Her eyes widened. "You think I'd blame you if I started drinking again?" she whispered.

"Mom." Dammit. My voice was all raspy too. Emotions were blocking my throat. "You tried to kill yourself. I couldn't—don't ever do that again. Please don't. I can't—" Grief rose up, taking me over. I couldn't function.

Who was this person? I didn't like her much. Her was me. I was talking about myself.

"Okay. First." My mom's voice rose, getting sharp. "I did not try to kill myself."

I paused because . . . huh?

"You didn't?"

She shook her head, a whole look of wisdom shining through. I knew I'd never seen *that* side from her. Rehab did do wonders. "No." She was firm. "I didn't. I was drunk, and I got mixed up with what meds I could take with alcohol and which ones I couldn't. I had a splitting headache that wouldn't go away, so they were wrong in their initial assessment, but they also weren't wrong because I did almost kill myself. It was by accident. I've done a lot of therapy to know that I'm not suicidal. I'm not built that way, but I am angry, bitter, and getting older. I have a lot of regrets and yeah. Holy shit. I thought I'd have some time before doing this with you."

I flinched. Again, it was my fault. Again, I was the problem.

"Okay. I'll . . ." What would I do?

Go to Trace's?

"You what?"

I shook my head. "I don't know. Trace and I got back together, or I think we did. I can go to his place."

"No. I don't know what you're talking about. My god. Do we have anything here to drink?" She went to the kitchen. I trailed as she was opening the fridge. "And everyone can relax because I'm not asking about booze. Tea? Something." She was looking at what was inside. "Oh. You said you cleaned everything out, not that you stocked the whole place up again. Lots of green juice. What are these things?" She pulled out a bottled drink.

"It's a probiotic drink. They're healthy for you."

"How the fuck you pronounce that? Komb-agch-aw?"

I laughed. "Close enough." I moved around her, moving the water aside. "There's lemonade, and I have a whole pitcher of tea."

She was looking at me.

I stepped back. "I remembered how you used to love tea when I was little."

"You remembered that?"

I shrugged, looking away, not knowing what the hell was going on. Where was Trace? Didn't take a half hour to put her bags away. "You made the stuff all the time. Tea in summer. Then it was hot tea in the fall and winter. I loved that shit too."

"Thank you."

I paused, hearing the break in her voice.

She was fighting back tears, and she touched her hand to my cheek.

I froze. I couldn't remember the last time she'd touched me like this. With affection.

"You always did take care of me back then. Nice that you're doing it again. I started drinking tea again at the treatment center. I think it soothes my soul or some shit like that."

I cracked a grin, getting a glimpse of my old mom there. "That's good to hear, Mom."

Her eyes grew watery again, and she pulled her hand away. "You cleaned. You remembered how I used to love tea, and now you're calling me Mom again. How'd I luck out getting a daughter like you?"

Oh-kay. I was fully frozen in place. The old Chelsea Montell would next be spitting out how I ruined her life. Or something like that. I was waiting for it, already hardening up inside.

"I got a lot of apologies to make, a lot of regrets that'll haunt me forever, but you. You being here. You still taking care of me. I never did anything to deserve this. Thank you, Jess. I mean it." The tears started to fall from her eyes.

I frowned. "Mom?"

She ignored them, regret flashing bright in her gaze. "I'd love for you to stay as long as you want. This place will always be yours, and I mean that. Literally. I changed my will when I was in treatment. Got ahold of my lawyers and had them put the house in your name. You're the owner. Your man helped make all that happen."

She said that almost casual, off the cuff, as she reached for her tea and took it to the cupboard. She opened one, reached for a cup, and asked, grabbing a second one, "You want some?"

I let the fridge door shut behind me. "What'd you just say?"

She put the second cup down on the counter. "I was asking if you wanted some tea?"

"No," I ground out. "About the other stuff."

"The house? You own it. You've been paying the bills. It's your house. I mean, look at the place. You're the one who cleaned it up. You're already putting your stamp on it, but it's yours."

"No." Everything in me tensed up. "About the other shit, about my man making this all possible."

She frowned. "He didn't tell you?"

"No." My voice was hoarse because what did that mean? Any of it? All of it? "He did not."

"They weren't helping her." Trace was in the doorway, and he eased in as if he'd been listening for a while. "Bear and Leo weren't going to help her. I pulled strings, saw the proposed treatment for her. Thirty days, but she wouldn't be in a facility. She'd stay here and go in every day for individual and group therapy. It wouldn't have worked. She needed more, so I made it possible."

"You paid?"

"I paid. I did everything. She needed intensive long-term therapy, and it's not done. She's not done. She has daily group therapy, and she sees a counselor three times a week. She's also going to do community service. I believe she's volunteering at a local animal shelter."

I had no idea how to process any of this. I turned to my mom, who had frozen in place too. She shrugged, holding up a hand. "I thought you knew."

"An animal shelter?"

"I loved animals. You remember when we had that dog when you were little?"

"Barnabee."

"Yeah. Such an idiot. Not a clue his breed, but didn't matter. He was the best thing that we got in this house. Besides you kids, of course."

"He took off one night. I never knew why."

"He didn't take off. I gave him away."

"What? Why?" How many more punches could I take today?

"Your dad would've killed him. Always threatening. Didn't like how you took to him, how I took to him. Even Isaac loved him. Your dad wasn't one to believe someone or something else was getting more love than him. I found him a good home so you'd not grow up knowing your dad killed him."

I was rocked by all of this. "What family?"

"He passed a few years ago, but we can go over there. They send me Christmas cards every year. I'll show you the pictures they sent of him. They have three kids. The little girl had bad depression, and Barnabee helped her a lot—that's what they shared with me. Seems right judging by the photos. He's half on the girl's lap in every one of them."

A choked sob ripped from me.

I couldn't begin to comprehend any of this.

"I have to go. I need to do . . ." something. Anything. I needed to not be here. "I don't know. I just can't be here right now." I shoved forward, but Trace reached for me.

"Hey." He stopped me, his hand resting on my hip.

My skin burned where he was touching me. I didn't want to be touched right now, but that wasn't the truth. I did. I needed it, but I didn't feel worthy of being touched. It was a hard pill to swallow, but I fought it, taking his touch.

I soaked it in, needing it, and I touched him back, resting against him.

"Hey. Hey." My mom came forward, her voice insistent. "Listen to me. Okay? Just listen."

I turned, slowly.

Now she looked how I felt moments ago. Uneasy. On edge. Cautious.

A twinge of desperation lined her voice too. "Listen. I thought you knew about your man helping me. I did."

"I asked to come see you. I wanted to be there for you. You blocked me from the visitor list."

"I know." She grimaced, her face twisting up. "I was going through a lot. The therapy dredges up everything. I didn't want you coming and seeing me going through that because I didn't want to do more damage. I know how I am, how I can be. I wasn't handling everything the right way, you know, where I take accountability. It's easy for me to lash out, especially at you, but I'm wrong to do that. I needed to go through everything and get a grip on myself before seeing you. I just didn't want to hurt you anymore. I've already done so much to you. I'm sorry, Jessie. I am." More tears were sliding down her face, but her voice was strong.

"I'm happy you're here, and please don't leave. Please. Stay. I . . . I got a lot of years to make up to you. Let me start by, I don't know. Making new tea? How about that? I'll make you that chai stuff you like."

It was so ludicrous that I barked out a laugh. "I hated chai tea. Isaac liked that stuff."

"What? He did? You didn't?"

"I didn't. Never. I like the sweet tea you always make, but not chai tea."

"Oh. I never knew that."

Oh, good Lord. And I was actually talking to Him. Some of the tension eased from me, like a leaky toilet bowl. It was messy. So much crap had happened inside it, but it was slowly emptying out. Such a waste in some ways too.

"You'll stay? This tea you have is good. I can work with it, make it like the sweet stuff."

"Okay."

"You'll stay then?"

I nodded. "I'll stay."

Her smile was blinding.

I didn't know this woman. I don't think I ever met her in my life. But I shared a look with Trace and went to sit at the table while she busied herself in the kitchen.

I think I wanted to get to know her.

CHAPTER

SEVENTY-THREE

TRACE

Ashton: I know you're still enraged with me, but you need to call me. We got movement happening and I'm not totally sure what it all is.

I got that text and eased out of the living room. Jess and her mother had cooked a meal together. There'd been a good conversation over the dinner table, and now both were on the couches. A movie was on the television. Each had a blanket over her lap and a bowl of popcorn in hand. Plus, sweet tea. Lots of sweet tea being drunk between the two of them.

I knew Jess had questions for me about being the one to push for her mother's treatment, but all in all, it didn't matter. I had high hopes for their relationship being mended.

I called him from the burner phone when I went upstairs to Jess's bedroom.

"Where are you?" he asked, answering.

"What movement are you talking about?"

"One of our warehouses is on fire. And I just got a call saying that someone drove by Katya, shooting inside." We both heard a beep on his end.

He cursed.

"What?"

But my phone was beeping too. I read the text sent.

Pajn: Shots fired at your uncle's house.

Pajn: We're under attack.

Ashton was cursing, but I was on the move. These were synchronized attacks, coordinated to happen at the same time. I grabbed my gun, my coat, and my keys. "I'm on the way."

"Where are you?"

"Does that really matter?"

"Yes! I know I fucked up with Jess, but I'm still your brother. Where are you? I can't send guys to protect you if I don't know where you are."

I frowned. "You don't have to know. I'm coming to you. I'll call when I'm on the way."

I heard him cursing as I hung up and headed downstairs.

Jess met me at the bottom of the stairs. "What's going on?"

I forced myself to take a second before I moved in. I touched her shoulders and leaned down, pressing a kiss to her forehead. Her mother watching us from the couch. Her blanket was half pushed off of her. She was clenching it, pale in the face.

I rested my head against Jess's, for just one second. I needed this touch. I needed to remember this touch.

"We're under attack."

"What?" Jess started to jerk back.

I held her in place, my fingers curling around her shoulder. "Please."

She let out a swift curse but stayed. Her hand touched my chest. "Trace. Let me help."

"You can't. You know you can't. I have to go and take care of this, but I made a call for Kelly and Justin. I didn't tell you, figured you could have an evening with your mom, but a 411 representative got back to me. They've agreed to hide Kelly and Justin. They'll be okay." I angled my head back, taking her in. "The meet is tomorrow. Call Kelly. Tell her to pack one bag, that's it, and be ready by nine in the morning. When I get more instructions, I'll let you know, but also know that sometimes the 411 Network will move on their own timeline. Meaning that they might move in and take them before I know, you know, or anyone. That's the point of hiding them. I wouldn't be surprised if they're already on their way here and will make contact before any of us are notified."

My phone kept buzzing. I had to go.

"I love you."

She nodded, blinking back tears, and lifted up on her tiptoes to touch her lips to mine. "I love you too. Be safe."

I headed out but had to stop one last time. One last look because the truth was that I had no idea what would happen tonight. I just knew it was time for war.

Me: I'm on my way.

Ashton calling.
I picked up, getting into the vehicle. "Wha—"
"Tr—" Bang!
I froze. "Ashton?"
Nothing.
Silence.
. . . *Bang, bang!*

CHAPTER

SEVENTY-FOUR

JESS

The sound of glass shattering woke me up.

My training took over, and I was on the floor before I could fully comprehend what I was hearing.

More glass shattering.

Jesus Christ. Someone was breaking in.

I was barefoot, but Mom. Where was Mom?

We were both upstairs. Her bedroom was down the hallway.

There was silence, so I didn't know what that meant, but I grabbed for my phone, dialed 911, and put it in my back pocket. I grabbed for my gun—not my government-issued gun but my own. I had no badge. I had no vest to wear, but this was my house. That was my mom.

I moved across the hallway, and I could hear them in the house now. They were on the first floor. No voices. No talking, but they were moving swiftly.

Professionals, if I had to guess.

I went to my mom's room, laid a hand over her mouth. When she woke, she gasped, but I held her down. She went still, her eyes bugging out. She grabbed for her blanket.

There was more shuffling.

Goddamn. They were going fast. They were on the stairs.

I laid a finger to my mouth, but she heard them. Her head twitched, and she started to jerk toward the door.

I eased it closed, thanking Trace for putting WD-40 on the hinges. I'd been complaining about everything that squeaked. It swung shut, and it did it quietly. I moved over, turning the lock.

My mom was scrambling off the bed.

I motioned for her to come toward me. Opening the closet door, I pointed for her to go in there. There was a hidden crawl space that ran the length of the house. It bypassed the stairs and connected to my room, going into my closet. If a person knew the house, they'd know that was there. If they didn't, they'd have no idea.

I was hoping we had guys that didn't have a clue about the house, but just in case—I eased over to the other side of the room, my gun drawn but pointing downward. I opened the window, then moved back and went into the closet behind where my mom was.

Glancing back, but I couldn't see anything.

I heard her shuffling, moving something back there.

I was praying she was going for the crawl space.

A second later, as I heard them come up to the second floor, I felt her tapping on my foot, and I moved my foot back, exploring the area. She was in the crawl space. I moved over, feeling down there, finding her, and I pushed her a little back into the space. She went in, and I reached, finding the covering. I moved it in place.

"No," she whispered when she realized what I was doing.

I shut the covering and moved in front of it. They'd stop at me. I wasn't going to let them get through me, but I eased forward, back to the closet door.

It was one person, not two. I was hearing only one set of feet moving around.

This person wasn't a burglar. If he or she was, they'd be stealing and leaving. This person was looking for my mom, but they'd gone into my room first. They knew about me, knew I was here.

Anyone friendly would've called out my name. I was assuming that meant this person was here to kill me, my mom, or both. Trace was heading into something, which I knew about. I'd let him go because that was his life. Not mine, but this was a fight being brought to my front door, literally. This time, I was wading in. I was all in, and whoever was coming through on the other side of that door—I took the safety off of my gun and lifted it.

I would shoot to kill in this situation.

I moved the closet door open a tiny bit so I could see, so I had line of fire, and I waited. This was my position I was taking.

I waited.

The door was locked.

I wasn't hearing more than one person.

The quiet game was done. He couldn't bust through the door and not alert us, but I hadn't been in my bed. He knew, if he was smart and knew who he was going after, that the chances I was in here were high.

He had only one option, and I waited because he was going to shoot the lock, kick the door open, and then he'd charge in, probably with guns blazing.

I waited for him to make the decision.

My arms were up. I was ready. No one was behind me.

Pop, pop!

Now.

He kicked the door open and barged in. Gun drawn.

He flipped the lights on.

I saw him in the mirror on my mom's dresser.

He was in all-black clothing, a ski mask. Square, medium height, built with broad shoulders. He moved in, his gun aimed at the bed, and he cursed.

I frowned. Was that . . .

He cursed louder, going to the opened window, then he whirled toward me. His gun was up.

I shot him before he could shoot me, and I shot him again and again until he was down. His gun clattered, and I ran over, finding it, kicking it away.

I knelt down, checking his pulse.

He was alive, but barely. His pulse was thready.

"Jesus Christ!" That came from behind me.

A second person?

I whirled, one knee on the floor and my arms raised. My gun was still drawn, but at seeing it, Leo reared backward, his hands in the air. "I'm unarmed. Jesus! Put the gun down, Jess."

Leo.

It was Leo. He was friendly.

Things weren't making sense, but it was my boss, my mentor. His hands were empty and in the air.

I lowered mine, and I moved away from the man.

"Jess?!" My mom's voice rose in a high-pitched cry, and Leo cursed, sparing me a look before he went into the closet.

I moved over, unable to let go of my gun, and watched as he was helping my mom out of the crawl space.

Leo looked from her to me and back again. He was shaking his head. "What the hell happened here tonight, Jess?"

"What are you doing here?"

He shook his head, shock still on his face. He was holding my mom, his gaze going from her to me to the man on the floor. "I—I was coming over and heard a call go over the scanner. Recognized the address. Front door was open."

Everything was coming at me at once.

The glass. A break-in. My mom. My gun. The window. The closet. The crawl space. Where I decided my stance would be. I would've given my life for my mom. I'd been fully prepared to engage in a gun battle. It was my job to protect her, and not because she was my mother. Because she was a civilian.

It was my job, but now the shakes were coming in, and I had to sit down for a moment. Just a moment.

"Jess. Jesus. Okay."

I waved him off, going back and standing over the fallen man. Job. My job. I would do my job. Didn't matter that this happened in my house.

"Jess. I got it." He motioned toward my mom, who was huddling in the doorway. "Get her out of here and sit tight."

"I need to finish my call."

"What?"

He had his gun drawn, aimed at the guy in case he moved.

I holstered mine and pulled my phone out of my back pocket. I put it to my ear. "This is Officer Montell." I gave them my badge number and where I worked and told them my location.

The operator replied, "We got other calls as well. Your address was pulled up, and you should have squad units showing up right now." As she finished talking, red and blue lights filled the air outside the window. I went over and saw two squad units parked. Four officers were heading for the house.

I began going for the hallway to wave them in and upstairs.

"Jess. No pulse."

I stopped, turned back.

Leo was kneeling at the guy's head, his hand down where I couldn't see.

"Hello! This is the police. Anyone in the premises?"

"Jess, I want to know."

I frowned, but as they began clearing the house on the first floor, Leo pulled off the guy's ski mask.

My mom screamed.

Leo cursed.

And me, I had no idea how I reacted because *now* I was in shock.

It was Bear.

CHAPTER

SEVENTY-FIVE

JESS

I . . .
   . . . Bear.

———

I killed Bear.
   It'd been Bear . . .

———

Bear!
   It was *Bear*, and I'd *killed* him.
   Time needed to stop.
   I needed to stop feeling.
   Right. Now.

Business.

Take care of my mom.

Trace—Trace!

I needed to find out what was happening with Trace, tell Trace, and then I'd deal.

I'd deal later.

———

"They got my uncle. They tried to kill Ashton."

"What?" I was on the phone, but this time we were at Leo's house. I was in his study while he was in the living room with my mom. I needed some time, and I wanted to check in with Trace. I also just wanted to hear his voice because that was the sappy-fool-in-love part of me now. I supposed I'd need to resign myself to this pattern. Something happening and me needing to feel connected to him so I felt more centered.

Also, I was worried. "The cops filled me in, said they had calls coming in from all over the city, that something was going down."

"Stephano's dead, and they tried to kill Ashton. Remmi called, said two guys tried to shoot her. We're still taking inventory of what all they hit."

His uncle? The head of the West family?

I didn't even know how to process that. I frowned. "They tried to shoot your sister in Vegas?"

"Not Vegas. Apparently she's here, staying with my father. She's been there this whole time."

"Your dad?"

"She said he wasn't there. She has no idea where he was, but her security guards got off a couple shots. They got away, nothing substantial against them or who they were."

A really horrible thought was coming to me. "Trace." I felt sick, thinking about it.

"What?"

"You said there's a leak. What if it was Bear?"

"I don't see how it could've been unless he was working with someone else in my family. Bear's connected to the old neighborhood, but the information leaked about our warehouses was all new information, info that he couldn't know unless, again, he was getting that information from someone else on the inside."

"You said information was leaked to law enforcement. He could've been the go-between."

"He could've, but if he was, then we're still looking for a second leak. I didn't know Bear. Ashton didn't. The leak is someone we know. That's basically the only thing we do know." He dropped his voice. "Are you okay? I'm worried about you."

I drew in a breath; my insides were starting to shake. A little. "I am. I mean, I killed Bear. My mom is a wreck, and right now, I'm just focusing on her and doing what I need to do. Bear—I'll process that later. My focus now is hoping that my mom doesn't start drinking again."

"How's she handling it?"

"She hasn't stopped sobbing. Leo steps away from her, and she breaks down all over again. She's in his living room, wants all of us to sleep there together. She's too scared to be without one of us around her."

"How did Leo know to go to your house?"

"I put a call in. He said he heard it on the scanner."

"That was fast."

"He said he was already coming over." I let out an unsteady breath. "What are you doing tonight?"

He was quiet at first, then lowered his voice. "Are you asking because you want to know? Or are you asking because . . . I don't know. What are we doing here?"

I shook my head, leaning back and resting it against the back of my chair. "I don't know, Trace. I just know that my mom is alive. I killed her childhood best friend, and you're the first person I called as soon as I could. So whatever that means to you is what it means to me."

He chuckled, softly. "I'm glad you called. It means something. I think we might be getting serious."

I grinned, holding back a laugh because that felt inappropriate. "Don't say things like that. A girl might get all kinds of ideas."

"Maybe I want this particular girl to get those ideas."

"Then maybe you should say more."

He barked out a laugh. "I love you. I'm assuming since you're at Leo's house that I'd not be welcomed to come and slip into bed with you."

I let out a quiet laugh, standing. "I do not want another reenactment like what just happened at my mom's house, so no. I'll see you tomorrow?"

"I'll see you tomorrow."

"Hey, Trace." I was heading for the door and turned the light off before I opened it.

"Yeah?"

"I'm sorry for what happened to you guys tonight, but I'm glad that they didn't try to shoot you."

"They didn't know—" He stopped, cursing swiftly.

"What?"

"They didn't know where I was. No one knew. I slipped my guys because I wanted to see you, and I didn't want to be bothered with the business. I didn't want to bring my guards with me. No one knew where I was."

We both were quiet, letting that sink in.

I murmured, "You were at my house all day."

"Yeah. Bear brought your mom home there late afternoon. He knew I was there."

"You were there until late evening."

We were both arriving at the same conclusion.

"He's not the leak—"

"—or they would've come for me at your house."

"Yeah." Shit. Shit!

"What does that mean?"

I shook my head. "I have no idea."

"You sure you want to stay at Leo's house? I could do with feeling reassured there are no bullet holes in you all night long."

"Me, too, but no. I need to stay here for my mom. It'll be fine. Leo's family."

"Okay. I love you."

I said the same and put the phone away. I was replaying the conversation in my head, opening the door. The hallway was dark. The light was on in the living room from the television.

"Jess?"

A shadow flashed across the living room, and my mom came to stand in the doorway, looking down to where I was at. Everything was dark except the living room, so I moved forward a step.

"Mom?"

"Oh, there are you." Her relief was clear. Her hand went to her chest. "I must've dozed off and just woke."

"Oh. No." I held up my phone. "I went to call Trace, but I thought Leo was with you."

"No. He's not. I got scared. You both were gone."

I stopped dead in my tracks. "What?"

She gave me a look back. "What?"

"Leo left you?"

She nodded, motioning behind me. "He's gone. I don't know where he went. Looked through the house, but I couldn't find him."

That was . . . That was not right.

My gut shifted. Something was wrong.

Something . . . I couldn't put my finger on it. He wouldn't have left her. Maybe be in a room away, but within earshot. He wouldn't have totally left. He wouldn't put her through that, if she woke and no one was around.

"Mom," I murmured, distracted, and starting to look around.

"Hmmm?"

"Do me a favor?" I began guiding her backward. "Go into the bathroom."

"Bathroom?" she echoed, sharply.

"Yeah. Just to be safe."

"Be safe?"

I moved her back, found the door to the bathroom, and pushed her inside. "Stay here."

"Jess—" She grasped onto my hand, as if to hold me in place.

I needed to find Leo. Something was off. I needed to figure it out. I said to her, trying to be gentle, "I'm going to close this door. You're going to be fine."

"What are you doing, Jess?"

I couldn't explain. There wasn't time. I moved back, shutting the door, and I whispered through it, "Lock it. Just to be safe, Mom."

"Jess—"

"Lock it!"

I heard the lock click into place, and then I turned.

Leo was family.

She said she looked through the house. So, he wasn't in the house.

I started for the back, mulling in my head.

Leo was family, but so was Bear.

And Bear wasn't the leak, but someone was leaking information to the police. That could be anyone.

But Leo was family. Bear was family.

What was I doing? I was making a mountain out of a molehill.

But where was Leo? He wouldn't have disappeared on her.

Leo had told me he checked on my mom. Bear had said the same. Both had lied. Trace had said it himself.

"What is your problem with me, Travis?"

"Nothing except I don't like dirty cops."

He'd looked at Leo as he'd said that.

Leo.

Not me.

Leo.

Leo was dirty.

But, no. No. That was crazy.

Right?

I looked down.

My gun was out. I didn't remember pulling it, but I grasped it with both hands and started thinking.

Jesus. I wanted to be wrong. I needed to be wrong.

He'd go where he couldn't be heard. Outside. His garage. He kept a fridge out there, a ready-made excuse if he needed one.

He must be. I was betting everything on it, but my heart was pounding.

This wasn't like last time. I'd just gone through this. The adrenaline spike had hit me, carried me through shielding my mom. The shock had hit me later, then had worn off, and right now my body was tired. It didn't want to go through this again, but as I eased to the side door, my heart began speeding up.

The sound was loud in my eardrums.

My breathing sounded like it could shatter glass.

One foot. Two. Three. I kept going, reaching for the door, finding it unlocked.

I was right. He'd gone out this way.

I opened it, and it made sense. It was the quietest door; there was no sound.

I eased out. No lights were on outside, but there was one in the garage. I saw it and moved toward the building.

Gun drawn. I didn't have my phone this time. There'd be no backup. It was just me.

After moving to the side of the building, I stood so I was as small as I could be, heading for the door.

There was a window open, and I paused, right underneath it.

"—no! They're here. Yes. She's here. No. I don't know. He got there before me. He was probably there to stop me. Who the fuck knows. I'm aware, boss!"

Boss.

He was there to stop him? "He" as in Bear?

The air was suddenly sweltering around me. My body began moving, weaving.

Stop. I felt impending doom coming on, but no. No way. I shoved that shit down. I had a job to do.

"It's not my fault that everything was fucked. Bobby fucked up too. Your kid never took the 'Mom is alive' bait. That whole idea was for nothing. Now this tonight? You made a move tonight, and nothing happened. Killing Jess makes no sense. Yeah. *Okay.* I'll do it. I know! I know. I'll do it, but I gotta figure something out to say to her mom. The job was never for me to kill them both—because I already killed the dad! He was my best friend."

I was wheeling.

Leo was the mole.

He—I gripped my gun tighter, making sure I wouldn't drop it.

"Okay. Okay! I'll take care of it. I'll *take care* of it. Say I got word and need to show her something. She'll go with me. She trusts me, always has. Yeah, yeah. We'll deal with her mom later on. Fine." He began cursing to himself, moving around the garage. A door opened, shut, but it wasn't his.

I eased back, waiting, but—I had a different idea.

Fuck this. I was done.

Done.

I opened the door, stepped inside.

He froze, then started to bring his gun back up.

I shot at it. Not him. His hand. He dropped his gun but started to fumble around. He had a carton of milk in his other hand but threw it at me as he swooped down, grabbing for the gun with that hand.

I stepped aside, dodged the milk, and as soon as he touched the gun, I shot at that one too.

"*Aaghh!* Why are you doing this? Stop, Jess!"

He was bleeding from both hands. He had no other options, except—he considered barging at me. I raised my gun. "Don't do it." I said it softly, calm. I was locked down. My heart was pumping. I could hear it going fast, but it was like it was outside of my body. "I'll put you down."

I would. He knew it, looking at me. I knew that he knew it.

I raised the gun to his forehead. "Sit. Down."

He looked around, groaning as he kept bleeding out, but he moved to the red couch behind him. It was a piece-of-shit couch, moved out here for when he liked to have beers with his buds. I thought the color of it fit the theme perfectly tonight.

I'd never liked it before. I loved it now.

He lowered himself, grimacing from the pain. "Jess. I'm going to bleed out. Call an ambulance."

"You suspended me. Right?" I was taunting him.

"Oh, come on. Jess! Please!" He tried to raise his hands up.

"I'm sure that'll help with the bleeding."

"Come on. I'm going to die if you don't call for help." He was panting now. Sweat broke out over his face. He'd be woozy soon.

"Who's your boss?"

He frowned at me. "Huh?"

"I heard your call. Who is your boss? Who made the move tonight?"

"Oh, God. Jess. Seriously. Call 911. You don't want to kill me. I know you don't. You already killed Bear. That'll be two of us. They're going to ask questions, but I can . . ." He had to stop, catch his bearings. The room should be spinning for him now. "I can cover for you. I will. I promise. I'll say whatever you want, but call 911. I'll tell you everything."

"You'll tell me everything now."

"Jess! Come on!"

"Now, Leo. Before you bleed out."

"Jess! Now!"

I waited. I was finding that I wasn't having a moral dilemma here. Not one bit.

"Agh! Come on! Are you serious?! Fine! *Fine!* I work for Dominic West. Always have. I went in undercover when I was a cop. It's how I met your dad. How we got close. He was my target, but things got complicated." He choked off, breathing hard. Harder. He began slumping down. "I . . . I . . ."

"Why?"

"What do you mean?"

"Dominic was behind the hits tonight, wasn't he? The ones against Trace and Ashton?"

He moaned. "Jess, I don't have long."

"Then tell me everything. Now!"

He raised his head, squinting at me a little before sighing. His head fell back down. "Yes. It was Dominic and Nicolai Worthing.

Nicolai's been trying to push in. He gave your uncle a proposition, but Stephano didn't bite. But Dominic, *he* did. He made the call tonight that everyone was going to go. Everyone. He'd take over the family business, and he'd work with Worthing, let them in on their deals."

Right. Okay. That was a lot to process, but I'd deal with all of that bullshit later. "Did you kill my dad?"

He nodded, frowning, eyes fluttering like he couldn't see straight anymore. "Yeah. That was a long time ago. Stephano ordered it, but Dominic's been holding it over my head the whole time. Said he has evidence on me. Forcing me to keep working for him, giving him information."

"How?" That word ripped from me.

He drew in a deep breath, then began coughing. Blood was coming up. "D-d-doped up your brother, made him think he killed him. He was all broken up about it, why he didn't fight the conviction. Said he had to go in, pay penance for you and your mom."

"Why did he want me dead? Why tonight?"

"His kid wasn't killed tonight. Couldn't find him, so he gave me this order to hurt him. Trace is in love with you, but Jess, I didn't want to do it. I wasn't going to. I was going to figure something else out. I swear." Other liquids were seeping down his pants, and he groaned. "Jess, I don't have long here."

"Then hurry the *fuck* up." Cold. Ruthless. I was out of my body, not recognizing who I was, but she wasn't fucking around.

"Aghofhygod. Please, Jess! Please."

"Talk!"

His eyes rolled up, then around. "Oh my god. I'm dying. Everything is going black. Jess. Come on. Please . . ." He was whimpering. The life was draining out of him before my eyes.

"What was the plan?"

"Dominic was the one giving information to Worthing, who's got cops on his payroll. Said he had to make it look like they tried for him, too, had them shoot his own house when he wasn't there."

"What does this have to do with Bear? Why was Bear there tonight?"

"I don't know. I think he was there for me, knew I was coming to kill you tonight. Only thing that makes sense. He knew Dominic West too. Fact, I always thought he was being paid to keep tabs on your mom. Like I was paid to keep tabs on you. It's why I recruited you to be a PO for me."

I was sick, all over again.

He'd set me up. Everything.

Everything he was showing, panting, chest heaving, liquids coming out of him, was what I was feeling inside. The difference was that it wasn't my body dying. It was my soul.

"Why were you supposed to keep tabs on me? Why was Bear supposed to watch my mom?"

"I don't know. I really don't." He couldn't lift his head up, so he rolled it to the side to see me. "Oh, God. Jess. I'm dying. Please call for help. I swear. I swear . . ."

He didn't finish, and I didn't care.

Maybe I would. One day.

Not today.

I turned to go and braked.

My mom was at the door, and she had her phone in hand. "Yes." She spoke, giving them Leo's address. "We need an ambulance to the garage. There was a shooting." I could hear them asking more questions, but she pulled the phone back and hit the button. She ended the call.

I didn't blink an eye. "How much did you hear?"

"Enough. Too much. You shot Bear in self-defense, but I won't let this piece of shit's death be on your conscience."

I had to blink twice to make sure this was my mother in front of me. She was standing, looking calm, speaking clear. There were no hysterics like before. "Why are you suddenly so calm? You were pissing your pants ten minutes ago."

She studied me a moment. "I think I'm in shock. Again."

CHAPTER

SEVENTY-SIX

JESS

Maybe I shouldn't have gone.

I'd been the one to pull the trigger, but Bear was still family no matter the circumstances of why he was coming into the house, wearing a ski mask. The running theory was that he knew about Leo's involvement and was there to stop him. Leo had said it himself to me, overheard by my mother, and we'd both given that account to the authorities.

How that made me feel—I couldn't think on it because that meant I'd killed . . .

I couldn't think on it. I would someday, but that wasn't today. That's where I was.

Because of all of that, Leo's funeral was disgraced, and barely anyone went to it.

Bear's was another story. He had a few relatives, not many, but a few. They wanted to keep the funeral small. I'd gone, but I'd sat in the back. The after-party at his pub was over capacity, but no one was going to report it. Not on this day, not for Bear.

That's where Detective Worthing found me, at one of the back booths in Bear's place.

Val and Reyo had just left. He went to the bar for drinks, and Val went to the bathroom. I saw Brian when I first walked in, but considering that it was out about Trace and me, he'd not come over. I wasn't expecting it.

"Surprised you showed up tonight."

I cocked my head to the side. "What do you want?"

His lip curved up, and he let out a small laugh. "Right." He leaned back, his hands going into his jacket's pockets. "My brother's missing—"

I shot forward. "Did you coordinate those raids on behalf of OC or your family?"

He stopped talking.

Then Detective Worthing jerked forward, and his eyes got mean. "You wanna point fingers here? Whose bed did you get up from this morning? Whose bed are you going to be in tonight? You want to bring *my* family into this, news flash. They *already* are. Where's my brother?"

I leaned back, my eyes narrowed. "I was cleared of both shootings. I was also asked to return to my job. I am not dirty."

He snorted, mirroring me and leaning back too. "Not yet. The only reason you're allowed to come back to work is because you didn't warn your boyfriend. That was a test. Now. Where *the fuck* is my brother?"

"The 411 Network has them."

His eyes widened, and he went still.

"Kelly reached out to me, said they were scared for their lives. She did not go into detail, and I didn't ask, but considering she came to me, I'm thinking they weren't running for their lives from Trace's family."

"You're lying," he said through gritted teeth.

"I'm not. And you know as well as I do that when the 411 Network gets involved, those people are smoke. Your brother and my best friend are gone."

Worthing sucked in a breath, making a hissing sound.

"They're alive, but they're gone."

His gaze was heated, but he didn't move for a moment. Then, slowly, he raised his head up, almost looking down his nose at me, but he was conflicted. That made me feel a bit better about Detective Worthing.

He didn't say another word, but he stared long and hard. "You know. Bear didn't know you were staying at your mother's. Ever think about that?"

I went still. Stock still.

No.

What Worthing was implying—no.

I shook my head, the words spilling out because he was wrong. He was guessing and making a go at me. It wasn't working. It wouldn't work. "You're lying. What you just said. You're lying."

His eyes flashed. "You sure about that?"

Leo was sent to kill me. Bear was . . . he was wrong. "We got into his phone. Leo was at his bar earlier, and he overheard Leo's conversation. He was there to stop him. That's why he was fully masked, because he was trying to get the drop on Leo. And he thought I was back in Manhattan. That's why he didn't notify me. He didn't have enough time. It's all on his phone, in case something happened to him."

Worthing blinked once. "Right. Whatever helps *you* sleep at night, Montell, but you know he would've had time to send you a text. Or dial 911. You know he had time."

What a dick. How dare he say this to me about Bear, in his bar.

But—no. Bear was good, and I'd killed him, and I'd have to carry that cross from here on out. I growled, "Get the fuck away from me."

After sliding out of the booth, he stood at the end of the table. He was *still* studying me.

Val was coming back, about to slide in where he had vacated. She paused in midsquat, taking in the silent perusal between us until she moved in. Reyo was behind her, coming in with a beer for himself and a beer for me. He slid in, also taking in the stare-off before he slowly placed the drinks on the table.

He cleared his throat. "What's going on, guys?"

Worthing's eyes narrowed to slits, right before he turned, and I watched him make his way right back outside Bear's Pub.

"Do we need to know?" That was Val's quiet question.

I was still watching the door. "You don't want to know."

"That's not what I asked."

Her seriousness filtered through to me, and I turned to see her watching me back, just as serious.

"I'll ask it again. Do we *need* to know what that was about?"

I'd not made my decision if I was coming back to work. Val knew. She knew everything at this point, but there was something nagging me. A little voice whispering in the back of my head, but I couldn't make out what it was. The feeling of something coming, something more happening, was in my stomach, and it was growing along with those whispers.

Maybe it was because of that feeling that I hadn't said when I was coming back or if I wasn't.

Leo's betrayal had rocked me, to the point where I couldn't talk about it.

I would have to. I knew that day was coming, but not yet. Leo had been like my father, and all the revelations from that one call—I was off balance.

The foundation under my feet was cracked.

I didn't know where to tread anymore, but hearing Val's question, I couldn't tell her about Justin and Kelly. When I told her, it hit me when I was leaving.

In a way, Kelly and Justin were the true innocents here.

CHAPTER

SEVENTY-SEVEN

JESS

My phone was ringing when I left Bear's.

I answered as I got into my own car. "You tracking me again?"

Trace chuckled, but the warmth of his voice slid over me, and I welcomed it. I needed it. He'd been a rock for me in the midst of everything. "I got a notice that you were leaving. How was it?"

I reached to start the engine but paused and sat back. Maybe I'd just take this time and enjoy a phone call with him. Felt nice. Felt like a momentary sanctuary.

I knew it wouldn't last because we were both in this weird place.

Ashton had offered to take over Trace's family business. The fallout from that night had hit everyone, including Trace, Ashton, and me.

All of Ashton's uncles had been killed. Trace's father had disappeared, and his uncle Steph had been gunned down by one of his own men, Bobby. I didn't know who that was, but Trace said his name with such derision that I knew that betrayal hurt.

Bobby worked for Dominic. Bobby had also lied about Trace's mom, telling him that she was still alive. It'd been a whole ruse to distract Trace even more, but it hadn't worked. I knew it wouldn't have. Trace didn't operate like that. He researched. He took his time. He had the capabilities to be a mastermind, which his father so clearly wasn't.

But while Trace was stepping into his uncle's position temporarily, until he decided what he wanted to do, Ashton made his own decision. He was the new head of the Walden Mafia family. That's where his offer came in. While I'd not seen Ashton since the torture session and Trace was having minimum contact with someone he used to consider a brother / best friend, Ashton offered to take over what both families handled. Whereas most times those offers would be a sham, extended as a "favor" but in reality they wanted the power, it was not the case this time. There was a lot I didn't know or want to know about Trace's family business and especially Ashton's, but Trace explained to me one night that their two families had always been linked.

They were almost a yin and yang sort of deal.

His family handled the businesses, the shipping yards, the distribution in the city. Ashton's handled the law enforcement and the bribes. For one family to take over all of it would be a lot of change and chaos. It'd take time.

I hadn't wanted to know. I'd been keen to keep that boundary because of my job, but it didn't seem to matter as much anymore. Not if Trace was going legit, like he'd been planning.

"It was okay. Good to see Val, a few others."

"They're not turning their backs on you?"

I hesitated, but what was the point? "A lot of them have. It's obvious, but not Val."

"If you go back, will that be a problem?"

"Yeah. We need each other in this work. I get iced out, and that could be dangerous."

"Okay, you know you have my support no matter what you decide."

I did. Warmth spread through me. "I know. I love you."

"I love you too. Are you going back to your mom's right away or . . . ?"

Another smile from me, even though there was so much bad that had happened that maybe I shouldn't be smiling at all. But I was because there'd been one surprising silver lining out of everything. "That gallery called, and they want a few more of my paintings."

"Really?"

"Yeah. I guess the ones she had in her gallery sold, so she's asking for more. And I got an email. An art magazine wants to interview me."

"That's great. I'm not surprised."

The gallery owner saw my paintings while I'd been moving them out of the studio the day I was moving into my mom's house. She'd asked, then and there, for a few, and I'd been in such a mess that I'd forgotten about the whole deal. I'd gotten the call when I was leaving Bear's funeral.

I hadn't even told Val.

"I think I'm going to go to my mom's and do some more painting. I'm feeling the need."

"Sounds good. You want to sleep there or at my place tonight?"

My mom seemed like a new person. Maybe it was the therapy, or maybe it was because we knew everything: about my dad's death; about Isaac, whose lawyer thought we should try at getting him an appeal considering Leo's confession. We didn't have it on tape, but since everything else was treated as evidence, his confession about my father's murder should be treated the same.

It was a long shot, but it was a shot. Either way, my mom had a new purpose in her life.

"I'll probably paint late tonight."

"Your house it is tonight."

I smiled, warming. "I'll see you tonight."

"Love you."

I smiled, my voice cracking because I felt this down into my core. "I love you too."

EPILOGUE

TRACE

A month later

"Are you sure you want to do this?"

I was on the phone with Ashton, and I was looking down at the ring in my hand. "Yes."

"Okay. Things have been quiet, but it's time to hit back. They won't be expecting it now."

I put the ring back in the box and back into my pocket.

Ashton was talking about the payback we still had due. We'd found out that my father had organized the hits against us, whereas the Worthing family had organized the hits against Ashton's family. We'd been waiting with payback against the Worthing family, but we couldn't wait with my father.

Dominic West officially went missing twelve hours after Jess killed Bear. He went missing in the "very dead" sense of the word.

We had to move fast, but now we were finalizing our plans against the Worthing family.

"There'll be fallout."

I went to my window and looked out over the city. "There's always fallout. They're starting to make moves into our territory, thinking we're not going to hit back. It's time. They've come out of hiding."

"We should meet for the final details."

"I agree."

There was silence after that. I knew neither of us wanted to hang up.

I missed my best friend, but our relationship was strained after I'd learned what he'd done to Jess. I knew the reasoning, knew he did it to protect me, but I hadn't been able to forgive him for it. We were cordial, still working together, but we weren't the same.

"How are things with—" His voice was tentative, and I knew who he was going to bring up.

I cut him off. "Let's meet tomorrow. Before everything happens."

His tone changed, growing more distant. "Of course. I'll let you—"

"Ashton."

"What?"

"You have to make it right with *her* first."

"I know."

—

JESS

I chose painting.

Or, I don't know. A part of me might've just been choosing not that old life anymore. No more law. No more being a parole officer, but that meant no more being Val's partner. In the end, it was a better choice for her too. I'd lessened the target on her back, and there *was* one because she'd stood by me. She would remain doing that.

Though, and there was a big "though," the other side of me choosing painting was that it gave me different freedoms. Different options.

I chose my time. I chose my paintings. No more orders. There was nothing dangerous about what type of paint color I picked. I suppose I'd miss the adrenaline, the camaraderie, and the action. I'd miss helping the parolees that wanted help. But my art, this was me. All me. A new me.

I'd just started. I had a whole future ahead of me, and this time, it actually looked bright.

I could see the hope, the light.

Painting had been an escape for my mind, from my job, but now, I was choosing a different path.

I resigned my position, and it was a full month later with no more drama. That, possibly, was the best part of my choice. More and more of my paintings were selling. I'd like to see that as a sign from the universe, but I didn't. The jaded part of me would always be in me. I'd seen too much shit in my life, but it still felt nice.

The other nice things happening in my life? My mom.

Chelsea Montell was doing good, and sober, and she leaned into her therapy versus going back the other way. Currently, she was all aflutter because Trace was coming over tonight. I didn't know the reason for the nerves. He'd been over for dinner on multiple occasions by now, but I was in the basement working. She'd insisted on cooking dinner tonight.

It smelled delicious, whatever she was making.

I heard the doorbell ring.

My mom's footsteps crossed the house, and I had to laugh a little because Trace had a key for the house. He used it often when he slipped inside and came to my room. I brought up the idea of selling because of Bear, but my mom wouldn't have it. Instead, she was sleeping in my room while we were renovating the master bedroom. New carpet. New everything. A new closet was being put in.

We'd turned the back office into our new bedroom as well. Mine and Trace's. We used it when we stayed here. The relationship with my mother was still in a delicate balance, so we stayed here a couple nights a week, for times when I wanted to spend the evenings with my mom or if I wanted to paint late into the night. All the other time was at Trace's downtown place.

A whole host of other renovations was also happening on the house. My first paintings were paying for some of it. The other part was a gift from Trace, but it felt nice. The house was being taken care of, and this way my mom had a choice. She could sell, because in my mind, she was still the owner. Or I'd sell, if that's what she insisted. It was a nice conversation to have. We had options. Both of us and she wasn't hating me. I mean, I knew there were people out there who believed in working through family trauma, et cetera, whether it was done to us or done between us, but that wasn't who we were.

We kept trucking forward, and if apologies were made and felt along the way, then even better. We were those kind of people, but something was going on.

I could hear my mom's voice, and it went up a whole octave. She'd been like this all day today.

I don't know what was happening, but I assumed it had something to do with Trace since she was also so insistent on cooking a whole feast for tonight. And she'd told me to dress nice too.

What was that about?

But she was happy. I was happy. Trace was happy with me, and he would get there with the rest, with whatever he decided, because I didn't think he'd fully decided. He said after tonight, he'd have closure, and he could decide if he'd take Ashton up on his offer.

My mom was pacing, her footsteps going all around the kitchen.

I could hear Trace's voice; he was more calm.

He wasn't coming down, so I went back to my painting.

Chelsea made pasta, rolls, every dish of vegetables there was. Mashed potatoes. Yams. She was trying the vegetarian route, so we had a lot of meat that wasn't meat, but it still tasted like meat, so I didn't care.

My mom carried the conversation that night. She was talking a mile a minute, her eyes darting to Trace every thirty seconds.

After twenty minutes, I'd had enough. "Okay." I scooted my chair back. "What's going on?"

Trace went still.

My mom gasped and started chewing on her bottom lip.

I narrowed my eyes, looking between the two. "Something is obviously going on. You asked me to dress nice. You're wearing a dress. Trace, well, you look the same since you always look good." And he did. A Henley and jeans, and his hair was messed up in a seriously hot way that was speaking to my vagina.

"Well." Trace stood up, his hand going into his pocket.

My mom gasped.

I frowned, but then my phone started ringing.

"Leave it." Chelsea waved a hand at it.

But, no. It was Val.

I showed Trace the screen, and he nodded. If she was calling, it was important. We weren't friends that phoned.

I answered. "What's up?"

She let out a nervous breath.

That was my first clue.

I straightened, all focus on this phone call now. "What's wrong? The baby?"

"No, no. This little kicker is still in me, but uh . . . I gotta tell you something."

That was my second clue.

"What? In person?" I was racking my mind, but I couldn't guess what it was about.

"Uh. We could do that, but this news is going to spread fast, and I want to make sure you hear it from me first."

"Now you're worrying me."

"I know."

That was my third clue. There was no reassurance. Nothing.

My stomach officially dropped, and I closed my eyes, preparing myself. Or I was trying.

I felt Trace next to me.

"Just tell me, Val."

"Two bodies were found up north in New York. No one was notified down here because it's not our jurisdiction. But they asked me to be the one to tell you."

I was going through the list.

Who was here. Who wasn't.

No, no, no.

I knew, I *knew* as she said it.

"DNA matches. It's Kelly and Justin."

ACKNOWLEDGMENTS

Writing Jess and Trace's story was such a whirlwind! Literally. I remember starting out writing this story but then talking to a parole officer (which I am so thankful for!) and realizing how much Jess's personality was going to change. She was such a different character for me to write, and I loved it! Thank you to Kimberly, Lauren, and Lindsey for working with me and helping to make Jess and Trace's story the best I could. Thank you to the entire Montlake group that helped put this book together. I truly appreciated it so much. Thank you to Crystal, Amy, Chris, and Kimberley for helping me every time I message. You guys always make time, and I appreciate it so much.

A big thank-you to my readers in Tijan's Crew. You guys uplift me with your posting in there, and you have no idea how much I am thankful for you all. Thank you to Debra Anastasia, Helena Hunting, and Rachel Van Dyken just for being. Lol!

Last, thanks to the B-man. Your constant tail wags and cuddles and licks make my world go round, even when you're tired of me writing and just want to go for a walk! Love you so much.

ABOUT THE AUTHOR

Tijan is a *New York Times* bestselling author who writes suspenseful and unpredictable novels. Her characters are strong, intense, and gut-wrenchingly real with a little bit of sass on the side. Tijan began writing after college, and once she started, she was hooked. She's written multiple bestsellers, including the Fallen Crest series, *Ryan's Bed*, *Enemies*, and others. She is currently writing many new books and series with an English cocker she adores.

You can join her reader group on Facebook, Tijan's Crew, or at www.facebook.com/tijansbooks. Follow her on Instagram @tijansbooks, on Twitter @TijansBooks, and on TikTok @tijan_author. And don't forget to check out her author site, www.tijansbooks.com.

Tijan is represented by Brower Literary & Management Inc.